T.M. BROWN

ADVANCE PRAISE FOR

PURGATORY: A PROGENY'S QUEST

"Amid the patchwork of furrowed cotton and peanut fields...downhome country fun at its finest....But when one of Shiloh's citizens purchases an armored limo with a checkered history at a Sheriff's used-car auction, the town's tranquility is shattered by the accumulation of dead bodies and broken hearts. Here's a story that will keep you reading to the wee hours."
—**Jedwin Smith**,
I AM ISRAEL, Our Brother's Keeper, and *Fatal Treasure*

"Purgatory: A Progeny's Quest is the third novel in the excellent Shiloh Mystery Series and is the best yet. I've enjoyed reading all of T. M. Brown's books, but I think he really knocks it out of the park with *Purgatory*. It's a stunning blend of mystery, inspiration, and authentic characters and setting...I highly recommend this novel."
—**Lee Gimenez**, award-winning author of the J. T. Ryan series and Author Academy Award finalist

"Having read the first two books, this last in the series exceeds all expectations and, as expected, many of the delightful characters so carefully described before have returned. Theo and Liddy are trusted residents of Shiloh, frequently called upon for advice and guidance. Barbequed brisket, coffee from grounds carefully measured into a pot, and celebrations such as the Lightning Bug Festival brighten their days. Just when you think it all a little too perfect, a founding family's bloodlines are redefined and a new resident arrives. Your heart races when two mysterious strangers intrude and skulk around town. When lives are threatened, the town joins local deputies to discover their identities and motives. Of course Theo is smack dab in the middle. Where else would he be? There's more than sweet tea and moss-covered oaks to this tale and Mike Brown has done Shiloh proud."

—**Linda J. Pifer**, author of the Windows Trilogy and *Sandpiper Run*

"Mysteries beset the citizenry of a small Southern town that exudes contagious, country-fried wholeness. As you approach the finale, better hold on to your hat!"

—**Jameson Gregg**, Georgia Author of the Year, author of *Luck Be a Chicken, A Comic Novel*

"T. M. Brown writes with subtlety, compassion, and understanding….and the denouement is more than satisfying. The story is funny and sad, the language clever and poetic, and the book is nothing less than a gem. With skill and finesse, Brown moves the story forward at a measured pace as he introduces believable and sympathetic characters, and each of these brings depth and sometimes gentle humor to this finely crafted story. *Purgatory: A Progeny's Quest* is a story of growth and change and hope and renewal. It is a story of forgiveness. It is an extraordinary tale written by an exceptional author. I will read this book again."

—**Raymond L. Atkins**, author of *Set List, Sweetwater Blues*, and *Camp Redemption*.

"In *Purgatory: A Progeny's Quest*, T. M. Brown delivers another satisfying read of Southern fiction with a strong sense of place

and memorable characters. Theo and Liddy Phillips right the wrongs of broken lives and hearts with Christian hope."
—**Johnnie Bernhard**, author of *Sisters of the Undertow* and *A Good Girl*

"The long-awaited finale of the series doesn't disappoint. With barbecue, lightning bugs, and delightful dialogue, T. M. Brown delivers a gem of a Southern novel to his faithful followers."
—**Renea Winchester**, author of *Outbound Train*

"A page-turner suitable for all audiences."
—**Dana Ridenour**, award-winning author of *Behind the Mask, Beyond the Cabin,* and *Below the Radar*

"Small-town shenanigans, Southern style. Theo Phillips and his wife Liddy live in Shiloh, Georgia, a town graced with a mess of colorful characters and a passel of predicaments. Whether he is writing an article about the Miss Shiloh contest, advising a friend on fatherhood, pondering the political future of the town's mayor, or struggling with how to best help an orphaned teenager, Theo faces all life throws at him with his wife Liddy by his side and his faith to guide him."
—**Christopher Swann**, author of *Never Turn Back* and *Shadow of the Lions*

PURGATORY: A PROGENY'S QUEST

Copyright © 2022 T. M. Brown
Published by Blue Room Books | Decatur, GA
BlueRoomBooks.com
For permissions email: blueroombooks@outlook.com
Subject line: Permissions for Purgatory

T.M. BROWN
PURGATORY, A PROGENY'S QUEST
BLUE ROOM BOOKS | DECATUR, GA
978-1-950729-19-7

Original Cover design and interior: Olivia Croom Hammerman
Current cover art and interior layout: Angela K. Durden
Barn photograph © johnnychaos/iStock; tree courtesy of Pixabay.com
Editors: Tom Whitfield and Angela K. Durden
Printed in the United States of America

T.M. BROWN

Shiloh Series Character List
By family grouping: Name, Age in *Purgatory: A Progeny's Quest*

Phillips:
Theo, 64
Liddy, 64
Teddy *"Junior"*, 39
Kari, 36
Eddie *"Bubba"*, 13
Conrad, 6
Tommy, 37
Stacie, 34
Teddy, 13
Sissy, 10
Elton *"Buzz"*, 6

Priestly:
Zack, *d.* 2007 (69)
Betty, *d.* 2010 (63)
John, 43

Edwards:
Wiley, *d.* 2016 (85)
Malvinia, *d.* 2016 (80)
Wilson, 36
Cassandra *"Cassie"* Davis-Edwards, 35
Keith *"Woogie"*, 17

Adams:
Zeb, 66
Miriam, *d.* 2000 (40)
Jay, 29
Jim, 29

Archer:
Harold Archer, Sr., *d.* 2014 (62)
Delilah Dixon *"Dixie"*
Archer/Arnaquer, *d.* 2014 (56)
Harold, Jr. *"Hank"*, 37
Hal, 35
Phillip, 25
Maddie, 74 (housekeeper)

Arnaquer:
Beau, *d.* 2013 (59)
Maude, *d.* 2016 (82)
Sallie Mae *"Pepper"*, 16

Wright:
Arnold *"Arnie"*, 62
Judy, 59
Hillary Wright/Rutherford, 35

Masterson:
Marie, 60
Joseph *"Joe"*, *d.* 1976 (23)
Jessie, *d.* 2010 (34)

Simmons:
Sam, 56
Susanna, 54
Pete, 30
Mary Scribner/Simmons, 29
Andy, 29
Megan Archer/Simmons, 30
"Lil Jessie", 1
Jeannie, 26

PURGATORY: A PROGENY'S QUEST

Arians:
Joseph *"Joe"* P., 45
Melissa *"Missy"*, 40
Elizabeth *"Lizzie"*, 11
Lucille *"Lucy"*, 11
Nick, 39
Tammy *d.* 2007 (30)
Lucinda *"Momma"*, *d.* 2014 (69)
Barnabas *"Barnie"*, *d.* 2007 (68)

Scribner:
Larry, 57
Martha, 56

Davis:
"Hub", 60
Marcellus, 39
Byron *"Bobo"*, 16

Thompson:
Benjamin, 37
Hannah, 36
Tim, 15
Vickie, 8

Waller:
Roy, 35
Vickie, 32

Michelle *"Mickey"*, 13

Shiloh Police:
Mitch Johnson, *32*
Tyler *"Hawk"* Hadley, 21
Camille Gaines, 25

Bubba's BBQ:
Robert *"Bubba"*, 64
Barbara *"Barb"*, 52
Cecil, 56
Cora, 56

The Butcher Shoppe:
Silas Thrope, 53
Bernice *"Bernie"*, 52
Alex Thrope, 23
Amanda *"Mandy"* Baggett, 25

Shiloh High School:
Phoebe Thatcher, 40
Esther *"Kay"* Kathleen
Abernathy, 57
Ray Abernathy, 58, postmaster

Cyrus *"Cy"* Riddell, 41

Samuel G. *"Gus"* Appleton, 64

T.M. BROWN

For
Noah, Brannon,
Natalie, Eli,
and Dillon

PURGATORY: A PROGENY'S QUEST

T.M. BROWN

T.M. BROWN

A PROGENY'S QUEST

PURGATORY

from the author of "SANCTUARY" and "TESTAMENT"

"...stunning blend of mystery, inspiration, and authentic characters and setting...
Lee Gimenez,
award-winning author of the J. T. Ryan series and Author Academy Award finalist

PURGATORY: A PROGENY'S QUEST

1

WILSON EDWARDS ONLY INVITED A FEW CLOSE FRIENDS TO THE house following his grandfather's funeral because his grandmother's recent passing still weighed heavy on so many folks in town. There would be no traditional church supper following the interment service at Shiloh Cemetery. However, Wilson anticipated the ladies of the church would still drop off casseroles, side dishes, and desserts. Inviting a few close friends over would provide conversation and help Wilson consume the cornucopia born of Shiloh's good intentions that would undoubtedly fill his kitchen by the end of this sun-drenched afternoon.

Liddy's peach cobbler, fresh out of the oven, made the already hotter-than-usual late May afternoon even more uncomfortable by the time Judy Wright, the pastor's wife, greeted us at the front door of the Edwards home.

"Smells scrumptious," Judy said, extending her hands. "Theo, please allow me to take that for you. Y'all head on into the living room. Wilson and Woogie are there."

Liddy peeked down the long hall into the kitchen. "Looks like the church ladies outdid themselves again."

Inside the living room, Wilson chatted with Zeb Adams, Hub Davis, Joe Arians, and Arnie Wright. Catty-corner across the room beneath the ornate built-in bookshelves, Woogie's lighthearted youthful cackles and broad smile caught my attention. He and Coach John Priestly joked with each other about this past football season. Liddy accompanied me into the living room long enough to make our arrival known before her attention diverted to high-pitched giggles reverberating from the kitchen and dining room.

Wilson interrupted Zeb's lighthearted story and greeted Liddy with a warm embrace, extending his hand to me. "I'm so glad y'all made it. Woogie and I cannot tell you enough—"

"Don't say another word, Wilson." Liddy took hold of Wilson's hand as she glanced at Woogie's laughter-filled face. "By the looks and sounds of it, Woogie appears to be handling the sudden loss of his great-grandfather fairly well."

"You'd think so at first glance, but he's like most teenagers putting on a good front while still reeling inside. That cozy armchair he's curled up in is where Grandpa slipped away while watching the Braves go extra innings with Cincinnati. Woogie still feels somehow responsible because he followed me upstairs that night rather than hang out with Grandpa."

"I understand Wiley died from broken-heart syndrome," I said to Wilson but glancing at Woogie.

"It's likely Grandpa allowed himself to follow Grandma." Wilson's upper lip began to quiver. "He had no known heart issues according to Doc Lucas. It appears he slipped away in the wee hours. When Woogie came downstairs the next morning… he found Grandpa slumped in his chair, TV still on."

Liddy draped her arm across Wilson's shoulders. "I hope you and Woogie realize you couldn't have prevented his departure. It sounds as if God beckoned and his heart and soul answered."

Wilson glanced at Woogie. "Funny, by the looks of it, Woogie understands better than I do." He exchanged a tight smile with his son, who likewise raised a thumbs-up.

"Hey, I got another story on hold over here about ol' Wiley," Zeb barked with a jovial grin.

Liddy walked over to Woogie and kissed him on his forehead before she disappeared into the kitchen. I didn't hear what she said, but I saw Woogie mouth, "Thank you, ma'am."

I joined Zeb, Arnie, Hub, and Joe as they swapped tales of more memorable antics and foibles of Wiley Edwards. I felt like an outsider since Liddy and I had moved to Shiloh less than three years ago. Wilson's open-mouthed look mirrored my own as each story unfolded. I remembered Wilson's years of self-inflicted exile from Shiloh. Those ended only a few months ago when he and Wiley reconciled. Wilson was named sole heir of Wiley and Malvinia's estate; even had his father's barber chair bequeathed to him. That marked the first real opportunity for Wilson and Woogie to enjoy their life as father and son in over a decade.

Before that, Wilson struggled to remain a dutiful husband to his drug-dependent wife, and had faced legal and financial woes until she abandoned him and Woogie and wound up in prison. Now they had some measure of stability. Wiley and Malvinia had even created a college trust fund for Woogie with some of the proceeds earned when Malvinia sold her gift and card shop.

An hour slipped past while Zeb, Joe, and Arnie continued to reminisce before John Priestly tapped my shoulder on his way into the dining room. By the time I managed to excuse myself from the conversation, earning a curious squint from Zeb, John had disappeared.

In the dining room, Phoebe Thatcher, Hillary Wright-Rutherford, and Missy, Joe Arians' wife, giggled amongst themselves at the far end of the table. Phoebe nonchalantly pointed toward the kitchen where Liddy leaned against the countertop near the sink absorbed in conversation with Judy and Marie Masterson.

Liddy winked at me and bobbed her head toward the back porch before reverting her attention back to Judy and Marie. John was hunched over on the weatherworn porch swing, appearing to be lost in his thoughts. His blank stare appeared aimed at the deep peach glow touching the horizon.

I stepped onto the porch, eyed the darkening indigo sky. "You needed a break, too?"

He clasped his hands behind his head and lounged back against the swing's sun-faded and peeling green slats. A series of crackles and creaks in the rusted chain links followed in the swing's gentle sway. "Take a seat, my friend. You're just the fella I needed to talk to."

"Don't mind if I do." I plopped into the emerald metal patio chair adjacent the swing.

John looked at the back door. "Do us a favor. Pull the kitchen door shut. I'd rather not compete with all their giggling."

I got back up, pulled the screen door open, and gripped the doorknob. Liddy's eyes met mine and we exchanged curious glances as I pulled the back door shut.

"Thanks, Theo. You're the only one I feel I can trust to give me the answers I need."

Those words caused me to squirm in my seat. At once I remembered how nervous I felt when we first met almost three years ago. Joe Arians had arranged for me to visit John in prison. Though Joe managed to gain John's release and eventual exoneration, the initial chill I felt cut clean through me when John entered that stark concrete interview room. His first icy cold stare thankfully melted over time, but on that memorable afternoon, he minced no words about the lack of trust he harbored.

I double-checked the closed kitchen door and said, "Whatever's on your mind must be important."

John chuckled. "You might say that." He released his firm grip on the back of the wooden swing and planted his feet square on the porch deck. The swing's chains rattled and popped once more as he scooted to the edge of the seat and leaned forward. He motioned me to come closer and whispered, "Do you think it's too late for me to become a father?"

John's inquiry made me adjust my seat closer still. A look of uncertainty had swept across his more familiar stoic confidence. I muttered almost inaudibly as a wrinkle or two creased my brow. "You and Phoebe aren't—?"

"Oh, hell no!" John's unmuffled retort spurred him to glimpse over his shoulder at the kitchen window. John inched closer, placed his hand on my shoulder. "Theo, Phoebe's more than just a close friend to me." He stammered. "I don't need to tell you the last six years wreaked havoc on any notion I held about getting hitched and starting a family. And those three years stuck in prison scarred me." John pounded his heart.

"But, John—"

"Hold on, Theo. Let me finish what I gotta say." I sat back a bit in my chair and slapped his kneecap to continue.

"It's no use. I've tried my best to live up to all sorts of expectations I just can't deliver, no matter how hard I try."

"What expectations? I don't understand," I said, leaning forward again and trying to lock eyes with him.

"The kind of expectations that haven't allowed me to consider the prospect of marriage or starting a family."

"John, you can't get back those lost years, but let me answer your original question. No, it's not too late. Have you considered Phoebe may be asking herself the same question?"

John shook his head, but his eyes stared into mine. "I've been afraid it may be too late for both of us. I'll turn forty-four this year and, well, Phoebe ain't much younger."

"Stop and listen to me. More than anyone I know, you deserve to be a father and not just a father figure." I eased back into my chair and waited.

PURGATORY: A PROGENY'S QUEST

John's eyes pleaded as he wiped his cheeks with his fingers. This feeling had him in an unfamiliar place. Rather than having the answers, he was searching for them.

"You really want my advice? Quit dilly-dallying around and sit down with Phoebe. She's the only one who can give you the answers you deserve to hear. She's been on this merry-go-round with you far too long."

John looked up. "I reckon you're right. I've almost mustered the courage to ask her a couple of times, but the thought I'd let down everyone who put their faith back in me as their coach has been a huge stumbling block."

"The only stumbling block is you."

"I know, but I couldn't forgive myself without considering the faith they placed back in me. For that one reason I finally realized something that has been hard to admit. After last season fell short of the playoffs—again—I did some deep soul searching and dissected my coaching. I'm no longer the coach the school needs or deserves."

"Now hold on! You're the best dang coach I've been around, and there's a host of others more knowledgeable than me who will attest to that fact."

John rose to his feet. "I appreciate it, but Shiloh's glory days were not all my doing. Those back-to-back state championships happened after Jessie Masterson came on board. After I lost my job, Jessie even had the team headed there again before he died in the damned courthouse fire."

His confession rattled me. I felt at a loss for words.

"No matter how hard I might try," John said, pounding his chest, "I can't fill the gap he left after he died."

"What, or should I say, who can?"

"Andy Simmons can. He and I talked on the phone last week. He's added two commendable years on Georgia Christian's staff, but he and Megan are ready to come home." With a satisfied smile, John sat.

"Why would Andy give up all he has going for him at GCU to come back to Shiloh?"

"Andy's head coach is about to announce he'll be the next head coach at Nebraska. He's asked some on his staff to come with him. Andy's one of them, but he doesn't want to go all the way out to Nebraska. It's much too far from family."

"Why not stay at GCU?"

"He's not sure the new coach will ask him to remain. Besides, he told me Megan finished her degree work and wanted to find a high school where she can teach and coach cheerleading."

"Do you think Andy can fill Jessie Masterson's shoes?"

"No one can fill Jessie's shoes, but I believe Andy's the right person to take over. He played under Jessie and experienced the consecutive state championships this town idolizes."

"Did you offer Andy a position?"

John smiled. "Not yet. I'll be meeting the school board later this week."

"Let's get back to Phoebe."

Before John could answer, Zeb opened the kitchen door and yelled back inside, "They's still out here." He stepped onto the porch. "Speaking of Phoebe, that young lady's looking for you. You two got school in the morning, and Theo, I'm pretty certain Liddy's ready to go home, too."

John slapped me on the back as we followed Zeb inside. "Thanks," John whispered. "You're a good friend. Please keep this between us for the time being."

2

LIDDY SCURRIED OUT THE DOOR IN HIGHER THAN USUAL SPIRITS. It was her second school year as Shiloh High's art teacher, and her students had three days left to present their semester portfolios. She also anticipated more of her students would register for the school's new Summer Art and Music Camp she and Phoebe Thatcher would be conducting.

After Liddy left, I headed for The Butcher Shoppe. Though I held no regrets about leaving Atlanta and the hustle and bustle of suburban life, savoring Bernie Thrope's frothy Mediterranean brew turned into a regular habit on many mornings. For all the steadfast homegrown traditions and tastes one could rely on in a small town like Shiloh, the Greek menu of The Butcher Shoppe provided an unexpected yet delightful exception.

My ears had even grown accustomed to hearing the Greek accents and slang of the owners, Silas and his wife Bernie. Likewise, what appeared Greek to me when Liddy and I first entered The Butcher Shoppe—Tzatziki, Falafel, Souvlaki, Moussaka, not to mention their special gyro and wrap options—I now ordered with far less hesitancy. Though barbecue reigns in the South, Silas and Bernie's Athenian hospitality and mouth-watering fare had carved its own unique niche at the center of our small town.

"*Kalimera*, my good friend," Silas shouted as I walked in.

"Good morning to you, my good friend. You think I can get my coffee to go this morning?"

Silas' salt-and-pepper, bushy mustache animated his upper lip as he yelled into the kitchen. "Mistor Theo's here and ordered his *kafes* to go this morning."

Amanda Baggett, Bernie's niece from Atlanta and one of Shiloh's newest residents, pranced into the restaurant like a high-spirited filly. She had on a pair of navy running shorts over neon orange Capri tights, and a sweat-soaked Auburn blue sports bra. A long-sleeved athletic shirt wrapped around her trim athletic waist. Her long black ponytail hung limp out of her baseball cap.

She leaned over with her hands on her knees to catch her breath, flicked her dangling ponytail off her shoulder, raised her head, and said between gasps, "Good morning, Uncle, and you too, Mister Phillips."

Silas grumbled. "Morning to you, Mandy. What can I get you to-go?" He glanced at his watch. "Did you have a late start today?" Silas peeked toward the kitchen.

Mandy nodded as she stood with a crooked smile.

"Your Aunt is not going to be pleased if you don't cover yourself, young lady."

"Yes, Uncle. I forgot." She untied the athletic shirt and slipped it over her head. As she adjusted her hair and cap, she turned to me and tendered a sheepish, coy smile. "Mister Phillips, I was sorry to hear about that sweet man, Mister Edwards. Your article about his legacy made me appreciate why I decided to move here. I'll miss his daily visits at the shop."

Before responding to her heartfelt words, I glanced over to Silas where he stood behind Mandy, and noticed his mustache-framed grin. "Young lady, your decision to reopen Miss Malvinia's Elysium Emporium meant a lot to Wiley."

Mandy's cheeks flushed deeper and her smile widened.

"Hey, I heard you'll be one of the Miss Shiloh contestants at this year's festival."

Mandy's coy look returned. "It sounded like a good opportunity to get better known around town. I don't expect to win, but—"

"Here you go, Mistor Theo. Be careful, my friend. It's still very hot," Bernie said with a warm smile that cooled as she inspected her niece. "And what might I get you, Mandy? I imagine you're in a hurry?" Mandy's schoolgirl grin did not impede Bernie's hasty retreat as she mumbled her disapproval in Greek. Mandy followed hard on her heels, apologizing.

Silas crossed his arms. "Mistor Theo, please don't misunderstand, but on mornings like this, I'm thankful God chose not to bless us with a daughter."

I handed Silas two dollars and glanced at a couple enjoying their own private conversation, seemingly unfazed by Mandy's arrival. "Go easy on Mandy. Most folks around here don't give a hoot and a holler about all the twenty-first century changes encroaching upon us. They only fuss at the changes that threaten their personal lives. I'm not so sure Mandy's modern, citified ways are that big of a threat. Besides, she needs them folks to patronize the Emporium, and, so far, she appears busy enough."

Silas laughed. "I know you are right but try convincing my wife. I think she's a bit hard on Mandy because our son is living with Bernie's sister while he finishes his degree work at Emory. I cannot help but wonder how he's adjusting to the lifestyle changes in Decatur."

"I wouldn't worry too much," I said, and sipped my coffee.

Mandy bolted around the counter with a cup of coffee in one hand and a paper sack in the other. "Thank you, Aunt Bernie. You too, Uncle. I gotta run home and shower."

I pushed the door open. "Enjoy your day, Mandy."

After she swooshed by, I looked back at Silas. Bernie stood behind him with her hands on her hips. I shook my head and said, "Y'all enjoy the rest of your day."

MY EMPTY CUP found the trash can beside Martha Scribner's desk after I entered the *Sentinel*. She looked up with a wrinkled scowl. "Mister Grumpy's in the breakroom pouring his coffee."

"Well, thank you...I reckon," replying with a marked hesitation as I walked past her desk.

Mary's exasperation showed in her snippy greeting. "I hope you're bringing good news. Dad's been a royal pain in my you-know-what this morning."

"Your dad? A royal pain? What's up?"

Mary's tight lips eased as the corners of her mouth rose. "Doc told him after his physical he needed to schedule a colonoscopy."

Recalling my own examination last fall, I swallowed an emerging chuckle. "I'll see what I can do to ease his fears."

As I approached and rapped on his open door, Larry's grumbles grew louder.

"Since when do you knock anymore? I suspect you heard the news?" Larry groused, slumping in his plush executive chair.

"What a short memory you have when the shoe's on the other foot. Who ribbed me last fall when I had my last checkup?"

Larry nodded without giving up his grimace. "That was different. You'd already had a couple of them invasive backside procedures."

I sat in my usual chair in front of Larry's desk. "Then take it from a pro. The prep and waking with an echo chamber for a stomach are the hardest parts of the whole procedure. You'll sleep through the actual examination."

"Yeah, I got that. Doc suspects a false-positive from the lab work. What if —"

"Larry, at the worst, Doc might find a polyp or two—he'll nip them in the bud."

Larry's head swayed back and forth in reply.

"Look, this will be nothing more than another reason to take a day off from the office."

"I know you're right, Theo." His coerced grin revealed a lingering skepticism.

I leaned forward and took the morning paper laying folded on the corner of his desk, opened it to the only obituary listed, and placed my finger on the name. "I'm curious. Tell me more about this Matilda Mae Arnaquer's obituary."

"Hold on. Before you ask what I figure you're about to, Martha took a call from some odd-named priest at a Catholic Church in Mississippi last week. She told him what he wanted to know about sending an obituary notice to the paper, but before she could get any additional information, he thanked her and hung up. Until this obituary arrived in the mail, none of us gave the call another thought."

"That's it? Why would someone send a notice of Matilda Arnaquer's death all the way from Natchez to Shiloh?"

Larry rolled his eyes and shrugged. "I reckon news about Dixie's untimely demise never reached whoever wanted the obituary sent. Does that satisfy your curiosity?"

"For the time being." I scratched my chin a moment and shrugged. "On more pressing news, I ran into Mandy Baggett at The Butcher Shoppe this morning. Did you know she entered the Miss Shiloh contest?"

Larry's contorted grin morphed back into his more recognizable sneer as he pulled a document from a folder on his desk and slid it toward me. "Miss Baggett's revival of the Elysium

Emporium's storefront exposed how weathered our own building's exterior has become. It stirred up Mary and she's been bugging me with expensive notions of sprucing up the *Sentinel's* charming facade."

"You old miser. A coat of paint on some of the storefronts around town would be welcomed. Don't be such an old skinflint."

"Save your breath. Mary and Martha already got their pound of flesh out of me. As for the Miss Shiloh contest, Mary's the pageant chair this year." He pointed to the printed list he had pulled from the folder on his desk. "Arians Realty and Property Management sponsored Jeannie Simmons again. Our Police Chief sponsored his new clerk/dispatcher, Camille Gaines. And The Butcher Shoppe entered Amanda Baggett."

"They're the only contestants this year?"

"Looks like it, but I've already heard there's a swelling of support for each of them. To spice things up, Mary's included a popular vote that'll carry equal weight with the judges' decisions this year. In fact, Mary's printing something in Friday's edition announcing the Miss Shiloh contestants alongside the full schedule for the festival." Larry chuckled. "You oughta know, she's going to ask you to write a piece on each of the contestants."

"Me? May as well ask me to dance on a bed of red-hot coals."

"Don't blame Mary, it was my suggestion. She's now Jeannie's sister-in-law, and let's face it, by extension that excludes Martha and yours truly, too. Undoubtedly, we'd be viewed as biased. Besides, you're the most respected journalist in town."

"You patronizing old conniver. Just when I was about to let you in on some juicy breaking news."

"What juicy breaking news?"

"We can't make this public until it's a done deal, but John's stepping down as head coach."

Jaw dropping, Larry's eyes bulged.

PURGATORY: A PROGENY'S QUEST

I stood and leaned over Larry's desk, and whispered, "He already has his replacement in mind, too."

"Dagnabbit, Theo!"

"Sorry, but I can't tell you quite yet. Of course, writing this story will make up for the Miss Shiloh article you wrangled me into? Will I see you at church tonight?"

Larry grumbled. "Nope. I'll be prepping for tomorrow's backend inspection. And if I don't make it out of the operating room tomorrow, I swear I'll haunt you for the rest of your days. Now get on out of here, you ol' news hack."

I DREADED BREAKING the news to Liddy. Though Mary apologized, I had to hand her my article on the Miss Shiloh contestants by the next afternoon. Liddy's frown added to my guilt by the time she drove off to church Wednesday evening without me.

I took refuge on our front porch and settled into one of the rockers with pen and legal pad in hand. A reminiscent sweetness infiltrated the still country air, a reminder that beyond Shiloh's town limits a patchwork of furrowed cotton and peanut fields stretched for miles.

In spite of the fact Memorial Day remained a handful of days away, green leaves already sprouted atop South Georgia's hallowed sandy-red Tifton soil. From my limited front porch vantage, what I could not see my senses captured: Fertile images my mind's eye knew to be real. An unharmonious chorus of crickets and garden frogs grew louder as the sun set and moths fluttered overhead lusting after the porch light.

I contemplated the task at hand and realized all three contestants were unique. An initial sketch of each contrasted their backgrounds and attachment to Shiloh.

Jeannie Simmons proved to be both the easiest and the most challenging portion of this assignment. Liddy and I had met her on this very same front porch our first morning in Shiloh when she greeted us for the walkthrough before we closed on our home. Since then, she and the entire Simmons family had become dear friends. We've shared church pews and broken bread on many occasions with Susanna and Sam, her parents. Brothers Pete and Andy provided insightful if not hilarious tall tales about growing up in Shiloh.

Despite being only twenty-five, Jeannie's reputation grew as she stepped out of the shadow of her two older brothers. She had become invaluable to Nick Arians, the owner of Arians Realty and Property Management, and he had recently entrusted his Shiloh-based business affairs into Jeannie's more-than-capable hands after he decided to open an office in Saint Simons. Jeannie's quick-witted business acumen helped her brother Pete and his wife Mary purchase Nick's former stately home not long after he relocated to his family's longtime summer house in Saint Simons. In January, Jeannie also orchestrated the purchase of the Elysium Emporium by Amanda Baggett.

I chuckled as I pondered Jeannie's personal relationship status. Her and Phillip Archer's outward platonic friendship had continued without any signs of blossoming further—as far as Liddy or I could tell or the gossip mill had yet revealed.

However, Chief of Police Mitch Johnson broached his liking Jeannie during some conversations with me in recent weeks. Then again, Phillip and Mitch have another suitor to compete with for Jeannie's affection: Career ambitions.

As for the next contestant to write about, Amanda "Mandy" Baggett arrived in Shiloh last Autumn. Bernie Thrope's brother-in-law, a well-to-do real estate attorney in Decatur, gifted Mandy with the down payment and capital she needed to purchase the Elysium Emporium.

During Mandy's graduate studies, her parents divorced, which, according to Bernie, precipitated her decision to leave Decatur. Bernie had also insinuated that her sister, Mandy's mother, orchestrated Mandy's ill-fated engagement to an eligible dashing young bachelor, but it had come to an embarrassing abrupt end with plenty of hurt feelings. Though Mandy shared her mother's olive complexion and alluring features, I am fairly convinced her father's Scotch-Irish sense of intrepid individualism had prompted her to strike out on her own and move to Shiloh.

The third contestant I had only met in passing. Right after Mitch Johnson organized the Shiloh Police Department, he received permission from our new mayor, Hal Archer, and the City Council to hire a clerk/dispatcher to run the office, and a night shift patrol officer. Tyler "Hawk" Hadley, a graduate from Shiloh High, got the patrol officer position. but Mitch had difficulty finding someone to suit his professional expectations in the office. Two previous hires for the clerk/dispatch position lasted no more than a month or so before Mitch, with some reluctance, interviewed a young woman, Camille Gaines, who Zeb Adams recommended.

Camille's father was a diesel mechanic and moonlighted doing vehicle and equipment repairs for Zeb and his sons at the lumber mill. Camille was new to Shiloh and still lived with her father and mother in Mossy Shoals, about twenty miles or so outside of town. I also realized I had never seen her in other than blue jeans and boots with a tucked-in Shiloh Police Department uniform shirt. It became quite obvious she should be interviewed first thing in the morning.

The rumble of Marie Masterson's sunbaked green-and-rust farm truck broke my concentration as she pulled into our driveway. Backing back out, Marie honked and waved.

"Thanks, Marie," Liddy yelled. "We'll see you this weekend."

I looked at Liddy. "What's going on this weekend?"

"It's Memorial Day Weekend, silly. We got invited to a cookout at Marie's place after church." Liddy greeted me on the porch steps, placed her arm around my waist and squeezed. "Let's go inside, and I'll tell you about Arnie's sermon tonight."

PURGATORY: A PROGENY'S QUEST

DAWN'S STILLNESS AND NEAR CLOUD-FREE CANOPY PORTENDED another ordinary, late Spring day in South Georgia. It was another scorcher once again. I scooted a cozy rocker closer to the porch rail, propped my flip-flopped feet on the railing cap, and opened my devotional journal to Thursday, May 26.

Liddy shared a passage from Genesis that Arnie shared in last night's lesson. After mulling it over I felt a kinship to Abraham's odyssey. He had left his native soil, his family, and familiar surroundings in search of new lands and opportunities promised by God. Forty-four years earlier, I too had packed my bags and followed my heart's desire when I left for college to discover what doors might open for me there. On the University of Georgia's sprawling Athens campus, I met Liddy who, like me, had left her beloved South Georgia roots.

We fell madly in love and got married. Upon graduation, Liddy encouraged me to chase my boyhood dream of becoming a journalist like my father. After a couple of years cutting my teeth with a publishing firm near Savannah, I experienced a brief foretaste of my dream when Liddy and I moved back to my boyhood home to help my father salvage his beleaguered *Douglaston Dispatch*.

During those months, my father asked me to write a weekly column on the cultural changes affecting Douglaston. He also urged me to investigate and expose the social injustice that had become a cancer wreaking havoc in far too many towns throughout the South in the late 1970s. These opportunities honed my love of writing, but providence sent us down another path. The stork visited Liddy shortly after Garnet News purchased the *Douglaston Dispatch,* red ink and all. The buyout provided a nest egg for my parents' retirement. I once again left my hometown and found myself as an editor at Cornerstone Publishing outside of Atlanta.

I crawled my way up the ladder until, four decades later, Liddy sat me down one day and whispered, "Let's retire while you're young enough to chase your dreams of being the writer you always wanted to be."

On the one hand, I felt blessed that our move to Shiloh facilitated our everblooming circle of new friends and unexpected opportunities for Liddy and me to pursue our passions. Part of me, on the other hand, wondered why God had stuck me in Egypt like Abraham for all those years. Then I stared at Liddy's scribbled sermon notes.

Though God drafted the blueprints for our lives, we cannot expect God to reveal all the details beforehand. At the bottom of the sermon notes, she added, *God leads us one step at a time. We must take each step by faith before he shows where the next one leads.*

While I added Liddy's notes in my journal, a burgeoning chorus of yips, yaps, and yelps indicated the *Sentinel* would soon land at the foot of my porch stoop. Tim, almost fifteen now, pedaled down Calvary Street. Each rolled edition flew to its appointed target with an effortless flip of his wrist. I stepped away from my rocker in anticipation of the paper's arrival when I heard the squeal of brakes and snap of his bike's kickstand.

In one fluid motion, he dismounted and walked toward me carrying my paper. "Good morning, Mister P. Here ya go."

"And what, pray tell, earned me such service this fine morning?" I asked, unfolding the paper.

"Ah, come on, Mister P. You're my most favorite customer. Besides, we both work for the *Sentinel*."

"Thank you all the same, Tim." I tucked the paper under my right arm and rested my left hand on his broad shoulder. "I just had a flashback to meeting you for the first time. Of course, you were a head shorter then."

"Yes, sir. I guess I've grown a bit over the last couple of years."

"Looks like Coach's workouts have benefited you, too."

Tim instinctively flexed his biceps and eyed his arm. "Teams will find out this year I won't be so easy to bring down. Those late-season losses were my fault after Coach put me in as quarterback when Quentin got injured."

"Don't you fret none. By the looks of you, I don't think you need worry about getting tossed around this fall. With Quentin leaving for Valdosta, you think you'll be ready to be the starting quarterback this year?"

"Yes, sir. Coach Priestly sat down with me right after spring practice ended and told me as much." Tim paused and stared at his shoelaces. "That leads me to tell you I'll be turning my paper route over to someone else."

"Don't blame you a bit. You've got a bright future ahead."

Tim stood speechless for a moment and then beamed as he said, "Thanks, Mister P. Please tell Missus P I'll see her in class. I gotta run." He popped his kickstand, straddled his bike, and looked over his shoulder before he pedaled. "Woogie appreciated your write-up on his great-grandpa."

"How do you know Woogie liked it?"

"He told me so." He vanished around the corner before I could say another word.

SHORTLY AFTER BREAKFAST, I followed Liddy onto the porch, gave her a gentle squeeze, and pecked her on the cheek before she scampered down the steps to our vehicle, eager for another day at school. Not long after she pulled away, Pete's well-preserved, cherry-red pickup pulled up out front. To my surprise Zeb Adams sat behind the wheel.

"Good morning, Theo," Zeb barked above the idling engine.

"What in tarnation are you doing driving Pete's truck?" I stuck my head in the open passenger window.

"It ain't Pete's any longer."

The mere thought of Pete Simmons selling his prized truck left me lost for words.

"Before you go off thinking I bought it, let me set ya straight. Jim told me Camille Gaines needed some new wheels to replace her old beater, but she don't have enough money saved up to purchase another and hers kicked the bucket yesterday. As fate would have it, Pete asked me this morning if I knew anyone who'd consider buying his truck. So, I'm taking it over to show it to Camille right now."

"But what's Pete going to drive?"

No sooner than I got those words out, a horn honked, and I bumped my head yanking it out of the window. Pete honked the horn of Mary's sky-blue hatchback again. Mary punched Pete's arm and yelled, "Quit it!"

"Sorry to startle you, Theo." Mary clutched Pete's arm as if he needed an old-fashioned maternal scolding. They greeted us on the sidewalk.

"Pete, what's this about you selling your pride and joy?"

Pete stared at Mary with puppy dog eyes until she murmured, "Go ahead, you big galoot. You might as well tell Theo and Zeb."

Pete grabbed Mary's hand and said, "Mary and I are heading to Albany to buy us a four-door, family-friendly truck. We already talked to the salesman at the dealership and he's expecting us later this morning for a test drive."

Zeb let out a belly laugh with an exaggerated wink. "A family-friendly truck? Are y'all two about to be three?"

Mary giggled and Pete's cheeks turned to match the paint on his old truck. Pete pulled Mary closer and nodded as any expectant father would. I remember that same look on my two sons' faces fourteen years ago when within months of each other they shared their great news.

I stepped forward with arms spread. "Congratulations! Do y'all's parents know yet?" Both shook their heads.

Pete finally said, "We're going to tell them this evening after we get the new truck."

Mary snickered. "We figured showing them a new truck would kinda break the ice so we can tell them. Daddy's no spring chicken, so we figured showing him the new truck first might temper the shock."

Zeb and I could not help but laugh.

"I'm not too worried about Pete's parents. They already have one grandson. But Mary, your Dad's expression will be priceless—if it don't send him into cardiac arrest," I stumbled out through the laughter.

Pete looked at Zeb. "Think Camille will like it?"

Patting the truck's tailgate, Zeb said, "Absolutely. Knowing her and her daddy like I do, they'll take good care of it, too."

"Thank you, Uncle Zeb. You tell her she can pay me as we agreed. I ain't fretting about getting paid right away. She can pay me a little now and then as she can. Remember, not a word." Pete looked back and forth at Zeb and me. "We gotta scoot."

"Theo, my friend, I'm mighty proud of that young fella. If you'd have told me ten years ago ol' Pete would have turned out like he has, I'd have thought you were plumb crazy. Talking about crazy, how'd you like to take a drive with this crazy old fool tomorrow morning? There's a certain vehicle I've had my eye on. It's been advertised at the Sheriff's auction in Coffee County. Ain't it your old stomping ground?"

"It sure is. What kind of vehicle?"

Zeb stroked his gray beard. "A one-of-a-kind former foreign dignitary's limousine that fell into the wrong hands and got confiscated when the driver got arrested for drugs. I'll know more tomorrow, but the description and pictures lead me to believe it'd make a fun vehicle to tinker with after I clean it up real nice and give it a good coat of wax. I might even drive this year's Miss Shiloh in it during the Lightning Bug Festival parade."

"Sounds great. What time you want to leave?"

"I'll pick ya up about eight," Zeb said, slapping my back and climbing into the truck. "We'll go in my Bronco. This truck's going to its new owner."

THE PHONE INTERRUPTED dinner. Liddy stood with the receiver to her ear and mouthed, "It's Susanna." She shook her head as she said, "That's great news, Susanna. What did Sam say?"…Liddy nodded…"Has Pete told Andy?"…Her giggles crescendoed until she took a deep breath…"Do you think he'll wait until Andy arrives with Megan and Jessie this weekend?"… Liddy gasped…"All the better. Pete won't have to wait as long if they're arriving tomorrow afternoon. I can't wait to tell Theo the good news, too. Thanks Susanna, and give Sam, I mean PeePaw Simmons, a big hug from me…Bye!" She hung up.

"Let me guess. Pete and Mary are expecting."

"When did you find out?"

My shrug and silly grin got Liddy to grab a potholder and toss it at me. "Why didn't you tell me!"

"I'm sorry, but I promised not to say anything until Pete and Mary told their parents. By the way, are Andy and Megan arriving tomorrow?"

"That's what Susanna said. Why?"

"No particular reason. By the way, I'll be tied up with Zeb all day anyway."

"Oh, no. What trouble are you boys gonna get in now?"

4

THE BEEP OF ZEB'S HORN SPURRED ONE FINAL GULP OF COFFEE. Liddy grabbed her keys eager to head off to school for her last day before the summer break began. We stepped off the porch after a quick kiss. She climbed in our SUV while I climbed in the passenger seat of Zeb's maroon Bronco idling at the curb. His classic ride still looked as if it had just left the dealership showroom, though the instrument panel and cassette player dated it. The unblemished chaparral leather interior exemplified his reputation for babying his vehicles.

"Zeb, y'all will be back by sunset?" Liddy asked as she pulled alongside before driving off.

Zeb smiled reassuringly. "Don't you fret none. We oughta be back before supper."

"Theo, you've got your phone don't you?" Liddy shouted as she crept forward.

Zeb honked while I slid my cell phone from my shirt pocket and stuck it out the window. Zeb and I chatted idly until we stopped for gas and coffee. Our conversation shifted as we pulled onto the Willacoochee Highway and drove toward Douglaston.

In the midst of Zeb telling me what he discovered about the limo he wanted to bid on, he blurted, "What do you think about that new gal in town, Silas' niece?"

I took a moment to absorb the question. "You mean Mandy?"

Zeb bobbed his head. "That's her."

"It appears she's adjusting to the slower pace of our little community pretty well considering her upbringing among the social circles of upper-crust Atlanta. Why?"

Zeb adjusted his hands on the steering wheel. "I want only the best for both my boys, and God only knows how earnestly I pray for each of them to find the right girl." A loud *harrumph* followed.

"So, you think one of your boys has his eyes on Mandy?"

"Let me say it this way. Out of the blue Jay's been buying and reading all sorts of books."

"Why does that make you believe there's more going on than Jay renewing his interest in reading?"

Zeb slapped the top of the steering wheel. "He's got a growing stack of Southern classics on his night table. *To Kill a Mockingbird, All the King's Men, God's Little Acre*, others I've never heard of. You'd think he joined a book club or something. Ain't like Jay."

"I agree it's highly possible. Jay and Jim are eligible bachelors. And, let's face it, Mandy's not only a pretty young woman, she's pretty darn smart too. Of course, her store's growing book collection won't hurt Jay none, no matter what happens."

Zeb scratched his beard, clearly in deep thought, not uttering another word. I settled back in the seat and reflected upon how much our friendship had blossomed since Liddy and I arrived in Shiloh. We realized his family's deep roots and long town history the minute we entered Adams Feed and General Hardware for decorations and a tree for our first Christmas in our new home.

For generations, Zeb's family had preserved their original Old General Store. Though over the last few decades, they had constructed the larger Adams Feed and Hardware retail store and warehouse enveloping the original building. The museum-like Old General Store now remains accessible only from inside the main retail area. Its lost-in-time artifacts on display serve as a reminder of the long legacy of the Adams family dating back to the establishment of Adams County in the early 1800s. In researching an article on the Adams' legacy in Shiloh, I learned that during the bleakest days of the Depression they had stood in the gap on more than one occasion to safeguard the economic well-being of Shiloh's tight-knit community when other business enterprises faced financial ruin.

After Zeb lost his wife, Jay and Jim's mother, he had instilled the same selfless values in them he'd learned from his parents. Whether blood-kin or not, folks throughout town looked up to Zeb as a wise and influential Town Father.

I shifted in my seat. "Have you heard anything more about John and Phoebe?"

"Like what?" Zeb asked, breaking his straight-ahead gaze with a quick glance at me.

"Do you think John will ever pop the question? It sure isn't any big secret they're more than friends."

"I understand your question. I happen to know for a fact they were about to get hitched before those trumped-up charges cost him three years of his life. It's such a shame too. I'm afraid John believes it's too late for him and Phoebe. Why do you ask?"

"Suffice it to say John mentioned something to me recently that leads me to believe God's stirring John to rethink what the future might still hold for him and Phoebe. So, you're thinking...?"

Zeb smiled. "Time'll tell. For now, we need to turn right up here. Our destination will be on the right just down that road."

THE SIGN IN front of the open chain link gates directed us to the Coffee County motor vehicle garage. A handful of used car dealers walked amongst the five vehicles on tap for the morning auction. After Zeb registered, we inspected all of them.

PURGATORY: A PROGENY'S QUEST

Zeb pointed and whispered, "Them three are dog-tired county pickups." He led me to the stake-body truck and declared as if I was deaf, "Don't look half bad. I wonder how she runs?"

I tugged Zeb's sleeve, "This doesn't look like any limo to me."

"Shh! Lower your voice. The limo I want to bid on is right over there. I want to see who's kicking its tires before I let anyone know I'm interested." Zeb winked and we climbed into the cab of the stake-body truck.

A deputy walked among the vehicles and announced, "We'll begin at eleven o'clock sharp. Y'all have only a few more minutes to inspect these vehicles before we begin this morning's auction. If anyone hasn't registered yet, ya better hurry over there." From the truck's cab, Zeb kept his eyes focused on the limo. Only one person seemed particularly interested in it. Zeb nudged me and pointed. We climbed out of the truck and walked to the dust-laden black and chrome stretch limo. Despite its appearance, its engine purred.

Zeb pulled open the front passenger door. "Theo, come over here. Feel this door. I didn't realize it'd be an armored limo. Doors are at least six inches thick. Windows must be an inch."

With my curiosity piqued, I asked Zeb for his copy of the vehicle's details. Being not an aficionado of older vehicles, especially Cadillacs, I discovered this was a one-of-a-kind 1982 Fleetwood Brougham that underwent after-factory modifications to become armored. Its conversion had been completed by Hess & Eisenhardt International, Ltd. in Ohio, and sold to Spiros Kyprianou, President of Cyprus, for $146,874.

The odometer recorded only 15,623 original miles on the 368 cubic inch V8 engine. Under a layer of dust and dirt, it appeared in near mint condition and mechanically sound. The armored design made it nearly impregnable or, as its paperwork stated, it had "no soft spots." A red ink note stated its console-controlled tear gas system had been deactivated.

I raised my head after studying the paperwork.

Zeb smiled. "What do you think?" He pointed to the roof. "This limo's got a removable roof hatch above the rear compartment of the vehicle. Can you envision Miss Shiloh riding up there in the Lightning Bug Festival parade?"

"Well, she'll be safe enough, that's for sure."

"Ladies and gentlemen, please gather over here." The county's auctioneer stood next to a Sheriff's deputy who held a clipboard. "We will begin this morning's auction with this 1998 Ford stake-body."

We listened with interest as each of the first four vehicles found new owners before the county auctioneer stepped in front of the 1982 Cadillac. "This vehicle was seized a year ago, and now this one-of-a-kind custom limo is ready for a new, law-abiding car collector to take her home. What do I hear for an opening bid?"

The man we saw earlier inspecting the car shouted from the rear of the vehicle, "Five-thousand dollars!"

Zeb measured the well-dressed bearded man and said with a smug grin, "Six-thousand."

Zeb and the stranger exchanged smirks. The auctioneer interrupted the silence. "I have six-thousand dollars. Are there any other bids?"

The stranger stepped to the driver's side of the limo. He caressed the chrome door handle before he removed his sunglasses, and glared at Zeb. "Ten thousand."

Zeb stroked his beard. "Mister, I don't know if you're buying this for someone or not, but I sorta figure there's going to be a young lady perched atop this vehicle next weekend."

Zeb eyed the auctioneer. "Twelve-thousand dollars. Of course, I assume we can drive this out of here today with all the necessary paperwork and a proper tag so my friend here can drive it back to Shiloh for me."

The auctioneer looked at the Sheriff's deputy. "Should be no problem—as long as the new owner has a valid driver's license and proof of insurance," the deputy told him.

Zeb folded his arms across his chest. "Well, Mister. I'm retired and got nothing better to do than dicker with you for this vehicle. So, unless you've got a hankering to fiddle away this sunny morning, you might as well make your best offer so we can get this over with. Me and my friend are getting hungry and have an afternoon drive ahead of us."

"Old man, I got twenty-thousand reasons in my pocket to help you and your friend get on the road right now."

The auctioneer smiled at the man as he slid his sunglasses back on. "Is twenty-thousand dollars your offer?" The stranger nodded coldly.

I looked at Zeb and whispered, "Are you sure this vehicle is worth it? Nobody else appears interested in entertaining a bid."

Zeb placed a reassuring arm on my shoulder. "Mister, that's a mighty fine and respectable offer for this old beast, but gosh, I'm partial to this particular classic Fleetwood. So I figure, since I asked you to give your best offer to end this finagling, I'm obliged to do likewise."

He peered at the auctioneer. "If my friend on the other side of this car agrees, and no one else objects, I'll end this at twenty-four thousand dollars. Besides, I'd like to get inside where there's some air conditioning and something cold to drink."

The stranger smiled and stretched his hand across the hood toward Zeb. "Do me one favor. Tell me where you're from. I'd at least like to know where this fine automobile will call home."

Zeb smiled at the stranger as the auctioneer looked at the others still milling about. "I have a final bid of twenty-four thousand dollars. Going once, twice." He hesitated one more moment before he smiled and yelled, "Sold for twenty-four thousand dollars."

Zeb grabbed the stranger's hand. "My name's Zeb Adams, and this here is my friend, Theo Phillips. We'll be headed back down to Shiloh over in Adams County as soon as we get the formalities over with. Stop by anytime."

"If it means anything to you, you bought yourself a pretty special vehicle. My name's Cy."

The Sheriff's deputy reached out to Zeb. "If you follow me, Mister Adams, we'll get you and your friend on the road quick as we can."

I followed Zeb and the Sheriff's deputy. Cy climbed into the passenger side of a black Cadillac Seville in sore need of a good wash. I got Zeb's attention before we entered the office.

"Looks like your new pal is partial to Cadillacs."

An hour later, Zeb tossed me the keys to his Bronco. "You don't mind if I drive the Caddy? I'll buy lunch at that whistle-stop cafe we passed coming in. This black beauty is sitting on less than a quarter of a tank."

SUNDAY MORNING, PETE HONKED THE HORN OF HIS NEW FOUR-door, vermillion-red pickup as Liddy and I crossed North Main Street walking to church. The only competition to the truck's sparkling appearance came from the gleam of Pete's wide-eyed look as he hopped down from the driver's seat.

"Mister P, Missus P! What do you think? Do you like it?" he asked, scurrying around to the front passenger door.

Mary pushed her door open and stepped onto the truck's running board. "Pete! For heaven's sake. Quit your gloating."

Liddy greeted Mary with welcoming extended arms. "How are you feeling this morning?"

Mary frowned at Pete before responding, "Thank you, but I've felt better." She glanced at her watch. "Oh my, gotta go. I'm going to be late."

Mary's curled lip directed at Pete became a playful smirk as Liddy took her arm. "I'll walk inside with you. They'll be in shortly. Come on, we don't want Arnie to fret looking for you before the service begins."

Pete ranted on about all the features of his more spacious new truck. I watched Liddy and Mary disappear into the church before I pulled open the rear passenger door and climbed inside.

"Pete, this backseat's big enough for triplets with room to spare," I said, crossing my legs.

"That's a fact. But if you don't mind, I'd prefer to fill the backseat one at a time."

I stepped out and closed the door. "Of course, I was speaking figuratively. How about you and I scoot on inside? We don't want Mary to think you like your truck more than her."

In the church foyer, Hillary stood outside the nursery preoccupied with checking in another batch of infants and toddlers before the service began. Pete walked over to his dad and his father-in-law, Larry, who were engaged in conversation along with Zeb and his son, Jim.

Hillary pushed a lock of hair from her face and smiled as I approached. "Good morning, Theo. Liddy and Mary just went into the sanctuary."

"Have you heard from Hal? Will he be back today?"

Hillary offered a guarded reply. "He called last night and assured me he planned on heading straight to Marie's place later this afternoon. Why do you ask?"

"Just curious. I figured you'd likely know." I shared an equally guarded tight-lipped smile.

Hillary placed her hands on her hips and stared at me. "What do you suspect Hal's been doing in Atlanta? Have you or your newshound buddy heard something?"

"Should I have heard anything? You and I both know this trip sprung out of the blue and came smack dab on the heels of the scandalous resignation of Congressman Stevens."

"Theo Phillips, Hal wants nothing to do with the high-cotton, unsavory political party wrangling, especially if it has anything to do with the current raunchy, swamp-water intrigue of Washington." Before I could respond, Hillary's eyes diverted, and her wrinkled forehead disappeared. "Megan! Let me see that little young man."

Andy Simmons walked alongside Megan holding Jessie, their one-year-old son. Hillary swooped Jessie into her arms while Andy and I exchanged a brief man-hug.

PURGATORY: A PROGENY'S QUEST

"When did y'all get in?"

Andy said, "Not soon enough for me or Megan. We sure have missed everyone."

Martha arrived with Liddy, who greeted Megan. "My goodness, Little Jessie is getting so big. Is he walking yet?"

Megan giggled and nodded. "Actually, it feels as though he's gone straight from crawling to running—a real-life Forrest Gump the way he attempts to run and run and run. He wears me out keeping up with him throughout the day."

Zeb announced, "Service is about to start."

Hillary looked at Megan. "Y'all go inside. We'll see you after."

She looked down at her fashionable running shoes and gave a hoot of laughter. "See, Jessie and me will be just fine."

I tapped Zeb on the shoulder before we scooted into our pew. "Jay not coming?"

"He went to the Methodist church with Mandy this morning." Zeb shrugged and added, "I reckoned when he heard Coach Priestly would be there to hear Phoebe sing he thought he oughta go as well, but I'm not so sure that was the real reason."

I cleared my throat to smother a laugh. "Yep, I'm sure he went because of John."

Zeb slid into our usual pew and settled in on the other side of Liddy, next to Larry Scribner. Arnie rose from his pulpit chair right after Mary stepped down from her piano and nestled beside Pete on the front pew. For the next forty-five minutes, Arnie's Memorial Day sermon dwelt on all the lives sacrificed to protect and defend the freedoms we enjoy in this country.

He decried mankind's celebration of bloodthirsty wars, and addressed how wars should not garner the same lasting, celebratory honor as those who died and deserved to be memorialized. Arnie described life as a precious gift from God, and mankind's battles by design extract life as the price of defending life. He stepped out from the pulpit, closed his Bible, and said with emphasis, "All who take up the sword will perish by it. May the anvils echo the death knell of war with the pounding of swords and spears into plowshares and pruning shears so wars will be forever forgotten."

After the service ended, Liddy tugged on my arm. "We've got to hurry along. In case you forgot, we walked to church and need to change before we drive to Marie's place. You can chitchat all you want with Larry and Sam this afternoon."

BY THE TIME WE slowed to cross the rickety one-lane bridge spanning Shiloh Creek and drove through the open fence gates onto Marie's farmstead, Liddy had filled me in on the buzz going around town about the upcoming Miss Shiloh contest that my article, to my dismay, had spurred. The ever churning gossip mill inferred this year's popular vote inclusion had instigated a trifurcated split within the community.

Liddy confessed, even after listening to the tittle-tattle before and after church, she couldn't say which of the three young women held an advantage over the others. Jeannie's popularity rested upon the fact she was the home-grown girl everyone knew, but Mandy's recent visibility around town had earned her share of support, too.

Liddy smiled as she spoke about Camille Gaines, the outsider and lesser-known of the three. She identified Camille as the dark horse in this year's contest. Mitch Johnson, the well-liked Chief of Police and Camille's boss, as well as Zeb Adams had cast their support for the demure police clerk and dispatcher.

The buckling of timbers and loose planks spanning the stream near Marie's farmhouse announced our arrival. We parked along the fence line adjacent the barn. Sam and Zeb acknowledged our arrival but kept busy tending the meat on the smoker. Larry sat on the porch with Joe and Arnie guarding the cold drinks. Liddy grabbed her bowl of potato salad from the rear floorboard before she shoved the door closed with her hip.

I retrieved our ice chest and said, "I'll catch up later. I'm going to drop this off beside the cold drinks on the front porch."

Marie greeted Liddy at the kitchen door before both disappeared inside.

After looking around, I asked Sam and Zeb, "Is John here?"

Tending to the meat on the smoker, Zeb said, "Marie ain't heard hide nor hair from him since he drove off to church this morning, but she promised he'd be along shortly."

Larry rocked back in his chair as I dropped off the ice chest on the porch. "We were just talking about Hal's impromptu invite to Atlanta. Have you heard anything?"

"Hillary mentioned this morning he might stop by later this afternoon." I spied Larry's confident smirk. "Why? What have you heard?"

Joe leaned forward in his cane chair. "I've got it from a well-connected lawyer friend in Atlanta that there's some closed-door, smoke-filled-room caucusing underway up there. The party's power brokers are struggling to name someone to fill Congressman Stevens' seat and Hal's name popped up on the list of candidates being tossed around."

I stared at Joe and Larry. Then Arnie said, with raised brow, "I'm not sure he'd be interested in wallowing in the rancid swamp engulfing Washington."

"I agree with you," I said. "I can't picture Hal being anyone's lackey either."

"However, the fact remains: Hal's on their shortlist," Joe said.

"Word's out they're desiring a new face to mend the damage Stevens inflicted with his dalliances. The governor asked them to come up with a bona fide eagle scout who'll bring a sharp mind and immutable moral compass."

"With elections this fall, they want someone who can help the party hold onto the voters' trust," Larry said.

Joe nodded. "In my opinion, Hal won't get the nod because he's single. They'll want a candidate with an upstanding wife who'll be up to the task of quelling the media's sensation-driven voracious curiosity."

"Let's hope you're right," I said.

Pete's arrival in his new red pickup interrupted our speculating over Hal's political future. Andy pulled in right behind Pete, driving his late-model metallic-gray GMC truck. A moment later, Andy carried Little Jessie in one arm and a grocery bag in the other. Megan pulled a diaper bag from the backseat as Mary greeted her, and they went inside. Pete joined us on the porch, but Andy and Jessie stopped off to visit Sam and Zeb.

Arnie reached into one of the ice chests and pulled out a Coke. "Sit down. Take a load off. We're only chewing the fat like usual."

Pete popped open his drink. "Coach here yet?"

Arnie said, "Not yet. Do you know what's up?"

"What makes you think I know anything?" Pete peered at Andy talking with Zeb and their dad as he swigged some Coke.

Arnie smiled and said, "This year's Miss Shiloh contest is gonna be interesting. Mary commandeered yours truly as one of the judges."

Pete began to campaign for his sister until Zeb hollered, "These butts are about done, and not too soon. John just pulled up with Phoebe. One of y'all let the ladies know the meat's done."

After we all helped ourselves to seconds and dug into the large bowl of banana pudding, John stood in front the sofa where he and Phoebe had eaten their dinner. "Sorry I got here a bit later than I had hoped, but I'm glad all y'all made it here. I only wish Jim and Jay were here, but I've no doubt they've got good reasons for passing up all this good food. And that reminds me, I want to thank Marie for hosting this cookout." John laughed as he added, "Frankly, my place ain't quite big enough."

John walked across the room and nudged Andy's arm, encouraging him to stand. John gawked at Larry and me and said, "Before this makes the paper, I want to share two bits of news to my friends and family." He sank his hands into his pants pockets. "I've decided to step down as the head coach and athletic director at Shiloh."

Zeb and I smiled. Larry jumped up. "You're leaving Shiloh?"

"I ain't leaving my home, but I am allowing someone else to lead the program." John slid his arm across Andy's broad shoulders. "It's official, Andy here is moving back to Shiloh as the school's new head coach and athletic director."

Mary asked, "I'm glad Andy and Megan will be moving back, but why the change? What're your intentions?"

John grinned. "The good news is Andy asked me to remain on his coaching staff."

Andy chuckled as he glanced back at Megan, who tried her best not to giggle. "Y'all need to understand that I accepted John's offer only after he explained his reasons. Let him tell you himself."

"First of all, though I wanted to bring Shiloh back to its glory days…" John eyed Marie then said, "I realized this spring what's missing is someone like Marie's son, Jessie Masterson. He made the program excel to the heights it enjoyed, not me."

Marie smiled and dabbed at tears from her eyes as she stared at Jessie's framed photo perched side by side with John's on the mantle. Though cousins, Marie and John had developed a bond that went well beyond blood kinship. On the opposite end of the mantle a picture of her uncle and aunt, John's parents, served as a reminder that this home and much of the farmstead property came as a timely gift from them. John built a modest cabin home two years ago at the far end of the fenced pasture that has allowed both to take care of each other as they recovered from separate yet connected tragedies.

John eyed Pete and Andy. "You two understand the impact Jessie had on our championship teams. After God opened the door for Andy and Megan to return home, my decision became crystal clear. His coaching experience at GCU has prepared him, much like Jessie years ago. Besides, I need to slow down and spend more time away from the locker room and ballfields."

I peeked over at Phoebe's pursed lips, and asked John, "Is there anything else you might want to share?"

Marie immediately shouted, "Who wants some banana pudding? I'll put a pot of coffee on, too."

I apologized to John about prodding him with my question.

He said, "One step at a time, my friend."

TUESDAY'S *SENTINEL* FORECASTED THE SWELTERING MEMORIAL Day weather would carry into the coming week. Farmers in the Flint River Basin welcomed such early summer-like forecasts so their crops could bask in abundant sunshine. Yet the same sizzling weather slowed the pace of life for everyone else. The farmers might welcome their burgeoning green fields, but as for me, I had been mowing my yard every week since before Easter and likely would continue the weekly ritual until Halloween.

Liddy's shoulder-length ponytail swayed as she hopped off the back porch. She had on a gray Shiloh High V-neck top over her favorite faded jeans and a pair of navy canvas slip-ons. Her students might have begun their summer vacation last Friday, but teachers and support staff had two more days of paperwork and meetings to bring the school year to an official end.

I shut off the mower's engine. "You sure look mighty fine, ma'am. You scooting off to school?"

"I'm proud of you for getting this done before it gets too hot." She put a jug of ice water on the stoop. "I'll likely not get home until after four today. Phoebe and I want to organize and plan for our summer camp. I pulled some pork chops from the freezer for tonight. Will you set them in the fridge when you come inside?"

I climbed off the mower and stepped toward Liddy with my arms extended for a hug, but she jumped back. "Save that for tonight when you're not so yucky."

She blew a kiss and walked toward the front driveway.

CITY HALL'S CLOCK chimed ten right after I blew the last blade of grass off the sidewalk and stowed the blower, weed whacker, and mower in the storage shed. For another week our lawn and gardens would rival the other properties throughout our neighborhood. There's something about residing in a tight-knit, long-established community that spurs each homeowner to do their part to help the overall appearance of the neighborhood.

Not hearing any news about Hal's trip to Atlanta caused an uneasy feeling about my hasty assumptions. Right after lunch I decided to swing by the *Sentinel* and then City Hall.

MARY HAD CLIMBED out of her sky-blue hatchback and popped her tailgate when I walked up the sidewalk to the *Sentinel*. She reached for a cardboard box in the back of her car when I gently grabbed her arm. "Young lady, allow me to carry that in for you."

Mary stepped aside and sighed. "Thanks, Theo. But, Hell's bells. Who do you think put it in the car in the first place?"

"I don't doubt it for a moment, but if Liddy caught wind I allowed you to tote even a box of tissues for the next few months, I'd never hear the end of it. Please, you're doing me a favor."

One whiff of the box revealed Mary had been on a lunch run to Bubba's Barbecue.

Mary chuckled as she held the front door open. Larry looked up, hunched over Martha's shoulder as she sat at her desk. "About time. Your mom and I thought you got lost."

"Oh, Daddy. Phillip Archer was there. We talked for a few minutes while I waited on our lunch order."

"Did he say anything about Hal's trip?" I asked.

"Thanks, Theo. You took the words right out of my mouth," Larry said, staring at Mary.

— 41 —

PURGATORY: A PROGENY'S QUEST

Mary reached into the box and removed a white Styrofoam take-out plate. "As a matter of fact, no. He did say Hank should be home from the VA Hospital in Augusta in a couple of weeks." Mary proceeded to her desk and removed the lid on her lunch. "I'm famished. So unless you want to harass me some more, I'm going to enjoy my lunch."

"I'll share mine with you if you'd like," Larry said. We walked to his office.

"No thanks. Smells good, though. I'm still digesting the Dagwood sandwich I made before I left the house. I'll grab a Coke with you, though. What do you want?"

"Let's sit down in the breakroom. My desk's a train wreck. I'll take a Dr Pepper."

I slid onto the picnic table bench opposite Larry and twisted the lid off my Coke bottle. Larry dumped some of his fries on a paper towel and pushed them across the table. "I can't possibly eat all this anyway."

"I'm taking it you've not heard anything more about Hal?"

Larry shook his head as he stuffed a couple of French fries in his mouth. "Sounds like our deaf and dumb peckerheads in Atlanta are in a conundrum and can't get a consensus for any one name to recommend to the Governor."

I chuckled briefly at Larry's colorful depiction. "Be that as it may, I'm about to see Hal in a bit. Maybe, just maybe, he'll give me an indication of where he stands should his name get put forward." I washed down a cold fry with a swig of Coke. "In the meantime, why don't you put together an article about Andy Simmons being named Athletic Director and Head Coach at Shiloh High? Once folks realize John's not leaving and that he recommended Andy, they'll see the wisdom behind the decision."

Larry chewed a bit before he swallowed. "Already working on a piece about that. Do you think John and Phoebe will finally quit playing their cat and mouse relationship game? They've been dodging the inevitable for close to a decade."

"When John hesitated to say more, I'm thinking he's not as ready as we'd believed."

MANDY KNELT IN the Elysium Emporium's cramped display window. She dabbed her forehead with her sleeve and mustered a perfunctory but rather brief smile when I waved. A colorful lightning bug poster provided the backdrop for her eclectic display of jewelry, figurines, coffee mugs, and festival t-shirts along with a cute children's book featuring a cartoonish lightning bug on its cover. She even had tiny lights flickering inside painted bottles and mason jars. It reminded me of when I used to collect lightning bugs as a youngster. The Elysium Emporium appeared ready to attract more than its fair share of curious customers during this weekend's festival.

While I walked across Adams Avenue, I looked over my shoulder at Edwards Barbershop. Wilson hovered over a customer in his grandfather's old barber chair. Hub and his son Marcellus appeared equally busy with customers in the other two chairs. A handful of familiar faces sat in chairs along the opposite wall and thumbed through magazines. Although Liddy had bugged me about needing a haircut, waiting for a better time seemed like a good idea.

I walked across Town Square with its manicured lawn and brick walkways. Trimmed red-tip shrubs, azaleas, and crape myrtles with colorful annual flowers nestled in lush beds of pine needles invited visitors to the main entrance. Jessie Masterson's once pristine bronze memorial on the far Main Street corner had acquired a golden-brown patina since its erection three years ago.

PURGATORY: A PROGENY'S QUEST

Inside the Masterson Administration Building, I walked across the city's emblem embedded in the marble-floored lobby and headed for the Mayor's office.

Hillary walked out of Hal's office clutching a folder against her chest. She looked back into Hal's office and said, sounding a bit exasperated, "Yes, I'll get right on it."

"Is this a bad time to ask if our illustrious Mayor is available?" I craned my neck to try and catch Hal's attention as Hillary sat at her desk.

Hillary puffed a couple of wild hairs from her frazzled brow. "He's all yours," she said but signaled me to wait a second. She grabbed her phone and pushed the intercom button. "Mister Mayor, Mister Phillips would like an audience with you. Should I let him in?" Her words spewed a tinge of sarcasm, but she didn't even wait for a reply and nodded toward the open door with an impish smirk.

Hal stood at his office doorway, sleeves rolled up and tie dangling. As he inspected the tuck of his dress shirt he said, "Can't say I wasn't expecting you. Come on in but excuse my office. I've been pretty busy catching up after being away all last week." He turned the two padded armchairs in front of his cluttered desk so we could face each other.

"By the looks of things, you've got a lot of catching up to do, so I won't beat around the bush. Larry's fit to be tied, and you know how he can get."

Hal propped elbows on knees as he leaned forward. "I guess that means he expects you'll weasel out of me what went on in Atlanta the last few days?"

"Pretty much. With all we've been hearing while you've been away, a lot of folks are wondering if this town is about to lose a mayor to gain a U.S. Congressman." Hal held his steadfast gaze until I added, "Larry's frustrated that none of his so-called well-connected buddies in Atlanta have been helpful."

Hal straightened up from his hunched position and leaned back in his chair with fingers interlocked behind his head. "Yes, I got pulled into a couple of hush-hush meetings, but you know me well enough by now. I'd never kowtow to their whims and wishes like some yes-man. My dad would crawl out of his grave and smack me silly first."

"That's about what I said to Larry, but—"

"Before you say anything more, I slammed the doors shut before I left. There were plenty more qualified names mentioned while I was up there—excellent fellas with impeccable reputations. So why don't we move onto the topic of my brother Hank coming back home in a few days?"

"Is he going to stay here in Shiloh?"

"Guess we'll all have to see after he gets back. He told me last week he has no immediate plans other than enjoy getting back home." Hal stood beside his chair and stretched out his hand.

I stood and we shook. "Thanks, Mayor. By the way, is Hillary okay? She sure looked frazzled."

Hal laughed. "Hilly and I got into a rather enthusiastic difference of opinion about the upcoming Miss Shiloh contest."

"Let me guess. She's supporting Camille since she works right down the hall in the police department office?"

Hal walked me to the door. "My friend, if I hear anything more about what's happening in Atlanta, I'll call you or Larry."

Hillary looked up from her desk and said goodbye as I stepped out of Hal's office, but I noticed a sparkle in her eyes seemed more intended for Hal, who stood in the doorway. Hal said, "Hilly, please, no more interruptions for the rest of the day. I gotta find the top of my desk before I go home tonight."

DURING OUR CONVERSATION at dinner, Liddy asked, "Did you talk to John today?"

"No. Why?"

Liddy sighed. "Phoebe wasn't her usual self this afternoon. When I asked her what's the matter, she said John had been acting peculiar ever since the cookout."

"Did she explain what she meant by *peculiar*?" I asked.

"She said when he drove her home, he grew distant and quiet and, for the last couple of days, she feels he's been avoiding her. She's convinced John might be regretting stepping down."

I reached across the table and placed my hand on top of Liddy's. "I'm pretty sure John's still struggling with bottled-up emotions he's kept a cork on for quite some time. If he's got any regrets, they've nothing to do with Andy taking over."

We ventured onto the porch, lay together in our hammock, and watched the streetlights flicker on in the neighborhood. Liddy nestled her head against my shoulder and whispered, "I remember a young man who struggled with his fancy dreams and wondered if getting married might alter those dreams. Does he still have any regrets?"

"Nope. Looking back, I thank God a certain young girl said yes when I finally mustered the nerve to propose to her."

7

WEDNESDAY'S *SENTINEL* INCLUDED A FULL-PAGE COLOR INSERT highlighting Friday and Saturday's festival schedule and listed the Miss Shiloh judges: Kay Abernathy, Shiloh High School Principal; Dr. Arnie Wright, Pastor of Shiloh Baptist Church; Barbara Patterson, Co-Owner of the Shiloh Motel and Bubba's BBQ; and Dr. John Matson, Pastor of Shiloh Methodist Church. Mary had not only cajoled them into serving as this year's judges but had also kept their identities under wraps until this morning.

Minutes after Liddy drove away for her last full workday before a well-deserved—albeit short-lived—break, I prepared to leave the house to get my overdue haircut at Edwards Barbershop. With an ocean-blue clear sky overhead this first day of June, I chose to wear khaki shorts, a red polo, and casual hiking sandals since I had no office visits planned. On the way out the front door, I grabbed my UGA safari hat and sunglasses from our wall-mounted coat rack.

I knew if I arrived right after Wilson opened, my wait would be brief, though I planned to dawdle long enough to glean the latest buzz going around town—no different than when Wilson's grandfather ran the shop. Though many of the wilier patrons flipped through stained and dog-eared magazines cluttering the waiting area, with few exceptions everyone felt the obligation to insert their two cents about the latest goings-on in town. Whereas Adams Feed and Hardware Store encouraged prolonged chatter over a rousing game of checkers and, more often than not, the ripest scuttlebutt became more urgent than the next strategic move. Gossip-mongering at Edwards Barbershop, on the other hand, tended to slow the pace of each haircut. The fact is, like many rural towns, whenever two or more folks gathered in any of Shiloh's establishments you pretty much could be assured the latest juicy news came with an ample supply of opinions.

Intent on getting my haircut, I ran into Mitch Johnson in front of Arians Realty and Property Management where he greeted me with a hearty smile. His smile lingered as he inspected my exposed knobby knees.

"Good morning, Mitch. Can I buy you a cup of coffee?"

I gestured to The Butcher Shoppe. I had not been able to catch up with Mitch recently. This seemed as good a time as any. Eighteen months had passed since Hal and the City Council hired Mitch to reactivate the Shiloh Police Department. He appeared tireless in his efforts to make the most of the limited resources earmarked to support the town's three-person police force.

While we waited for Bernie to bring us our two large to-go coffees, Mitch asked, "Are you taking the day off? You don't usually dress this casual around town."

I removed my glasses and hat and finger-combed my mussed and greying light brown hair. "My only plans today involve a haircut and harassing Zeb into a friendly game or two of checkers at his store." I pointed to the nearby table. "If you've got a few minutes...?"

Mitch smiled and grabbed his handheld radio. "Camille, I'm grabbing coffee at The Butcher Shoppe." He chose a seat facing the front of the restaurant.

"Here you go, my two fine handsome friends." Bernie placed our coffees on the table. "Can I get you anything else?" She pointed to the pastry behind the glass display on the counter.

Mitch shook his head with a polite grin.

I said, "No, thank you. Your pastries are mighty tempting for this old man, but I better pass."

"You and Miss Liddy have any vacation plans this summer?"

"Nah, we're sticking around town. Our two sons are bringing their families down for the Independence Day Jubilee, and after the rest of the family leaves, our two oldest grandsons will be staying with us for a couple of weeks. Besides, Liddy will be tied up with the school's art and music summer camp."

"What about your other grandkids?" Mitch asked.

"Sissy, our twelve-year-old granddaughter, will be going to Camp Chippewa near Blue Ridge while the boys are here. The two youngest ones will be making sandcastles on Jekyll Island with their parents." I leaned back in my chair, sipped my coffee. "Yep, everyone's doing something exciting this summer except me."

Mitch nodded, smiling. "Aren't you going to enjoy hanging out with your grandsons while they're here?"

"Oh, I reckon I'll get a pair of coveralls dirty pretending to be a farmer for the sake of my grandsons. Marie suggested I bring them out to her farm. They're city boys. I plan to show them how to dig for worms and go fishing and catch crawdads in Shiloh Creek. Marie said she'll expose them to life outside of their electronic games."

Mitch leaned to one side as his eyes darted to the door and then stood up.

"Sit down, Mitch," Jeannie said with a sheepish look. "I only stopped in to buy a cup of coffee. I forgot to buy more coffee grounds for the office."

Mitch slid a chair out. "Join us while you're waiting."

Jeannie shook her head. "No, thanks. I need to get right back. Don't let me interrupt your conversation. Miss Bernie's already poured a to-go cup for me."

Mitch sat back down and smiled as Jeannie left.

"How's Tyler handling the graveyard shift for you?" I asked to regain Mitch's attention.

"Tyler? Oh, yeah. Hawk's Mister Gung-ho. Of course, after the sun goes down, our town rolls up its sidewalks and stays pretty quiet anyway," Mitch said, fingering the rim of his coffee cup.

"Is that why you don't carry a gun?"

Mitch reached for his handheld radio. "It's in my vehicle, and I hope I'll never have to use it."

"For everyone's sake, I hope not as well. So tell me, does Camille like her new truck?"

My inquiry sparked a cockeyed grin. "Lord, have mercy, yes. And with Pete's old truck, the girl would give the Dukes of Hazzard a run for their money with her heavy foot."

"Funny, when I interviewed her last week I struggled to get much more than a polite yes sir or no sir."

Mitch laughed. "She does thrive in her introverted domain at the office. Most would go bonkers keeping busy without a lot of folks to chat with throughout the day, but not Camille. Even when I'm in the office, I hardly know she's at her desk unless the phone rings. Mind you, something tells me she'd be a real hellcat if someone ever got her dander up."

Camille's voice came across his radio, "Mitch. You there?"

He grabbed his handheld. "Yep. What's up?"

"The Mayor called and wanted you to stop by his office."

"10-4. Tell Hillary I'll be there in ten." Mitch got up and clipped his radio back onto his belt. "We need to meet for coffee more often, Theo."

I shook his hand. "I'd like that. Oh yeah, one more quick question. What do you think about Camille's chances in the Miss Shiloh Contest? Jeannie and Mandy aren't by any means wallflowers."

"I really can't say," Mitch said, brow arched. "I ain't ever seen her without faded jeans and boots. Heck, she doesn't even wear makeup, and her glasses don't do her any justice either. Guess we'll both see whether Cinderella shows up Friday night."

AFTER DINNER, LIDDY sat in her cozy armchair, feet stretched out on the ottoman. I sat across from her, my reddened and once sun-starved legs propped up on my recliner's extended footrest. Our Tiffany reading lamp cast a soft amber glow on the bay window as darkness arrived a tad tardier than the previous evening.

"Did you use the aloe cream like I told you after you showered?" Liddy asked.

I responded with a feeble, simpering nod.

"Theo Phillips, how many times do I have to remind you to use sunscreen, especially on those sexy, but sun-deprived legs of yours? Our grandsons will be here in one month, and you're gonna have to make sure they protect themselves too. I'd hate for them to waste any of their time with us nursing a nasty sunburn."

"Message received loud and clear, my darling. How did it go with John Priestly in his first day as the new Vice Principal, especially since Kay flew the coop for a few days?"

Liddy's eyes sparkled and smile widened. "Phoebe and I kinda enjoyed the fact he kept busy settling into his new office across from Kay Abernathy's. When he made the morning announcements, applause and whistles filled the halls. Mind you, Andy paraded past my room headed to John's office at least three or four times throughout the day. Phoebe told me Andy reminded her of Jessie Masterson's first days on campus."

"I hope everyone's expectations won't be influenced by Jessie's bronze image reminder on town square. Jessie Masterson can't be replaced. Besides, who can keep pace with a legacy that grows larger with each passing year?" I said, glancing at a copy of *Jessie's Story* on my bookshelf. "If I have any regrets since we arrived here, capsulizing Jessie's heroic life in the darn book would be one of them."

Liddy squirmed in her seat and hugged her knees. "Why would you say such a thing? What you included in the book about Jessie helped Marie swap a mother's grief for a treasure trove of fond memories. Others who mourned Jessie's tragic death would agree your portrayal of Jessie's life helped them, too."

"I know you're right, but whenever Andy's name got brought up today around town, Jessie got mentioned right along with it."

"Oh, fiddlesticks! John knows the weightiness of those expectations. He'll make sure Andy gets the kind of support he'll need to succeed, whether it includes a championship right away or not." Liddy climbed out of her cozy perch, walked over to me, and planted a big kiss on my cheek. "Why don't you find us a movie to watch while I perk some coffee?"

Liddy returned with two mugs and sat down on the opposite end of the sofa so I could rest my feet across her lap. While she rubbed more aloe on my legs, I scrolled for a suitable movie to watch on television.

She sipped her coffee. "Any more news about Hank?"

I shrugged. "How about *The Quiet Man?*"

Liddy slapped my sunburnt shins. "You and your John Wayne movies. Well, at least this one doesn't have anyone getting shot at."

8

THE FLURRY OF ACTIVITY ALONG THE STREETS BORDERING TOWN Square piqued Liddy's curiosity. City workers erected barricades at the intersections and hoisted Lightning Bug Festival banners throughout town. Right after lunch, she pestered me to take a walk with her into the center of town to get a firsthand look at the festival preparations before crowds filled the streets later in the evening. At the corner of Broad and Main, Liddy tugged on my hand and accelerated her pace. On the Arians Realty and Property Management door Jeannie had posted a sign reading *Closed for the Festival*. Next door, Silas examined the hustle and bustle in Town Square from his restaurant's doorway.

"What do you think, Silas?" Liddy said as we stopped and observed the transformation of the city's flatbed trailer into the festival's main stage. City workers affixed the red, white, and blue skirting to hide the trailer's underside. Others anchored steel steps to the tail of the trailer near Jessie Masterson's bronze statue and convenient to a ten-by-ten white canvas enclosed canopy. Under another white canopy at the opposite end of the stage, wires connected stacked sound equipment to microphones and speakers onstage.

Silas shook his head. "Why is it, Miss Liddy, we make such a big fuss each year about such a little bug?" He pointed to the street corners on both sides of Town Square. Traffic barriers now sealed off Adams and Broad streets from all vehicle traffic.

PURGATORY: A PROGENY'S QUEST

With a sigh, Silas said, "And this year, since Bernie decided to give her niece a hand at the Emporium, I might as well close early today, too. Of course, we both will want to watch the Miss Shiloh contest tonight. Who knows? Mandy might win. I know that'd make Bernie very happy."

Liddy squeezed Silas' hand. "Please tell Mandy we wish her good luck tonight."

Then Liddy dragged me to Adams Street where Edwards Barbershop and other shops and businesses had long been closed. A carnival company filled the barricaded street with kiddie rides and game booths. Liddy particularly enjoyed the gigantic painted lightning bug with its blue illuminated tail perched atop the roped-off entrance to the children's rides and games. Food vendors were interspersed among the arts and crafts vendors along Broad Street between City Hall, Shiloh Baptist Church, and the Shiloh Library. On both Main Street corners out front of Town Square sat two purple-painted post office mailboxes labeled, *Cast Your Ballots for Miss Shiloh Here.*

BY FIVE O'CLOCK whiffs from the succulent vendor offerings and a cacophony of carnival noises coaxed us to walk the two blocks into the center of town. Giggles and laughter of children intermingled with mechanical noises from kiddie rides as barkers cajoled young men to show off their skill for a chance to win a prize. Hillary and Mary sat behind a table in front of the festival's official tent handing out extra copies of the *Sentinel's* full-color festival pullout. Along Main Street, folks unfolded chairs and spread out blankets to reserve their spots in anticipation of the six o'clock Miss Shiloh contest.

Mitch Johnson talked with a Sheriff's deputy at the northern end of the blocked off Main Street. At the opposite end of the traffic-free street, Tyler dangled his feet from the tailgate of his Shiloh Police truck. He'd parked his patrol vehicle parallel to the traffic barrier redirecting traffic coming south on Main Street to the circuitous detour taking vehicles around the center of town.

Liddy grabbed my hand as we weaved our way through the crowd and crossed Main Street to visit Hillary and Mary. "This turnout sure is crazy," she said, standing in front of the table.

Hillary looked up after she handed another stack of Miss Shiloh ballots to Mary. "Isn't this great? I can't remember such a huge crowd like this on Friday night. The bigger crowd usually turns out for Saturday's parade. If this is any indication, tomorrow's turnout should create a parking nightmare around here." She looked up to her apartment above The Butcher Shoppe and snickered. "I just joked with Mary that I should sell tickets for folks to watch the parade from my living room window."

"Where's Hal hiding?" I asked.

"He's still in his office handing out last-minute instructions to Jeannie, Amanda, and Camille. They arrived a while ago and went in to get dressed for the pageant."

After Mary instructed a young couple about where to cast their ballots later this evening, she said, "I'm just glad we decided to hold off until tomorrow to announce the winner. It looks like it'll be a late night tallying the ballots. Want to lend a hand?"

I clutched Liddy's hand. "I'm sure hungry. Let's grab a bite before the contest gets started."

"Chicken!" Mary called out as we walked away laughing.

Liddy looked back and said with a concocted apologetic pout, "He'll be sound asleep by the time the festival shuts down this evening anyway."

We found a seat atop the steps leading up to Shiloh Baptist Church's main entrance while we each munched on a deep-fried turkey leg. From our elevated vantage point, we could watch most all the activity filling Town Square.

"Mister and Missus P, why aren't you down there in the crowd?" Pete Simmons asked. He stood on the sidewalk with Phillip Archer and Jay and Jim Adams.

I lifted my Styrofoam cup of iced tea. "Enjoying dinner."

Caught taking a bite out of her sandwich, Liddy swallowed and wiped her mouth. "What about you four? What are all y'all doing milling about?"

"Hal just chased us out of City Hall," Phillip said as Jay elbowed him.

"Now why would Hal do that?" she asked, stiffening her back.

Pete looked at Jim and Jay and said, "Just showing our support for this year's Miss Shiloh."

I couldn't help but laugh. "And who might the next Miss Shiloh be? You know something all those folks down there don't know yet?"

Phillip blurted, "His sister, of course!"

Jay shoved Phillip against Pete and said, "What do you mean? Now hold your horses one cotton-picking minute. I thought you agreed Mandy has just as much chance as Jeannie this year?"

Jim stepped between Phillip and Jay and draped his arms across their shoulders. He then looked up at Liddy. "This is why Hal asked us to leave."

Unable to stop laughing, I said, "Would the four of you mind if the rest of us enjoy the suspense that's about to unfold in a few more minutes?" I pointed to the City Hall portico. "It appears Hal's about to get the show started."

"Come on guys. Let's find a spot to watch from Main Street." Jay looked at Liddy and me. "Y'all coming? Looks like it'll be a standing-room-only crowd in front of the stage."

I glanced at Liddy and said, "I think we'll watch and listen just fine from right here."

At the first stroke of six on the City Hall clock, Kay Abernathy, Arnie Wright, Doctor Matson, and Barbara Patterson climbed the steps onto the stage and took their assigned places behind a crimson-draped table at the far end of the platform. Hal followed and stood at the podium. The PA system's feed of music faded as his microphone let out an ear-piercing squeal. The crowd whooped and whistled until Hal stepped away from the mic and held his hands high in the air.

"Thank you. Thank you. We've got three young ladies eager to share a few minutes with you this evening." More whistles and cheers briefly interrupted Hal. After a pause, the crowd settled down as he continued. "Before I introduce each of our beautiful contestants, I'd like to introduce our other very important guests this evening."

Hal introduced each of the four judges. My attention diverted to Mitch Johnson engaged in conversation with a young woman wearing a floral embroidered denim dress. She appeared flustered as her arms flailed about as she spoke. Mitch listened, arms folded across his chest, occasionally nodding, or shaking his head while the young lady continued to speak.

Liddy yanked on my shirt sleeve. "The girls are about to come out. Are you paying attention?"

"Hold on one sec. Mitch appears to have his hands full with another young lady." When I looked again, Mitch walked up the sidewalk in our direction with the young woman one step behind.

Liddy asked, "Who's that girl?"

Mitch stopped and asked, "Have y'all seen Gus Appleton anywhere this evening?"

"Sorry, Mitch," I said.

Mitch tendered a half-hearted smile. "Miss Sarah says she's a family friend and just drove in from out of town. She figured she'd find him here since he wasn't at home."

I got to my feet, craned my neck, and pointed to the parking lot behind City Hall. "I think you'll find him smoking a cigarette beside his old Lincoln."

Liddy tugged on my pants leg as Mitch and the young lady walked away. "Sit down. I think Mitch can handle getting Miss Sarah and Gus together from here. Jeannie just walked onto the stage. Let's listen to Mary's introduction of the three contestants."

Jeannie waved a greeting to the crowd while Mary described her yellow halter evening dress. Her light-brown hair bounced on her shoulders. Amanda followed wearing an all-white summer dress naturally setting off her Mediterranean complexion and black hair. She wore a magnolia blossom in the white ribbon securing long dark hair falling halfway down her back.

The rowdiest *oohs* and *aahs* came when Camille appeared on the stage wearing a full-length, red floral evening gown. Her pale auburn hair hung across her back in a loose French braid. I looked over to Liddy and whispered, "I think Cinderella showed up."

It was now time for each contestant to explain why they should become Miss Shiloh. Jeannie took the microphone first.

"Having grown up right here in Shiloh, I recognize so many of your faces. I went to school with many of you. I'm proud to be considered once again for this honor, and if I earn your support this year to become Miss Shiloh, I will cherish every opportunity to represent our town throughout the year."

Amanda accepted the microphone next. "I can't say I recognize all your faces yet, but I can say I am tickled to be up here tonight. Everyone I have gotten to meet since I moved into Shiloh and reopened the Elysium Emporium has been so supportive and kind. I kind of feel I have already won, just being invited to participate in this year's pageant. I want to say a special thanks to my Uncle Silas and Aunt Bernice for making this evening possible. Thank you, and please feel free to call me Mandy whenever you stop in at the store."

Camille accepted the microphone from Mandy and stared at it for a couple of seconds before she raised her head with an uneasy look stymying her first words.

"I ain't very good at giving speeches, or for that matter standing in front of so many folks. Like Mandy, I don't know too many of y'all, and most of y'all don't know me real well either. I want to thank Miss Jeannie and Mandy for being so kind and helpful. Heck, they're far more comfortable wearing these fancy dresses and walking in these high heels than me. If all y'all vote me to be your next Miss Shiloh, I'll do my very best to make you good folks proud you chose me."

The three waved as they departed the stage. Mary reminded everyone to cast their ballot for who should be the next Miss Shiloh. The final decision would factor in the weighted votes of the four distinguished judges along with all popular votes cast that evening. Mary ended with, "Anyone needing a ballot, please stop by the official festival tent. Please place your ballots in either of the bright purple mailboxes just beyond the ends of the stage."

Hal returned to the podium. "We want to thank Missus Mary Simmons and all those who helped tonight. Please enjoy yourselves the rest of the evening. We look forward to seeing everyone tomorrow for the festival parade at eleven o'clock when we all will find out who will be this year's Miss Shiloh."

Liddy stood and wiped the backside of her jeans. "You about ready to head home for a cup of coffee and a slice of carrot cake?"

"I think so. We can take in more of the festival tomorrow. Right now, coffee and cake sound good to me."

PURGATORY: A PROGENY'S QUEST

Before we crossed Main Street, I saw Pete next to Mary at the table in front of the festival tent. Jim, Jay, and Phillip pestered Hal and Hillary behind the stage. Mitch Johnson walked among the dispersing crowd and appeared to head to the far side of Town Square where the carnival rides continued to stir plenty of laughter and screams. The PA system boomed calliope music throughout downtown.

Liddy looked up to the second-floor window of the Arians Building. "Theo, look up. Joe and Missy are waving." Liddy waved and giggled like a giddy schoolgirl. "Now I know why we didn't see Sam and Susanna Simmons tonight."

"I bet Sam arranged their vantage point to temper Susanna's proud mother exuberance for Jeannie," I chuckled.

"Heading home?" John Priestly asked as he approached, his arm around Phoebe's waist.

Liddy asked, "You want to join us for coffee and cake?"

Phoebe wrapped her arm around John's waist. "Thanks, Liddy. But I think we're going to wander around before we call it a night."

The streetlamps flickered on as we left Main Street and strolled down Broad Street's sidewalk toward home. Liddy squeezed my hand when she heard Gus Appleton across the street beside a pale blue Buick sedan with Louisiana tags talking with the young woman we'd seen with Mitch earlier in the evening.

"Evening, Gus. We're glad your young friend found you," Liddy said with a cordial but inquiring inflection in her voice.

Gus seemed startled as he turned. "Oh! Hey, Mister and Missus Phillips. Enjoy your evening." He waved briefly and turned his attention back to Miss Sarah, who rubbed her eyes and shook her head ever so slowly. She appeared to avoid direct eye-to-eye contact with Gus or us.

NOT LONG AFTER Liddy and I had finished off our carrot cake and sat down to relax on the porch listening to the sounds of the festival, two cars pulled around the corner. The first, Gus' black, well-worn Lincoln, pulled up alongside the curb. The other, the blue Buick we saw earlier, parked behind the Lincoln.

We watched as Gus and the young lady came up our walkway. "Mister Phillips, I apologize for stopping by this late and unannounced, but I need your help," Gus said, fumbling for the right words.

"What can we do for you, Gus? Should I include Sarah?" I asked, eying his nervous look. Sarah reached into her pocketbook and pulled out an envelope.

Gus uttered as if he feared what I might say, "Mister and Missus Phillips, I didn't know where to bring her, but after you walked past us earlier, I took it as a sign from heaven above."

All three of us looked at Gus with raised brows.

"Gus, what's wrong?" I asked. I stared at Sarah clutching the envelope even tighter.

Sarah tried to speak, but Gus spoke over her. "This young woman is Miss Sarah Mae Arnaquer, Dixie's daughter."

PURGATORY: A PROGENY'S QUEST

9

SARAH SEEMED TO SENSE OUR AWKWARDNESS AND RELUCTANCE after Liddy offered her a gracious smile and invited them into our living room. But Gus hesitated, seeming more interested in his vehicle than accepting Liddy's invitation.

I edged closer to Gus and whispered, "Does she know about Dixie?" I nudged him across the threshold and he shook his head.

Liddy pointed Sarah down the hall to the bathroom. Gus gnawed on his lower lip. With one eye on the hallway, he said, "When she explained who she was and why she showed up here, I didn't know how to tell her about Dixie. I'm still uncertain why she sought me out. I'm not sure what to say or do. She can't stay in my apartment." His desperate frown spoke volumes.

"Can I get you a cup of coffee?" Liddy asked Gus as I sat down in my recliner opposite him seated in Liddy's cozy armchair.

"Thank you, Missus Phillips. I guess a cup of strong black coffee would suit me," Gus replied, appearing unsettled in Liddy's plush armchair. The way he fidgeted you'd have thought the seat cushion was carved of stone. He planted his feet square on the floor and stared at the ottoman offering his knees little wiggle room between it and the front of the chair.

When Sarah reappeared, she dismissed Liddy's offer for coffee but asked for ice water instead. She took a seat on the sofa but seemed as uneasy as Gus. Her eyes danced from the magazines displayed on the top of our coffee table to the family pictures spanning the mantle and scanned our bookshelves.

"Here you go, young lady. I've also got some carrot cake if you'd like."

With a sheepish look, Sarah muttered, "That'd be nice. Thank you, ma'am." Birdlike, she took a sip of her water, looked to place the glass down on the coffee table and hesitated. I climbed out of my chair and slid a coaster in front of her.

After Liddy served Sarah and Gus, she sat at the opposite end of the sofa and glanced at Sarah. Liddy's "My, oh my!" broke the silence deafening. "So, you're Dixie Arnaquer's daughter?"

Sarah swiveled her hips to look at Liddy better. "Yes, ma'am. Do you know her?"

Liddy's eyes darted at Gus and me with a look I knew well. The next words would come from my mouth, not hers. I scooted to the edge of my seat, stroked the corners of my mouth with my fingertips to buy a few seconds.

Sarah's thirst for answers drew her focus to me. "Wh-wh-what's wrong? What's happened to Momma? Where is she?"

I felt compelled to stand, looked across the room at Sarah's wide-eyed stare, and put into words what she needed to hear. I glanced over at Gus, but he shrank further back into the chair as his head drooped. Liddy inched closer to Sarah, but her eyes encouraged me to respond.

"Miss Sarah, there's no easy way to tell you. Your momma died in an accident over a year ago. You never knew, did you?"

"No!" Sarah burst into tears.

"I'm dreadfully sorry we're the ones to break the news to you like this. My wife and I got to know her when she visited Shiloh, but she never mentioned anything about having a daughter."

Liddy crept beside Sarah and draped her arm around her. Tears streamed down Sarah's cheeks as she moaned, "I've got no one. Everyone's left me. I hate you, Momma. I hate you."

Liddy stroked her shoulder. "What do you mean, everyone's left you? Who's been taking care of you?"

Sarah tilted her head to Liddy. "Maude was my father's mother. She raised me for as long as I can remember. She was more of a mother than that woman who bore me." The last words arrived harsh, brimmed with bitterness.

I stepped closer and knelt down on one knee to capture her blank tear-filled stare. "What happened to your Maude, if you don't mind me asking?"

Her reddened eyes locked onto mine. "I buried her last week. Cancer took my Maude from me."

"I'm genuinely sorry. So why did you come to Shiloh to find your momma?"

Sarah retrieved the envelope from her pocketbook and handed it to me.

"Is it okay if I read this?"

Sarah nodded. The powder-blue embossed stationary I pulled from the envelope identified Maude as Mrs. Matilda Mae Arnaquer, 2916 Levee Road, Vidalia, Louisiana 71373. Though written with an unsteady hand, the indigo penned message originated from a loving heart. I read the letter out loud.

My Darling Pepper,

Seeing as you are reading this, my body has surrendered to the battle I tried with all my might to win. I would have gladly embraced my prolonged suffering to see you graduate and take your first steps as the independent young lady I know you already are. I want you to know I have asked God to send his guardian angels to help you complete the task I could not.

Please pray for my soul. There are sins from my past only the Heavenly Father can wipe away and free me from a prolonged stay among the throngs in Purgatory. I believe with all my heart that your fervent prayers and God's eternal love will release me to watch over you myself, in due course.

There is a shoebox in my closet with your name on it. Inside you will find a keepsake for you. Also, Father Aloysius knows my wishes for your care and has agreed to provide guardianship until you reach your eighteenth birthday. I asked him to give you this letter in person upon my death.

I have not heard any more from your mother since she wrote from her hometown of Shiloh, Georgia. I suggest you locate Mr. Gus Appleton, Attorney-at-Law in Shiloh. If anyone knows how to contact your mother, he will. I pray Dixie might yet prove to be the mother you deserve.

These words of wisdom have sustained me for many years. Cherish them. May they guard you through the years to come:

"Just as we do not understand the coming and going of the spirit of life, nor how the bones are knitted together in the womb of a mother, so neither can we grasp the works of God, the Maker of us all. Therefore, leave the past behind you, embrace each new day as if it is your last, and never claim ownership of tomorrow because it rests in God's hands."

Please know I'll forever be waiting and watching.

Maude

I refolded the letter and slipped it back into the envelope filled with far more questions than answers.

Gus stood and scratched his scraggly, peppered red beard. "I'm sorry, Sarah. It's getting late. I've gotta work on finding a place for you to stay. The Shiloh Motel is most likely sold out due to the festival." His eyes bounced between Liddy and me.

Liddy looked up at me, still attempting to console Sarah.

"Miss Sarah, or do you prefer Pepper?" I asked.

With a tight-lipped half-smile, she said, "Pepper, thank you."

"Well, Pepper, Miss Liddy and I would be honored if you wouldn't mind staying right here. We've got two guest bedrooms upstairs and you'd have your own bathroom. We'll even throw in breakfast in the morning. That'll give us more time to talk. No doubt you've got a lot more questions."

Liddy patted Pepper's hand. "Is there anyone you need to call or let know where you are?"

Pepper shook her head. "I've got my stuff in the car."

"Can I help you with anything? I'm going to walk Gus out to his car anyway," I said, pointing to the door.

Gus approached the front door but stopped and said, "Miss Pepper Arnaquer, I believe your grandmother's prayer got answered. I'll stop by tomorrow. Good evening and thank you, Mister and Missus Phillips."

I DON'T KNOW what time in the wee hours Liddy climbed into bed, but it was about midnight when she shooed me off to bed. The dawn's early light eased into my bedroom when I crawled from bed out of habit more than want or necessity. A few minutes later, I sipped on a piping hot mug of coffee and ventured onto the porch to fetch the paper. I took a seat in a rocker and savored my coffee when I realized my edition of the *Sentinel* did not lie at the foot of the steps. I surmised Tim must have had a late evening, and my paper would arrive before long. Since he made his first delivery not long after we moved into this house, Tim had been late only a handful of times.

The caffeine began to set in as I contemplated Pepper's revelation from last night. I stared at her powder-blue Buick parked out front, squeezed my eyes tight, and mumbled, "God, I don't understand. Why did this girl, the daughter of a woman who almost killed my friends—and me no less—end up here? Why now? Lord, I'm not questioning Your will or Your ways, but I am asking for a little clarity. What should I say when she inquires about her mother's death? Isn't it bad enough she lost her father in a suspicious drowning accident? She's still reeling inside from losing her grandmother Maude, the one person who evidently loved and cared for her. The news has bankrupted her emotions. Lord, please guide our hearts, souls, and minds as we try to help Pepper realize she's not alone. Please prepare Hal and Phillip for the news about their half-sister. Oh, Lord, I almost forgot: Hank, too. I know it wasn't by accident she found her way here. Help us avoid what could become a train wreck for all concerned. Amen."

The barking of neighborhood dogs signaled the paper's imminent arrival. I left my rocker to pour more coffee when a sleepy-eyed Pepper greeted me at the front door.

"How long have you been up, young lady?"

Wearing a pair of jean shorts, a faded, threadbare green t-shirt, and flip-flops, Pepper looked more like the freckled sixteen year-old than she appeared at first last night, especially now with her long red hair braided into pigtails. "Not too long, but I didn't want to disturb you. You looked as though you were praying and talking to yourself."

"I'm getting some more coffee. There's also orange juice and milk in the fridge. What would you like?"

Pepper's dimples deepened. "I'd like a little coffee if that'd be okay? Miss Liddy and I stayed up until after one o'clock."

"How do you like your coffee?"

"A little milk with a spoonful of sugar, please."

PURGATORY: A PROGENY'S QUEST

I pointed to the rockers. "Go grab a seat. I'll be right back."

A moment later, I handed her a mug of coffee just as Tim pedaled down Calvary Street chucking papers. He stopped and straddled his bike after I waved and called his name.

I looked at Pepper and said, "Come on. I've got someone I'd like you to meet." She hesitated briefly but placed her cup on the table between our rockers.

"Good morning, Mister P. Sorry about being late this morning. Woogie, Bobo, and me kinda lost track of time last night after the festival wrapped up." Tim handed me the morning edition; he glanced at Pepper with an awkward but curious smile.

"Excuse my manners. Tim, this is Pepper. She's visiting from Louisiana. Pepper, this is Tim. He's not only the best paperboy in the entire State of Georgia, he's also the quarterback of the Shiloh Saints." I'm not sure whose dimpled cheeks turned red the fastest.

Tim nodded and offered his hand. "Nice to meet you, Pepper. Are you going to be staying here long?"

Pepper shook his hand before she looked at me and said with uncertainty, "I'm not too sure yet, at least a couple of days."

"Did you catch any of the festival last night?" Tim asked.

"I didn't get a chance to see much of it. I got in last evening."

"If'n Mister P doesn't mind, me and a couple of friends will be hanging around Town Square by the time the parade starts, if you'd like to join us, I mean."

The distraction appeared to be a godsend and would allow Liddy and me a chance to get some advice before catching Hal and Phillip at the right moment this afternoon. I glanced down at Pepper's eager, wide-eyed look.

"If Pepper wants to hang with you guys for a while this afternoon, I don't see why not. That is, if *she* wants to."

"Sure. Sounds fun to me," Pepper said more to him than me.

"Tim, we plan to be on Main Street before the parade gets underway anyway. I'm sure we'll see you," I said as Tim put one foot on a pedal, ready to push off.

As Tim rode off, he said, "We'll be hanging around the barbershop. See ya later."

Pepper and I walked back to the porch. "Pepper, trust me, you'll like Tim, Woogie, and Bobo. They're pretty popular guys around town, and you won't have to worry. They'll make sure you have plenty of fun."

"Woogie? Bobo? Those are odd names."

I chuckled. "Well, Woogie's real name is Keith. His dad owns the barbershop, and he's an exceptional football player, too. He'll likely wind up playing for some big-name college after he graduates. And Bobo, well, his real name is Byron, and he's Woogie's cousin. His father is one of the barbers, too. Bobo's going to college, but I'm not sure he'll play any football after he graduates. He's pretty smart though and should get an academic scholarship anyway."

"They sound pretty cool. I play basketball and soccer at my school. I don't think I'm good enough to play in college, but Maude always told me I was because most of the boys couldn't run as fast as me."

I sipped on my coffee while I stared at her car. "Let me guess, that's Maude's car. It doesn't look like the kind a young girl like you would prefer to drive."

Pepper giggled. "I've been driving it since I was fifteen because Maude couldn't drive herself any longer. I had to drive her across the Mississip' into Natchez where we did most of our shopping and went to Sunday Mass. That's where I attend school." She stopped as though she ran out of words and then stared off into the distance.

I started to speak but swallowed the last of my coffee instead.

Pepper looked at me with her green eyes. "Miss Liddy told me about what happened to my momma the day she died. Is it true she almost shot you before she drove off?"

Her stone-cold look caused me to stop rocking. "People can do some mighty strange and inexplicable things when they allow their mistakes to overtake them."

"Who was Hank…the man momma shot?"

I then realized Liddy had not told her Hank was her oldest half-brother. "You'll get to meet him in a couple of days if you'd like. He's been away for the last few months, but he's on his way back home. Let's just say if it weren't for Hank and a courageous dog named Ringo, I might not be standing here with you."

"I hope to meet him. I'm glad he's okay. I feel like I should say something to him. I know Momma could be pretty mean, but kill someone?" Pepper shook her head.

The storm door opened, and Liddy asked, "Who wants some breakfast? I'm about to whip up some eggs, bacon, and biscuits."

"How about we all pitch in? Do you like to cook, Miss Pepper?" Pepper responded with a cheery nod.

10

WHILE WE WAITED ON THE FRONT PORCH FOR PEPPER, LIDDY rubbed sunscreen on the back of my neck. "Stand still," she barked. "It's going to be another hot one by this afternoon."

I pointed to today's headline above the photo of the three contestants standing with Mary—*Miss Shiloh Outcome Remains A Parade Mystery.* "Have you heard from Susanna or Judy?"

Liddy squirted a dab into my hand. "Please rub it on your face." She then rubbed the residue left on her hands onto her exposed arms. "Nope, not a peep."

Pepper opened the storm door. "Do you want me to shut the front door?"

"Turn the lock button when you do. Thanks," I said.

Pepper secured the front door and latched the storm door. "I didn't pack a lot of clothes. Will this be okay?" She had on the same rolled-up-cuff jean shorts from earlier this morning but had changed into a sleeveless cotton top and leather sandals.

Liddy gave her an approving nod. "Your necklace is so pretty and unique. Where did you get it?"

Pepper removed the double-wrapped string of carved cinnamon-red beads attached to a matching heart and showed it to Liddy. "Maude left it to me. She told me it used to be a rosary. Each bead was hand-carved from the nuts of a special palm tree in South America, but I never saw the crucifix that belonged to it. It's been missing as long as I can remember." A restrained smile rose across Pepper's face as she ran the beads through her fingertips. "Maude knew I always had an eye for it," she said, slipping it around her neck. "It kinda makes me feel closer to her."

"Well, Maude must have given it to you for that very reason. Besides, it looks so nice on you," Liddy said.

"Ladies, we need to skedaddle. We promised to find Tim and the gang before the parade starts," I said as I gave both a gentle nudge toward the porch steps.

LIDDY SPOTTED MARIE MASTERSON sitting with Little Jessie in front of The Butcher Shoppe. "Where's Andy and Megan?"

Marie eyed Pepper standing between Liddy and me. "They're over by the church. Megan wanted to buy a couple of snow cones. It sure is getting warm again today. I volunteered to keep an eye on Jessie so Andy could help Megan." Marie's attention returned to Pepper. "And who might this young lady be?"

Pepper looked to me as I thought about how to respond. I knew the truth would race through town before I had a chance to catch up with Hal and Phillip. "This is Pepper. Have you seen Tim or Woogie?"

Marie pointed to the corner of Town Square nearest Edwards Barbershop. "They stopped by only a minute ago looking for you as well. They said they'd wait outside the barbershop." She smiled at Pepper. "Glad to meet you, Miss Pepper. This is Jessie." Marie looked down at Jessie in her lap and raised his arms. "Jessie, say hello to Pepper."

Pepper knelt down. "Hello, Jessie. Glad to meet you." She looked at Marie. "Is he your grandson?"

She hugged him. "No. I'm his Aunt Marie."

"Marie, if you'll excuse us, I promised Pepper she could watch the parade with Tim, Woogie, and Bobo, and I need to find Phillip and Hal."

"Don't fuss looking for Hal and his brother. They're both in the parade. You'll have a better chance catching them afterward. But if you hurry, you should be able to find the boys."

Before Marie had a chance to ask more about Pepper, we scurried across Main Street. The center of town was free of traffic as everyone anticipated parade vehicles to turn onto Main Street near the Sentinel Building. Parades in Shiloh never traveled far but were likewise never in a hurry to make their way through town either.

On the sidewalk in front of the barbershop, Tim introduced Woogie and Bobo before they dashed off to claim a spot to watch the parade. Liddy and I snaked our way across Town Square to snatch up the same vantage point we had last night in front of the church. I knew Arnie Wright would be in the parade, and I'd feel better consulting him before I slipped away to talk in private with Hal and Phillip.

Liddy tugged on my sleeve right after we sat down atop the steps. She squinted as she looked around at the crowd settling in up and down the street. "You could've at least picked a seat out of the sun."

"I'm sorry. Right after Arnie's vehicle passes by, we can leave here and catch up with him in the church parking lot. Besides, why are you belly-aching? We can see all the way down Main Street from here. I'll tell you what. How about a frosty snow cone? What flavor do you want?"

Liddy sighed. "How about blueberry? Bring back some extra napkins too. I don't need blueberry stains on my white shorts."

I climbed down the steps and weaved my way through the crowd migrating in the opposite direction toward Main Street. The moment I stepped up to order our snow cones, the gentleman ahead of me did an abrupt about-face, apparently more concerned about munching his snow cone than paying attention to me. His arm jostled my opposing arm as he spun around. We instinctively looked at each other as he brushed shaved ice from the front of his Ralph Lauren navy polo shirt.

"I'm sorry," I said, realizing what had happened.

The man looked up and said, "No harm, no foul. It was my fault. I should have watched where I was going." He walked across the street to a young woman with long, dark hair, her slender face hidden behind oversized dark sunglasses. He handed one of the cones to her, then glanced back before they strolled toward Main Street.

"Do you know them?" Liddy asked, wrapping the bottom of her snow cone in an extra napkin.

I looked for the couple, but they had already blended into the crowd along Main Street. "I don't think so." I had the odd feeling I'd seen him before but dismissed the thought as Liddy's hand shot in front of me. Her sudden reaction near about caused me to topple my liquefying blue snow cone.

"There's Phoebe walking alongside the Saints marching band. See her?"

I nodded but lowered her hand flittering about in front of my face to catch my attention. "Easy, girl. I see her."

The festival's Lightning Bug float crept along behind the band. Shiloh High cheerleaders ran alongside the trailer tossing candy to children waving eager little hands along the curb. Liddy's art students had repainted the lightning bug mascot's oversized head as an extracurricular project before school ended.

Liddy said this year's honor of being the mascot fell on the cheerleaders. In this heat, I felt for whichever cheerleader ended up with the distinction of wearing that costume. Whoever had accepted the honor pranced and waved atop the float, and every so often she wagged her bright blue illuminated tail.

A couple of local groups marched by before Pete's red truck towed the trailer with the four judges sitting on hay bales. Banners with *Miss Shiloh Pageant* in blue letters dangled from both sides of the makeshift float. Dr. Matson and Kay Abernathy waved from one side while Arnie Wright and Barb Patterson waved from the other. Zeb's washed and waxed black limousine inched along farther back. As it completed its slow turn onto Main Street, the vehicle's tinted windshield and polished chrome glistened, but we could still make out Zeb's jovial grin amidst his grizzled beard behind the steering wheel.

I remained unconvinced whether the vehicle's tortoise pace served to protect his precious cargo on the roof or to soak up the cheers from the crowd for his new prized automobile. Sitting aloft, Mandy, Camille, and Jeannie sat squeezed together in their evening gowns. The Miss Shiloh white ribbon sash adorned Camille's shoulder. The three giggled and waved, feet dangling into the rear compartment of the limo. They held onto one another as the car inched its way up Main Street.

Not far behind, Mayor Hal Archer rode atop a city utility bucket truck driven by Gus Appleton, followed by the city's dated fire truck and a bright yellow emergency vehicle. They all blasted their horns, squealed their sirens, and flashed their lights. Mitch Johnson brought up the rear of the parade riding shotgun in the Shiloh Police Department white pickup, its blue lights flashing, driven by Tyler. Mitch and Tyler wore their new short-sleeve, Kelly green polo shirts and matching baseball caps with a gold embroidered SPD logo visible across the bridge of their hats and on their shirts.

As soon as Zeb's limo passed out of sight, I squeezed Liddy's hand. "I need to scoot around to the church parking lot for a few minutes. Will you keep an eye on Pepper and the boys? I need to speak to Arnie before getting with Hal and Phillip."

Liddy brushed herself off. "I thought you wanted me to go with you?"

"Hun, you need to keep Pepper and the boys preoccupied at least until I've spoken with the Archers. I'll come find you as soon as I can."

Liddy walked down the steps to the sidewalk and made her way in the opposite direction across Town Square. I circumvented the crowd clogging Main Street and hightailed it up the narrow alley between the library and the church.

Parade vehicles serpentined their way into the church's rear parking lot. Pete's bright red, family-sized truck stood out amongst all the other vehicles. I found Arnie talking with Kay Abernathy, Jeannie, and Pete beside his truck.

"I'm sorry you didn't win this year, Jeannie," I said, looking at the beads of perspiration on her forehead and her rosy cheeks, her once-meticulous coiffured hairdo also a victim of the heat.

"Thanks, Mister P. All's good. Camille deserved the title this year. She's not only a good-looking country gal, she's actually a barrel of laughs, too. She's more like me than I'm comfortable admitting. I imagine we'll be spending more time getting to know each other better."

Kay said matter-of-factly, "Any one of them could've won. It was that close. Only a couple of votes made the difference."

Pete hugged his sister. "Well, lil' sis, I'd say better luck next year, but you won't be eligible next year. We'll have to figure out something else for you to run for."

"How about City Council President? That'd also make you the head of the City School Board, too," Kay said as she placed her arm around Jeannie.

Jeannie punched Pete in the arm and turned to Kay. "We'll see. I kinda got my hands full at the moment. Right now all I want to do is change out of this dress, take a long shower, and put on some shorts."

Arnie stared at me. "Do you have something on your mind, Theo? I don't believe you wandered back here by chance."

I looked at the others with a crooked smile. "If you'll excuse us, I do have to speak with our illustrious preacher for a moment." I placed my hand on Arnie's shoulder and whispered as we turned away. "I need your advice and prayerful help with a delicate but urgent matter. Can we step inside the church office for a minute?"

Arnie nodded but with obvious hesitation. "What's all this about, Theo?"

"Last night, Gus brought Dixie's daughter to my house."

Arnie stopped and said, "Did you say Dixie's daughter?"

"She drove into town from Louisiana yesterday evening with instructions to find Gus, but he didn't know what to do after talking with her. He saw Liddy and me walking home from the festival, then showed up at our house a few minutes later."

Arnie shared the same expression I felt last night when I first met Pepper. After tugging on his chin a moment, he asked, "How do you know she's Dixie's daughter?"

"She drove into town driving an old Buick with Louisiana plates and handed us a letter signed by her grandmother, Matilda Arnaquer, who Sarah—or Pepper, as she prefers—calls Maude."

"I recall seeing her obituary in the *Sentinel* not long ago and wondered if there was a connection," Arnie said as we headed into the church office.

At his office door I said, "The letter she showed me directed her here to look up Gus Appleton, but she identified him as an attorney with connections to her mother."

Arnie closed the door and plopped down on the sofa in his office. "Does she know her mother is dead?"

PURGATORY: A PROGENY'S QUEST

I nodded and then said, "Gus appeared as caught off guard as us. We broke the news to her last night. Since Gus didn't know where Pepper could stay the night, which I figured is also why he came knocking at our house, we invited her to stay with us. As we talked, it became clear she knows nothing about the Archers, nor do I imagine Hal and Phillip know she even exists either. Liddy and I—"

"Where's Liddy anyway? Is she with this Pepper?"

"I introduced Pepper to Tim this morning, and he invited her to hang out during the parade and afterward with him, Woogie, and Bobo. Liddy's keeping an eye on them until I figure out what the next step should be, which is why I'm sitting here with you, O wise pastor and pal."

Arnie's tight-lipped smile inverted into a grimace faster than it first appeared. "We, meaning me tagging along for moral support, need to talk to Hal and Phillip."

"Thanks, Arnie. I knew I could count on you. You know this could hit Hal and Phillip like a midnight tsunami."

Yelling near Zeb's limousine caught our attention as soon as we left Arnie's office in search of Hal. The same stranger I bumped into earlier walked pell-mell past us grumbling to himself. He never made eye contact, but looked and sounded mighty perturbed. Arnie jogged ahead when he saw Zeb and Hal consoling Camille. I arrived a step behind Arnie.

"What happened? Camille okay?" Arnie asked.

Zeb's deep-set brow and narrowed eyes revealed a side of good-natured Zeb few folks had seen before. "Who does that upstart think he is? One thing to pry into places you don't belong, but to mistreat a young woman. I've got half a notion to give that guy more than a piece of my mind."

Hal had his arm around Camille. What I thought were tears were nothing more than free-falling beads of sweat. Her once fancy French braids hung half unraveled. Her white ribbon sash lay on the floorboard of the limo's backseat next to her shoes.

Hal looked at Arnie. "That nutcase bulled his way into the backseat after he asked to look inside, after she told him he would need to talk to Mister Adams first. He insisted it would only take a moment and ignored Camille's plea to wait a minute. That's when he muscled her aside. Camille grabbed him by his belt and yanked him back. She identified herself as a police officer, but he demanded to see her badge. Camille said this guy snarled at her when the ruckus started to draw so much attention and Zeb arrived to see what had happened. He bolted as soon as he saw Mitch and Tyler climb out of their vehicle."

Zeb stared at me. "Theo, I'm certain that was the same fella we met at the auction. The same one who wanted to buy my limo and asked all those questions."

"I knew he looked familiar." Zeb gave me a blank look. "We sorta bumped into each other by the snow cone vendor. He walked away with a thin dark-haired woman. I couldn't place him then, but yeah, now I know why he looked familiar."

Camille thanked Hal and assured him she was all right. She stepped to Zeb. "Mister Adams, thank you. I'm pretty sure you scared him off, but I still better report the incident to Mitch." She walked barefooted over to Mitch and Tyler. A minute later, Tyler dashed toward Main Street.

Arnie patted Zeb on the back. "Who in their right mind would tangle with you?"

"Thank ya kindly, Arnie. Truth be told, I'm still trembling. I think I'll head back to the house and call it a day."

Hal shook Zeb's hand. "Thank you, Zeb. I know Camille's glad you showed when you did. This guy has hightailed it out of town, I'm sure."

Zeb cranked the limo and maneuvered out of the still crammed parking lot.

I looked at Hal. "Got a second? Arnie and I need to talk to you and Phillip. Is he around?"

Hal eyed me and Arnie. "What's wrong? I don't know where Philip is at the moment. Why?"

"There's someone I would like you to meet."

11

HAL HUNG UP THE PHONE IN HIS OFFICE. "MITCH WANTED ME TO know Liddy is on her way with the young girl, Pepper. He also reported they haven't been able to find the lunkhead who tried to intimidate Camille. Mitch figures he's long gone at this point."

Phillip walked in, pulled a chair from the conference table, and sat next to Arnie. Hal leaned back in his leather swivel chair and said, "Okay, what's this about? Who's this girl you needed Phillip to be here to tell me about?"

Arnie offered the moral support he promised and sat mum waiting for me to answer.

"I reckon there's no easy way to tell you two, but it seems you have a sister—well, at least a half-sister. Her name is Sarah Arnaquer, but she goes by Pepper. She drove in from Louisiana last evening with instructions to contact Gus Appleton because he supposedly would be able to help her find her mother or, as we know her, your mother, Dixie."

Hal straightened up in his chair and edged forward with his elbows and clenched fists on top of his desk. He stared at Phillip, who rose from his chair and stepped around Hal's desk to stand beside Hal.

"How do you know this? Does she know Dixie's dead and that Gus had been in cahoots with her?"

Arnie broke his silent support. "Hal, you know Theo well enough to know he'd not go through all this drama to tell you and your brother unless he wasn't convinced of who she is."

PURGATORY: A PROGENY'S QUEST

I left my chair, placed both hands on the edge of Hal's desk, and leaned closer to make my point. "She drove here in her deceased grandmother's Buick. It's got Louisiana tags, and at the moment it's parked at my house. Pepper handed me a posthumous letter she received from a Father Aloysius who, as it appears, is her designated guardian back in Vidalia, Louisiana, which lies right across the Mississippi River from Natchez, Mississippi. Her grandmother raised Pepper for as long as she can remember. Needless to say, it appears Pepper came to Shiloh looking for information about Dixie. As far as she knows, she has no other immediate family left. Her grandmother's handwritten letter indicated she knew Pepper would seek out her mother."

"Does Pepper know what happened to Dixie, if she was, in fact, her mother?" Phillip asked.

Feeling ruffled by his inference, Hal and I peered at Phillip before I said, "We told her she died in a tragic accident. We dodged telling her anything more until we could talk to both of you. It appears you two and your brother Hank are her only family. Please don't lay the sins of the mother on this girl. From what Liddy and I can tell, she's been far removed from her mother and father. Of course, this Father Aloysius of St. Mary's Catholic Church in Natchez may be able to validate Pepper's story. Before I introduce you to her, understand she's still grieving over the loss of the one person who mothered her all these years."

Hal looked up at Phillip hovering over his shoulder and let out a long, deep audible breath. "Lord help us. We might as well meet our baby sister, but understand what you've laid on us is still being digested and remains hard to swallow for a multitude of reasons. We'll do our best to remain open-minded until we talk with her ourselves."

Arnie left his chair and went to the door. Liddy entered with an understandably confused and wide-eyed Pepper by her side.

Phillip placed another chair beside the empty chair he had been in. Pepper's eyes surveyed the office until her focus locked onto the framed painting of Harold Archer hanging on the wall.

Hal walked over and extended his hand. "I'm Hal Archer, and that red-haired gentleman standing behind my desk is Phillip, my younger brother." She placed her hand in his, but Hal must have sensed her uneasiness and offered only a brief gentle squeeze. Her eyes diverted back to Harold's stoic face. Hal, too, turned and looked up at his father as if seeking his guidance. "My father passed away not long before your mother died. He was a great man and a far better mayor than I'll ever hope to be."

Pepper turned to Hal. "Did you know my mother?"

Hal broke his distant gaze and held Pepper's hand. "Phillip and I knew her. She abandoned us also, long before you were born. You see, she was our mother, too."

Phillip remained frozen. His lips quivered, but his tongue failed him. Liddy stepped beside Phillip and whispered to him as she placed her arm around him.

Pepper took an extended look into Hal's eyes, and her deep-set dimples sank a little deeper as a curious grin appeared. "You have the same blue-gray eyes she did." She turned to Phillip and stared at him for a moment. The two exchanged modest grins as she fingered her own red hair. "And you've got the same color eyes, too."

Hal smiled. "Well, your smoky-green eyes are pretty special, too, but those dimples sure remind me of her. What do you think, Phil?" Phillip nodded but remained speechless.

Arnie stood and said, "Liddy, Theo, let's allow them some time to get better acquainted."

Hal said as we were leaving, "I'll bring her by your house later. We've got a lot to talk about. She doesn't even know about Hank yet."

PURGATORY: A PROGENY'S QUEST

LIDDY AND I STOPPED by Mandy's book and gift shop before going home. Bernie Thrope greeted us as she leaned over the counter next to the cash register. The store's shelves and displays provided ample evidence of a busier-than-expected day. The once stacked and sorted festival t-shirts lay heaped in random piles on the counter. As revealing, Bernie's lack of enthusiasm defied her trademark feisty self. She remained propped on her elbows as we took stock of the aftermath that would have yielded a gratifying smile on most proprietors. In the rear of the store, Silas mumbled and leaned on a broom and reset toppled books on the shelves.

Liddy looked at Bernie, "I thought you closed the restaurant to enjoy the festival this year?"

Bernie's obviously sarcastic chuckle and disappointed sway of her head said otherwise. "In hindsight, my friend, we would have seen far more of the festival and the parade tending customers from our restaurant than we did from here today."

"Where's Mandy?" I asked.

Silas shrugged and turned away amidst more of his incoherent murmuring.

"She got back a few minutes ago and is upstairs changing," Bernie said, straightening herself and looking at the stairwell.

Without saying a word, Liddy began folding and re-sorting piles of t-shirts. "I'd say it's been a rather hectic day all around."

Mandy appeared at the bottom of the stairs, surveyed the displays and shelves, and tied a red bandana around her pulled-back ebony hair. Her wide-eyed *uh-oh* expression belied the smile she mustered. "Aunt Bernie, Uncle Silas, I can't thank you enough for your help."

Silas grumbled loud enough to be clearly understood. "You can thank us by telling us to go home now."

Bernie flashed a look stirring Silas to slide the push broom toward the back of the store, but not before he shot Bernie a juvenile hangdog pout with a playful glint in his eyes.

Mandy walked straight over to Liddy folding another t-shirt. "Miss Liddy, you don't have to fuss with those. It's past closing time." She took the t-shirt from Liddy. "Besides, I'm going to spend tomorrow putting the store back together again." Mandy glanced at Silas, now only pretending to sweep. "Uncle, you can take Aunt Bernie home, too. You've been lifesavers today."

Silas set the broom aside, brushed his hands off on his khaki pants, and with renewed energy stepped toward the front of the store. "Mistor Theo. I heard there was quite a ruckus after the parade ended. Anyone get hurt? They said my friend, Mistor Zeb, he chased the scoundrel away."

"Yes, he did. I didn't actually see it all unfold, but Camille looked a sight afterward, though she did her best to laugh the whole incident off. From what Mitch Johnson said later, this stranger must've left town in quite a hurry. No one has seen hide nor hair of him since."

"What do you mean Camille looked a sight?" Mandy asked.

"Her fancy braided hairdo came undone, and she came clear out of her shoes during the scuffle. Otherwise, she and her dress survived unscathed."

Mandy groaned an *oh-no*, then said to Liddy, "I heard your friend, Miss Thatcher, spent a couple of hours last night helping her with her makeup and getting her hair just right and helped her again this morning before the parade. What a shame, but I'm glad Camille's okay. She seems to be a real sweet girl. I hope the run-in didn't ruin the rest of her day as Miss Shiloh."

Liddy shook her head. "She looked unfazed right after lunch. Her hair and makeup looked good as new."

Bernie turned to Mandy and arched a brow. "Weren't you supposed to be with her this afternoon?"

"No, ma'am." Mandy's cheeks flushed as she stumbled through her words, "I took off with Jay right after the parade ended. I didn't even know what happened after I left until Mister Adams got home. I'm sorry. I sorta lost track of time after Jay took me to his house for lunch. Please believe me, Aunt Bernie, I meant to get back here much sooner than I did."

Bernie untied her apron and placed it on the counter. "Come on, Old Man. Now I don't feel so bad about leaving this mess behind for my niece." Bernie's good-natured feistiness returned. Smiling at the door, she sighed, "Oh, it's so true, youth is wasted on the young." Her eyes rolled in the direction of Silas waiting in the doorway stroking his bushy salt-and-pepper mustache.

After Bernie left, Mandy said, "Go on home. I'm locking up anyway. Thank you for stopping by."

"Did Zeb drive his limo home?" I asked.

"He parked it in their old workshop behind their house." Mandy giggled and added, "I thought the three of us would have fallen more than once sitting on the car's sunbaked rooftop, but I'll never forget riding up there with Camille and Jeannie."

TRAFFIC ON MAIN STREET had resumed, and the crowd had dispersed from Town Square by the time we headed home. As we passed City Hall, Liddy squeezed my arm and asked, "I wonder how much Hal and Phillip told Pepper?"

"I guess we'll find out when they bring her by the house."

Phillip's Jeep Wrangler and Hal's pickup remained parked next to each other behind City Hall.

A COLUMN OF gray clouds had swept northward overhead and pulled refreshing Gulf breezes with it as the sun began its descent in the western sky. Phillip called from Bubba's BBQ and said they would be by the house about eight o'clock. Liddy whipped up some of her pecan-chicken salad and served it on a bed of lettuce with two wedges of dill pickle for supper, and we ate on the porch. Our conversation focused on speculating what Hal and Phillip might have shared with Pepper and what she likely told them about their mother.

Phillip pulled his Wrangler in behind Pepper's Buick as promised. Pepper climbed out of the backseat giggling with Phillip and Hal as the threesome came up the walkway to the porch. Liddy greeted them at the top of the porch steps while I grabbed an extra chair from the kitchen.

Phillip and Pepper sat beside Liddy, but Hal remained standing. When I pointed for him to take the chair on the other side of Liddy, Hal said, "It's been a long day. Phillip and I don't want to stay too long. I'm sure Pepper's pretty tuckered out, too."

Liddy squeezed Pepper's hand. "By the look on all three of you, I'd say we all had an exhausting day."

"Yes, ma'am. My brain feels like my stomach right about now—stuffed." Pepper then patted her stomach and rolled her eyes as her head bounced back and forth. "I'm still trying to digest all Hal and Phillip told me about our mother. I'm a little jealous because I never knew her like they did." She fingered the brownish-red beads on her necklace.

"From what little time we got to know your mother, I'd have to say, looking at you three, I can see some of your mother in each of you. Whatever differences y'all experienced can't change that fact," Liddy said cupping her hands around Pepper's hands.

"I meant to ask you, Pepper. Where'd you get that necklace?" Hal asked.

"Maude left it to me. Why?"

"I don't know for sure. I guess I'm only curious because it complements your freckled rosy cheeks."

Pepper lifted the beads to examine them closer with a reticent, sealed-lip smile.

Phillip asked, "Would it be okay if you brought Pepper over to see our house tomorrow after church?"

"I don't see why not," I said, catching Liddy's affirming nod.

Hal said, "On that note, Phillip and I are going to beg your pardon. It's starting to get dark, and I still need to make some phone calls after we get home."

Pepper and Liddy walked with Phillip toward his Jeep. Hal lingered behind and put his hand on my shoulder. "You ought to know we haven't told her any details about Dixie's death. We did tell her a little about how she took care of Dad before he died, but we couldn't tell her everything that led to her death."

"I understand. She's still getting a grip on the fact she's got older brothers from her mother years before she was born."

"Has she spoken to anyone back in Vidalia? What about this Father Aloysius?"

I shook my head and shrugged my shoulders.

"I'm going to call Joe Arians this evening and get some legal advice before we tell her too much."

"Sounds like a good idea. See you in church in the morning then. I hope she doesn't mind coming to a Baptist church." Hal and I laughed as we caught up with the others.

Pepper offered Phillip and Hal a warm hug. "Thank you. I know I'm going to have a bunch more questions tomorrow."

T.M. BROWN

12

THE PREDICTABLE TRIVIAL MURMURINGS IN THE CHURCH FOYER
fell silent right after Liddy and I escorted Pepper into Shiloh
Baptist Church. Though Maude had raised her as a devout
Catholic, Pepper admitted she had attended other churches from
time to time back home with her friends. Nonetheless, her gait
shortened and eyes widened the moment we stepped from the
bright sunshine into the foyer. She wore the floral embroidered
denim dress she had on when she first arrived in town. Her
grandmother's beaded necklace adorned her neck and appeared
to offer some comfort as she stared at all the strange faces who
inspected her as though they had never seen braided red hair and
freckled dimples on a teenage girl before.

"Good morning, and you must be Pepper. I'm Judy Wright,
the pastor's wife." Judy's warm smile, calm voice, and gentle
touch seemed to settle Pepper's fluttering butterflies.

She smiled. "Yes, ma'am. Nice to meet you, Missus Wright."

"My husband told me you're from Vidalia, Louisiana."

Pepper's pearl-white smile shone as she engaged Judy. "Yes,
ma'am. It's a small backwater town along the banks of the
Mississipp' across from Natchez. Do you know where it is?"

"Why, as a matter of fact, I sure do. My husband and I took a
riverboat tour from New Orleans a few years ago. Will you be
staying here much longer?"

"Ma'am, I don't know exactly what my plans are at the
moment. You see, until yesterday, I thought I'd lost all the family
I had, but then I discovered I've got brothers—well, half-brothers.

Turns out my mother was also their mother. My head's still kinda spinning while I'm trying to make sense of it all."

Judy's even-keeled demeanor gave way to a broad smile. "Are these the two young men you were talking about?" Judy placed her hands on Pepper's shoulder and got her to turn around.

Pepper beamed seeing Hal and Phillip standing beside us..

"Good morning, Pepper. Phillip and I wanted to know if you'd like to sit with us this morning." Hal glanced at me and received an affirming wink.

Pepper grabbed ahold of Hal and Phillip's arms as they stepped toward Hillary, who was preoccupied attaching a nametag on each child before they scampered through the children's area door.

Judy said, "I feel so awful for that girl. I can't imagine coping with all she's had to digest in the past month. Did she say anything more after talking to her new brothers? She seems to feel comfortable around them."

"She didn't say a whole lot about what they talked about yesterday," I said. "She sure asked a lot of questions though about Hal, Phillip, and Hank. We tried to be selective in what we told her, and mostly discussed the Archer family history. Of course, we also prepared her to meet Maddie when we visit with them this afternoon."

ARNIE'S MESSAGE addressed our responsibility to safeguard our God-given legacy of the land. He constructed his sermon around two biblical passages. The first came from Leviticus on the obligations of redeeming the land as a gift from one family generation to the next. While he expounded its application to the congregation, I kept an eye on Pepper, who sat sandwiched between Hal on the aisle and Phillip with Jeannie on his other side. In the second passage, Arnie drew upon Ruth's story to exemplify the obligation of a kinsman-redeemer to restore any property that by rights belonged to a family member.

Arnie concluded his message by saying, "Our town's long heritage remains tied to the land, but let us take heed. As we are reminded in Leviticus, we do not own the land, God does. We may possess it during our lifetimes, and even prosper from it, but ownership remains with God. Each generation also rises out of the sweat-drenched soil of the land but, without exception, each generation also returns to that same fertile soil. God gifted each of us, just as he did the generations before us, the same fertile fields that have been plowed, planted, and harvested for generations as our inheritance."

Liddy squeezed my hand and whispered, "Not all of us have remained where we were first planted. Couldn't this message also refer to prospering wherever God plants you in life?"

I patted the top of Liddy's hand and smiled, then surveyed familiar faces around the sanctuary.

Arnie's voice grew louder as he emphasized each word to follow. "Yet, the moment we value the land we hold dear above our obligations to family and neighbors, we risk our God-given rights to possess the land we claim as our own. Let us be mindful as we leave here today—relationships should always remain treasured above real estate."

THE BLACK WROUGHT IRON, monogrammed gates swung open. I followed Phillip up the landscaped drive until we reached the circular concrete drive in front of the Archers' palatial plantation home. Though Liddy and I had visited their estate several times, their pillared mansion still drew me back to the genteel era of the Old South. Spanish Moss dangled like forlorn tears from the evergreen live oaks lining the estate's winding drive. The centuries-old thick trunks anchored gnarled branches arched overhead like protective arms of ancestral guardians. Where the live oaks failed to cast their shadows, manicured azaleas, holly trees, and tall crape myrtles flourished. Little grass survived around the front of the house, but in the rear of the property, an immaculate lush-green lawn flourished.

Neat gardens filled with a variety of roses, daylilies, assorted flowers, and hydrangea made the brown pine straw mulch appear like a painter's palette filled with daubs of bright colors. Though their father had passed away, Phillip and Hal maintained the grounds throughout the year just as their father before them. The shame of such splendor was that none of the three Archer sons had wives or offspring to enjoy it with.

Pepper exited our SUV and took a slow look around before she saw Hal and Phillip. "This is all yours? I've only seen the outsides of two plantations where I grew up. I don't recollect ever seeing one this nice up close."

Hal smiled, pointing to the porch. "Come on inside, then."

As the door opened, Maddie's pearly smile welcomed us. "Mister Hal, you didn't tell me how pretty this young lady looked." Maddie gave Pepper a head-to-toe inspection. "Child, your pretty hair and freckles remind me of Phillip at about your age, but he doesn't have your soulful green eyes. Miss Pepper, forgive me. Where are my manners? I'm Maddie. Won't you please come on in. I sure hope you like fried chicken."

Pepper giggled as her reddened cheeks glowed. "Yes, ma'am. Thank you." She held onto Liddy's hand as we entered between the double-stair foyer into the Archers' panoramic great room with its floor-to-ceiling stone fireplace.

Pepper outpaced Liddy and had to let go of her hand when she saw the view of the manicured gardens and lawn beyond the spacious veranda.

Sad but true, only one woman had enjoyed the grounds and magnificent Archer home for the past five decades. Maddie's no-nonsense, mother-hen ways had served the Archer family since Harold had been a youngster. Though she had served as housekeeper and cook, the Archers revered her like family. On several occasions, Liddy and I saw firsthand her maternal chastisement of all the Archer men whenever she deemed it necessary. She treated them as if they were her own.

Liddy speculated Maddie was well into her seventies because of the stories she told, but her feisty spirit and lively gait would wear out grown men half her age. Her only child died as an infant while Maddie had still been a teenager. Her beloved husband had lost his life in the early seventies tending to the estate's former turpentine distillery. Because of that terrible accident, the Archer family had guaranteed Maddie a place in their home.

From the railing on the second floor above, Phillip said, "I'll be right back down. I wanna get rid of my tie and jacket."

Hal slid open the nearest glass sliding door. "Come on out. It's pleasant enough this afternoon."

Liddy lowered her sunglasses from the top of her head back onto her nose and followed Hal onto the rear deck. I waited for Phillip when I heard him bound down the stairs. Pepper stepped out to the wooden railing on the veranda deck and used her hand to shade her eyes as she gazed at the view.

Hal stood beside Pepper and pointed as he talked, but I couldn't make out their conversation. After Phillip joined Hal and Pepper, Liddy and I sat beneath one of the umbrella-covered tables on the deck.

"Do you think Pepper's a little overwhelmed?" I asked Liddy.

"Weren't we the first time we visited out here?" Liddy grinned as she focused on the three siblings getting acquainted.

The French door behind us swung open. Maddie stood on the threshold, hands on hips, and called out, "Mister Hal, Mister Phillip. Y'all wanna eat inside or out here on the veranda? Dinner's ready."

Phil looked at Hal. "We'll be more comfortable inside. Thank you, Maddie. We'll be right there."

Maddie had set out bowls of potato salad and coleslaw before she hoisted a large platter of fried chicken over our heads and placed it in the center of the dining room table. After pouring each of us some iced tea, she set two pitchers on the table and wandered back to the kitchen.

Pepper swallowed a mouthful of potato salad, and asked, "Miss Maddie, aren't you going to eat with us?"

Maddie hesitated but then said matter-of-factly, "No child, but thank you for asking."

"Maddie, won't you please join us," Hal said as he wiped his mouth with his linen napkin and stood. He looked at Phillip. "Pull a chair out for Maddie."

Liddy got up and grabbed a fresh plate and silverware from the buffet along the wall, leaned across the table, and handed them to Phillip. He slid his plate and silverware over to where he had pulled out a chair. He then pointed to the place between Pepper and himself.

Liddy said, "You must join us now, Miss Maddie. I bet Miss Pepper would love to hear some stories about Hal and Phillip."

Maddie's dark-complexioned cheeks turned as candy apple red as her lipstick. She untied and lifted her apron over her head and folded it across the back of a chair at the far end. Phillip stood holding the back of the chair as she scooted up to the table.

She looked at Hal and then Phillip before she said to Pepper, "What'd ya' like to know?"

Liddy motioned Maddie to remain seated twice throughout the next hour and kept our glasses topped with iced tea. Later, she stepped into the kitchen to serve the dessert—Maddie's fresh baked pecan pie with a scoop of vanilla ice cream. During dinner, Pepper egged Maddie to expound on a couple of hair-raising tales involving Hank and Hal. Though more than a dozen years separated him from his brothers, Phillip did not escape without a couple of stories causing him to duck his head as Pepper's laughter caused him to blush.

"Miss Maddie, did you really make Hal and Hank remove their muddy clothes and hose them off on the back stoop?"

Maddie cupped her hand over her mouth but still cackled out loud. "Yes, child. The older two musta been thirteen and fifteen. They pranced about giggling in their mud-stained BVDs so much Phillip, who musta been about almost three at the time, ran under the water spray, yanked his shirt over his head, dropped his shorts, and yelled 'Wash me, too!' When Mister Harold heard the commotion, he joined us on the porch and began roaring before he called to all three of them, waterlogged and all, and they filled his lap with laughter. Mister Harold paid no mind that his shirt and pants got mud-stained and soaked neither."

In the midst of the story, I noticed both Phillip and Hal continued to laugh but their eyes glossed over, a fact I am sure Maddie considered as she got up and cleared the dishes.

As we prepared to leave, Hal took Pepper's hand at the door. "Is it possible for you to stay until Hank gets home Wednesday?" He made eye contact with Liddy and me. "That's assuming Mister and Missus Phillips don't mind. I'll be glad to make some calls in the morning if that'd be okay with you?"

Liddy said, "We'd be glad to have her stay a while longer. It's kinda nice having a young lady around the house."

"It's probably a good idea to call Father Aloysius. I'm sure he's trying to check in on me by now," Pepper said before she bit her bottom lip.

"I'll bring her to your office about nine o'clock," I said, walking to our car.

Hal yelled back, "Make it more about ten. I've got to make a quick stop before I get to City Hall."

I waved and nodded and slipped into the driver's seat.

13

A LITTLE BEFORE TEN THE FOLLOWING MORNING, PEPPER AND I drove to City Hall and stopped in at the Utilities Department. Pepper wanted to thank Gus. The visit lasted only a couple of minutes, but two of the office workers gawked when Pepper and Gus embraced before we left.

Gus walked with us into the hallway. "Pepper, thanks for stopping by. I pray everything works out for you with your brothers and whatever lies ahead for you. Stop back anytime." As we walked away, he shook his head and disappeared back into his office.

Outside the Shiloh Police Department, Pepper tugged my arm and stopped in her tracks. She pointed inside and muttered, "Is that who I think it is?"

I laughed. "Yep, Miss Shiloh. Her name is Camille Gaines."

"I hardly recognized her with her hair tightly braided and tied back and those dark rim glasses hiding her pretty face."

I knocked on the open door. "Miss Gaines, I've got someone who'd like to meet you."

I stepped back as Camille and Pepper shared smiles and compliments. Camille looked at me as we were about to leave. "Thanks for stopping by. How long is Pepper in town?"

Pepper looked up at me as I considered the appropriate response. "Well, Camille, we're still talking about that exact question right now, but I imagine Pepper will be here at least a few more days. Why?"

"Mitch talked about her this morning. I guess Mister Appleton was able to help her find what she came here looking for?" Camille asked, looking at Pepper.

"I'd have to say that's pretty accurate. In fact, we said hello to ol' Gus a minute ago. We're about to go to the Mayor's office to discuss some related concerns Pepper has developed."

Camille waved with a polite grin beneath an inquisitive wrinkled brow.

HILLARY SAT AT her desk immersed in conversation with her father outside of the Mayor's office.

"Arnie, checking on your industrious daughter this morning?" I asked in jest.

Arnie turned. "Good morning, Miss Pepper. I was pleased to see you in church yesterday, but I didn't get to meet you properly. I'm Arnie Wright." He offered her his hand.

Pepper shook Arnie's hand. "Thank you, sir. I enjoyed your sermon—and meeting your wife."

"Thank you, young lady." Arnie then turned his attention to me. "Unless he's changed his mind, Hal's expecting both of you. We just finished talking with Joe Arians a moment ago." Arnie looked at Hillary. "Why don't you plan to have dinner with Mom and me this evening?"

"Of course, Dad. Tell Mom I'll be there." She turned to me. "Theo, you and Pepper can go on back. Hal's waiting on you."

Hal left his executive chair and walked around his massive desk. He greeted Pepper and me and pointed to the two armchairs I knew well, positioned side by side in front of his desk. He pulled over an extra armchair and sat facing us, his back to the desk.

He leaned forward, propped his elbows on his knees, and fidgeted with his interlocked fingers as he gathered his thoughts.

Pepper squirmed in her chair as she glanced at me and looked at Hal. For the life of me, I had no idea what caused his prolonged silent hesitation. Pepper fingered the beads of her necklace and stared at the top of Hal's head until his eyes crept upward.

"Pepper, I have a simple question for you, but I'm pretty certain the answer may not be so simple," Hal said. "Now that you know about our mother, it appears you have no other immediate family members, except for my brothers and me. What do you think will happen when you go back to Louisiana? I mean, you're not old enough yet to live all alone, even in your grandmother's house."

Pepper's eyes watered and her lips quivered. She leaned forward with her hands clasped around her knees. She shook her head. "I have no idea at the moment. I came here hoping to find my mother, but—" Tears trickled down flushed, freckled cheeks. "I'm sorry." She dabbed at tears with her bare forearm.

I reached into my hip pocket and handed her my handkerchief. She unfolded it, wiped her cheeks, and then squeezed it tight with hands in her lap.

Hal placed his hand upon hers. "I know about your father's unexpected death and the raw deal you got dealt when our mother and your father decided you'd be better off being raised by your grandmother. No matter how mother-like Maude tried to be to you—trust me, I understand—there's a void in your heart that can only be filled by the mother who brought you into this world. In your case, not having your father there for you only made the void twice as hard to fill."

Hal touched Pepper's chin to lift her face as she fought to control her crying. "Have you spoken with this Father Aloysius? I understand Maude named him your interim guardian. Do you know what his plans were for your care?"

Pepper shook her head again and dabbed the tear-filled trails on her face with my beleaguered handkerchief. "He told me Maude instructed him to investigate if her brother and his wife would take me, but I don't want to live with them. They live somewhere in Arkansas and they're old and sickly, too."

I scooted my chair closer to Pepper's and patted her shoulder.

"I don't think anyone intends to send you off to somebody that's not able or willing to be the kind of guardian you need. Heck, in a couple of years or so, you'll be old enough to decide for yourself where and with whom you want to live."

Hal stiffened his back and ran his fingers through his hair. "With your permission, Pepper, I'd like to ask Pastor Wright to get in touch with Father Aloysius. We should let him know where you are and, though you've learned your mother is dead, you've discovered you have family right here in Shiloh. Would that be okay with you? Pastor Wright can be pretty persuasive when he has a mind to do so."

Pepper and Hal shared hopeful smiles before she confessed, "I'm not sure what I'd say to Father Aloysius. He's nice and all, but he can be—well, let's say he can be a well-meaning stick-in-the-mud from time to time." The image she created for us stirred a small snicker from Pepper.

"In that case, Pastor Wright is without a doubt the person to talk to him for you," I said with a reassuring smile.

"In the meantime, Phillip and I enjoyed the time we shared yesterday," Hal said. "Like you, we're both absorbing the revelation we've got a baby sister."

Pepper stiffened her back and pushed her lower lip out. "I ain't no one's *baby* sister."

"Oh, Lord, no. Forgive me. I meant to say *younger* sister," Hal emphasized in quick verbal retreat as he let out a chuckle and leaned back, arms extended in full apologetic surrender.

Pepper giggled at Hal's animated defensive response. "Apology accepted."

Hal stood and extended his arms toward Pepper. "I'm not particularly good at being an older brother, but I imagine a hug is in order."

Pepper shot up from her chair and embraced Hal. "I'm not used to having older brothers, either."

Hal pulled back from their hug and stared at her necklace. "Where'd you say you got that necklace?"

Pepper stared down at the necklace and rubbed the beads with her fingers. "Maude left it to me along with a few other things of hers. I like wearing it because it reminds me of her."

"I hate to break up this family reunion moment, but I promised Liddy I'd be home for lunch," I said.

"Hold up one sec," Hal said to me and then hollered, "Hilly, will you come in here a minute?"

Hillary appeared at the doorway and huffed, "Did you just yell for me? Is the intercom broke?"

Hal had one arm across Pepper's shoulders. "Would you mind if Pepper joined you and me for lunch today?"

Hillary inspected the glint in Pepper's eyes. "Camille asked if she could go to lunch with us, too."

"I hope I don't end up regretting this," Hal said with a shameless grin. "If you don't mind, Theo, I've got a lunch date with three pretty ladies. I'll call later to let you know what time I'll bring Pepper by your house."

Pepper's eyes lit up as she looked at me. I shrugged to show my approval. "How could I possibly say no?"

Hillary said, "Give me five minutes. How about Bubba's?"

A few minutes later, Hal walked away with Hillary on one arm and Pepper on the other. Camille waited for them outside the SPD office door. I felt as though I had won the office pool as I skipped across the marble floor of the Masterson Administration Building's rotunda and out the front door.

DURING LUNCH, I filled Liddy in on how the meeting went with Pepper. Afterward, I pulled out the mower and attended to my weekly appointment in my own yard. While I blasted the last of the grass clippings from the driveway, Liddy caught my attention from the kitchen stoop, holding out our house phone.

"It's Joe Arians!" she hollered.

I shut down the blower, walked to the stoop, and took the phone from her. "Joe, what's up?"

Liddy hovered over me as I sat on the top stoop step and dabbed the sweat from my face with my shirt sleeve.

"Hal asked me to fill you in on the results of two calls I made today on Pepper's behalf."

I peered over my shoulder at Liddy's dying-to-know glare.

"Okay, I guess, but why do I need to know about the calls?"

"Arnie gave Father Aloysius your and Liddy's contact information so he or his parish office could talk directly to Pepper later this afternoon. I confirmed your contact details when I inquired about Pepper's official school records from St. Mary's Catholic School. Thankfully, Father Aloysius agreed to release what we requested after he learned about Pepper locating family in Shiloh."

"What information of Pepper's were you looking for?" I asked, which drew Liddy to lean even closer over my shoulder.

"This morning, I advised Hal that before he and his brothers made any decisions it would be advisable to document Pepper's claim of who she is and whether, in fact, Dixie and Beau Arnaquer were her parents and Pepper's grandmother held legal guardianship at the time of her death," Joe stated in a lawyer's matter-of-fact manner. "If so, as I explained to Father Aloysius, Matilda Arnaquer's bestowal of guardianship to him would be validated and honored."

"Sounds all legalistic to me, but what should we expect when Father Aloysius calls?"

"Your good buddy, our Right Reverend Arnie Wright, assured Father Aloysius that Pepper's arrival and claim of being Dixie's daughter caught everyone by surprise, but he confirmed what we know so far to be true. He would just feel better if he could talk with Pepper. I suggested he call about five o'clock our time. In case you forgot, they're on Central Time in Mississippi."

I looked at my watch. "I got it. Liddy and I both would feel better if Pepper talked with Father Aloysius, as well."

Liddy tapped my shoulder. "Hal's here with Pepper."

"Joe, I gotta run. Hal's out front." I set the phone down on the kitchen counter and followed Liddy to the front of the house.

Pepper jumped out of the passenger side of Hal's truck, but Hal leaned out his open driver-side window. "Theo, did Joe call?"

I walked up to Hal as Pepper disappeared with Liddy around the side of the house. "I just hung up with him. It sounds like Arnie smoothed things over with Father Aloysius pretty well. But what's all this about getting copies of her records sent?"

Hal rested his hand on my shoulder. "If Phillip, Hank, and I are the only family she has left, then we need to consider what's best for our sister, whether or not she's but our half-sister. Joe's only being a good lawyer and making certain we have all the facts before we say or do anything.

"Besides, Arnie already counseled me this morning. He advised me to consider the possibility that God may have had a hand in Pepper driving five hundred miles by herself in search of her mother. Although she learned about our mother like she did, God revealed she wasn't an orphan but had brothers instead. I also believe God had a hand in Arnie's conversation with Father Aloysius today. So, whatever decision Phillip, Hank, and I may yet make about Pepper, it appears God placed the final say in the hands of Father Aloysius. That's why Joe wanted to also call him and gain his cooperation so we could proceed judiciously with Pepper's best interest in mind."

"Liddy's definitely enjoying Pepper being around, and I gotta confess, me too. I hope God's got something special in store for her, whether it's here or back in Louisiana or Mississippi. She seems to be a great young girl and a pretty gutsy kid at that."

Hal grinned as he put his truck into reverse. "I have one question only God can answer. If she winds up here, would we have to drive her to the Catholic church in Alexandria, or will Father Aloysius object if she attends Shiloh Baptist with us?"

"Good luck getting God to answer you on that one. Of course, you've got a bigger question to get answered."

"What's that, pray tell?" Hal quipped, ready to pull away.

"What do you think Hank's gonna say about all this when he gets home Wednesday?"

Hal chuckled to himself as he pulled out of the driveway and waved at Liddy and Pepper sitting together on the kitchen stoop.

PEPPER CONVERSED MORE THAN AN HOUR ON THE PHONE WITH Father Aloysius last night. After she had hung up, she apologized and disappeared upstairs looking glum and disheartened. Liddy and I tried to comprehend what might have been said that caused Pepper to walk away as if her spirit had been broken. By the time we went to bed, we felt whatever burdened her would likely come out in the morning.

Those unanswered questions induced a restless night. I crawled out of bed a little after four and slipped into a pair of warmups and a t-shirt. Liddy wrestled beneath the covers as she mumbled an inquiry about the time but drifted right back into a deep sleep before she heard my reply. At the foot of the stairs, Pepper's bedroom door was closed. Only the guest bathroom night light's spectral blue glow illuminated the upstairs darkness.

Two minutes later, I relaxed in my recliner enjoying a warm mug of coffee. The Tiffany reading lamp provided the only light I needed. I reached for my devotional journal and Bible. At the top of the page for June 7, I read the verse from Psalm 68: *Sing praises to God! Raise your voice in song to him who rides on the clouds! The Lord is his name—rejoice. He is the guardian of orphans and defender of widows wherever he dwells. He provides families to the lonely.*

I reread the passage, then paused and looked down the still dark hallway toward the stairs. A calmness filled my troubled heart and set my mind at ease.

PURGATORY: A PROGENY'S QUEST

It became clear to me God already had a plan in place for Pepper's future, whether in Shiloh or back in Vidalia. Over the past four days, Pepper learned of her mother's tragic accident, leaving her motherless as well as fatherless. Yet God had introduced her to brothers she never knew existed, nor they, her. I pondered how, without actual family back in Louisiana, Father Aloysius could offer Pepper a better option to her newfound family in Shiloh. Yet, all she had known—her church, her school, and her friends—remained five hundred miles away. Would she choose the familiar over family? Could that dilemma have been behind her woeful retreat last night?

I started to jot down my thoughts when the sound of shuffling feet and a stifled yawn caught my attention. "Mister Phillips, you're up awful early," Pepper managed at the back end of an extended yawn. Her mussed long red hair hung free and veiled much of her face.

"Did I wake you?" I asked.

"Not really. I didn't sleep very well last night anyway." She pulled the wayward strands from her eyes. "The smell of your coffee got me out of bed, though. It smells like the coffee Maude used to perk each morning."

I chuckled as I left my recliner with my mug for a refill. "How about a cup? It's a chicory blend your mother served us. I thought you'd appreciate it this morning." I pointed to the kitchen table.

"That'd be nice, thank you."

"Sugar and milk?" I asked, grabbing another mug.

"Please."

We sat across from each other at the kitchen table. She cradled the mug between her hands and took tiny sips every so often while we talked. She asked about Hal and Phillip at first, but the conversation shifted to her oldest brother, Hank.

"Why would my mother actually shoot him?" Pepper asked, nose and forehead scrunched as though she braced for more pain with the answer.

"It happened more by accident and reflex than intent. I would even testify your mother felt hemmed in by her past and the pressing reality of mistakes she had made. I do know she wanted to take care of family matters in Louisiana before she planned to leave the country. I don't know if this makes you feel any better or not, but it sounded to me as though she wanted to see you before she left."

Pepper stared into her half-empty coffee mug. "I know my mother and father were far from perfect. But Momma had her moments. She'd pop in for a quick visit and take me for ice cream. She'd always remind me to make her proud and mind Maude before she'd kiss me on my cheek and leave almost as fast as she arrived. I don't reckon she ever knew I saw her crying whenever she drove off. Before long I accepted the fact that she left as she did to hide her tears. That's when I added her to my daily prayers. I still ask God to credit what little good she had in her to keep her from the eternal agony beyond Purgatory."

Pepper squeezed the ceramic mug as she spoke about her mother. "I gotta believe that as long as she remains in Purgatory, there's something I can do that God will accept as an acceptable indulgence to save her."

"Wow. I'm not too familiar with such matters, but I do believe God's mercy and grace applies for even the worst of us sinners. Who of us can boast we are without sin? From my way of thinking, a sin is a sin. It doesn't matter how big or small. What matters is we recognize our sinning nature and never give up believing in God's mercy and grace."

Pepper's brow crumpled. "The Church teaches some sins are forgivable, but there's some that even absolution from the Church can't release us from. Are you telling me all sin can be forgiven?"

"Not exactly. The Bible says it plainly, there's but one unforgivable sin."

Pepper's eyes widened. "What's that?"

"Refuse to revere God's presence or spirit within each of us. If anyone condemns God's gift, then what forgiveness can we expect from God? This is so important for each of us to understand. Jesus said as much, and I don't think it matters which Bible might sit on your nightstand. If we love God with all our heart, soul, and mind, God's love resides in us no matter what."

Pepper's eyes popped. "God might forgive my mother?"

"I ain't God, but from where I stand the answer is always yes with God."

"Young lady, I can assure you, Theo Phillips ain't God! Although, he's been accused of acting like it from time to time," Liddy said with a smirk, exiting the shadows wrapped in her blue terry robe with matching fuzzy slippers on her feet. A pink plastic clip kept hair off her face.

Pepper broke into a spate of giggles that harmonized with Liddy's early-morning snickers. I shook my head in denial of Liddy's humor at my expense, but inside I felt Pepper found a little relief she surely needed.

Neighborhood dogs cued me the paper would land on the foot of the porch steps at any moment. This morning, Pepper jumped up before I got out of my chair. "I'll get the paper, Mister Phillips."

Liddy and I smiled as we watched Pepper trot down the porch steps to the sidewalk. She pushed her hair from her face and off her shoulders as Tim rode up the street on his bike. When he reached Pepper, he stopped and straddled his bike. He handed

her the morning paper and the two bantered back and forth before Pepper stepped back and waved as Tim rode off.

As Pepper climbed the steps onto the front porch, Liddy said, "It appears she likes our fair-haired young paperboy."

AFTER BREAKFAST, a blanket of cotton-white cumulus clouds brought a refreshing, midmorning Gulf breeze. Pepper climbed into the porch hammock while Liddy and I sat in our rockers. I read Mary's feature article about Hal Archer's formal decision to remove his name from consideration for the vacant Congressional seat. Below Mary's front page story, Larry Scribner wrote about Zeb's limousine he drove in the festival parade. A photograph of Zeb beside his new vehicle accompanied the article.

On the sports page, below the latest Atlanta Braves doubleheader results and box scores, a staged photo showed John Priestly with an uncharacteristic toothy grin handing a football and whistle to Andy Simmons in front of the coach's office. The ceremonial picture showed Andy donning his new monogrammed Shiloh High coach's shirt and shorts on the business side of the old wooden desk in John's former office.

I pointed to the photo. "Liddy, I wonder how awkward John must have felt posing in his old locker room office wearing a short-sleeve dress shirt and slacks."

Liddy raised her sunglasses and stared at the photo. "It looks to me Andy's the one who's uncomfortable. By the way, did I tell you John's planning a birthday party for Phoebe out on the farm?"

"When's her birthday?"

"June 30, I think. Just before the holiday weekend. I also noticed in the school office John's requested vacation from the last Wednesday until the following first week in July," Liddy said with a grin. "And Phoebe seems afraid to say anything because it isn't like John either to make such a fuss like this."

Pepper rolled onto her side, propped her head with her arm, and asked out of the blue, "Can I ask the two of you a question?"

"Of course," I said.

"Last night, Father Aloysius told me Maude had named him executor of her last will and testament. As such he was instructed to notify me Maude had a $100,000 life insurance policy with me as the beneficiary."

"That was very generous of Maude," Liddy said.

"Father Aloysius also said he had instructions to arrange for the insurance money to be deposited into a trust account she opened in my name with almost $250,000 in it to pay for college and provide me a monthly allowance until I graduated."

Surprised by Maude's provisions for Pepper's future, I had to clear my throat to spit out my words. "Wow! That was more than generous. What did he say about the rest of her estate?"

"She named St. Mary's the beneficiary."

"So the house and property are to go to the church?"

Pepper nodded. "I'm grateful for the money and all, but the memories I shared with Maude in the old house will be lost."

"I understand, but still, it's a lot of money she left for you. Sounds like she wanted you to get a college education," Liddy said with a reassuring smile.

"Yeah, I guess. But Father Aloysius also said he promised Maude St. Mary's would arrange for a suitable foster family for me. Does that mean I can't live in my old house anymore?" Pepper's despondent long face returned.

Liddy left her chair and sat on the edge of the hammock. She stroked Pepper's hair and said, "It sounds that way, but I'm sure it's because he knows you can't live all alone."

"But it's the only house I've ever really known. I don't want to live with some family I don't know."

I leaned forward in my chair and asked, "Are there any friends whose parents might let you live with them?"

"I thought long and hard about that last night. I just don't know." Pepper slumped in the hammock and threw her arm over her face. "It's just not fair!"

Liddy continued to stroke her hair. "We'll help as best we can to sort this out with you. You only have one more year of high school, and didn't you tell me your birthday's in August?"

"Yes, ma'am. I'll be seventeen on August first." A little smile appeared on her sad face.

I stood up and stroked my chin. "What if I talked to a couple of friends of mine? From what I heard you say, Maude provided well for you, but there are other options for you to consider. I don't know diddly-squat about Louisiana laws, but I know two good friends right here in town who might be able to help."

Pepper scooted herself up into a sitting position and held Liddy's hand. Liddy offered a warm maternal smile. "Why don't you let Theo see what he can do?"

Pepper looked up at me. "Would you, please?"

"Absolutely. I'll do it right after lunch. How's that?" Liddy patted Pepper's hand. "While Theo does what he does best, how about you and I drive over to Alexandria and do some shopping? I'd love to buy you some more clothes. I don't think you packed to stay this long."

Pepper's freckled dimples sank a bit deeper as she nodded. "We can drive in my car if you don't mind."

PEPPER PULLED MAUDE'S Buick out of our driveway not long after lunch. Though Liddy didn't appear to have any reservations letting Pepper drive, she waved from the passenger window gnawing her bottom lip. I waved with a reassuring smile. At the same time, I had a flashback to driving with our two sons when they were sixteen. Neither started driving at fifteen out of necessity either nor had driven five hundred miles all by herself. Liddy was in good hands.

Not long after they left, I drove to the *Sentinel* rather than hike across town since the earlier morning cloud cover had dispersed and the unobstructed sunshine catapulted the temperature once again into the high nineties. The air-conditioning in our Expedition worked just fine; there was no sense in not taking advantage of it. Martha's desk was unoccupied when I arrived at the newspaper office, but Mary appeared from her dad's office sipping a Coke.

"Where's your mom?" I asked Mary when she returned to the editor's desk.

"Taking the afternoon off. As far as I know, she drove over to Alexandria to do some shopping."

"I read your article this morning. Sounds like you squeezed a little more out of Hal about his decision."

Mary smiled. "Hal seemed relieved to have this behind him. I also learned a little more after I got to chitchat with Hillary, but what she told me didn't make the article."

Leaning over the counter, I asked, "What does that mean?"

"You know I'm not going to divulge a confidential conversation. I can say it sounds like Hal's mulling over more pressing family concerns."

"But—"

"Theo, no buts! When Hal wants the likes of you or me to know something, Hillary promised he'll tell us."

As I ventured back to Larry's office, I tried to decipher the cryptic reference to *more pressing family concerns*. I considered the possibility of Pepper being one of those family concerns but dismissed it when I deduced Hal had already made his mind up about the vacant Congressional seat before he even met Pepper. Hank's return after eighteen months in two Army hospitals, hopefully now set free from his Afghanistan nightmares, could surely qualify. Since I first came to Shiloh, Hal had served as his older brother's keeper even when he hated all the wrongs Hank had inflicted upon him, their family, and others. It made sense Hal wouldn't abandon Phillip, the youngest of the Archer brothers, to handle Hank all alone. Of course, Pepper's unexpected arrival likewise added to Hal's *pressing family concerns*.

"Since when does Theo Phillips stand in my office doorway waiting for permission to enter? You look lost in thought. What's up?" Larry bellowed from behind his desk, atop of which his feet were perched.

"Mary said something interesting about Hal's decision, but I'm here on another point of interest far more pressing and yet germane to Hal and his brothers."

"You're referring to Dixie's daughter, I imagine," Larry said with a smug grin as I sat in one of the wooden armchairs in front of his cluttered desk.

"Miss Sarah Mae Arnaquer, or Pepper as she prefers, appears, in fact, to be the sole legal progeny of our dearly departed and somewhat infamous Delilah Dixon Archer and her presumed and otherwise deceased Louisiana husband, Beauregard Arnaquer. After hosting Pepper these last few days, I find myself scratching my head. She's a genuinely good kid—which I attribute to the fact Dixie and Beau did manage to do right by Pepper when they allowed Beau's mother to raise her. Maude Arnaquer by all measure kept Pepper far removed from all Beau and Dixie represented, at least until she passed away last month. The girl drove five hundred miles in search of her mother only to discover she died in an accident after nearly killing a brother Pepper never knew existed."

"I presume you're talking about Hank. And I likewise presume she has now met her other two half-brothers."

"That's why I'm here," I said, crossing my outstretched legs at the ankles. "Without going into all the details, suffice it to say Pepper had a very gracious and loving grandmother. From what she told Liddy and me this morning, her grandmother left her with a generous trust account, supplemented further by a sizable life insurance policy. But she's lost the house she was raised in. That home along with the rest of her grandmother's estate has been willed to St. Mary's Catholic Parish in Natchez, Mississippi. Of course, Maude Arnaquer bequeathed her estate under the proviso that Father Aloysius serve as Pepper's interim guardian until she reached her eighteenth birthday."

"What do you want me to do?"

"Pepper's pretty torn right now. She's got no real family to take her, outside of the Archers, but that's still up in the air pending Joe Arians getting his hands on Pepper's records to confirm she is, in fact, Dixie's daughter. Although, at this point, I have no reason to believe otherwise. So, in the meantime, I was wondering, could your buddy at *The Times-Picayune* do a little digging and shed a little light on Pepper and her grandmother? Maybe look into their relationship with St. Mary's Catholic Parish, which also runs the school Pepper has attended since elementary school in Natchez, Mississippi."

As I talked, Larry scribbled notes, then he asked, "What's Maude's full name? And do you have her house address?"

"It's Matilda Arnaquer." I pulled out from my satchel the notes I scrawled before leaving the house, then shared the pertinent details I had acquired about Maude with Larry.

"Let me see what I can find out. How soon do you want to hear something?" Larry asked.

"See if they can get us something to share by Thursday morning. The poor girl is betwixt and between a rock and a hard place and deserves some answers before she faces an arduous five-hundred-mile drive back to Vidalia where even more uncertainty awaits her as a ward of the Catholic Church."

"I can't make any promises, but let me get right on it. I'll call you as soon as I hear something."

SUSANNA SIMMONS GREETED me when I walked into Joe Arians' office. Without missing a beat, she pointed to the waiting area after telling me he had Hal in his office. A cup of coffee later, she said, "Theo, you can go back now."

Hal stood as I entered and greeted me at the conference table in Joe's private office. Joe sat at the head of the table and pointed to the chair across from Hal.

"Sorry we kept you waiting as long as we did. Hal and I went over Pepper's records the school faxed over. Everything appears in order, and you may have already guessed she's an honor student and recently completed her junior year. She's a standout soccer and track athlete, too. And more importantly, we have copies of the court papers naming Matilda Arnaquer as Sarah's legal guardian twelve years ago."

I looked at the faxed copy of the court order and saw it was the same address back then appearing on the handwritten stationery Pepper showed us when she first arrived. I laid the paper down and glanced at Hal and Joe, "Where's the *but* plastered all over the two of you?"

PURGATORY: A PROGENY'S QUEST

Hal reached across the table with the faxed copy of Sarah Mae Archer's birth certificate. It stated Pepper was born at Tulane University Hospital in New Orleans, August 1, 1999. I read *father unknown* where the name of the father should be, and *Delilah Dixon Posey* in the space for the maiden name of the mother. I looked up at Hal and then Joe.

Hal pointed to his mother's name. "This was her name before she married Pop. If Beau Arnaquer had been the birth father wouldn't his name be there?"

PEPPER AND LIDDY arrived at the house a little before sunset. As soon as I caught the first whiff of Bubba's mouthwatering ribs, I knew they spent more than an afternoon in Alexandria, but their giggle-filled enthusiasm made it all worthwhile. Pepper must have raced up and down the stairs five or six times modeling new blouses, skirts, jeans, shorts, and shoes. The priceless look on Liddy's face reminded me we raised two sons, and our only granddaughter was not quite eleven. I sensed Pepper's beaming approval when I applauded and commented on her new clothes.

After we enjoyed Liddy's banana pudding, Pepper thanked Liddy for the umpteenth time then said goodnight. A moment later, she raced down the stairs, gave me a hug, and whispered, "You really didn't mind she bought me all those clothes?" I smiled and shook my head. She kissed my cheek. "Thank you, Mister Phillips." She waved at Liddy and bounded upstairs.

Before we turned off the lights to retire for the evening, Liddy whispered, "I think that young girl relished all the attention you provided her tonight. Thanks for being such a sport about all the clothes I bought for her." She blew me a kiss from her chair.

"Thank you for the ribs and banana pudding. Now, would you like to hear what I learned about Pepper today?"

Liddy wrapped her arms around her knees. "I'm all ears."

I looked down the dark hallway before I whispered, "Beau Arnaquer is not her birth father. She was born Sarah Mae Archer."

Liddy's once-sleepy eyes grew wide as I shared with her what appeared on Pepper's birth certificate.

TIM AND WOOGIE STOPPED BY THE HOUSE TO INVITE PEPPER TO grab some lunch and see a little more of our sleepy town. Liddy stepped from the kitchen, folded her arms across her chest and, with the voice of a concerned mother, said, "I trust you two will mind your Ps and Qs while you show her around. Please make sure to get back by four o'clock. Church tonight."

Tim and Woogie both said, "Yes, ma'am. Four o'clock. Church. No problem."

"Where you taking Pepper for lunch?" I asked.

Tim blurted out, "My house. Mom's fixing some sandwiches and was the one who suggested we invite her."

Pepper's eager wide-eyed look reminded me how she was very much a typical teenage girl. I said, "Y'all go have fun. Why don't you introduce her to Uncle Zeb over at the Old General Store? Miss Marie should be there, too."

The three bolted out the door and had hit the sidewalk by the time the storm door closed behind them.

PEPPER AND LIDDY fretted over the prospect of walking to church in the early evening heat and humidity, so I drove us up Broad Street to church and parked between Pete's truck and Larry's Buick. While we climbed the church steps, I noticed Hal and Hillary speaking to Gus near his old Lincoln in the City Hall parking lot.

At the top of the steps, Pepper looked back as Phillip parked next to Pete's truck. "Is that Phillip's oldest brother with him?"

Hank stepped out on the passenger side, at least twenty pounds lighter than we last saw him, sporting a trimmed full-face beard. His trademark aviator sunglasses shielded his dark eyes. He adjusted his untucked blue and white checkered dress shirt and cream-colored chino slacks. He draped his arm across Phillip's shoulders as they stepped in unison across the street. To witness the two of them relaxed in idle chat with one another brought a smile to my face.

"Mister and Missus Phillips, I'm glad to see you this evening," Hank said, shaking my hand. He shifted his attention to Pepper fidgeting with her necklace while she stared at Hank with a shy but curious look. "Well, this pretty redhead must be Pepper." He leaned a little closer as he lifted his mirrored sunglasses. "I sure don't know where you got those pretty green eyes, but you sure have Momma's charming bright white smile." Hank motioned to her red braids. "It's also plain to see, you and Phillip share the same red hair genes. Of course, yours looks a whole lot nicer."

Hank mussed his brother's hair, which riled Phillip until Pepper's giggles become contagious.

Inside the air-conditioned foyer, Hank wandered over to where Pete stood in conversation with his brother Andy and Megan. Handshakes and hugs exchanged were in stark contrast to the hostility once existing between them. Megan pointed to the children's check-in before he walked away with his hands sunk into his pants pockets and a satisfied look on his carefree face. I could only imagine he inquired about Little Jessie.

Pepper disappeared with Phillip after he had invited her to sit with him and his brothers. We meandered over to Sam and Susanna Simmons, who likewise watched Hank's exchange with their sons and daughter-in-law.

PURGATORY: A PROGENY'S QUEST

"Whatever those doctors did with Hank, it sure looks like it worked. To see him greet Pete and Andy like that and then offer a smile and hug with Megan—who'da thunk it possible?" Sam said, shaking his head.

The sound of Mary Scribner playing the prelude on the piano stirred everyone to head for their seats in the sanctuary. Following the singing of a couple of familiar hymns, Arnie left his place behind the pulpit and stepped down from the dais.

He stood at the head of the center aisle and said, "Before I share with you tonight's message from God's Word, I have an announcement. It's been far too many years since we held a community-wide social to raise money for the outstanding ministry work of the Shiloh Cooperative Church Fellowship. So this morning, the churches in town agreed: In lieu of the old-fashioned camp meetings like we used to do for this purpose, this year we decided to host a musical jamboree at Priestly Park, last Saturday of this month. I hope all y'all who won't be on vacation then will enjoy a special evening of foot-stomping music, food, and fellowship. It's sure to be fun for all, and rumor has it there'll be special entertainment for the youth."

Arnie opened his Bible.

"In the Greek language the word for time is not singular. There are actually three Greek words translated as 'time' in our Bibles. The first is *chronos*. It refers to a measurable duration of time, such as an hour or minute, or even a day, month, or year. *Aion* is the second, and it refers to an extended period of time such as an age or era. You know, an indefinite, extended length of time, whether pointing us to the distant past or distant future. However, there's a third I'd like to speak about tonight, *kairos*.

"*Kairos* refers to a definitive moment in time. Or, you might say, an opportune point in time. Its proper definition says it is the fleeting rightness of time that creates conditions for action whether by deeds or words, or both. We all have experienced and will yet experience a handful of *kairos* moments—crucial times in our lives where a life-altering decision awaits."

Arnie referred to several examples of *kairos* moments in the Bible and even referenced two moments in modern history such as D-Day in World War II when General Eisenhower seized the crucial window of opportunity in history altering the war, though his instincts and intuition said otherwise. Arnie reminded us that only yesterday our nation celebrated the seventy-second anniversary of that event, then asked for folks to speak about *kairos* moments in their own lives.

Liddy stood up and said, "For Theo and me, it was the day we made the decision to purchase the home that brought us to Shiloh. We trusted God and are most thankful we did."

Andy Simmons said, "When Coach Priestly called to discuss the opportunity he offered for me to return to Shiloh. Before that life-altering call, Megan and I were bound for Nebraska."

"For me," Marie Masterson said with reluctance at first, "my crucial opportunity arrived when you first brought Theo Phillips with you to my farmhouse." Marie teared up as she took a deep breath. "When God brought Theo and Liddy Phillips back into my life after thirty-five years and for me to recognize him like I did. I don't know about you, Pastor Wright, but I know that crucial moment set me back on the road to recovery from a lonely, bitter time in my life. Thanks to Theo and Liddy, and others in this room, I can now look at the bronze memorial across the street of my son, Jessie, without the bitterness and emptiness I used to feel inside."

The sanctuary fell silent when Hank stood up. "Pastor Wright, this is my *kairos* moment." Hank turned and looked at all the familiar faces. "This is hard to admit, but there isn't a soul in this room except one who I hadn't offended or wronged over the years. I want all y'all to know I'm taking this opportunity to ask for your forgiveness. Over the past eighteen months, I discovered a lot about my inner demons warring within me, but I can stand here with you tonight and assure each of you they all have received their eviction notices. I admit I'm still a work in progress, but the old Hank Archer no longer exists." Hank stared at Arnie. "Preacher, I think that's the most I've ever said in this church." Hank sat back down, head slumped.

An eerie stillness occupied the sanctuary for close to a Southern minute before Arnie pointed to Mary. She left the front pew and returned to her place at the piano, but she sat with her hands in her lap staring at Arnie who said, "Hank, thank you. I reckon it's the right time to close in prayer."

As the pews emptied and folks filled the aisle, Mary played a respectful postlude. Liddy and I stood in the aisle and thanked Marie for her kind words.

Larry grabbed my arm. "Come see me in the morning."

"What?" I asked.

"Not now. Stop by about ten-thirty tomorrow morning," Larry said before he turned and followed Martha to talk with Mary and Pete.

Hank and Pepper remained seated and talked, while Hal, Hillary, Phillip, and Jeannie walked up the aisle headed out of the sanctuary into the foyer. Liddy and I followed.

"Are Pepper and Hank okay?" Liddy asked Hillary.

"My guess is she's looking for answers as much as Hank about what their future holds," Hillary replied. She looked at Phillip. "Tell Theo what Pepper said to you about Woogie."

Phillip eyed the aisle and saw Hank and Pepper lost in conversation as they made their way up the aisle. Phillip leaned closer and whispered, "Did you hear? Woogie claims he saw his mother at the festival and again this afternoon, driving a Caddy past Zeb's store going toward River Road."

"No. How did you find out?"

"Pepper told me."

"Did she say anything else?"

"Only that Woogie got upset after they stopped to see his dad at the barbershop. She and Tim stayed outside while Woogie and his dad went in the back of the shop for a few minutes. Pepper said when Woogie reappeared he looked confused. His father had told him he had to have been mistaken. The woman he saw could not have been his mother."

Megan and Andy joined us with Marie holding Little Jessie by the time Hank and Pepper left the sanctuary laughing. Jessie squirmed in Marie's arms.

"Andy, is this Jessie?" Hank asked, and stared at Jessie's rosy cheeks. Jessie reached out to touch Hank's dark beard.

Megan took Jessie from Marie and knelt down to allow Jessie to stand in front of her. Hank dropped down on two knees and joined them. Jessie looked back at Megan and then up at Andy. Hank wiped a tear with his sleeve and looked at Andy, "Congrats. Jessie would be pleased." He then looked up at Marie, "He kinda looks like Jessie, doesn't he?"

Megan hoisted Jessie back into her arms as she stood before she handed him back to Marie. "Thank you, Hank. I know that wasn't easy for you."

"No. God gifted him to you and Andy. Can't deny it. What happened is in the past. I'm good. I'm even better now I realize how happy you are with Andy." Hank patted Andy's shoulder.

Zeb smacked Hank on his back. "That was mighty fine of you to say what you did tonight. Your daddy would've been proud."

"Thank you, Mister Adams."

"Now that you're back, does this mean you're goin' back to work at Archer Construction?" Zeb asked.

Phillip turned to catch Hank's reply. "Nope. Don't think so. From what I've heard, Phillip's been doing a bang-up job running the business. I'll find something else to do to keep me busy out on the estate. Hal and Phillip already suggested I take over as caretaker and manage the property. With the lumber mill growing like it is, it'll need a bigger supply of timber. We've still got plenty of mature loblollies ripe for harvesting, too. Besides, me and ol' Maddie need to mend our fences. I reckon my time will be best served out there." Phillip exhaled and then offered an affirming nod and smile.

Hal wrapped one arm around Hillary's waist and said, "Hank just got home. There's plenty of time to sort the future out. For right now, let's consider this an opportune moment for us all to say goodnight."

Pepper hugged Hank then joined Liddy and me standing beside our vehicle. I wondered how all this might change after I visited with Larry the next morning.

T.M. BROWN

16

PREPARED TO HEAR WHATEVER LARRY MIGHT SPRING ON ME, I
sat straightaway in my customary chair while he finished his
phone conversation. I pulled out a fresh legal pad from my
leather briefcase and clicked my ballpoint pen. As I doodled on
the corner of the pad, I noticed a folder labeled *Sarah M Arnaquer*
on his desk. Larry ran his hand over the top of the manila file
cover as he exited his call and hung up.

He sank into his leather swivel chair, stroking the folder.

"What's in here took a little digging by my newspaper buddy.
He used the ruse that *The Times-Picayune* wanted to publish an
article on Matilda Arnaquer. Although he began in Vidalia, his
inquiries led him back to New Orleans in no time—and even
Baton Rouge. Want to know what's inside?"

I prepped my pen in my hand and nodded. "Of course." I had
not shared anything Joe Arians had shown me about the birth
certificate with Larry. I felt it apropos to use that information to
test the info Larry had found out.

Larry pulled out a copy of Pepper's birth certificate, identical
to the one Joe had produced in his office, and removed faxed
copies of two other legal papers and handed them to me. "Are you
certain Beauregard Arnaquer fathered this young girl? According
to the birth certificate, the father's name was not provided."

I examined the birth certificate again, although I knew what it
said, and then the other two legal documents. Both were court-
approved State of Louisiana Petition for Name Change forms filed
in St. Tammany Parish.

— 125 —

PURGATORY: A PROGENY'S QUEST

On October 10, 2006, Delilah Dixon Archer became Delilah Dixon Arnaquer, and her daughter, Sarah Mae Archer, became Sarah Mae Arnaquer.

These documents answered a lingering question from Dixie's return to Shiloh two years earlier. We had never found any records of her and Beau Arnaquer's marriage, but she had a Louisiana Driver's License with Arnaquer as her last name.

I lifted Sarah Mae's petition and asked, "How about any record of adoption?"

Larry shrugged. "They checked and found nothing except this name-change petition. Dixie and Beau didn't even file Pepper's birth certificate reissued after the name change. Sounds like Beau avoided becoming Pepper's father or stepfather." Larry handed me one other legal document. "Furthermore, though I'm not surprised, not even a year later in Concordia Parish, where Matilda Arnaquer and Pepper resided, this petition for Voluntary Transfer of Custody granted Matilda full custodial care of Pepper with Dixie's consent."

"Where did they find this?"

Larry smiled. "Her school records provided a copy, along with her name-change petition."

I stared at Larry for a moment. "May I use your phone?"

I called Joe Arians. Larry leaned forward and planted his elbows on his desk as I described to Joe what Larry had dug up. Joe acknowledged that copies of Pepper's name-change petition and legal guardianship papers were among the items he received as well, but his focus had been on the birth certificate. He listened with interest when I told him there evidently was never any marriage certificate filed between Dixie and Beau Arnaquer, only a name-change petition for both Dixie and Pepper. He asked for copies of everything Larry had gotten. I hung up.

Larry asked with arched brows, "What did Joe say?"

I tried to grasp the significance of all this. Yet I wanted to be sensitive to Pepper's situation. I mumbled as I gathered my thoughts, "He asked me to get copies of what you have, so he can match it up with what he got from the school."

Larry tucked papers back into the folder and handed it all to me. "Let Joe make copies of what he needs, but keep me informed. What do you think this all implies about the young girl?"

I slid the folder into my briefcase. "I'm a bit confused. It appears Beau Arnaquer was neither Pepper's father nor likely even her legal stepfather. I'm not sure how all this is possible, but then again we are talking about Louisiana."

Larry left his chair and walked around the desk shaking his head. "I once heard that in Louisiana a few dollars here and a favor there greases the wheels of backwater bureaucracy. Now I believe it more than ever."

"IT'S GETTIN' MIGHTY late. What time did the boys say they'd have Pepper back here?" I asked Liddy.

"Quit your fussing. Pepper enjoys the distraction those boys are providing her," Liddy said, but her voice tapered as concern slowed her words.

The tantalizing aroma of Liddy's meatloaf filled the house, though, along with a bowl of mashed potatoes, it remained in the oven to stay warm in anticipation of Pepper's return. I didn't need to recheck my watch. The growing grayness told me it must be almost nine o'clock.

The click-clack of her rocker became louder with each passing minute. "I don't understand it, Theo. They've always been respectful of the time. I sure hope nothing bad has happened."

Liddy adjusted her crossed arms, but her gaze remained focused on the street.

"Kids will be kids. I trust Woogie and Tim, but all the same, I agree with you." I had already left my rocker and started pacing the porch as the streetlights popped on.

Headlights soon turned off Broad Street onto Calvary. A moment later, Pepper hopped out the front passenger side of Mitch Johnson's SPD truck. Woogie and Tim piled out from the backseat. The boys helped Mitch lower the tailgate and remove Pepper's bike from the rear of the pickup. Pepper ran past me to Liddy's open arms. Her face and outfit looked as though they had wrestled in a dirt pile. Trails of drying blood ran down from the scrapes and abrasions on her knees, shins, and arms. I walked toward Mitch but gawked at Woogie and Tim. They also carried their own bloody scratches and scrapes beneath a layer of South Georgia brownish-red dirt. The boys looked a sight with sweaty, dirt-filled hair littered with flecks of debris.

"They flagged me down on River Highway about a mile outside town. Tim's bike chain had busted, and they were about to stash it in the drainage ditch until they saw me," Mitch said, watching the boys standing alongside the bike I'd let Pepper use.

Tim pushed Pepper's bike closer to me. "Where should I put this, Mister P?"

Woogie then said, "I'm sorry, Mister P. We should've been home a couple of hours ago. It was my fault."

"What do you mean it was your fault?" Though I stood with a measured scowl, I tried not to jump to any conclusions until I knew more.

Tim piped in. "Mister P, like I told Mister Johnson, if it weren't for Woogie we might still be stuck under that old mansion."

Liddy held Pepper close then pulled her head back and, with a dose of motherly consternation in her voice, said, "Did you boys take Pepper out there? You know it isn't safe. What happened?"

Woogie wiped his mud-caked eyes. "I saw my momma pull up to the old plantation house in that same Caddy with some guy. We were just showing Pepper the cotton fields and exploring the woods out there. Honest, I didn't plan for her to step anywhere near that glorified rat-trap, but—"

Pepper shouted, "It was my fault, Mister Phillips. I knew how bad Woogie wanted to be sure it was his momma, so I encouraged him, and Tim agreed."

Tim nodded. "She's exactly right. I know Woogie still felt bad because his dad convinced him it wasn't his mother who he saw driving through town the other day. Woogie needed to be sure this time."

"After we snuck around to the front of the old mansion, the guy started ranting and cussing up a storm from near the back of the house," Pepper said. She left Liddy's embrace to stand beside Woogie and Tim. "We crept around to the far side of the house until we could peek around the back corner. The guy was leaning against the front end of their car. He waved his arms around, yelling at someone on the phone. The woman came off the back porch with two cans of beer. That's when Woogie said he thought it was his momma, but she didn't look like he remembered."

"Mister Johnson, I could have been wrong. The woman did kinda look like my momma, but my momma was never that skinny. I also don't remember her having tattoos on her neck and arms. But still, I'm pretty sure she was my momma."

I surveyed each of them standing side-by-side in dire need of soap, water, and a few Band-Aids. "So what happened? Why did it take you so long to get back home, and why do you look like you crawled through the cotton fields?"

"Well sir, Woogie decided he needed to get closer and see for sure. He told Pepper and me to stay put. As soon as Woogie stepped out from the corner of the house, the guy pulled a gun from his belt and yelled for Woogie to stop. The woman stared at Woogie, dropped her beer can, and grabbed the guy's arm."

"What did Woogie do?" Mitch inquired.

Tim said, "He turned and hightailed it as fast as he could across the cotton fields bolting for the woods. That's when I pulled Pepper underneath the house. We were scared, so we scooted as far back as we could to hide."

"Yeah, it was creepy too," Pepper said. "Spider webs were everywhere. I just about screamed when a huge, nasty brown spider crawled onto my shoulder, but Tim swatted it away. That's when the woman started to walk around the house. We scooted even further back and tucked behind a brick column. In the distance, we heard the man calling after Woogie. It felt like an eternity had passed, but he eventually returned and stood beside the woman. We couldn't see any more than their legs, but I almost squealed when I saw his gun." Pepper looked at Tim. "That's when I tasted century-old dirt on Tim's hand."

Tim smiled at her. "Sorry, but you would've given us away."

"How'd you get out of there?" I asked.

"It felt like hours, but before long, the man and woman drove off. Woogie showed back up right after. We ran as fast as we could through the cotton fields into the woods. We were afraid they may come back." Pepper looked up at me. "That's when we got most of these scratches on our legs."

Pepper looked at Mitch and said, "We decided at first to risk riding our bikes back to town, but Tim's bike chain snapped. Thank God we saw your truck and waved you down."

"Theo," Mitch said, "I don't know why those two were at the old mansion, but Hawk and I will check it out first thing in the morning. I'm also still uncertain who they were, but based on what the kids said, our troublemaker from the festival is still hanging around for some reason. I'll let you know what we find." Mitch looked at Tim and Woogie. "Y'all hop back in, and I'll run you home."

Pepper went straight upstairs and took a long shower while Liddy got dinner together. When she came back downstairs, Pepper continued to relive her adventurous afternoon long after we had dinner.

PURGATORY: A PROGENY'S QUEST

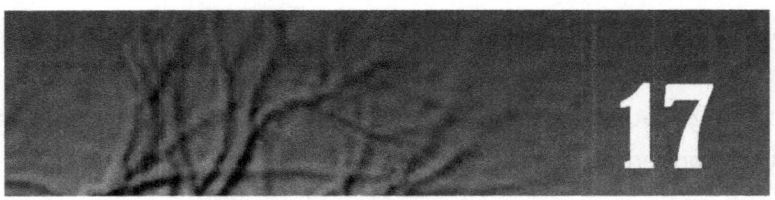

WE ALLOWED PEPPER TO SLEEP IN WHILE WE ENJOYED A QUIET breakfast of toasted bagels, orange juice, and fresh coffee. Her harrowing ordeal with Tim and Woogie out at the old mansion yesterday earned her a little extra time in bed.

When the phone rang, Liddy jumped up so fast she grabbed it during its first ring. She hung up and said, "Hal and Hank are on their way over."

A few minutes later, Hank pulled along the curb in his black pickup with Hal in the passenger seat. Mitch parked his SPD white pickup right behind him. I pointed to the porch rockers and asked if they didn't mind talking outside since Pepper was still asleep. Mitch opted to remain standing by the steps while Hank leaned against the porch rail, arms folded.

Mitch asked, though not more than a whisper, "How was Pepper when she went to bed last night?"

Liddy winced a time or two as she spoke in a muted, considerate voice. "Her scrapes and scratches looked a sight better after she scrubbed all the dirt off her. I helped her put some ointment on the nastier scrapes on her elbows and knees, but I didn't think any of them even needed a bandage."

"She kept us up quite late rehashing everything that happened. No doubt, the guy with the gun upset her the most. I guess I'd have been pretty shaken, too," I added.

Mitch peered at Hal before he said, "Hawk and I combed the old mansion and the surrounding grounds first thing this morning. Outside of a few empty beer cans and cigarette butts near the back stoop along with a set of tire tracks, this mystery couple left nothing that would indicate they stayed out there for any length of time. It makes me wonder why they even ventured out there in the first place."

Hank butted in. "This time of year, only rows and rows of green cotton plants surround that old vermin-infested house and its kudzu-draped toolshed behind it." Hank then focused on Hal. "We oughta level what's left of it once and for all before someone gets seriously hurt out there."

Hal smiled at Hank. "Big brother, I agree. Even though we own the property, Dad honored his ongoing gentleman's lease agreement with the Akridges to farm cotton on the land. We can't bring heavy equipment out there to demolish anything until after the harvest this fall."

Hank chuckled. "Who's talking about bulldozing anything? It'd be a whole lot easier to light up the old place and its outbuildings."

Hal said, "We don't need any more buildings burned down around here."

Hank throttled his laugh. "I was only joking. Nix the fire suggestion."

Hal stared at Hank with a contorted, unimpressed look, "Good idea." He glanced at Liddy. "Miss Liddy, we actually have another reason to be here this morning. Do you think Pepper likes it here in Shiloh? I mean, does she talk much about missing her little river town in Louisiana?"

Liddy rocked back and peeked over at me. "I don't think Pepper feels like she has any good reasons to go back to Vidalia. She knows she can't return to the home she grew up in. She hasn't even asked to speak with Father Aloysius the past two days. I believe she's afraid what may be waiting when she goes back."

PURGATORY: A PROGENY'S QUEST

Hal and Hank stared at one another before Hank winked and nodded. Hal left his rocker and stood beside Hank with his arms crossed over his chest. "Joe Arians told me last night that from all he's seen in her records, we—meaning Phillip, Hank, and me— are her only real next of kin. Which means there's nothing stopping us from inviting her to stay right here in Shiloh with us. Joe's already posed the possibility with Father Superstitious, or whatever his name is. Appears the final decision is Pepper's."

I asked, "Is there any of the Arnaquer family to consult?"

Hank replied, "Nope. There's no reason to chase that rabbit. Besides, you well know her father wasn't Beauregard Arnaquer anyhow. Now that her pseudo-grandma has passed away, there's also no reason to hold onto the name the court gave her. She's an Archer. Her birth certificate confirms the fact. Her name change can be undone without much fuss if she wants it done."

Opening the glass storm door, Pepper mumbled, "If who wants to do what? Besides, how do you know my father was not my real father?" She stepped barefoot onto the porch. Her exposed knees bore quarter-sized dried blood scabs on them. Less noticeable scratches left reddened streaks across her arms.

Liddy left her rocker and walked to Pepper, who had already instinctively embraced the only person she seemed to fully trust— herself. Liddy put her arm around Pepper's shoulders, which seemed to soften Pepper's scowl. "We're sorry. We didn't mean to upset you like this."

Pepper began crying and glanced at each of us. "I've pretty much known for awhile that the man I knew as my father was not my real father. I hardly saw him...hardly knew him...got no memories of sitting in his lap or holding his hand. Only the photos Maude on the mantle reminded me what he even looked like."

Liddy pulled Pepper closer and stroked her pigtail braids. "God inspired you to travel here in search of your mother. She's gone like your Maude, but see what's happened? You've discovered family you didn't know you had."

Liddy stared at Hal and Hank. "They too were taken by surprise, like you were, Pepper. So they instigated an investigation into the truth. They discovered you are in fact Delilah Dixon Archer's daughter. Of course, it's also true Beauregard Arnaquer gave you his name as he did your mother. Your birth certificate identifies you as Sarah Mae Archer, born to your mother in Tulane Medical Center, New Orleans, Louisiana, almost seventeen years ago. It's quite obvious to us Maude loved you and wanted nothing but the best for you. But there's one thing you must realize—you are, in fact, Sarah Mae Archer by birth."

Tears raced down her cheeks as she pushed a few stubborn unkempt strands of hair from her face.

Hank asked her, "Where's the necklace Maude gave you?"

"Upstairs."

"If you wouldn't mind, please go get it. I want to show you something that'll help you grasp all this." Hank then shoved his hands deep into the front pockets of his jeans.

Pepper returned a minute later holding the strand of brownish-red carved beads. She offered them to Hank, but he pulled one hand from his pocket and raised one finger for her to wait a second. He removed his other hand from the other pocket and concealed something in a closed fist.

"Pepper, I want to prove to you that we are family. Would you like it to be true?" Hank asked, sharing wistful looks with her.

Pepper wiped the corner of her still moist, reddened eyes with the sleeve of her blue cotton top. "Yes, but—"

Hank extended his clenched hand and relaxed his fingers as he turned his hand palm up. He revealed a crucifix attached to a short tail of reddish-brown carved beads. "My mother kept this among her prized jewelry. When I saw your necklace that first day, I knew right then why she had tucked it among her most valuable jewelry." Hank reached for the necklace in Pepper's hand. He slid his fingers along the length of it until he reached the carved heart that had a small metal ring attached. He pried open the metal ringlet at the end of the short strand of matching beads attached to the crucifix. A moment later, he handed the restored rosary to Pepper.

Pepper took a long look at the rosary. Her tears returned along with a reserved smile.

Hal stepped next to Hank and Pepper. "Maude must've known someday the two parts of Mom's rosary would come back together. If you ask me, that's why she gave it to you with the note to come to Shiloh to find your mother."

Pepper opened her arms and hugged Hank and Hal. "I want to be Sarah Mae Archer. I would like to be your sister." Hal and Hank's arms swallowed Pepper.

Mitch cleared his throat. "I hate to interrupt this kumbaya family reunion. I need to get to the office before Camille thinks I'm playing hooky this morning."

Hal lifted his head and said, "Tell Hilly I'll be a little late. A family emergency came up."

THAT AFTERNOON, LIDDY took Pepper to see Joe Arians. She wanted to understand what would happen if she decided to accept Hal, Hank, and Phillip's invitation and remain in Shiloh. Afterward, Liddy took Pepper to visit Shiloh High School to meet Kay Abernathy and John Priestly. If Pepper indeed decided to remain in Shiloh, she would attend Shiloh High for her senior year, a far cry from the parochial school she had attended. Liddy felt meeting the principal and getting a tour of the campus might erase any preconceived notions she had of what a small-town public school would be like.

As for me, I walked to Edwards Barbershop for a haircut and a chat with Wilson. When I arrived, he and Hub occupied their respective barber chairs.

Wilson rustled from his chair. "Mister Phillips, did you come in for a haircut or do you want to talk about yesterday?"

I ran fingers through my hair. "Both."

Wilson wiped off the seat and backrest with a towel and prompted me to take a seat. He adjusted the barber chair and secured a pinstriped cape around my neck. "The usual, I presume?" I nodded and he ran a comb through my hair. "What exactly did the kids say to you and Liddy about yesterday? I couldn't get a straight answer out of Woogie last night."

"Do you remember the commotion two weeks ago after the festival parade?"

"You referring to Camille getting accosted?"

"A woman accompanied him then and yesterday. He's also the same character who tried to outbid Zeb at the vehicle auction. I also distinctly remembered a woman behind the wheel of the black Cadillac this guy Cy drove off in that day, likely the same car the kids saw yesterday."

Wilson clamped a swath of my hair between his fingers, ready to be trimmed. "Why are you connecting the link between this woman and this guy?"

"It strikes me she very well might could be the woman Woogie saw driving through town."

Wilson snipped scraggly ends between his fingers. "Are you insinuating the woman might've been Cassie, Woogie's mom?"

"Well, could it have been?"

"Like I reminded Woogie last night, Cassie went back to prison three years ago for drug possession and prostitution right after I got out of jail myself. Besides, Woogie's only really known a handful of foster mothers before I arranged to get him to Shiloh under my Grandparent's guardianship a couple of years ago. Could the woman have looked like his mother? I guess, but I don't think it's likely. Even if she's out of prison—"

Wilson placed his hands on my cheek and turned my head so I could see Hub absorbed in our conversation. Hub leaned forward in his barber chair and checked the front door.

"Cassie may have once been my daughter, but she's been dead to me for a long, long time, Mister Phillips. She knows if she ever steps one foot inside Adams County again or attempts to contact Woogie, she'll be arrested." Hub's sad, shame-filled eyes sank to the floor.

"I'm sorry, Hub. I realize there's history of hard feelings between y'all. I merely figured the way Woogie described her and her actions made me feel she could've been Cassie."

Hub muttered, "I know you didn't mean no harm. I just don't want any misunderstanding. There's a part of my heart that prays daily against hope that she'll someday be freed from Satan's dark, cold grip. Until it happens, and this may sound heartless, I plead almost daily with God: If she cannot be resurrected back to life as the daughter I once knew and loved, might she find peace from misery through her death. May God forgive me for even asking such a thing."

"I sense you're facing a level of grief I pray I never may have to face in my lifetime. As hard as it may be for us to understand, there are worse consequences in life than death itself. I had this discussion with Pepper not long after she arrived. We talked about the reality of Purgatory. The Catholic Church taught her Purgatory awaits us after death, but I told her Purgatory exists in life. The way I tried to explain it, the reality of Purgatory imprisons us as a result of the selfish and harmful choices we make in life. Without the persistent intercession of others, death offers the only escape for anyone imprisoned in the Purgatory they created for themselves."

Wilson returned to cutting my hair. "That's pretty deep but sounds an awful lot like the life Cassie's carved out for herself. The girl I married and who gave birth to our son no longer exists. Whoever Woogie thinks he saw, she was not his mother."

"Did Woogie tell you that when the guy pulled a gun on him, this woman screamed and grabbed the man's arm? Why do you think she did that?"

Hub looked at Wilson with a puzzled stare. Wilson looked at me in the mirror with a conciliatory shrug.

"I'll concede what you're implying, but if she's in fact here, it's because she hooked up with another manipulative loser. If that's the case, he brought her here for some other reason. She's not made any effort to talk to Woogie, or anybody. Am I right, Hub?"

Hub looked out the front window, lost in his own thoughts, until Zeb Adams pushed open the door and limped inside. Hub looked at Zeb. "Mister Zeb, what's wrong with your foot?"

"My blasted bunion flared up on me."

Wilson, Hub, and I burst into a welcomed chorus of laughter as Zeb hobbled over to Hub's chair.

"This ain't no laughing matter. This daggum bunion has finally gotten to be more than I can tolerate. Doc Lucas scheduled me to see a foot doctor in Alexandria first thing Monday. In the meantime, I can't even stand to wear regular shoes." He lifted his left shoe, a faded black canvas sneaker. The canvas had been cut to accommodate his swollen big toe. "Outside of flip-flops, these are the only shoes I can get around in without pain rocketing straight up my leg."

The rest of my visit taught me far too much about Zeb's incapacitating, alien affliction.

PURGATORY: A PROGENY'S QUEST

THE MOUTHWATERING AROMA of andouille sausages on the stove caught my attention as soon as I walked inside. "Where's Pepper?" I asked Liddy as she scurried about the kitchen.

Liddy turned from the stove and wiped her hands on apron. "Getting her things together."

"What's going on?" I asked, turning my head toward the stairwell. "Everything okay?"

"Yes, silly. Joe gave her the news she needed to hear. He discussed the legalities involved for her to remain in Shiloh as Sarah Mae Archer. Joe's already received approval for the three Archers to become Pepper's legal guardians until she turns eighteen. And Pepper hit it off with Kay Abernathy. Kay gave Pepper a grand tour of the campus, and they even got to catch up with Tim and Woogie. Both became quite animated when they learned Pepper would be remaining in Shiloh and attending Shiloh High."

"Was John there?" I asked.

"He was with Andy at the stadium. After we brought him up to speed about the change in Pepper's status, he took her to meet Phoebe. It seems Pepper expressed an interest in joining the choir. Andy also made sure she left the school wearing a brand-new green and gold SHS t-shirt after he learned of her sports interests."

"Sounds as though she'll fit right in," I said as I heard Pepper bound down the stairs.

She joined us in the kitchen. "Mister P, would you like some red beans and rice tonight?"

"I already answered for you, dear. Now, go on out into the living room while we finish in here," Liddy said, stirring the rice on the stove as Pepper took over cooking the sausages.

"Smells good. So how soon are you going to move in at the Archers' place?"

Pepper said, "Tomorrow morning. Hank called this afternoon. They're working out plans to take me to get my things from my old house in Louisiana next week. All this is happening so fast. It almost feels like a dream come true."

PURGATORY: A PROGENY'S QUEST

18

WE FOLLOWED IN OUR EXPEDITION AS PEPPER DROVE MAUDE'S powder-blue Buick to the Archers' estate. Her suitcase and new clothes were folded neatly in a cardboard box on the backseat. At the Archer Estate, the open ornate wrought iron gates welcomed us onto the property. As we pulled up to the house, Hank and Phillip stepped off the front portico and helped Pepper bring in her belongings.

Maddie greeted us at the foot of the stairs in the foyer. "Phillip, please take her things straight up to her room." She opened her arms wide and said with a teary-eyed smile, "Young lady, I'm so pleased God has brought you here. You're an answer to prayers. Mister Harold had three fine sons, but I always wished he had an Archer daughter. Let me show you upstairs."

After being warmly embraced, Pepper said, "Yes, ma'am. That'd be nice."

Hank looked at Liddy and me. "Hal's out back on the veranda with Hillary. He's been on the phone making arrangements for me and Maddie to take Pepper back to Vidalia."

"You're taking her, Hank?" Liddy asked.

"Yes, ma'am. Since I've nothing better to do, I volunteered to make the trip. Of course, leave it to Hal, he wanted Maddie to go along. He felt the road trip would allow her and Pepper to get better acquainted."

Liddy greeted Hillary, who looked jilted. They got lost in girl talk under one of the umbrella-covered tables.

At another table, Hal had his phone propped against one ear while he jotted notes. Hank and I sat down in the chairs across from Hal, but he ignored us. By the time Hal finished his call, Pepper had joined Hillary, and Liddy and Phillip sat down at our table. Not a minute later, Maddie rolled a serving cart out from the kitchen with an assortment of bite-sized fruits and vegetables, chips, and two pitchers of lemonade and iced tea. She disappeared back inside to prepare lunch, but not until she welcomed Pepper's offer to join her in the kitchen.

Hal looked at Hank and then at his notes. "Y'all can leave Pepper's car in the rear garage, but make sure to get the paperwork on it so we can transfer the title after you get back. Father Aloysius promised to give you all the documents she'll need before you leave. He'll call on y'all at Pepper's old house first thing Tuesday morning. By the sound of it, you should be able to get on the road home by Thursday. That sound okay with you?"

"Assuming no surprises, it works for me," Hank said leaning back, fingers interlocked behind his head.

"Just wanted to make sure you're up to a long day of driving."

"I got it covered, little brother. I've spent the last eighteen months getting rested up. Besides, my truck can use a good road trip. I'll also have Maddie and Pepper to keep me company."

Phillip said, "If you want, I'll take time off from the office."

"Thanks, Phil. I appreciate it, but I'll be fine. You stay and help Hal around the house since Maddie's coming with us."

Hal chuckled. "You take care of those two." He stared at Pepper and Maddie through the glass sliding doors as they prepared the table for lunch. "Phil and I will be just fine until y'all get back."

PURGATORY: A PROGENY'S QUEST

"If you two are afraid of messing up Maddie's kitchen, you can join Liddy and me for dinner," I said as we scooted our chairs back and headed in for lunch.

After we devoured our fill of chicken fingers, tater wedges, and slaw, Hal slid his chair back from the table, crossed one leg over the other, and patted his stomach. "It's a bit short on notice to some of our friends around town, but how about a welcome-home party for Hank and Pepper next Saturday? Arnie liked the idea and promised to announce it during church. Bubba's Barbecue agreed to cater our little shindig."

Hillary smiled. "I already invited the Arians, all the Simmonses, Marie, John, Phoebe, and even Gus."

Then I said for all to hear, "If Mandy comes, Jay'll be here for certain. That means we need to make sure Jim and Zeb come, too. Lord, let's not forget ol' Zeb. We'd never hear the end of it."

With a self-conscious look, Hank asked, "When was the last time Zeb Adams was out here?"

"I can't say exactly, but it's been way too long. I'm going to call ol' Zeb right now and invite them myself," Hal said before he disappeared into the study.

When Hal returned he said, "Zeb and his sons will be here. If y'all think of anyone else, feel free to invite them. Let's make use of this big old house and its backyard next week. What do you think, Pepper? You and Hank will be the guests of honor. You'll get to meet half the town it sounds like."

Pepper giggled so hard the freckles on her dimpled cheeks glowed as she nodded approval. Maddie leaned over and whispered to her, stirring up an even louder outburst of giggles.

"HUN, MANDY SAID she'd make certain her uncle and aunt will be at the Archers' next Saturday," Liddy said as she carried two cups of coffee from the kitchen shortly after arriving home. "You got room for a piece of carrot cake?"

"Yes, ma'am. That'd make my coffee taste a whole bunch better tonight." While Liddy was still in the kitchen, I asked, "Do you ever regret we didn't have a daughter of our own?"

Without responding at all, Liddy turned off the overhead kitchen light before she handed me my dessert.

"Well?"

Liddy grabbed the TV remote and muted the TV after she sat down. "Theo Phillips, you ask the darnedest things. Why'd you ask such a hypothetical question? Pepper got to you, didn't she?"

I gave a reluctant shrug as my confession. In just shy of two weeks, Dixie's daughter redeemed the horrific memories I had buried of her mother. It appeared to me as though Dixie used up whatever good God gave her birthing three sons and Pepper. Sure, Hank had allowed his demons to haunt him, but Dixie's dark and devious grip on Hank lost its hold on him the moment the gun went off and she left, only to crash into Shiloh Creek minutes later. "Fess up. Did she get to you?" Liddy pressed.

"Pepper made me feel as though she saw us as the parents she never got to experience. You know what I mean?"

"Of course I do, silly. I felt it during our shopping trip. I could also tell Maude's unselfish love left an imprint on her soul, but every child deserves the kind of love and nurturing only a mother and father can provide. I sensed you felt it more than me because she needed a father figure in her life."

I felt the same lump in my throat listening to Liddy's response that I felt when we had driven away from the Archer Estate. In the rearview mirror, I couldn't help but notice how Pepper bit her lower lip as she waved goodbye with Maddie resting an arm across her shoulders. "I know Maddie will watch over her and offer any motherly wisdom Pepper needs. As for her brothers, I have no qualms they will respect and protect their new sister."

"Now, look here," Liddy said, peering at me. "If it'll make you feel any better, I told Pepper our door will always be open to her. More importantly, Hank walked over before that and said, and I quote, 'I know we can never be the father you may need, but you can trust me when I tell you that Mister Phillips over there is the real deal. If you ever need more advice than what I or my brothers can offer, I'm certain he'll be glad to talk with you.'"

"Hank said that? There's hope for him yet." I reached for the remote and unmuted the television.

The phone rang and stirred Liddy from the sofa. A minute later, Liddy said into the phone, "Thank you, Pepper. We feel the same about you too. Hold a sec." Liddy then extended the phone to me. "She wants to say goodnight to you."

I got up and grabbed the phone. "Everything okay?"

"Yes, sir. I crawled into bed and felt I should call you and Miss Liddy. I wanted to tell you how thankful I am that Mister Appleton brought me to your house. Kinda makes me feel that God made it possible for you and Miss Liddy to help me find out what happened to my mother."

"Young lady, you are most welcome. We were just talking about how much we enjoyed you being with us too. I agree: God has guided you on your quest. On that thought, will you be coming to church in the morning?"

"Yes, sir. Phillip offered to take me to Catholic Mass in Alexandria, but I like Pastor Wright. I figure God's the same wherever I go. I'll see y'all at church in the morning."

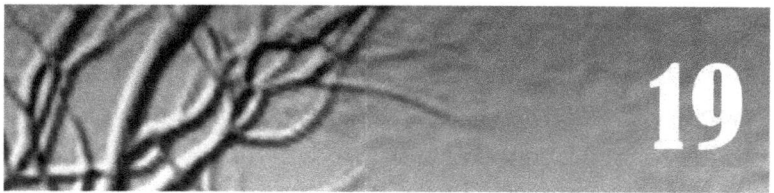

SUNDAY MORNING'S SHEER, CHIFFON-LIKE CLOUDS DRIFTED high over an otherwise vivid blue sky signaling no relief could be expected from another ninety-plus degree afternoon. Both Jessie Masterson's bronze memorial and the copper-clad cupola atop his namesake city administration building glistened beneath the late-morning sunshine as we walked into church.

Inside the air-conditioned confines of the church foyer, Judy walked up to Liddy. "I'm glad Pepper decided to stay in Shiloh."

"We are too. She and Hank are leaving first thing tomorrow with Maddie to retrieve the last of her things back in Louisiana. Kay Abernathy met her, and she's cleared to start her senior year at Shiloh High."

While Liddy and Judy continued to discuss Pepper's decision to attend our church, my attention drifted to Phillip and Hank engaged with Pepper in their own lively conversation that included Jeannie and her parents. Pepper stood out from the others with her chestnut, double-braided ponytail. I smiled at her choice of the mid-calf-length jean skirt. It covered the remnants of her scratched-up knees, but her short-sleeved, blue-striped, white cotton top failed to hide the scrape marks on her arms. Pepper's shouldered leather purse disguised Maude's rosary she weaved through her skirt's belt loops. Of course, in a church of dyed-in-the-wool Baptists, I doubt anyone much cared if a crucifix dangled from a decorative belt of ornate beads.

Hal appeared uncomfortable and rather helpless standing behind Hillary at the children's area entrance.

"Looks as though your new sister's enjoying the notoriety," I said to the relieved look on Hal's face when I walked up.

"Actually, I fathom Hank and Phillip are enjoying the attention she's receiving too, although it appears Hank relishes it a bit more than Phillip."

"Why'd you say that about Hank?"

"This morning Hank hounded us about leaving for church on time," Hal said, flaunting a satisfied smirk.

"Please don't distract my assistant, Theo. We still need to get these youngsters signed in," Hillary muttered under her breath, sporting a cordial smile as families waited in line.

I went back to rejoin Liddy when Larry motioned. "Have you seen Zeb or either of his sons this morning?"

"Not yet, why?"

"Tyler responded to a call involving a prowler at Zeb's house late last night."

"Did someone try to break in?"

"We'll need to ask Zeb or his sons. Nothing else came across the scanner last night. If they don't make it to church, will you drive out there? Find out if it's worth a story?"

"Liddy and I'll spin by Zeb's before we meet y'all at Bubba's after church."

As the choir finished singing, Arnie addressed the congregation from beside the pulpit about two upcoming events. After he talked about next Sunday being Father's Day, he requested Hank and Pepper stand.

"Folks, for those who missed the mid-week service, Hank Archer has returned home. I also would like to introduce the newest member of the Archer family, Miss Sarah Mae Archer, or Pepper, as she prefers. She's the daughter of Dixie Archer, and she's decided to move from Louisiana and live with her family in Shiloh. I've been asked to announce that next Saturday there's a welcome-home party planned at the Archer home for Hank and Pepper, and we all are invited."

A disjointed, brief round of applause followed, which caused an awkward wide-eyed look from Pepper. Hank stepped out into the aisle. "Folks, I can understand some of y'all being uncertain about my return home, and that's okay. I want you to know, though, the best thing that's happened to my brothers and me since our father passed away is Pepper coming into our lives." Hank smiled and nodded at Arnie. As he and Pepper retook their seats, the applause restarted with more enthusiasm until Arnie waved his arms.

"Before I delve into my message today, I have a second reminder. In two weeks, the city will be hosting the Music Jamboree at Priestly Park. I know the following weekend most of us will be back at the park for the town's annual Independence Day Jubilee, but this musical event benefits the Shiloh Cooperative Church Fellowship. When that tornado skirted our town a while back, we provided for a host of families, but it impacted our stock of canned and dry goods. This event will help restock those depleted pantry shelves. Besides, it always amazes me how much talent our town can brag about."

Arnie held his Bible by his side and gazed at the congregation.

"Today's message resounds the Apostle Paul's appeal to the church in Rome long ago. How many times have each of us been guilty of pretending to love others? How many times have each of us failed to genuinely love our neighbors and friends, and sadly even family members, as we should? How many times have we failed to hate what we know is wrong, not in our eyes, but in God's eyes? How many times have we failed to hold tight onto what is good and love each other with sincere heartfelt affection?

And how many times have we delighted in honoring each other as God has asked us to?"

As Arnie focused on his sermon notes, the sanctuary slipped into an eerie, deafening silence. For forty-five minutes Arnie captivated the sanctuary, sharing the power of honest-to-God genuineness versus two-faced hypocrisy. At his conclusion, he repeated the opening appeal, but this time he invited folks to stand if they felt convicted by past actions or attitudes toward others. I felt a tug on my heart and joined others who stood, though many hung their heads or stood with eyes closed.

Liddy left her seat and wrapped her arm around my waist. Time stood still while Arnie held his closed Bible in one hand at his side and watched in silence as one by one folks rose. His eyes sparkled when he invited everyone else to stand and join him in the Lord's Prayer to close the service.

One can never gauge every apparent heartfelt response, but when I looked for Hank and Pepper, well-wishers had swarmed them before they could exit their pew.

OUR QUICK VISIT to Zeb's house proved to be more social than sensational. According to Jim and Zeb, their phantom prowler disappeared as fast as he arrived. They credited Huckleberry, their bluetick hound, for the shadowy figure's hotfooted retreat. The consensus pointed to the intruder being a curious buck or brazen black bear who scampered into the dark right after Jim and Huckleberry stepped onto the back porch.

Once convinced the matter held little news value, I let Zeb ramble on about his throbbing bunion. He made it quite clear he clung to no notions about tomorrow's in-patient surgery going pain-free. The prospect of being sidelined for a month or more while his foot mended made him cantankerous. For a man as strapping and ornery as Zeb, we saw apprehension on his face and in his words which he refused to hide. Liddy volunteered to lend a hand during his recovery. Zeb thanked her but said Marie already promised to spend extra time at the store and check in on him at the house until he got back on his feet.

Jim mentioned that he and his brother planned to tag-team between the mill and the store. He confessed the most daunting task would be keeping their dad off his feet for at least four weeks.

We bid our farewells an hour after we arrived.

By the time we pulled into Bubba's near-empty parking lot, the after-church dinner crowd had dwindled. Cecil was busy ringing up a customer at the cash register when we arrived. "Good afternoon, Mister Theo and Miss Liddy. Y'all running a bit late ain't you?" Cecil's effervescent smile turned toward us as the young couple got their receipt and change and stepped away from the counter.

"Had to run an errand right after church for Larry Scribner," I said, scanning the cluttered but otherwise vacant tables.

"Don't worry. He's been waiting on you. Go on back. Cora's pouring tea at their table right now."

Liddy looked beyond the front counter to the smoke-pit. "Hey, Bob, do you still have any ribs left?"

Bob Patterson looked up, gripping his trademark wood-handled basting brush. Drops of thick, dark brown sauce fell onto the kitchen floor. He wiped his hands on a stained hand towel hanging nearby. "Miss Liddy, for you my darlin', I still have plenty of ribs. Now if you had asked about my brisket, that might'a got you another response."

Cora waved as she stood over Larry and Martha, who sat across from Pete and Mary at a corner table. A minute later, I occupied the chair next to Mary and Pete while Liddy took the seat beside Martha. "Y'all didn't order yet?" I asked as Cora poured tea into my glass.

"No, we haven't," Larry said, handing Cora their menus. "And Pete's been sitting on pins and needles waiting on you two for the last half-hour. Do you know what you want? We're ready to give Cora our orders."

While everyone else ordered, Liddy smiled and handed me her menu. I said to Cora, "Miss Liddy will have the half rack. I'll have a whole rack of Bubba's ribs today. And, beans and slaw for her. Fries and okra for me."

Cora grabbed another pitcher of tea and placed it in the center of the table. With her hand resting on Pete's shoulder, she asked, "Would you like me to bring some of Cecil's buttermilk biscuits while y'all are waiting on dinner?"

Pete gave Mary a pitiful look. Mary sighed. "Yes, that'd be nice, Miss Cora."

I then acknowledged Larry's curious stare. "Zeb and Jim said they definitely had someone or something snooping around their backyard. After Huckleberry howled and Jim shined his flashlight, neither Zeb nor Jim got more than a glimpse of a dark shadow disappearing into the darkness."

"I thought Zeb was still laid up with his foot?" Mary asked.

"Zeb's vantage point was limited to his bedroom window."

Pete raised his hands. "Hold up a sec. So what happened?"

"By the time Tyler arrived in his patrol vehicle, Zeb and Jim had dismissed the incident as nothing more than some animal snooping around. Zeb added they don't store anything of value in the rickety, old storage shed beyond a few tools and his vehicles. He joked that since he stowed his limousine in there, a full-grown man would find little room to maneuver inside the shed anyhow."

Pete chuckled as Mary asked, looking a bit disappointed, "Is there anything worth putting in the paper?"

"I don't imagine so unless you just want to fill a back-page column. Of course, if you want me to write a story on Zeb's bunion surgery, that's a horse of a different color."

A consolatory grin rose on Larry's face. Before he opened his mouth to speak, Mary blurted her stern opinion. "Daddy, I don't think we need to bring any uninvited embarrassment Zeb's way. I also will not condone you using the *Sentinel* to publicize your friend's unfortunate malady."

At Mary's admonishment, Larry and I raised hands in complete surrender.

Cora stopped back a while later and scooped up our dirty dishes. When she took away my platter full of meatless bones, she said, "This morning at church, Maddie told me that Miss Dixie's daughter has moved in out there. Of course, Maddie made no bones about the fact the girl ain't nothing like her momma, thank you, Jesus!"

Liddy interrupted Cora. "Her name's Pepper, and she definitely isn't like her momma. You'll get to meet her next Saturday at the Archers' homecoming party for Hank and her."

Cora pursed her lips and shook her head. "I'm sorry, Miss Liddy. I didn't remember her name. Although Maddie sure glowed when she went on about her."

Mary looked up at Cora. "You just gave me a great idea for a story this week." She looked at her dad and me. "Theo, while she's away with Hank and Maddie, why don't you work up an article to introduce Pepper to the folks around town? You and Liddy know more about her than anyone else."

"I agree, Theo," Larry howled. "That would be right up your alley. How about it? You can also add something about the homecoming party and throw in a little about Hank's return. He certainly isn't the same short-fused rascal we all steered clear of before he went away all those months ago."

Even Liddy joined in. "I'll be busy at school getting ready for the summer camp. You'll have plenty of uninterrupted time to write a really nice introduction piece about Pepper. She'll appreciate that it came from you as well."

"Mister Theo, it appears to me you can't say no," Cora said with a ruby-framed pearly smile.

T.M. BROWN

20

EARLY TUESDAY, LIDDY GULPED DOWN THE LAST OF HER COFFEE, abandoning all but a couple of bites of her eggs and toast as soon as John Priestly honked his horn.

She grabbed her shoulder bag and blew a kiss with one foot out the door. "I'll be home in time to cook supper. Use the quiet time to work on your article. Don't forget to put on your sunscreen, especially if you'll be walking into town."

As soon as Liddy climbed in the backseat beside Phoebe, John pulled out of the driveway and headed off toward an all-day educator workshop in Alexandria. Of course, to emphasize her point, Liddy left our car keys on the counter right beside the tan plastic bottle of Coppertone and my Georgia Bulldog straw hat.

After a quick shower and shave, I put on a pair of gray dress shorts and tucked in a red golf shirt before I slid into comfortable walking sandals. However, this time every square inch of exposed skin received a layer of sunscreen before I put my hat on and grabbed the car keys. I had no intention of suffering from another sunburn, nor Liddy's I-told-you-so look.

To learn a little more about Pepper and Maude's hometown of Vidalia, Louisiana, Shiloh Library would be my first stop. After reviewing the notes I'd jotted down yesterday, all I knew for certain was that historic Natchez, Mississippi, was directly across the mighty Mississippi. That's where Pepper and Maude had long attended church and Pepper's St. Mary's Catholic School was located. I felt confident after an hour or so scrounging around Shiloh Library's resources, I would have a better picture of where

PURGATORY: A PROGENY'S QUEST

Pepper had been raised. My article would focus mainly on her upbringing under the guardianship of her grandmother.

I wanted to downplay the fact her mother and father opted to pursue an estranged, distant relationship with her. My gut told me there was much more to the story behind their decision to give Maude custody rights, but none of that would come out in print.

The moment I stepped off the kitchen stoop, the sun's glare from my Expedition's dark blue hood and windshield forced me to squint. I jumped into the driver's seat, started the engine, and cranked the AC, but sweat broke out across my forehead before I drove across town to the library.

JUST BEFORE NOON I placed two pages of notes in my briefcase then tossed it in the backseat before I ventured across Broad Street. At the side entrance to the Masterson Administration Building, Gus pushed the glass door open. "Mister Phillips, what a pleasant surprise." He squinted as he stepped into the sunlight and held the door open.

"Thank you. How are you doing today? I'm headed to the Mayor's office."

Gus stepped back inside with me to escape the glare and heat.

"I'm doing pretty well, I guess, but I've got a quick question to ask since I've bumped into you."

"I hope I can answer it for you."

He started to say something but hesitated, mouth half-open before he managed to say with reluctance, "Well, now I think about it, maybe you won't have the answer anyway."

"What's on your mind, Gus?"

"I've been thinking about the party at the Archers'. That got me to wondering about what I heard about Pepper. Hillary said she's going to finish high school as a senior right here in Shiloh."

"Looks that way. Why?"

His eyes darted everywhere but at mine. "That makes her most likely seventeen, doesn't it?"

"As I recall, she'll turn seventeen on August first. Why?" I tried to measure Gus' obvious uneasiness.

"August first?" Gus paused and appeared as if deciphering something. His lips moved, but audible words failed to follow for a few awkward seconds.

I tapped his shoulder. "Gus, is anything wrong? Pepper will turn seventeen on her next birthday."

"I'm sorry, Mister Phillips. I gotta run, I'm on lunch break." He stuttered as he added, "I-I-I think I'll swing by the Elysium Emporium and see if Miss Bassett has any gift ideas for Pepper."

Gus checked his watch and, like a man on a mission, walked away into the sunshine without saying another word. My out-of-sorts exchange with Gus had been dismissed from further thought by the time I stuck my head into the police office. Camille shook her head and pointed to Mitch's empty desk.

"I was passing through, anyway. Sorry to disturb you."

Camille pushed her chair back from her desk. "Mister Phillips, hold up one sec. Are you and Miss Liddy planning on going to the Archers' party Saturday?"

"Wouldn't miss it."

"I ain't been out to the Mayor's house. What should I wear?"

"It's a beautiful old plantation home, but I don't expect you need to get all dressed up. For the most part it'll be outdoors, and they're serving barbecue. If you're still not sure, ask Hillary. She's definitely going. I'll probably wear shorts myself."

"Thanks. I'll check with Hillary. I've never been invited to a party like that before. I'd be much more comfortable in a pair of nice shorts, for sure."

"You'll fit in just fine, Camille. I'm stopping by Hillary's desk. Would you like me to ask her to call you?"

She giggled. "Don't bother her with such silly nonsense."

After a friendly shrug and nod, I continued down the hall toward the Mayor's office where I heard Hillary's contagious laugh inside Hal's office.

"Is this a private meeting or can a taxpaying citizen join your lively conversation?" I inquired from the open doorway.

Hal looked relaxed lounging in his leather executive chair with his hands folded behind his head. Hillary looked over her shoulder from her seat in front of his desk.

Hal waved for me to come in. "We were talking about you anyway. Grab a seat. Hank just called."

"Everything okay? Do they still think they'll make it back Thursday?" I asked and sat next to Hillary.

"Maddie and Pepper are sorting through Pepper's things and deciding what she wants to bring back here," Hal said.

Hillary smiled. "Hank's already decided he won't need to rent a U-Haul. He said more than once he's surprised how little she wants to take with her."

Hal chuckled, still sprawled in his chair. "Hank did take particular notice of a couple of keepsakes Maddie helped her pack away. In particular, her grandmother had autographed pictures of Jerry Lee Lewis posing with Maude from, I reckon, her much younger days."

"I didn't realize this until I visited the library this morning, but Jerry Lee Lewis was from Ferriday, Louisiana, a stone's throw up the road from Vidalia. He played in all the saloons and honky-tonk joints on both sides of the Mississippi during his early years. I guess old Maude wasn't as demure as I pictured after listening to Pepper's description of her. Pepper's feistier side musta come from her grandmother rather than Dixie."

Hillary said, "It sounds as though Pepper will need to go clothes shopping. She's leaving behind her Catholic school uniforms. And, according to Maddie, much of her other clothes have seen better days, or she's long outgrown them."

"With all Pepper endured helping Maude over her final weeks and months, I'm sure the last thing either of them fussed about was shopping for clothes." I looked at Hal. "How'd it go with Father Aloysius?"

"I guess it went well. Hank said they decided to execute a bill of sale to Hank for the automobile. They figured it would eliminate a lot of paperwork otherwise. He said he got Pepper's approval by promising her a vanity plate once it gets titled here."

"A vanity plate?" I asked, astonished.

Hillary blurted, "Why not Archer4?"

I looked at Hal and smiled as the significance dawned on me.

Hal lost his lighthearted grin. "Of course, Hank did learn something more interesting. Up until about a year ago, the Arnaquers had for generations been significant landowners in Concordia Parish. That is until Maude signed over all but the plot of land surrounding her home to an Indigo Bayou Management Company in New Orleans. Hank learned the land exchange took place about a year ago to make good her son's outstanding debts. Pepper thought Maude did it to pay off her growing medical bills."

I stared at the carpet between my feet, mind racing back to what Dixie said during the months she turned our town upside down and almost wrecked the Archers' family business in the process. It sounded as though Maude paid the debt neither Beau nor Dixie could resolve.

Hillary asked, "You okay, Theo?"

I gave a simple nod, but my sour-grape grimace matched Hal's. We understood the presumed truth behind Maude's baffling decision to relinquish her family's land holdings.

Hal left his chair and walked around his desk. "On a good note, Pepper can leave it all behind her. As an Archer she'll inherit a share in H. H. Archer Holding Co. That's going to be a surprise but, in a roundabout way, Dixie passed on something to Pepper that my dad made legal for her to pass on. Hank and Phillip have agreed and asked Joe to prepare the paperwork."

"I guess that means she can afford to do a little shopping when she gets back," I said with an approving nod matching Hal's.

"Join us for lunch," Hillary said as she left her chair.

"I'd love to, but I gotta swing by Adams Feed and Hardware and then Zeb's house. He had his bunion removed yesterday. Knowing him as I do, he's got to be making everyone around him pretty miserable about now. I figure I can get the lowdown from Marie at the store before I wander out to the house to check in on the old coot. Then I've got to get on to writing the articles I promised Larry and Mary about Pepper and Hank."

I DROVE THE three short blocks from out front of the library to Adams Feed and Hardware on Adams Avenue. When I stepped up onto the well-worn wooden loading platform, Marie propped open the front door holding a push broom.

"Theo, will you please give me a hand a second? I've finally got a few minutes to sweep these old floors in front of the store. I imagine General Sherman's blue-bellies could've trekked some of this dirt in." Marie handed me a well-used grain shovel. "Will you please lay that flat so I can dump this pile of dust and dirt?"

A few seconds later, a mushroom cloud of dust rose above the trash barrel on the store's loading platform. Marie grabbed the shovel from me and leaned it along with the push broom against the front sales counter while I closed the front door.

As I wiped my hands on the back of my shorts, streaks of sunlight from the overhead windows spotlighted the disturbed dust particles still flittering about after Marie's cleaning frenzy.

"How are you making out covering the feed and hardware customers as well as the Old General Store?" I asked.

Marie leaned against the glass counter with a tired but satisfied look. "It's not too bad. Jim and Jay swap in and out during the busiest hours. They scheduled Tim Thompson to shuttle between the mill and here, so he can give me a hand a few hours a day in the warehouse. Otherwise, most of the regular customers heard about Zeb's foot surgery and know he's gonna be out of commission for a month or so. For the most part, they're pretty understanding when we get a bit backed up."

"Well, that's kinda the reason I dropped by. How's the cantankerous old coot doing? Is he behaving?"

"Jay and Jim went with him yesterday. They figured their dad might need their combined assistance after the surgery. I went over last night after I closed up and fixed them dinner and helped get Zeb comfortable. I gotta confess, Zeb ain't exactly happy right now. That man pitched a fit like some spoiled, petulant child last night when the three of us scolded him for trying to hobble out of his bedroom. Mind you, the hospital gave us a set of crutches for him to use, but you know how hard-headed Zeb can get."

"I also know how hard-headed his two sons and caring cousin can be, too."

Marie laughed. "Jim called Doc Lucas first thing this morning and arranged for a wheelchair to be delivered. Zeb seemed more open to maneuvering around the house in a wheelchair than crutches...for now anyway. Jim told me this morning his dad is trying to figure how to get Huckleberry hooked up to pull him out onto the porch."

"Did the doctor say how long he'll have to stay off his foot?"

"No less than four weeks, and that's if he doesn't irritate the healing process by putting any weight on it." Her worry lines, more pronounced than usual, confirmed what I'd guessed.

"Is there anything I can bring out to him?"

"He's most likely sleeping about now. They gave him some pain pills that would put Stonewall, my old mule, out cold. Why don't you stop by tomorrow morning? He'll more than likely be better company by then."

The warehouse buzzer interrupted our conversation. When Marie returned, she said, "Gotta run. Tim needs a hand out back."

That evening, Liddy's promise to take care of dinner when she got home turned out to mean she'd toss a salad while I grilled steaks. We sipped iced tea and enjoyed sharing our mutually busy days on the deck as nightfall came. Before we went to bed, Liddy had baked and wrapped a dozen of Zeb's favorite chocolate chip cookies. She planned to deliver them after her first day of Art and Music Camp.

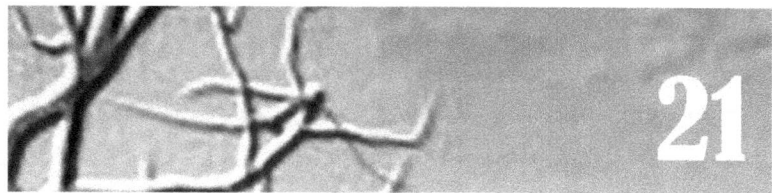

I CRAWLED OUT FROM UNDER MY BLANKETS BEFORE DAWN AND grabbed my robe. The coffeemaker made the only sound in the house. While I waited to pour my first cup, I read the message in my devotional journal for Wednesday, June 15:

A stain-free life that honors God our Father places the needs of orphans and widows above their own and remains unpolluted by the world's selfish focus on power, prestige, and possessions.

As I poured my coffee, the reading brought my own father's exhortations to mind. His words had long left an indelible mark on me, and I even shared the same message with my own sons as they were growing up.

"Believe with all your heart that God alone is the master of your life and then reflect that belief each day through every word spoken and deed performed even when it means unconditionally caring for the needs of others above your own."

Between sips of coffee seated in my recliner, I recalled how God had orchestrated Marie Masterson's life after she had become a widow as a young mother. He also had helped her heal after her only son, Jessie, died saving others. Likewise, I felt God's providential hand guided Pepper to Shiloh after death took her beloved Maude.

Though Pepper had already felt like an orphan long before she arrived, she masked any further despondency she may have felt once she learned about Dixie's fate and the scandalous behavior consuming her mother's legacy. Without God's help she more than likely would not have braved the long, lonely drive to Shiloh to discover she was not the helpless orphan as she had feared.

I struggled to grasp how I could use this revelation to introduce more about Pepper through my article. This community had accepted Marie many years ago and helped her through the tragic loss of her only son. With that reassurance, I hoped once again our town would rise up and accept Pepper without judging her by the sins of her mother.

I unscrewed the top of my pen and wrote my father's ingrained words beneath the passage in my journal. Writing each word calmed my heart as I asked God for clarity in choosing the words this community needed to read about Pepper. I also took a moment to pray for the safe return of Hank, Maddie, and Pepper. I could only imagine how unsettled Pepper would soon feel the moment they drove away from all she had known and as she anticipated what the future might hold for her in Shiloh. These thoughts made me thank God for the family Liddy and I have been blessed with in our lives.

The clink of a coffee mug drew my attention to the kitchen. Liddy poured herself a cup and asked, still holding the pot, "Need a refill?"

"Yes, ma'am. I'll be right there."

We walked onto the front porch to enjoy our coffee. I shared my thoughts spurred by my morning journal. Liddy offered warm, reassuring glances that spoke volumes as she listened.

She finally said, "Sweetheart, when I look back on our lives, in particular the last three years since we moved here, I truly have neither reservations nor regrets whatsoever over our decision to buy this house and call Shiloh our new hometown."

"Of course, I have to confess God had a hand in our decision."

"I agree. I'm also thankful for God unleashing your untapped talents to write for the *Sentinel*, and reawakening my passion for teaching. I knew we'd never enjoy a laid-back retirement, and I figure God knew it, too. Theo Phillips, I may not say it enough, but I'm so proud of my husband and best friend."

"I love you too, and pretty dang proud of you, too. What you're doing as a teacher with all those kids is pretty special. Let's also not forget how you've encouraged both Phoebe and John to realize it's not too late for them."

Liddy scrunched her nose and smiled.

"I wouldn't be surprised if John doesn't finally pop the question any day now."

"I sure hope so," Liddy sighed. "Phoebe feels more like Daisy Mae chasing Lil' Abner but never able to catch him."

"Just mark my words, my little matchmaker."

Sounds in the neighborhood broadcast the new paperboy's arrival. I decided today I'd like to get to know who took over Tim's route. I had tried to catch up to him a couple of mornings in the past week, but the paper appeared at different times from what I had grown accustomed. His accuracy also fell well short of Tim's reliable tosses.

Liddy pointed at a youngster swerving from side to side on his bike as he heaved papers end-over-end in the general direction of the walkways. When I stood to meet our new paperboy, Liddy giggled. "Theo, *that's* not a paper*boy*. We have a new paper*girl*."

Sure enough, a tail of dark brown hair swayed behind her ballcap. She had on a green and white, three-quarter sleeve baseball shirt, cutoff jeans, and faded black high-top sneakers. After coming to a squealing stop in front of me, she straddled Tim's old Raleigh boy's bike. I greeted her with a smile and introduced myself and Liddy, who waved back from the porch.

"Glad to meet you, Mister Phillips. I'm Mickey, Mickey Waller," she said, as she returned Liddy's wave. "I know her. She teaches at the school, doesn't she?"

"What grade are you?"

"I'll be in the eighth grade this year. We moved here from Alabama a few months ago. My dad and mom both work at the medical center."

"How did you end up with Tim's old paper route?"

Mickey lifted her hat and adjusted her hair. "We're neighbors. He recommended me to Missus Scribner when I asked if they'd consider a papergirl to replace him."

"I assume you play softball for the school?" I pointed to the front of her shirt.

She looked down and tugged at the green and gold Lady Saints emblem on her shirt. "Yes, sir. I play basketball, too."

I reached my hand out. "Mickey Waller, pleasure to know you. I hope you and your parents are enjoying our little town."

"Yes, sir. This ain't anything like Birmingham, and that suits me just fine."

"Miss Liddy and me understand. We moved here from Atlanta only about three years ago, too."

She handed me my morning paper. "I gotta finish my deliveries. Nice talking with ya, Mister Phillips. I don't want to be late the first day at the Art and Music Camp."

"Guess that means you'll see Missus Phillips later this morning. She'll be your art teacher."

Mickey rose high on her pedals as she pushed off. Turning onto Broad Street, she looked over her shoulder and yelled, "See you at school, Missus Phillips!"

BEFORE LIDDY SCOOTED out the door for her first day at the Art and Music Camp, Arnie called. He invited me to tag along with him to check in on Zeb. Liddy reminded me to let Zeb know she and Phoebe would stop over later in the afternoon with a tasty treat.

The rest of the morning I completed my article on Miss Sarah Mae Archer, but struggled as to what the community-at-large should know about Hank Archer's homecoming. His first welcome-home celebration took place eight years ago when the town welcomed Hank as an Army hero after serving in Afghanistan. Yet, this homecoming would be without the previous fanfare.

I wanted to address the real battle Hank survived fighting the demons that returned home within him after his tour of duty in the Middle East. I sensed Hank also would not want to explain away the wrongs he committed and the harm he caused in those many months following his first homecoming. Arnie's fortuitous invite offered an opportunity to get his wise counsel and advice before writing Hank's portion of the article.

Huckleberry sprang to his feet as soon as we pulled into Zeb's driveway, but his yelping simmered as soon as we exited Arnie's Tahoe. Zeb sat in his wheelchair on the front porch, his entire left foot bandaged and elevated.

Huckleberry's brown ears perked up when I allowed him to sniff my hand. Arnie patted the hound's speckled backside as he looked at Zeb. "I shoulda called to let you know we were coming, but I didn't think you'd mind a little company."

"You and Theo are always welcome. Besides, Huckleberry's a mighty fine listener but not much of a conversationalist. I tried watching a little TV but there ain't anything worth watching."

I nodded amidst a chuckle and asked, "So what have you been doing out here? Bird watching?"

"I've been out here paying mind to folks driving by. You know, I never realized how much traffic runs up and down Old Mill Road these days. Heck, I remember when you'd know a vehicle was coming by the dust it'd kick up, and back then it most likely was one of our neighbors coming or going. Arnie, your fancy Chevy is the first vehicle I recognized the whole time I've been sitting out here today."

Huckleberry curled up on the weathered porch deck between Arnie and me. Zeb seemed to enjoy the distraction of our idle small talk, but grimaced anytime we inquired more about his surgery. After enduring Zeb's drawn-out opine on John Priestly's decision to step down and pass the mantle to Andy Simmons, Arnie created an opportune moment to help me with my article on Hank Archer when he asked Zeb's thoughts about attending the Archers' homecoming party.

Zeb grabbed the shoulder straps of his overalls. "If Jim and Jay don't holler too much, I might reconsider going. The mistrust between our two families has kept us on opposing sides of this town long enough. Harold and I had our differences over the years, but not even Hank's unpredictable, hot-tempered past prevented his daddy and me from becoming friends before he died. Now that Hal and Phillip have done likewise, I'd like to think Hank's return this time will not change all our two families have accomplished for the good of the community."

"I don't have any reason to believe any different," Arnie said with a relieved glint in his eye.

"I get the sense Hank's demons have finally been exorcized. Do y'all agree?" I asked.

Zeb fiddled with his intertwined fingers resting on his belly. "I want to think so. And so far the best way to read Hank's present state of mind resides on Hal and Phillip's faces and their comments about him."

"Astute observation, Zeb. I'd have to say Hank's definitely experienced a noticeable metamorphosis, and in a big way. His treatment of Pepper has provided the clearest indication of it," Arnie added, rocking slowly.

"I trust your two opinions since y'all have known Harold's sons far longer than me. I'm writing a short piece in Friday's paper on Hank's homecoming to go with the introductory article on Pepper. Mary thinks there's an epidemic of curiosity spreading around town. My articles are intended to stave off idle gossip that's bound to spring up about them. As you can imagine, I'm discovering how guarded I must be expressing what needs to be said without rekindling the past that could haunt them both."

Zeb slapped his belly. "Theo, you worry too much."

"Zeb's right. The only suggestion I would offer lies in the wise old adage of less is more."

I reached down and ran my fingers along Huckleberry's ears.

"Arnie, you got church tonight, and Zeb, you'll have more company before too long, and they'll be bearing sweet gifts."

22

THE SOUND OF MUSIC IN THE KITCHEN STIRRED ME FROM MY BED Friday morning. Liddy had risen before me and listened to her favorite Dave Jackson country music album playing on her CD player. When I walked in running my fingers through my pillow-mussed hair, she pointed to the table with one of her playful smiles.

After I sat, she leaned over my shoulder and filled my coffee cup. Before pulling away, she whispered, "You're my only small-town Georgia man." She kissed the nape of my neck and swept her fingers through my hair.

When I felt her fingers gradually slide onto my shoulder, I clutched her hand and brought it close to my stubble-filled cheek. "You're still the prettiest girl in this old country town."

"I may like hearing the way Dave Jackson sings the words, but they mean more to me when you say them."

"What do you mean? You don't like the way I can sing?" I asked with an exaggerated, tooth-filled grin.

Liddy returned the coffee pot to the counter and turned the volume up on her CD player. "I prefer the way you swing, though." She cinched the knot of her terry robe as she swayed her hips, arms extended. We forgot all about our busy schedule and danced barefoot in our kitchen.

We exchanged a kiss and Liddy said, "Hold whatever thought you have until tonight. I gotta get a shower. You might want to see the morning paper. Mary put your articles on the front page beneath the fold. Enjoy your coffee before it gets any colder. I'll be right back."

Sure enough, Pepper's high school photo accompanied my article on her. Below my brief article about Hank's return home were the details for the Archers' homecoming party. By the time I got up to refill my coffee cup, Liddy paraded into the living room wearing tan dress shorts and a green polo shirt. She had pulled her peppered auburn hair into a ponytail, held in place with a green and gold scarf.

"What do you have planned today, hun?"

My heart preferred I go with her to school, but I said, "I figure I'll mosey into town this morning and catch wind of how folks are responding to my articles. I'm hopeful the gossipmongers will let sleeping dogs lie. I'd also like to hear if Hank, Maddie, and Pepper got home last night."

"If you hear anything, will you let me know?" She jiggled the car keys in her hand. "Meant to tell you, Mickey Waller is one sharp kid. She'll be a pleasure to get to know better over the next few weeks."

MORE THAN ITS rightful share of squandered lazy minutes filled my morning before I got dressed and headed toward Town Square. At The Butcher Shoppe, Silas greeted me with an offer to taste Bernie's latest Aegean brew. Though aromatic, its dark molasses boldness required a touch of extra sugar to suit my taste. What I intended to last but a few minutes lasted until well past ten. Mandy stopped by not long after I arrived, sweat-drenched from her morning run. This time, though, she had already slipped on her Auburn blue long-sleeve athletic top over her sweat-soaked sports bra. From behind the counter, Silas tossed her a clean, white hand towel and poured her a tall glass of iced water.

PURGATORY: A PROGENY'S QUEST

I listened as the two provided their own unique perspectives about Pepper and her Archer family roots. Mandy referred to her as a fresh face in town, and Silas recalled her mother's drama. He spoke well of Pepper but framed his cautious opinion with "time will tell" for her and Hank. Mandy admitted not knowing anything about Hank other than what others had said but revealed with a more than curious twinkle in her eye that she planned to close her shop early on Saturday to attend their homecoming party.

Jeannie Simmons stopped by as Mandy walked out the door. She ordered a cup of Bernie's new brew to take back to the office. Before she left, she said, "Mister P, I appreciate how difficult it must've been writing those articles."

I played with the rim of my demitasse cup. "Sometimes the past needs to be left where it belongs. I wanted to offer Pepper a clean slate for the good folks around town. It's going to be hard enough for her to learn what it means to bear the Archer name in Shiloh, but Hank, with a little help from his brothers, might make it a little less of a burden for her."

Silas said, "I pray for Hank's sake he will finally make his father proud."

"I'll add an amen to that, Silas," Jeannie said as she left.

I handed Silas my empty cup. "I gotta run. I've got two more stops before Liddy gets home this afternoon."

"*Ya-sas*, my good friend," Silas said with his hand extended. "With much regret, Bernie and I will not be able to attend the party tomorrow." He pointed to the counter, shrugged, and extended his lower lip in a sorrowful pout.

"Goodbye to you, too, my friend. I'll be sure to remind the Archers you and Bernie could not close the restaurant to attend. I'm sure they'll understand."

I walked across Main Street with intentions of visiting Hal and Hillary, but one of the City Hall clerks told me they had taken the day off. I checked my watch and stepped over to Edwards Barbershop. Both Wilson and Hub had customers when I stepped inside the shop's cozy air-conditioned confines and took a seat.

Wilson interrupted his conversation with Mitch. "Well, Mister Phillips. I didn't expect to see you this soon."

Mitch looked at my reflection in the mirror with his back to me. "Theo, I hoped to see you today. Hal called and asked to tell you how pleased Pepper and Hank were to be back in town. According to Hal, they both also liked the write-up in this morning's paper. He said he left a voicemail at your house, but he figured you might be out and about town anyway."

"If you talk to him later, thank him for me. I'm glad to hear they got back safe and sound. I'm gathering Hal and Hillary are out at the Archer place getting Pepper settled in and preparing for tomorrow afternoon?"

Wilson nudged Mitch's head forward and ran his clippers down the back of his neck. "I promised to take Woogie out there. I assume you and Miss Liddy are going?"

"Absolutely. Do you want us to give Woogie a lift for you?"

Wilson paused from snipping Mitch's hair. "Naw. Marcellus is filling in for me tomorrow afternoon. I'm interested in getting to know this young girl. According to everything Woogie and Tim have said about her, she definitely ain't nothing like her momma."

"I sure hope not. I'd hate to pull over the Mayor's sister for speeding around town," Mitch said, launching a deferential smirk at the mirror.

A chorus of snorting and snickering filled the shop. Even old Hub stopped clipping hair to regain his composure.

Wilson turned and, since I remained standing, said to me, "I figure you didn't stop to get your hair cut today."

PURGATORY: A PROGENY'S QUEST

"No, Wilson, I didn't, but you told me what I came here to find out. I best get out of your hair, pardon my pun, and let you finish trimming around Mitch's ears." I looked at the two gentlemen thumbing through a couple of dog-eared, outdated magazines.

"Sorry I distracted Wilson and Hub." Both looked up for a brief moment and then returned to eying the photos they likely had seen more than once already.

At Adams Feed and Hardware, Jay tossed two orange and white bags of livestock feed to John Priestly who stood in the bed of his pickup. Ringo, his floppy-eared sidekick, sniffed at the two sacks of dog food atop a half-dozen white salt blocks. John caught the second bag of feed and said, "Thanks, Jay. I got the rest. Besides, look who's here."

Jay turned with a hearty grin, "Mister P. How you doing?"

I stepped up onto the loading platform and wiped the sweat pouring from my forehead onto my cheeks with my handkerchief.

"Fine. Just fine, Jay. How's your dad today?"

Jay handed John a clipboard with an invoice to sign and then said to me, "If he ain't grumbling, he's mumbling. I reckon that means he's doing okay, considering."

"I guess it's a good sign," I replied. "He definitely struggled a little bit yesterday when Pastor Wright and I stopped by. Miss Liddy said he'd appeared quite uncomfortable when she and Miss Thatcher brought him some cookies a little later."

"Pop didn't say anything about any cookies. He musta had a miraculous recovery because Marie yelled at Pop more than once about trying to get out of his chair without help."

John stroked Ringo's side. "Your dad is as tough as they come, but if he doesn't mind the doctor's orders, he's goin' to find himself sidelined longer than a month. You can tell old Zeb that Marie said, in no uncertain terms, that she'll jerk a knot in his tail

— 174 —

if he does anything foolhardy enough to prolong his recovery one day longer."

"You and Marie going out to the Archer place tomorrow?" I asked, curious to learn how John felt about Hank's apparent recovery. He'd wrangled against the old Hank on far too many occasions. No one would blame him for remaining at arm's-length even from the new Hank.

John eyed Jay and then Ringo. "We haven't decided one way or the other. Marie and I haven't discussed it much yet. I imagine she's going to be stuck at the store though, but Phoebe wants to go. We'll just have to see what tomorrow brings. Fair enough?" He handed Jay the clipboard after ripping off a copy of his receipt.

John glanced at Ringo. "We still got things to do." He hopped over the side rail, landed flat-footed with a puff of dust beside his truck, and looked up to me. "What do you think?"

"Do what your heart tells you, not me. But, for what it's worth, Zeb put it pretty well yesterday when he said he wanted all this mistrust to end and leave the past in the past. You and Hank need to do likewise," I said as I grasped his outstretched hand.

"You've given me something to pray about." He turned and waved at Jay as he climbed into his truck.

Marie was behind the candy counter inside the Old General Store. We talked while I munched on a handful of South Georgia peanuts and downed a Moon Pie between swigs of Coke. I left sensing Marie wanted to forgive and forget the past, too, but her son's bronze statue on Town Square made it harder for her than most others. I understood her reluctance to bury the past.

NOT LONG AFTER Liddy climbed into our hammock, she nodded off while I cleared the dinner table and loaded the dishwasher. A late afternoon cloudburst brought welcomed relief from the afternoon's blistering temperatures. The downpour, though brief, drenched the sunbaked sidewalks and streets. I jostled Liddy from her nap as soon as Pepper pulled into our driveway with Hank and Phillip in her car. Before Liddy got all the way out of the hammock, Pepper scrambled up the porch steps way ahead of her brothers and toting two gift-wrapped packages.

"I just couldn't wait any longer to bring these to you. It was the least I could do for all your kindness and hospitality."

Hank and Phillip greeted me while Pepper handed Liddy the larger box wrapped nice in plain Kraft paper with a hand-drawn, red heart on the top. She had written across it, *Mister P & Miss Liddy, Thank you! Pepper.*

Liddy sat on the edge of the hammock with her feet dangling and inspected the package. "What did you go and bring us? Can I open it?" Liddy peered at me as she took her time peeling away the taped ends of the box.

Hank propped himself against a porch post near the steps. Phillip plopped down in the rocker beside me. Both enjoyed their sister's giddiness as she squealed, "Yes ma'am. Please open it now." Liddy removed the wrapping, seeming hesitant to rip or wrinkle the paper. Hank pulled his pocketknife from his pants pocket. "You might need this, Miss Liddy."

Pepper helped Liddy open the flaps of the cardboard box. Liddy raised a gift basket chock-full of Cajun seasonings and dinner fixings, as well as two bags of unadulterated ground chicory. Liddy looked at me and giggled, then set the gift basket back into the box and placed it aside before she stood and embraced Pepper. "Thank you so much. That was so thoughtful. You're gonna have to show me how to make some of these dishes the right way. Will you do that?"

T.M. BROWN

"Yes, ma'am. Anytime. I used to help Maude cook in the kitchen all the time." She glanced at me. "I brought this back for you, but I'm sure Miss Liddy will enjoy it just as much."

Without asking permission, I tore away the wrapping paper and stared at a hand-carved, red-mahogany frame with an old faded black and white autographed photograph of Jerry Lee Lewis. Underneath the framed photo were also two well-preserved Jerry Lee Lewis albums. I handed the framed picture to Liddy. "These were Maude's, weren't they? You sure you want to give them away?"

Pepper looked at Hank, who said, "Theo, she's got an antique footlocker full of old albums, 45s, and photographs of not only Jerry Lee Lewis but Mickey Gilley to boot. That Father Aloysius fella bragged that both of them grew up in Ferriday, just up the road from Vidalia. He confessed Maude and her girlfriends were known to have patronized a few of the old honky-tonks and music halls in the area whenever either of them performed there."

"Thank you, Pepper. These are genuine collector's items." I peeked at Liddy and smiled. "I'm glad we still have the old record player tucked away. Of course, we may need to purchase a new needle before we play these on it."

Pepper and Liddy went inside to better sort through the gift basket in the kitchen. Hank and Phillip remained on the porch with me. Hank offered a couple of lighthearted stories about Maddie and Pepper from their trip before Phillip brought up the articles in the *Sentinel*. "You should've seen the look on Pepper's face when she read about herself in the paper, but she didn't exactly fancy seeing her old school photo on the front page."

"You'll have to tell her Mary Scribner used the best photograph we had." I turned to Hank still holding up the porch post, arms folded across his chest. "Are you okay with what I wrote about you?"

— 177 —

Hank muttered, "Yep. I appreciated the pointed brevity, too. Maybe it'll help folks to let sleeping dogs lie and accept me as I am. Either way, I'm at peace for the first time in a bunch of years. I can't be responsible for what others might choose to think, but I can control what they see and hear from here on out."

"I'm glad you said that. A couple of folks said they can't make it to the party because of work obligations, but I want you to know Marie and John want to move on, too, but at their own pace if you catch my drift," I uttered a little louder than a whisper.

"I reckon I harmed them the worst, so I thank you for passing it on to me. I guess we all need a little time. Some wounds take longer to heal than others," Hank said, staring at the floor.

Phillip slapped his thigh. "Once you and John get straight again, Miss Marie will come around. You wait and see. In the meantime, Mister P, we'll see you and Miss Liddy tomorrow. If nobody else shows up, there'll be a heap of barbecue left over."

Hank stood tall and bellowed, "Come on, little sis, we gotta get home. There's still a lot to get ready for tomorrow."

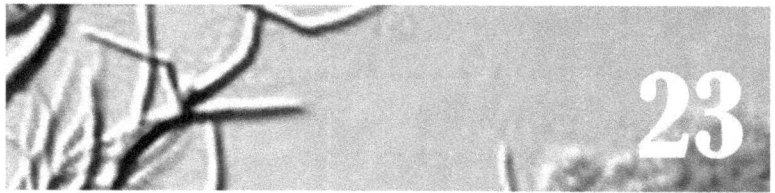

BY THE TIME WE ARRIVED, A HALF-DOZEN VEHICLES ALREADY HAD parked along the Archers' tree-lined drive. Tim and Woogie waved us around back beyond Camille's red truck and Hillary's white Camry tucked behind the garage. I followed the gravel road Harold had long ago used to show me their acres of loblolly pines beyond the family's *Better Homes and Gardens* picturesque lawn and gardens where cultivated pines provided an ideal habitat for quail and turkeys.

After we parked, Liddy followed me along the hedge-lined rail fence until we entered their beautiful backyard through the open gate. We walked past their horseshoe pit and four pairs of cornhole boards as aromatic smoke from twin smokers drifted overhead whetting our appetites. Bob had on his monogrammed white bib apron over a blue t-shirt. I waved, but he appeared preoccupied tending his charcoal black smokers, wiping his face with the once-white towel around his neck.

Liddy squeezed my hand and said, "Listen."

We climbed the stairs onto the veranda. Dave Jackson's undeniable baritone twang singing *Ain't No Place Like Home* came from speakers at opposite ends of their expansive deck. Familiar and unfamiliar faces mingled in lighthearted chatter and laughter. The French doors leading to the dining room, as well as the massive, panoramic sliding glass doors on either side of the decorative stone chimney, allowed guests to amble in and out of the Archers' great room.

I leaned closer to Liddy and whispered, "I wonder how many of these folks came only out of mere curiosity."

"Behave yourself." Liddy glared at me as if my nose had turned blue. Of course, her scrunched nose and pursed lips could not restrain her brief burst of giggles affirming she had likely come to the same conclusion.

Maddie scurried effortlessly between kitchen and dining room, but today she wore a vivid canary-yellow sundress decorated with a field of red roses, a noticeable contrast to her usual plain house dress and apron. Maddie's hairdo likewise earned a comment from Liddy. Her styled, shorter gray hair, freed from the confines of a hairnet, made her look more like the hostess rather than the beloved housekeeper.

Perched atop the veranda's back rail, Pepper looked at ease in her bib-overall denim shorts and a red-and-white cotton top. Her braided pigtails flopped about whenever she turned her head as she talked with Phillip, and Missy and Joe Arians. Nearby, the Arians' twin ten-year-old daughters, Lucy and Lizzie, their strawberry ponytails swaying in sync with Pepper's animated head turns, sat Indian-style at their parents' feet.

I grabbed Liddy's hand. "How about you and I go get something to drink."

Hal and Hillary were engaged with Barb Patterson when we took stock of the sweet tea, lemonade, and assorted bottles of wine. A large white insulated chest held plenty of beer, soda, and bottles of water in a bed of ice.

Barb's shrill voice greeted us. "Miss Liddy. Mister Theo. What can I get y'all?"

"Sweet tea for me, please," Liddy said before she glanced at me with a raised brow.

I pulled a Coke from the chest. "Where're Cora and Cecil?"

Barb smiled as she poured Liddy a glass of iced tea. "We couldn't afford to close down on a Saturday afternoon."

"Can we have a refill, please?" Hal handed two empty glasses to Barb and then looked at us. "Please join Hillary and me. Camille's making sure no one takes our table. Maddie shanghaied Hank a few minutes ago to help her in the kitchen, but he should be right back out."

We followed Hal and Hillary to their table, which offered plenty of shade beneath its blue, red, and yellow umbrella. Hillary's floppy sun hat and sunglasses may have shielded her face from the midafternoon sun, but her sleeveless jean top and beige shorts exposed her God-given bronze limbs to the sunshine. Camille's flaxen hair was tucked in a braided bun. Though a white halter top revealed tanned shoulders and arms, blue jeans covered her legs.

"Camille, look who we found," Hal said as we walked up to the table.

Camille slid her glasses off and stood. "Glad to see y'all. Go ahead and take Joe and Missy's chairs. Looks as though they abandoned us to hang out with Pepper."

Liddy scooted her chair out to allow her to stretch out her legs. Hal pointed at Phillip, Pepper, and the twins. "Look at all that red hair. What do you think?"

"You might have something there," I said. "All we need now is Pete to join them. You think we ought to take a closer look into their family tree?"

Hillary's father and mother walked out onto the deck from the great room. Arnie lifted his sunglasses and grinned as he looked down at Hillary, "What do you think, young lady? I promised I'd dress for the occasion." He ran his hand over the palm trees and seagulls decorating his beach shirt.

"If you ask me, I'm partial to those leather sandals you're wearing," Liddy said, looking at Judy, who wore a modest but casual summer floral dress.

"My traditional preacher-husband had to be reminded that Jesus and his disciples wore sandals, but it backfired when he refused to wear the nice khaki shorts I bought him."

"Oh, Dad," Hillary moaned.

Arnie crossed his legs and lowered his sunglasses to inspect the crease of his chino slacks. "Some folks simply don't appreciate the proper decorum for a pastor. I draw the line at exposing my hairy legs and knobby knees in front of folks who will gawk at me in the morning standing at the front of the congregation."

Hank's guttural voice reverberated from behind Arnie and me. "Preacher, may I remind you it's not our appearance but actions and attitude which define our character."

Hal looked across the table at Hank. "Brother, I am impressed. Those words of wisdom come from a man whose wardrobe consists of jeans, golf shirts, and boots."

Hank took a step back and spread his arms wide. "Methinks you're a wee bit jealous, little brother. At least I'm not sporting sun-deprived chicken legs in public."

Of course, Hillary suppressed giggles long enough to say, "Mayor, Hank's got a point. You sure do need to let them sexy legs see some sun more often."

Hal uncrossed his legs and examined them sticking out from under yellow shorts. He looked from those to Hank and Hillary and said, "What you might call pale chicken legs, I prefer to think of as the Official Mayoral Annual Parade of the Knobby Knees!"

A few minutes later, Pete, Andy carrying Jessie, and John Priestly appeared with Mary, Megan, and Phoebe close behind laughing among themselves. They joined Pepper and her growing entourage. Andy let Jessie play with Lizzie and Lucy while they greeted Pepper. Shortly afterward, I noticed Pepper left the porch rail and sat down beside the twins and played with Jessie.

It wasn't too long before Bob Patterson hollered from the lawn below where he had been busy tending the two roasted pigs. "Can I get a hand hauling these trays into the house? It's dinner time!"

Pete yelled, "Don't mind if I do! Come on, guys." Bobo, Woogie, and Tim followed Pete down the stairs while we got ready to step inside to eat.

Barb managed the buffet spread under Maddie's watchful eye. Guests took their plates and drinks to either the great room, back on the veranda, or down onto the back lawn. Just as Liddy and I looked for a place to sit and eat with the others in the great room, a commotion caught our attention. Mandy held the front door open as Jay walked behind his father. Zeb's growls and snarky comments left no doubt he did not like relying on his blasted crutches to get around.

"Thank you, son. You and Mandy go get yourself something to eat. I'll be okay from here," Zeb said, and grumbled under his breath as he made his way into the great room.

Gus sprang from one of the large leather armchairs. "Mister Adams, please sit here."

Zeb handed him his crutches. "Thank you, Mister Appleton."

As he sat, Zeb continued to examine the room and the railing overlooking the main floor. Gus placed the crutches beside the chair before he took his plate and drink outside. Hal left his seat on the matching leather sofa across from where Liddy and I sat with Hank and Camille and walked over to Zeb.

"I'm honored you were able to make it. It's been a long time since you were here." Hal extended his hand, and asked, "Can I get you a plate of barbecue fixings?"

Zeb shook Hal's hand and said, "It sure has been a long time since your father invited me here."

Jay shouted from the dining room, "Pop, Mandy and I are getting you something to eat."

Hank appeared with Pepper and introduced her to Zeb. "Pepper, if you ever want to know anything about the history of our little town, I suggest you catch up with Mister Adams. Most days you can find him at his feed and hardware store."

Zeb's harshness reverted to his typical congenial self as a grizzled, broad grin appeared. "Yes, little lady, please stop by anytime. There's always plenty of cold drinks and peanuts on hand at our store." Zeb took Pepper's hand. "By any chance, do you like to play checkers?"

Pepper bobbed her head enthusiastically.

"Well then, I can answer any questions you might have about Shiloh over a game or two of checkers in our Old General Store."

"Yes, sir. I'd like that," Pepper answered softly as she looked up at Hank and Hal beside her.

Zeb looked at her two brothers. "Jim decided to give Marie a hand this afternoon, but he wanted me to tell you that he did want to come."

Hank looked at Maddie and asked, "Do you think we can send a couple of plates home with Jay for Marie and Jim?"

After dinner, Phillip officiated a heated cornhole tournament. He grouped all who wanted to participate in teams of two. Zeb kept the participants apprised of the scores as he sat by the veranda railing surrounded by a host of others who preferred to watch. Liddy proved to be the better half of our twosome, but we got eliminated after our semifinal match with Hank and Camille.

We watched the other semifinal match: Pepper and Tim versus John and Phoebe. The winning couple would take on Hank and Camille. After the last bag landed and scored the winning point, I felt pretty confident Hank's crucial errant toss allowed an exuberant Pepper and Tim to claim the final victory.

Amid the celebration, I noticed Gus held a curious-looking smile as he sat by himself in a garden chair and shook his head as Pepper and Tim received hugs and high-fives for their victory. I walked over to him and asked, "Are you feeling okay? I didn't see you socializing much this afternoon."

"I'm okay, Mister Phillips. Thanks for asking. I just didn't feel like I fit in today, but I did enjoy talking a little with Pepper after dinner. You know, she looks a lot like her mother when she was about the same age."

I tilted my head with a raised brow.

"Oh, I know the Dixie you knew had out-of-the-bottle blonde hair, but in her younger years she was a natural strawberry blonde with the same cute freckles as Pepper." Gus went silent and kept staring at Pepper.

"I know you knew Dixie pretty well. Thankfully, I don't see Dixie's purported devil-may-care wildness in Pepper."

Gus broke his trance. "I'm sorry. What'd you say?"

"Pepper doesn't seem to have inherited Dixie's wild spirit. Would you agree?"

"Lord, no. It doesn't appear so."

WE ARRIVED HOME exhausted and crawled into bed early. Before Liddy switched off her bed lamp, we shared laughs as we recollected our afternoon at the Archers. I shared my brief conversation with Gus about Pepper and her mother's shared traits. Turning her light off, Liddy said with a half-hearted snicker, "I knew Dixie's blonde hair came straight out of a bottle."

Just before I dozed off, our bedroom phone rang. Without turning on the light, I sat up on the edge of the bed and grabbed the phone.

"Theo, this is Larry. Jim Adams is being taken to the hospital. Mitch Johnson's at their house right now."

"What happened? Is it serious?"

Liddy crawled over from her side of the bed and rested her head on my shoulder to listen.

"I only know what I heard on the radio. Zeb and Jay found Jim unconscious in their backyard when they got home tonight. I hate to ask, but can you head over to the hospital? I'm going to run by their house and see what I can find out from Mitch."

I stared at the illuminated 11:12 on my bedstand clock. "Sure thing, Larry. I'll drive over there in a few minutes."

"I'll go with you," Liddy said, sliding out of the bed.

WE PULLED BESIDE MANDY'S ORANGE MINI-COOPER CONVERTIBLE parked cockeyed across two spaces near the walkway leading into the hospital. As soon as we entered the ER waiting room, Jay and Mandy popped up from their chairs. Mandy had clearly rushed out of her apartment in a hurry. Besides the fact she stared at us through a pair of dark blue frame glasses, she had no makeup on, and her still-wet hair, secured into a hasty ponytail with a plastic clip, dampened the back of her black cotton t-shirt.

On the other hand, Jay had on the same faded jeans and button-down long-sleeved white shirt from earlier in the day. However, his shirt bore smeared dirt and blood stains on his shirttails and sleeves. He finger-combed his dark brown hair as he greeted Liddy and me. Liddy whisked Mandy aside and sat down beside her.

"Jay, Larry Scribner called with only a handful of sketchy details. How's Jim?" I asked.

"We're still trying to figure out what actually happened," Jay said, rubbing his weary eyes. "Pop and I dropped Mandy off at her place after we left the Archers and then drove straight home. Pop had half nodded off by the time we pulled into the driveway, but we heard Huckleberry snarling and barking up a storm out back. At first, we dismissed his carrying on as him scaring off a raccoon or some other unwelcome critter."

"It's obvious no critter did this to Jim. How'd you find him?"

"I managed as best I could to get Pop inside the house after Jim didn't acknowledge my yelling for him to lend me a hand. I got Pop into his chair and went onto the back porch. That's when I heard a loud clank in the storage shed, followed by a loud yelp from Huckleberry as he bolted out of the shed doors like his tail was on fire. I turned to get a flashlight from the kitchen, but Pop stood at the door holding the double-barreled shotgun we keep tucked behind the baker's rack and he flipped on the porch light."

"What'd he do then?" I asked, now more anxious about what happened to Jim at this point.

"He hollered for Jim. When he got no answer, he fired a round skyward. That's when I realized Huckleberry had not run off but stood near Jim laying in the shadows beside the woodpile. I jumped off the porch to check on him when a guy dressed like a dark-ops commando took off from the shed. He hightailed it around the far side of the shed just as Pop fired his second barrel. Jim was unconscious! I grabbed Huckleberry's collar before he could take off after our intruder. It took all my strength to prevent Huckleberry from chasing after the guy."

"Oh my, poor Jim," Liddy sighed.

"Yes, ma'am. Jim moaned when he sat up and grabbed the back of his head. When I saw the blood, I yelled for Pop to dial 9-1-1. A few minutes later, I saw Tyler's blue lights in the yard and then red and white lights signaled the arrival of the EMS vehicle."

"Did Mitch Johnson get notified?" I asked.

"Yes, sir. I was talking with Tyler while EMTs assessed Jim when Mitch walked around back with two Sheriff's deputies. Before I climbed into the EMS vehicle with Jim, I got hold of Mandy and told her to meet me at the hospital. Pop stayed at the house to fill in Mitch and the deputies on what happened."

Eyes wide and mind spinning, I asked, "Why in Sam Hill did this GI Joe character break into your storage shed?"

"It doesn't make any sense to anyone. When Tyler and I pulled the shed doors open, we found the limo's driver-side front and back doors unlatched. Tyler wouldn't let me touch anything or snoop around too much. As best as I could see, everything inside our garage seemed undisturbed. Tyler said it baffled him why this fella broke into the shed intent to get to the limo. From what we could determine, he didn't try to steal it or anything in it. But I'll tell you this much, I'm rethinking our prowler incident two weeks ago."

I ran my hand across my closed lips as I tried to make any sense of what Jim told me. "Let's wait to see what Mitch and the county boys find out. Maybe they can make more sense of why anyone would go through all that trouble just to snoop inside the old limo."

"Theo," Liddy whispered. "The nurse needs you."

I put my arm across Jay's shoulders and we crossed the waiting room floor to the nurse's station.

The nurse, holding a clipboard in front of her, offered a reserved smile. "You're Mister Phillips, aren't you? We haven't met before. I'm Mickey Waller's mother. She's spoken so much about you."

"Mickey's a nice young girl. Nice to meet you," I said, glancing at Jay's baffled but even more worried look. "I guess we're fortunate you're on duty tonight, Missus Waller. Can you tell us anything about Jim Adams? This is his brother Jay."

Missus Waller consulted the notes on her clipboard and then eyed Jay. "Your brother is going to be fine. He received a dozen stitches. The bats fluttering around in his belfry will more than likely cause him a terrible headache for a couple of days, at least until the swelling subsides, but Doc thinks he only suffered a minor concussion. To err on the safe side, we'll keep him here until tomorrow. If he doesn't experience any complications, he can be home in time to eat Sunday dinner at home."

Jay glanced at Mandy then asked Missus Waller, "Would it be okay for us to visit with him for a few minutes?"

She phoned the doctor, then hung up and said, "I'll take you back, but y'all can only stay for a few minutes."

The floor nurse propped Jim up in his bed so he could suck ice water through a straw in a Styrofoam cup. We watched from the doorway. With his bandage-wrapped head he looked like the Minuteman character he portrayed each Independence Day Jubilee. Mandy and Liddy remained in the doorway. I stayed at the foot of the bed. Jay pulled a chair up beside his brother.

Slowly Jim asked, "What happened? I went out to see what got Huckleberry...riled up when he, uh, when he wouldn't stop barking...I figured a curious critter...in the backyard...I let him out and—"

Jim paused longer to catch his breath. "So I followed him out, but...when I stepped off the porch Huckleberry's barking turned into snarls...I caught up to him near the, uh...the woodpile. Next thing I know, I'm staring at Jay's ugly puss...ha...and I'm strapped to a gurney. And I woke up."

Jim reached back and winced when he felt his bandage and the golf-ball-size lump on the backside of his head. "I don't think a four-legged critter could...ow...hit me like that."

"Best I can tell," Jay added, "Pop and I got home in the nick of time. Some guy dressed in dark camo with a Green Beret jungle hat and a blackened face ran out of the shed in a big hurry right after Pop fired his shotgun. So, I guess you're right, it wasn't any four-legged critter that clobbered you up side the head."

Jim squinted, furrowed his brow, and gritted his teeth. "What was he doing then?"

I said, "That's what Mitch and the Sheriff's deputies are looking into right now. It appears your commando critter had his sights on your Pop's limo, but outside of two of its doors being unlatched, nothing got taken or damaged."

"Sounds like you're pretty lucky. You could've been hurt much worse. The nurse told me your cowlick won't look the same once those stitches heal," Liddy said, giving a lighthearted wink.

Nurse Waller, in the hallway, finally pulled rank. "Sorry folks, doctor's orders. Mister Adams needs some rest so he can go home tomorrow afternoon."

In the parking lot, Mandy hugged Liddy, and Jay and I shook hands before Mandy drove him home. We were about to climb into our Expedition when Mitch pulled up and leaned out his open truck window. I told him Mandy left a minute ago with Jay. Then Larry also pulled up.

Before Mitch or Larry got out of their vehicles, Liddy grabbed my arm and said with a tired but insistent tone, "How about I brew some coffee? Y'all can confabulate all you want at the house. Missus Waller's not going to allow anyone to go back in there to talk to Jim until the morning anyway."

Mitch eyed Larry, who he caught in the midst of a deep yawn. "Sounds good to me," Mitch shrugged.

"Make it extra strong coffee, if you please, Liddy. I've got way too many unanswered questions to sleep anyway," Larry sighed.

MITCH STRETCHED HIS legs out on Liddy's ottoman after sitting in her armchair. Larry sat on the near end of the sofa. Liddy listened in from the kitchen while the coffee brewed.

Mitch flipped through his notepad, then peered at Larry. "If I miss anything, speak up. You saw about as much as I did while the deputies scoured the vehicle and the perimeter of the shed."

Larry nodded

"Theo, what did Jay and Jim say about tonight?" Mitch asked.

I recounted Jay's telling of how he found Jim out cold with Huckleberry standing next to him, and the mysterious camo-dressed intruder running away after Zeb fired a warning shot. Mitch asked if Jim said anything more, so I told him Jim's limited recollection of the events. Beyond investigating what had agitated Huckleberry so much to cause him to keep barking, Jim had gotten no further than the shadows of the woodpile when the lights went out.

"Did the doctors say anything about Jim's injury? Did he have a concussion?" Larry asked.

Handing the first cups of coffee to Mitch and Larry, Liddy said, "Nurse Waller told us Jim suffered a mild concussion. And they stitched the gash on the backside of his head. She said after the swelling subsides in a couple of days, his headaches will ease up as well, but they opted to keep an eye on him overnight before they let him go home. If he has no further complications, he'll be home tomorrow. If you ask me, Jim's attacker didn't care that he could've killed Jim."

"Crossed my mind as well," Mitch said, then savored a sip of fresh-brewed coffee. "Thanks, Miss Liddy."

Almost too fast for my tired tongue to spit the words out, I asked, "What I want to know is, did the deputies find any evidence this guy tried to hot-wire the limo? Why'd he bother to open the back door of the limo if he intended to steal it?"

Larry said, "I agree, Theo. If this guy didn't intend to steal the vehicle, what could make this 1980-something Cadillac limousine worth going through all the effort this guy did? What value could a thirty-year-old AM/FM stereo radio have? It can't be worth almost killing someone."

Mitch blew across the top of his cup and took a long sip before he spoke. "Fellas, I can't tell either of you anything more than I already have, but I'm glad Jim will be okay. Our suspect likely knows something we don't about this vehicle. Sheriff's Office is going to do some digging and promised to get back to me once they know something. In the meantime, I asked Zeb to consider locking the old car up somewhere else far away from his house."

Mitch turned to Larry. "That's why I wanted you here, too. Something tells me our car enthusiast is still around the area and might be desperate enough to try again. Will you write something in the paper about the Adams family moving the vehicle to an undisclosed location while the investigation continues?"

"Where should I say it's going to get moved?" Larry asked, wide-eyed.

"You aren't. Undisclosed. Look, I just prefer this guy know it isn't at Zeb's anymore." Mitch redirected his eyes to my inquisitive stare. "Theo, since you seem to have a reputation for digging up the past, can you see what you can find out about the vehicle's history? Didn't you go with Zeb to the auction?"

I nodded, feeling deep furrows of thought digging in across my forehead. "That reminds me. The man we met at the auction who bid against Zeb for the limo, also showed up at the festival. He showed more than a partial fancy to the limo. There's a good possibility he's also the same guy the kids ran into at the old mansion. I think his name was Cy or something like it. Come to think about it, a woman drove him away in a black Cadillac after the auction ended."

Mitch's sideways look told me he already realized the possible connection. "See what you can put together after you talk with Zeb and the boys. I plan to talk more with Camille about the incident in the church parking lot. Maybe she can recall more details about him to help with a positive I.D."

Larry asked, "Did the county deputies find anything when they searched it?"

"If you mean fingerprints, nothing they could use. If this Cy is the same guy or is connected with the break-in attempts, we'll need more. For now, I agree, he's a person of interest."

Liddy added, "Let's not overlook this Cy guy has been seen with a woman, and if he is the same one the kids saw, she may be Woogie's mother."

Mitch scribbled in his notebook. "I'll have a chat with Wilson and Woogie. I know there's a long, dark history there with Wilson's ex-wife. I hope for their sake, it's not her." He stood and handed his empty cup to Liddy. "Miss Liddy, thank you for the coffee. I don't think there's much more we can do for the time being other than try to get some sleep. Tyler's going to keep an eye on the Adams house until I relieve him later this morning." He glanced at his watch. "Mercy, it's nearly two. I'm sorry to keep y'all up so late."

Larry got to his feet, and said, "I'll try to be at church, but just in case I don't make it, let's touch base with Mary this afternoon about what to put in Monday's edition."

I walked him and Mitch to the door. "I agree with Mitch, we should only publish a brief recap of the break-in attempt as Mitch suggested. We can sit on what we know until we learn more."

Larry stopped on the porch, looked at Mitch, and said, "We'll do whatever you think is best. Mary's got a few good photos of the limo we can use to advertise that Zeb and the boys moved it off their property while the mystery behind the vehicle is being investigated." Larry raised a half-hearted tired smile. "I like it. We can publish more later about the vehicle and the break-in."

Mitch smiled with a slight tilt of his head.

Larry blurted, "We won't print anything without checking with you until this character is arrested."

Mitch put a tired hand on Larry's shoulder. "Mister Scribner, until you back your car out of their driveway, I can't leave. How about it?"

After Larry and Mitch drove away, I put out the porch light and locked the front door. I turned and looked at Liddy. "I sure hope Woogie's mother isn't involved in this. That'll crush him."

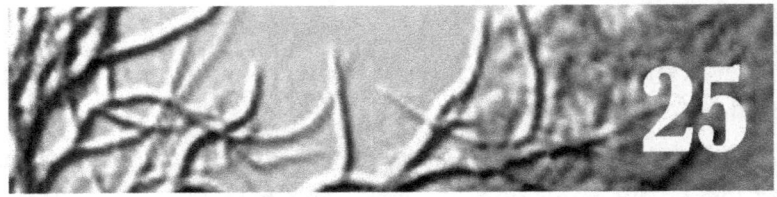

THOUGH A BLANKET OF GRAY LINGERED OVERHEAD AFTER much-needed rain fell during the wee hours, a pile of Father's Day cards greeted me on the breakfast table. Liddy also handed me a damp Sunday paper she had rescued while I poured myself some coffee. I enjoyed reading each card from our two sons and five grandkids.

Looking up at Liddy, and feeling a lot like the gloomy weather outside, I said, "I wish we could see them more often. Since we moved further away we just don't get together as often. And those kids are growing up way too fast." I stared at the family photos our sons included inside their cards.

Liddy reached across the table and squeezed my hand, offering a warm smile in the process. "They'll be here before you know it." She grabbed the calendar on the refrigerator and pointed. "See, the entire family will be here in two more weeks. Aren't you looking forward to spending a couple extra weeks with Teddy and Bubba? I know Marie's anticipating the three of you coming out to the farm while they're here."

The thought of hanging out with Teddy and Bubba set me off to smiling. "You're right. I'm looking forward to seeing how they handle giving Marie a hand on her farm. They've become spoiled suburb kids far removed from the rural life we enjoyed when we were their age." I chuckled and added, "How will they ever survive without access to unlimited Internet and reliable cell phone service?"

"They'll live, and it won't hurt them to eat some home-cooked meals rather than burgers, fries, and pizzas they're used to chowing down on."

Liddy carefully peeled open the damp paper and showed me the photos of the Archer Homecoming Party on page five across from Mary's article about the Summer Art and Music Camp. Liddy pointed to the picture of Pepper standing with Phillip and Hank. "I can only wonder what's going through Pepper's mind this morning while others are celebrating Father's Day."

I looked up from the paper, puzzled. Liddy got up and walked out of the kitchen. When she returned, she slid one more card along with a small, gift-wrapped box in front of me.

"What's this?"

"Read the card, silly."

Inside the Father's Day card Pepper had written, "Thank you." I shook my head and eagerly tore away the gift-wrap, opened the box, and pulled a personalized fountain pen from its fancy case.

"Pepper said you've got an obvious gift with words. She thought a wordsmith like you deserved a new fancy fountain pen worthy of writing your thoughts down in your daily journal." Liddy delivered the smile I envisioned on Pepper's face.

SHORTLY BEFORE ELEVEN, we scampered from our vehicle, sidestepping puddles until we entered the cozy confines of the church foyer. Once inside, we found the persistent drizzle failed to dampen the buzz within the church about the break-in at the Adams home.

Judy Wright greeted us, shaking her head. "Tsk-tsk, I just can't figure why some people need to be so melodramatic and stretch the facts to suit the importance of their opinion about the goings-on around town. If only Mitch and the Sheriff's investigators knew as much as our congregation claims to know."

Liddy smiled. "They don't mean any harm. All the same, some folks want to bend more ears than others even if it means exaggerating the truth to suit their needs."

Out of sorts with her usual cheerful self, Judy said, "Be that as it may, idle gossip can't be construed as being innocent. It almost always grows out of hand and whips up even more harmful, misinformed scandalmongering."

"Come on, it's Father's Day. Let's see what we can do to wrangle some of this misguided chitchat," I mumbled and grabbed Liddy's hand.

We found Hank and Phillip speculating on some of the wild notions already circulating about last night.

"Mister P, did you hear about Mister Adams getting into a gunfight last night?" Phillip asked as soon as we walked up.

Liddy and I smiled at one another before I said, "I guess you could say we heard our fair share about what happened out at the Adams place."

Hank asked, "How's Jim? I heard they transported him to the ER last night. After Mitch called earlier this morning, Hal ran out without saying any more about what happened."

"Where's Pepper?" Liddy asked, craning her neck to survey the foyer.

"Hillary invited her to lend a hand in the children's department."

Hank looked at me. "So, what about Jim?"

"Jim will be okay. They stitched up a pretty nasty gash on the back of his head, but you know how hardheaded those Adams boys are. It also wasn't exactly a gunfight. Zeb emptied his double-barrel, but both shots sent birdshot harmlessly into the air.

Jim got knocked unconscious when he and his hound went snooping around their shed after Huckleberry got all riled up."

Phillip turned from chatting with Liddy. "What do you think this fella was up to that warranted him cracking Jim's skull?"

"That's the big unanswered question. Possibly had something to do with Zeb's prize limousine he stored in their storage shed after the festival parade."

Hank's brow arched. "That old thing? It might be worth something to someone as a collectible, but it's not worth going to prison over."

"Mitch and the Sheriff's office are looking into that exact thing. They don't even know for certain who this person was," I said before Liddy could get a word in edgewise, which earned a curious stare from her. "I'm sure Hal may know a lot more when you talk to him later today."

Pete stepped away from Andy inside the sanctuary. "I got a message for you from Mister Scribner."

We stepped aside before I said, "I'm surprised he even got out of bed before you and Mary left for church."

"Shucks, he and Mary talked on the phone first thing this morning. She's gonna meet him at the newspaper office this afternoon. He wants you to call him after church—something about Uncle Zeb's limo."

"Is that all he said?"

"Yes, sir. Don't make a lot of sense to me, but he said you'd understand what he meant."

Mary's prelude music prompted the mass shuffling of feet into the sanctuary. Jeannie Simmons coaxed Hank and Phillip to sit between her parents and us.

After the choir marched down the center aisle and took their places behind Arnie on the platform, Hillary, Judy, Megan, and Pepper escorted the children into the sanctuary. Arnie stepped from his pulpit chair and sat among the youngsters on the platform steps. Jessie wriggled in Megan's arms and cried out with his arms extended toward Andy sitting beside Pete on the front row. Pete smiled while Andy appeared caught between his urge to respond and Megan's effort to distract Jessie. Lizzie and Lucy Arians sat on either side of Arnie. He addressed the congregation.

"The Bible declares that children are to obey and honor both their parents. Only last month we honored the mothers in our midst. So today it's the fathers who are being so honored." Arnie glanced at one-year-old Jessie and smiled at Andy. "Some fathers are just beginning to understand the daunting challenge ahead of them. For others here today, your children are now honoring you because they have developed a growing appreciation of the love you have invested in them over their lifetime."

Arnie winked at Hillary. "On this Father's Day, I'd like to express as best as I can, as a father myself, why living up to the expectations our Heavenly Father has placed upon us isn't always easy. To begin with, I believe it's safe to say, there's not a father in this room today who can declare they raised their children without any regrets along the journey. However, the love that grows between a caring father and his children serves as the salve that heals all wounds inflicted along the way. It's also true, fathering a child does not make you a father. Becoming a father is one of choice, not a consequence."

Liddy nudged and whispered, "Is Pepper crying?"

Arnie continued. "I'd like to take this time to suggest, if it's possible, talk to your father today. Thank him for loving you. For those who are unable to talk to their father, remember: God is your Heavenly Father. He promised to stand in the gap for those who lack a father's love in their life. During our fellowship time, parents, please make room for your children to sit with you this morning. This is not a day to be separated."

Marie Masterson stepped to the pulpit microphone. While she sang *How Deep the Father's Love for Us* accompanied by Mary, the children followed the choir members as they stepped off the platform and found seats with their families. When Marie finished, Arnie shared an embrace with her before she sat beside Pete at the end of our pew.

Arnie reminded the church about the Cooperative Fellowship Music Jamboree next Saturday evening. I looked at Pepper, who had squeezed in between Hank and Phillip and held their hands. She hung onto every word Arnie said.

When Arnie said Amen to close the service, Pepper left her seat to hug Liddy and me. During our embrace, I said, "Thank you for your special gift and card."

Pepper's eyes watered. "I may never know who my real father is, but I hope you don't mind me saying you've been an excellent father for me since I arrived."

Hank offered his arm to Pepper and said, "We need to catch up to Hal across the street in City Hall. He's waiting for us to go to dinner."

Right after they left, Liddy chatted with Hillary and Judy. I spoke with Arnie at the door. He said, "I stopped by the hospital earlier this morning. Sounds like God protected Jim last night."

"My thoughts exactly. There seem to be a lot of unanswered questions at the moment about what happened."

Arnie gripped my arm. "What do you mean? Are the Adamses in some sort of trouble?"

"I don't think they are. It's Zeb's prized vehicle that seems to be though."

"It's an interesting vehicle, but—"

"That's what we all said last night. Larry and I are looking into its history while Mitch and the county Sheriff's office are performing their own investigation. In the meantime, Jay stashed it away from their house for safekeeping."

"I'll check in on Zeb after lunch. Sounds like we will have a lot to chat about," Arnie said.

"Liddy invited Marie to have dinner with us at our house this afternoon. Afterward, I intend to curl up and catch a nap during the Braves game."

Liddy, Judy, and Hillary were caught up in a fit of giggles when Liddy turned to me and said, "Hal and Hillary are engaged." I gawked at Arnie.

Arnie chuckled. "Guess it ain't a secret no more. Hal wanted to announce it this morning, but Hilly asked me to hold off saying anything when he had to miss church."

Arnie and I shook hands. "Hillary, did you set a date?"

"Not yet. It'll be a small wedding. A few friends and family."

Liddy squealed. "Camille already asked if she could talk to Bernie and Silas about moving into Hillary's apartment over The Butcher Shoppe."

"Sounds like this isn't going to be a big secret much longer," I said with a laugh.

Judy said, "Not anymore."

THE FOLLOWING MORNING, WHILE JOTTING DOWN DETAILS OF my trip with Zeb to the auction, I heard footsteps on the porch. I set my notepad and pen aside and looked out the bay window but couldn't see who rang the doorbell. When I opened the front door, Gus Appleton stared back with an uncomfortable sour look. He had on his forest green Shiloh Utilities Department knit shirt and a pair of wrinkled khaki pants. Graying reddish-brown strands of hair, or at least what little he had left, lay aimlessly on his forehead rather than combed over his balding head.

After a frozen moment of indecision, Gus mumbled, "Mister Phillips, may I come in for a minute? I hope I didn't disturb you. In fact, if this is not a good time, I can come back."

"No, you're fine. Please, come on in."

I stepped back from the door. His hunched shoulders and droopy, long face bore undeniable evidence this visit was not a social one. His labored stride as he entered looked like he toted an eight-hundred-pound gorilla on his back, which caused me to pause and second-guess what he might want to talk about.

The once-cocksure Archer family attorney had lost his reputation and law practice when he got disbarred after his complicity with Dixie had come to light months ago, but at least he did not lose his freedom. A majority of people still scratch their heads when they try to make sense of how Dixie had played Gus like a fiddle to accomplish her ill-fated bidding.

The slippery slide that took him from strutting through town as the prestigious Archer family lawyer donning tailored three-piece suits to utter humiliation had only required the honey-sweet enticement of Delilah Dixon Archer-Arnaquer. After the dust had settled eighteen months ago, Judge Fitzgerald determined Gus had, in the end, undermined Dixie's efforts to defraud the Archer family. Although his fall came fast and hard, Gus managed to dodge a felony conviction for conspiracy and blackmail for coercing Wilson Edwards into breaking into our home as well as John Priestly's place.

However, this morning Gus had something much heavier weighing him down as he trudged slowly across our living room and sat on our sofa.

"Can I get you anything? I think there's still plenty of coffee — or perhaps a glass of tea?"

"No thanks, Mister Phillips. I need to get off my chest what I came here to say."

Still standing by my chair, I stared at Gus, though his attention did not include me. Interlocked fingers turned his knuckles white. Only elbows propped on knees prevented him from slumping further, as it appeared he looked for a trap door somewhere beneath our coffee table.

"Gus, what's eating you this morning? Is it the same thing that bothered you at the Archer place?"

He lifted his bloodshot eyes. "Yeah, I guess so."

"Do you want to talk about it?"

"That's why I'm here. You're the only one in town I can talk to about this."

"About what, Gus?"

"Sarah and Dixie."

I sat on the edge of my recliner and remained there, eyes glued to his sleep-deprived face. "I'm confused. How can I help?"

Gus fidgeted with the clasp on his watchband until he held it in his fingers and ran his thumb across the its backplate. "Sarah, or I guess I should say Pepper, will be seventeen on the first day of August. Is that right?"

I nodded. "Yes, I already told you that the other day."

Gus stood up and held his watch out. "Saturday, she confided that her birth certificate only identified her birth mother, but not her father." He leaned closer, watch dangling between his extended fingers.

"I can affirm it's true."

"Then please look at the back of my watch."

He dropped his brown leather-banded Swiss watch into my hand. It was not a Rolex, but its detailed craftsmanship screamed expensive. I read the engraving out loud. "Always remember what we gave each other, 08-01-99. D.D.A."

"Dixie gave me the watch not long after she returned to Shiloh. She told me we could never rekindle the feelings we once shared, but she wanted me to know she had not forgotten either. The inscription baffled me until Pepper arrived in town.

"You see, in 1998, I visited New Orleans for a conference the weekend before Thanksgiving. I called Dixie and invited her to dinner...old times' sake. Though I had not expected anything other than dinner, two lust-filled days later she kissed me and whispered how much she had enjoyed seeing me again, but she had already found someone special. I never heard anything from her again until she drove into Shiloh two years ago."

"So, you think you are Pepper's father? But, if Dixie had fallen for someone else about the same time, isn't it very possible he'd be the father?"

"That crossed my mind, but then I met Pepper face to face. I put the pieces together once I heard about her birth certificate and realized her birthdate."

"Have you said anything to any Archer...or even Pepper?"

PURGATORY: A PROGENY'S QUEST

"Of course not," he said and walked across the living room to sit facing me.

"What do you want to do about it?"

"Mister Phillips, I'm fifty-three, divorced, disbarred, live alone above my former law office, and I drive a Lincoln as old and tired as me. If it weren't for Hal Archer, I'd likely still be unemployed or have left Shiloh altogether. My ex-wife and I, thank God, had no kids of our own. I sure as hell have no business becoming a father at this stage of my life, especially to a child who's one year from heading off to college. Nor do I want to put an asterisk on her becoming an Archer after all she's had to endure. She doesn't deserve another crappy father. The way I look at it, she's better off without me cluttering her life."

"So? What now? What do you want me to tell you?"

"You and Miss Liddy had her under your roof for a couple of weeks. You also know the baggage I carry. If I approach the Archers and Pepper, my relationship with their mother might do far more harm than good, especially if they knew the full extent of our affair which caused her to leave Shiloh in the first place."

"Is there more you're not telling me?"

Gus collapsed back into the depths of Liddy's cozy armchair, his hands clenched white-knuckle tight again in his lap. Beads of sweat moistened his reddened and wrinkled forehead.

I sat straight and said, "I suspect it's true. I wouldn't be surprised to learn that Maddie's known all along."

Gus' eyes sprung wide open. "Knew what?"

"She said Phillip and Pepper could've been brother and sister except for their eyes. She reminded us that you once had a full head of red hair. I believe she's always known, or at least suspected, that Phillip may not have been Harold's son. When she eyed Pepper beside Phillip, she recalled the rumors about you and Dixie during her, let's say, younger, wilder days."

Gus twisted in the confines of the armchair. "If I confess about my relationship with their mother and tell Pepper I'm most likely her father, it'd be a short hop to speculate about how come Phillip came along when he did and why their mother left Shiloh twenty-three years ago."

"I'm not here to judge what happened all those years ago, nor what you told me about your visit to New Orleans. What you just told me though explains why you turned on Dixie after she came back and tried to sell the majority ownership in the family's business. You knew it would impact Phillip and you didn't want that to happen to your son. Am I right?"

"Yes, and for that reason again I'm caught in this inescapable conundrum. You see? It's not only a question about what Pepper will think about me telling her I'm her father but the likelihood Phillip will learn I'm his father, as well."

"All the same, no matter how well-meaning your motive, fostering a lie or harboring the truth are both wrong. Don't you think a genuine father should always try to do the right thing?"

"Harold proved to be Phillip's genuine father after Dixie abandoned them. I can't. I just can't allow Phillip to believe anything differently."

"I would never tell you otherwise, nor should you blur Phillip's memory of Harold as his father. However, is it fair to both Phillip and Pepper to deny them from knowing at least the truth about their birth father? In today's crazy, high-tech world, an innocent, curious DNA test could prove far more harmful unless you tell them the truth. I think you're selling Phillip and Pepper short. You're also selling Hal and Hank short about their reaction. Grant you, there may be some anger and confusion, but God places an enormous responsibility upon a father to say and do the hard things for the good of their children. Would you like to talk to Pastor Wright and get his advice too?"

Gus shook his head. "I've not been to church in decades. I don't think he'll say anything different from what you just told me anyway. You've given me a lot to think over. Will you please keep this confidential until I decide what to do?"

I nodded with a reassuring smile.

After climbing into his sunbaked black Lincoln, he glanced back and drove off. I felt as though I now carried a portion of the burden Gus had brought with him. What made it feel heavier: I couldn't dare tell Liddy what I now knew. I fell into the hammock and slowly swayed staring at the ceiling and praying.

Mary Scribner called as I munched on a sandwich I'd made for lunch. She invited me to go with her to visit Zeb. She wanted to take some more photos of the limo before he and I talked about what we knew of its background. Her blue compact hatchback pulled into the driveway a little after one o'clock. I climbed into the passenger seat, bringing only the yellow legal pad with my notes about the limo on the top page.

"I let Zeb know we were both coming over. I hope you don't mind me tagging along," Mary said as she pulled back out onto the street.

"Absolutely not. I wanted to drive out to Zeb's anyway but Liddy took our vehicle to school. How's your dear old dad today? Has he found out anything more about the limo?"

"He's been on and off the phone a good part of the morning. If he's learned anything, he hasn't shared it with me yet."

Marie's truck was parked out front of Adams Feed and Hardware when we drove by. Up the road further, Woogie looked busy unloading Jay's pickup at the lumber mill office. I surmised, since Tim already spent most of his day helping Marie at the Feed and Hardware, Jay hired Woogie to lend a hand at the lumber mill, especially while Jim and Zeb recuperated at the house.

As soon as Mary pulled in behind John Priestly's weathered pickup, Huckleberry and Ringo, John's hound, interrupted their lazy-day naps on Zeb's shaded front porch.

The howling duet continued until John pushed the screen door open. "You two, hush!" He smiled and joked, "Come on in. Welcome to the Adams Family Convalescent Home."

Zeb lounged in his green recliner with his feet propped up while Jim remained reposed across their once brightly colored floral upholstered sofa. John dragged two dining room chairs into the living room. He got Mary to sit in the cushioned rocker, then sat beside me. The continual slow whirr of the ceiling fans made the house tolerable as long as the front and back kitchen doors remained open and the afternoon breeze floated between the two screen doors.

Mary winced when she took a closer look at Jim's bandaged head. "How are you feeling?"

With a labored half-grimace, Jim said, "A whole lot better today, thanks. Doc Lucas said the throbbing headaches will subside as the swelling goes away. Then I can go back to work."

John laughed. "Be honest, Jim. You're afraid Tim and Woogie will do too good of a job filling in for you."

"Dagnabbit!" Zeb bellowed. "Jim's head is as hard as a rock. He's merely milking the little knot on his head to swindle a couple of extra days of TLC and rest. Y'all quit treating him like some wounded hero. Long after he drags his lazy butt off our sofa, I'm gonna be stuck hobbling around on these darn crutches until my blasted foot heals. Doc told me I was lucky I didn't aggravate the repairs they did on my big toe during all the excitement."

Mary rushed to Zeb's defense. "Everyone knows you were the hero." She eyed the double-barrel leaning against the baker's rack by the kitchen door. "Who knows what might'a happened if you hadn't ignored your foot and scared the fella off?"

PURGATORY: A PROGENY'S QUEST

Zeb's hoary beard couldn't hide his rosier-than-usual cheeks nor his widening smile. "Thank you kindly, Miss Mary. Now, how can I help you and Theo?"

Mary pulled a steno pad from the side pocket of her camera bag. "We want to do a couple of stories on your limousine. Folks are wondering where it came from and its prior history."

Zeb looked across the room at me. "Theo, would you reach beside you and open that top drawer?"

Inside the drawer I found the coffee-stained, dingy manila folder Zeb received when he bought the vehicle. I removed the vehicle's spec sheet and a news article about it.

"This is all I know about the vehicle itself other than what the Sheriff's deputy told me when I asked why it wound up in Douglaston of all places."

Mary leaned closer to Zeb. "Do you mind if Theo and I borrow those so we can look them over at the office?"

Zeb nodded as his fingers fluttered in my direction. "Theo, you can bring 'em back to me."

"What did the deputy tell you about the vehicle?" Mary asked, her pen at the ready to jot down notes.

"They didn't know exactly when or how it came back into the country, but them county boys took copies of the vehicle information, too. I bet they'll find out using their resources. But I do know the guy who made the mistake of speeding outside of Douglaston is in prison."

John chuckled. "For speeding?"

"Drugs, John. The idiot got stopped for speeding, but the deputy told us he was higher than a kite. To make matters worse, the fool had a rolled-up sack full of pot and heroin in plastic baggies stashed under the driver's seat, which is how the vehicle ended up in the county's vehicle auction. This fella tried to cop a deal, but when the investigators wanted to know the identity of the other person in the car, he refused. He's now a guest in one of Georgia's five-star prisons."

Mary asked, "How'd they know he had someone else riding with him?"

"The idiot kept saying *we* and *us* when he bragged how he picked up the car in Savannah and was already late driving it to New Orleans. He didn't know much about the vehicle, and to avoid a stolen vehicle charge confessed they had been paid to drive it, but only his partner knew the destination and name of the persons at either end."

John looked puzzled. "So, why were they hired to drive this limo to New Orleans from Savannah? Did they search the vehicle for any more stashed drugs?"

Zeb said, "I asked the question before I left the auction. I sure didn't want to own any drug vehicle. The deputy said the maintenance department went over the vehicle twice, and outside of being intrigued by the custom gadgets, they found no more evidence of drugs anywhere in it. Whatever reason they got hired to drive it to New Orleans is anybody's guess."

Zeb looked at Mary and then me. "If y'all learn anything more, please make sure I find out. We're owed an explanation as to why our mystery guy's been so intent on getting his hands on *my* vehicle. I paid good money for it, and I'd rather not have it stolen."

I asked, "Is it still here? Mary wants to take a couple more photos of it."

Jim scooted onto his elbows and looked over his shoulder at John. "John and Jay moved it to the maintenance garage at the lumber mill. It'll remain there for the time being."

I looked at Zeb, and asked, "You think I can swing by and ask Jay to let Mary take some pictures?"

"Sure, don't know why not."

Mary put her pad away and lifted her camera bag onto her shoulder. "Thanks, Zeb. And, you too, Jim. I hope both of you get better soon. I'll make sure Theo returns the vehicle information."

John walked us onto the porch. I told Mary I'd be right behind her, then whispered to John, "Can you keep a secret?"

John did a double take, but said, "Of course."

"Hal and Hillary are engaged."

John smiled. He whispered, "I know. *Supposed* to be a secret."

AFTER JAY BACKED the limo out of the garage at the lumber mill, Mary took several photos inside and outside of the vehicle. Liddy had just pulled into the driveway when Mary and I drove up.

Liddy waved at Mary as she left, then pointed to the bag of groceries in the backseat. "Busy day? Anything you want to tell me while I cook dinner?"

I mentioned that Gus had stopped by but said little more than he wanted to thank us for all we had done. I shifted the subject of our conversation to Mary's and my visit to Zeb. She giggled after I told her how John responded when I shared the good news about Hal and Hillary.

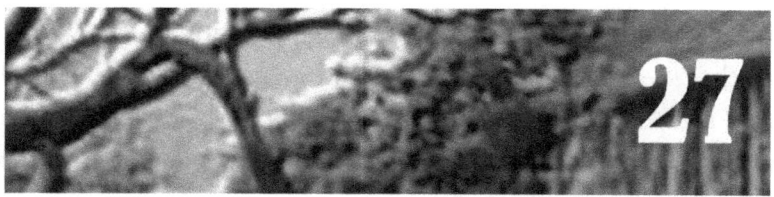

"LIDDY, IT LOOKS AS THOUGH LARRY COULDN'T HELP HIMSELF. Listen to today's headline: *Legendary Limousine Under Investigation.* That headline with its to-be-continued brief article and Mary's two accompanying side-by-side photos of the limo will, without a doubt, make heads spin and tongues waggle while they wait for the *Sentinel* to feed them further details about Zeb's infamous vehicle and why someone attempted to steal it."

I slid the paper across the table to Liddy. "Mary took these photos yesterday. Guess where Zeb moved the vehicle for safekeeping?"

Liddy stared at the photos, then read the article. "Larry didn't say where in his article." All of a sudden, a subtle grin emerged as she placed her finger on the second picture. "The Shiloh Lumber Mill."

"Why do you think that?"

"You can make out the SLM logo above the garage door. Thankfully, only local folks would probably recognize it. Besides, it makes sense it's where they would put it for safekeeping." Liddy remained fixated on the article before she asked with a certain degree of hesitancy, "Where's Cyprus? Isn't it an island near Greece?"

"Don't confuse it with the island of Crete, but you're close. I had to look it up myself. Cyprus is an island near the Lebanon and Turkey coastlines in the Mediterranean. It's been a nation engulfed in civil wars and bloody coups over the past century or so. Guess that's why this Spiros guy had figured purchasing a James Bond-like armored vehicle was a good idea."

I chuckled then said, "But it's the vehicle's low mileage that makes me scratch my head. I'd wager it's been tucked away in a garage or warehouse like a prized trophy. Maybe the authorities can tell us how it traveled from Cyprus to Savannah before its fateful drive to Douglaston. It sure didn't drive across the Atlantic. There's bound to be a paper trail."

An hour after Liddy scooted out the door for another day with her summer art students, I had folded a still-warm load of laundry and begun stuffing my shirts and shorts into my dresser drawers when Larry called. The official inquiries into Zeb's vehicle by the Sheriff's office had reaped more information.

When I inquired how he found out, he offered his pat answer, "My friend, trust me. Go visit Hal and Mitch this afternoon. I'm tracking down a lead on the vehicle's previous owners."

HILLARY POPPED HER head up as soon as she heard my footsteps echo across the rotunda's marble floor right after lunchtime. "Theo, we thought you'd show up."

"Before I seek an audience with his majesty, I think you and Hal getting hitched is wonderful news. How are your future brothers-in-law responding?"

Hillary beamed. "It came as no surprise to them — or Maddie for that matter." Her eyes hardened. "But it appears Pepper's still adjusting to her new-found life as an Archer. She seemed pleased with our news but asked if it meant Hal and me would be moving into our own home."

"What'd you tell her?"

"We plan on living at the estate. Hank's already made it evident he won't be living at the house much longer," she said with a pained look dimming the sparkle in her eyes.

"Why the down-in-the-mouth pout?"

"Pepper feels like she's responsible for Hank's decision. Hank assured her he'll be like a bad penny that keeps showing up, but he needs to establish a life away from Shiloh."

"Did Hank put a timeline on his decision?" I asked, scratching my chin.

She sighed. "He said he hadn't decided yet, but it'd be more like a few weeks rather than a few months. Pepper appears to have latched on to Hank. I almost think there's more of an odd father-daughter bond between them."

My heart throbbed as I conjured in my mind how Pepper might digest what I knew to be true. "I can see how it could be confusing for her. He's old enough to be her father, as is Hal. Speaking of Hal, is his majesty busy, or can I bust in on him?"

Hillary glanced at Hal's closed office door, then leaned forward and whispered, "Mitch must still be briefing him on the follow-up from what happened at the Adams place. I'll see if they're about wrapped up." A moment later, she hung up her phone, shaking her head. "Go on in. They want to talk to you."

I rapped on the door before I stuck my head in first. "Am I in some kind of trouble?"

Hal leaned against the front edge of his desk, sleeves rolled up, collar unbuttoned, tie loosened, a legal pad in one hand. He motioned for me to come right on in.

Mitch occupied an armchair in front of the desk, a file folder in his lap. He removed his SPD baseball cap and finger-swept his dark hair before he reset the hat on his head, bill angled upward.

"Mister Phillips, we were just talking about you. Mister Scribner said you were on the way."

PURGATORY: A PROGENY'S QUEST

Hal motioned to the second armchair in front of his desk. "Glad you joined us. Since you went with Zeb to purchase this black albatross that clearly a particular someone has taken a fancy to, I want to share with you what we uncovered so far, thanks to the resources of the Georgia Bureau of Investigation."

Mitch pulled a photograph from the folder in his lap. "This is a security camera picture taken a year ago last February at the ACL Import Cargo Terminal at the Port of Savannah. The nighttime photo is a bit grainy, but do you recognize the vehicle?"

"That's Zeb's limo all right." I handed the photo back to Mitch.

"Now look at this one," Mitch said, pulling another from the file. "It's at the same location a few minutes later."

The angle of the overhead security camera and the quality made it hard to make out the faces. "Looks like four men next to the vehicle."

Mitch hunched closer and pointed to the person holding what appeared to be a clipboard. "That's the ACL's import agent on duty that evening. The other three are our persons of interest." He pointed to the shorter one standing closest to the trunk of the vehicle. "Look harder. There's a woman wearing a knee-length overcoat and watch cap, but look at the long dark hair. We can't see her face, but we got a bit luckier with her two companions."

The third enhanced photo provided a zoomed-in headshot. "I can't recognize either of them."

Hal placed his finger on the clean-shaven, distinguished gray-haired gentleman, "That is Sergei Malakov. He's a suspected member of Bratva: Russian Mafia. ACL's files showed the vehicle traveled in a cargo container aboard a Greek-registered ship. It cleared U.S. Customs after inspection without issue as a personal vehicle for Sergei shipped from Corfu, Greece."

I gawked at Hal and Mitch.

Mitch said, "The GBI is still trying to identify the woman and man in the photo, but Zeb's vehicle has a checkered past."

"Why hasn't this Sergei fella been contacted after it got seized in Douglaston?" I asked Mitch.

"Three weeks after those pictures were taken, his body got pulled from the Savannah River."

Hal's awkward grimace broke the growing apprehension. "All this is off the record for the time being."

Mitch added, "The GBI feels the attempted vehicle theft or break-in may not have anything to do with its dubious past ownership. Although, until we know more about this fella you and Zeb ran into at the auction and after the parade, Tyler and I are going to keep an eye out. We've checked the vehicle from bumper-to-bumper and remain baffled. Outside its shady recent past, it is nothing more than a one-of-a-kind old vehicle with an interesting history, albeit with limited collectible value."

"I'm curious. Do you think the unknown man and woman in the photo are Cy and Cassie?" I asked.

Hal eyed Mitch. "Until we know otherwise, or our car thief tries again and we nab him, yes. There's enough to connect the dots. We just don't know anything about this Cy. We also are digging into Cassie's history to see if a connection pops up. Even though Woogie's the only one to see her, Mitch has spoken with Wilson and Hub. They know she'll be arrested if she shows up in town again."

Hal walked me to the door. "I've got a favor to ask. Will you head over to Adams Feed and Hardware? Pepper's there with Marie and Tim. Well, the news of Hank leaving Shiloh weighed on her this morning. She might also be trying to digest the news about Hilly and me."

"Sure. By any chance has Gus Appleton talked to you or Pepper today?"

"No. Why?" Hal asked.

"Nothing. He stopped by the house to thank Liddy and me for opening our home to her. I only thought he might've said something to you. I'll head straight over to see Pepper before I catch up with Larry. He's biting at the bit to hear what you guys found. He said something about following his own leads, too."

"Make sure to call me if he comes up with anything helpful. Ol' Larry never ceases to amaze me with his connections."

THE SUNSHINE BEAT down from the unobstructed midafternoon crystal blue sky. I quickstepped across two sizzling paved intersections and felt little relief from the oppressive heat on the cracked sidewalks. I began to envision myself as a slab of bacon dancing in its own fat juices in a hot skillet. The shaded wooden loading platform offered much-appreciated relief. Inside the feed and hardware store, swirling fans in the century-old rafters stirred the musty air enough to make its confines a tolerable refuge.

"Howdy, Mister P," I heard from a stool behind the counter.

"Jim! How are you doing? Except for the small, shaved patch of scalp on the back of your head, you appear almost good as new." I sank my hand into his firm grip.

"It didn't make no sense sitting around the house. My head feels a heck of a lot better. I figured I could at least mind the front counter and help customers on the main floor of the store. Can I get you something?" He relaxed his grip and leaned against the shelves behind him.

"Stay seated. Want a cold drink? It's a scorcher again today."

Jim lifted his green Sprite can and took a sip. I stepped across the aisle and stuck my hand into the ice-filled Coca-Cola red barrel to retrieve a Coke. "You can tell your Pop it turns out the old limousine has an interesting paper trail." I popped the aluminum tab and took a swig.

At that he popped upright on his stool. "Really?"

"Yep, and you can tell him I'm hoping Larry has dug up a little more on this Cy character by the time I stop in to see him in a bit. The GBI has drawn a blank so far on him."

"Mister Phillips," Pepper squealed, scampering through the archway from the Old General Store, Marie a few steps behind. Her contagious smile sparked one on my face.

"Miss Marie invited me to spend a couple of days on her farm. Isn't that great?"

My eyes drifted to Marie's approving nod. She put her arm around Pepper's waist. "Theo, this here is a bona fide country gal. Why didn't you tell me? I should've had her out to my place sooner. Do you think her brothers would mind?"

"I don't think so," I said and looked at Pepper. "Young lady, you have not fully experienced our little community until you've visited Miss Marie's farm and met Ringo. He's Coach Priestly's dog and wanders back and forth between Coach Priestly's cabin and Marie's place. They live not too far from one another on the farm property."

"Yes, sir! Miss Marie's been telling me all about both of them."

I turned to Jim and pointed to the phone beside the register. "Do you mind dialing City Hall?"

Jim grabbed the receiver and handed it to me while he dialed.

"Hal, hey. Someone wants to ask you a question." I handed the receiver to Pepper.

Marie giggled like a schoolgirl as Pepper filled Hal in about Marie's offer. Pepper then gave me the phone with a huge smile.

"Theo, one more thing before we hang up," Hal hollered. "Thank Marie for me. I assume Pepper will want to swing by the house and grab a change of clothes. Tell her Miss Marie doesn't have to drive all the way out to our place. I'll take her home and one of us will bring her out to the farm in time for dinner." Then he ended the call.

Tim slapped the dust off his shirt and jeans while he walked up front from the warehouse.

Pepper asked, "Would you mind if Tim and Woogie stop by?"

Marie looked at Tim, "You and Woogie wanna have dinner out on the farm tonight? Pepper's gonna spend a couple of days with Ringo and me."

"Yes, ma'am." He smiled at Pepper.

JIM DROPPED ME off at the *Sentinel*. Closing the truck door, I said, "Thanks for the lift. I bet thermometers around town touched the century-mark this afternoon."

A few minutes later, Mary followed me to her father's office. "Golly, I'm glad you're here. Dad's been pestering me every five minutes since he got back after lunch. He keeps asking if I heard from you."

"Thanks for the heads up. I've got two things about the vehicle he might be interested in hearing. The only hitch is Mitch and Hal want to keep the information out of the paper while the investigation continues," I whispered, holding the door for her so she could step into Larry's paneled office first. We sat in front of Larry's cluttered mahogany desk.

The phone rested on Larry's shoulder as he fumbled through papers on the credenza behind his desk. He then raised it to his ear and grabbed a pen. "Go ahead." After saying *uh-huh* three or four times, he hung up, spun around in his executive chair, and gave a smug, Cheshire Cat grin.

"What'd you find out, Dad?" Mary asked.

"Cyrus Riddell is our Cy fellow."

"How did you find that out?" I asked. "Please don't give me one of your cock-and-bull lines."

"I called the publisher over in Douglaston. I told him I'm working on a big story and asked if he could make some calls. It dawned on me that all auction bidders in Adams County have to provide identification before they're allowed to take part in monthly vehicle auctions. Turns out the same is true there, too. That last call got me to the clerk at the vehicle maintenance yard where you and Zeb went. After a little cajoling, she's faxing a copy of Riddell's Louisiana driver's license. I'm not sure this address is any good, but Cyrus has—or had—a New Orleans address."

Mary leaned forward with a puzzled look. "Great…I think. It still doesn't connect him with anything more than rude behavior at the festival, though. We don't know if he's the same guy who attacked Jim and tried to steal Zeb's limo."

"That's a fact, Mary," I said. "Let's make sure Mitch gets a copy. The GBI may be able to tell us if he's got a criminal record. I'd also like to find out if he has a connection to Cassie Davis."

Martha stepped inside Larry's office. "Are you looking for this?" She handed Larry a fax.

"Martha, would you make two copies first?"

Martha disappeared and I propped my forearms on my knees. "Listen, Larry. What I need to tell you must not make the paper for right now."

Larry's confident grin dissipated faster than it appeared. "This sounds serious."

"It's not only serious but also could bring a heap of trouble Shiloh's way. The GBI traced the vehicle to the night it left the Port of Savannah over a year ago. A Russian had it shipped to himself as a personal vehicle in Savannah." I checked my notes. "The guy's name was Sergei Malakov."

"Why did you say *was*?" Mary asked.

"They fished his body from the Savannah River not long after he and two others took delivery of the vehicle after it arrived and cleared U.S. Customs."

Larry slumped in his padded chair, folding his arms. "And?"

"The GBI found out he's a suspected Russian Mafia affiliate." Mary shushed us when her mother returned with the copies. As soon as Martha went back to her desk, Mary asked, "Zeb's relic from the eighties has been inspected and searched multiple times. It's nothing more than a thirty-year-old collectible oddity with a unique history. It doesn't make sense the Russian Mafia would risk getting caught stealing it."

Reacting to Mary and Larry's wide-eyed looks, I held up my copy of Cyrus' driver license. "Here's why Mitch and Hal want us to sit on this information until the GBI comes up with more," I said. "Let's let the boys at the GBI do what they are trained to do. The vehicle's safe for now at the lumber mill. Let's not stir up theories that may be proved wrong."

"Let's not put our heads in the sand either," Larry quipped. "I'll make sure this gets to Hal and Mitch on my way home."

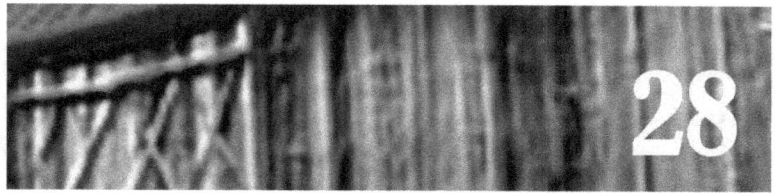

LIDDY HOVERED OVER MY SHOULDER REFILLING MY COFFEE MUG at breakfast. She said, "I'm curious. Considering everything you told me last night, it doesn't make any sense why anyone in their right mind would risk prison time to steal Zeb's vehicle. How far could they possibly drive without getting noticed?"

"Mary pretty much came to the same conclusion. You know though, it baffles me more that this Cyrus character had every opportunity to outbid Zeb. After he walked away, I figured that'd be the last we'd see of him. Then he shows up in Shiloh days later only to learn the hard way he should've shown Camille a little more respect when he bullied his way past her to stick his nose in the backseat."

I took a sip of coffee and continued. "If Cyrus turns out to be the guy the kids ran into, why would he draw so much attention to himself and then stick around? And, if he's Zeb's not-so-stealthy although persistent intruder, he must be pretty desperate. He's gotta be far more afraid of the vehicle's asserted Russian syndicate connection than what might happen if he gets caught stealing it."

My early morning stubble got a workout with my fingers as I tried to make sense of everything we had learned so far.

"That's a lot of speculative ifs, Theo. Permit me to add one more. What if Woogie is right and Cassie Davis is the guy's traveling companion? She has to know the risk she's taking being anywhere near Shiloh."

"Maybe the fax I gave Mitch will tell us more about Cyrus Riddell. I suspect a lot of this speculation will be cleared up when he hears back."

Liddy had bitten into her jelly toast when the sound of a car door closing made her jump up from the chair and look out the window. "Were you expecting Gus?"

"Nope, but I'm not too surprised."

Liddy glared at me. "You'll have to answer the door. I'm not presentable nor do I have the time for company. I'll go get ready for the day, so you two can be alone." Two steps into the hall she stopped and half-turned. "Do you know why he might be here?"

"I'll tell you later. It's about Pepper. Don't fret. Go get dressed. I'm sure this will only take a couple of minutes."

I walked out onto the porch and greeted Gus out of earshot of Liddy. Since I first met Gus three years ago, I never would have mistaken him for being a bastion for health and fitness, but this morning the strain of that same eight-hundred-pound gorilla he had toted on his back the other morning remained very visible.

He pulled his hand from his pants pocket and shook my hand. "Good morning, Mister Phillips. I apologize for imposing like this and so early too. I'm hoping you'd do me a favor."

"I'll try my best."

"As I told you the other day, I'm not a real religious person, but it might be a good idea to seek some confidential counsel with Pastor Wright. Can you help me?"

"I'll certainly see what I can do, Gus."

He raised his sunglasses to the top of his balding head. The dark bags beneath his deep-set, bloodshot eyes accentuated his graying strands of hair and the crow's feet marking his temples. I rested my hand on his slumped shoulder. "Arnie Wright has known the Archers a long, long time. You can trust him."

His weary eyes met mine. "I know, but will you help me to see him today?"

"Sure, Gus. I'll try to call him in a few minutes. Do you want some coffee or something?"

"No, sir. Thank you anyway. I've got to get to the office. I just felt I needed to ask you in person. Please call me on this number. It's my direct line." He handed me his business card. "I should be free by let's see—" Gus inspected his Swiss watch, "any time after ten. And, if it's okay with you, I'd like for you to go along."

"Why do you need me to go with you?"

"I'd feel much better if you went with me," Gus blurted, eyes opened wide in a desperate appeal.

"All right. I'll work that out as well."

His business card brought to mind my first encounter with Hal Archer when he handed me a similar Shiloh City business card. The only difference being the name above the City Utilities Department Director title. Hal had since risen to become Mayor while Gus groveled his way into the position with his tail between his legs after he was forced to close his law practice.

"I appreciate this, Mister Phillips." He lowered his dark glasses back onto his nose and returned to his car.

As he drove off, I felt a modest sense of relief. With Pepper still at Marie's place for the next couple of days Gus might be able to approach the Archer brothers first with his bombshell revelation. Phillip would surely take the news the hardest, so why have Pepper and Phillip together to hear what Gus intended to spring on them? Either way, it would be a meeting I definitely preferred to avoid. Arnie's relationship with Hank, Hal, and Phillip made him the logical one to accompany Gus.

"What did Gus want?" Liddy asked, standing at the front door, keys in hand.

"He asked me to arrange a meeting with Arnie. He's got something weighing on his mind and needs advice before talking with the Archers about it."

"Is there anything you're not telling me? You know I can tell when you're holding something from me," Liddy asked, arms folded across her chest, keys jiggling.

"Kinda. I'll tell you after I take Gus to talk with Arnie."

"Why do *you* have to go with him?"

"Gus asked me."

Liddy curled her lip. "Theo Phillips, now you're gonna have me wondering all day."

Her arms relaxed as I embraced her and kissed her forehead. "Will you just trust me on this?"

"Of course, you big galoot." She caressed my cheek and kissed me. "But that doesn't mean I won't stop worrying."

I ARRIVED A FEW minutes early and waited on a prayer bench in the shade of a centuries-old live oak until Gus parked his Lincoln in front of the church office.

He greeted me with a feeble handshake as his words stumbled over one another. "Thank you, Mister Phillips. I hope you weren't waiting too long."

"I just sat down a couple of minutes ago." Those drawn-out *couple of minutes* had allowed me to clear my thoughts and ask God for guidance. I glanced at my watch. "We've got another minute or so. Anything I need to know before we go inside?"

What Gus was about to confide to Arnie would soon test the relationships between the Archer brothers and their acceptance of their sister. Pepper's nascent future as an Archer, as well as her own understanding of her unsettled past, was at stake, too.

"If you don't mind. I'd prefer to get this over with."

Inside Arnie's spartan, dated office, Gus examined the wall of framed diplomas and plaques recognizing Arnie's thirty-plus years of ministerial and community achievements. Arnie walked from behind his green metal desk. Gus and I sat down at the unpretentious pine conference table in Arnie's office.

"I hope you two don't mind if I keep the blinds drawn. It helps keep my office more tolerable this time of the year," Arnie said, sitting across from Gus and me.

Gus looked as antsy as an alley cat who'd wandered into the dog pound. He peered over at me as if begging for more than moral support.

"Gus, Theo has told me you wanted to get some advice on a delicate matter." Arnie looked at the open office door. "Would you mind closing the door, Theo?" Arnie then addressed Gus. "Even more sacred than an attorney-client relationship, anything said here will remain sacrosanct—between God and us alone, if that's your wish. Right, Theo?"

Returning to my seat, I said, "Absolutely. In fact, if Gus would prefer, I'll wait outside while the two of you talk."

I stood and began to push my chair under the table, but Gus grabbed my arm. "You don't need to leave. I've already confided in you and trust you as much as I want to trust Pastor Wright."

Arnie motioned for me to take my seat, much to Gus' relief. "What's on your mind?" Arnie said, eyes honing in on Gus.

Once Gus got started, he needed little inquiry from Arnie or me to further the conversation for the next half an hour. Arnie's reassuring manner and affirming gestures sufficiently encouraged Gus. He rambled off details of his on-and-off relationship with Dixie. Arnie's lack of reactions surprised me— no wide-eyed looks, no double takes, and no raised brows.

PURGATORY: A PROGENY'S QUEST

Arnie maintained eye contact with Gus throughout the exchange except for an occasional glance toward me when I reacted to some of the sordid details Gus now felt free to share.

Toward the end of his revelations, Gus said, "Pastor Wright, now you can appreciate why I brought Pepper to Theo and Liddy. I didn't know then, but after I realized her mother was Dixie, my gut twisted tighter than a Gordian knot. The moment Theo confirmed her birthdate, I knew." Gus unstrapped his watch's leather band and handed it to Arnie.

Arnie slouched against the back of his chair and crossed his legs. He ran his fingers over the inscription. "Gus, I might as well tell you something I've known since Phillip came into this world, and you need to hear this. I hope it'll help you with what lies ahead for you. Harold confided in me long ago he was not Phillip's father. He never told me more. In fact, as far as I know, he never spoke about it to anyone again. I'm fairly confident none of his sons know he did not father Phillip."

Arnie planted his feet square on the threadbare carpet. "I mean no disrespect, Gus, but Phillip couldn't have had a better father than Harold Archer. Whatever needs to be unveiled between the two of you, Phillip must not lose sight of that fact. Fathering a child is not the same as being a father to a child."

Arnie's words undoubtedly smacked Gus right between his eyes because he squeezed them shut. "I understand. I would have never said a word to anyone about Phillip, especially to Phillip, if it hadn't been for Pepper. The way Maddie looked at me and her comments during Hank and Pepper's homecoming party made me uncomfortable, particularly after she saw me sit down with Pepper that afternoon. I wouldn't put it past the old woman to have known or at least sensed that the common denominator between Phillip and Pepper extended beyond Dixie."

Arnie paced back and forth at one end of the table. There was little doubt his gears were grinding, but his eyes remained focused on Gus, who wouldn't lock eye contact with either of us.

"Pastor, should I just keep this to myself? I don't want to cause any more harm. I'll quit my job and move away if it'd be best."

I stared at Arnie as he turned away, but then he said, his back to Gus, "What do you think would be best for you…and Pepper and Phillip?"

Gus turned his tear-filled eyes toward me.

"Gus, only one person can untie the knot tearing you up inside," I said with an emphasis on the *one person*.

Arnie waited in lingering silence, his back still to Gus.

Gus crossed his arms tight against his chest. "Doesn't it say in the Bible the truth will set you free?"

Arnie turned to him with a reassuring smile. "Yes, it does. And yes, it will."

"But I'm afraid what they'll say. I'm even more afraid what Hal and Hank will say and might even do."

"Whatever initial uneasiness and pain the truth may inflict, it'll be far less painful than the alternative," Arnie said with a hand on Gus' shoulder.

I said, "Pepper is supposed to remain at Marie's place at least until tomorrow or Friday. Might I suggest talking with the Archer brothers while she's out of the picture? I believe they will handle the truth better than you might expect. Especially when they understand how it implicates Pepper as well."

I then focused on Gus. "In the same way as you would not presume to step up as Pepper's father at this late stage in her life — until and if she's ready for it to happen—you might share the same thing to Phillip. I know you have no desire to usurp his memories of Harold as his father."

Arnie added, "Theo's got a point. It'll be about how you reassure them regarding your reasons for revealing the truth. The initial shock for Phillip and his brothers will not rip the bond they have for one another. If you ask them to help you tell Pepper, she'll better handle the impact of the truth. Her first concern will be her new-found life as an Archer."

Gus stood and shook Arnie's hand. "Will you go out there tonight with me?"

"Theo, would you mind standing in for me at church tonight? I might not get back in time."

"I-I-I guess so," I stammered, recalling the last time I got cajoled into serving as Arnie's fill-in.

"Relax. I'll leave notes on the pulpit about this weekend. You're more than capable of handling the usual prayer request time tonight. If I don't get back before that, ask Mary to use the time for a good old hymn request singalong."

Arnie returned his attention to Gus. "You and I have more to talk about. How about we let Mister Phillips mosey on out of here? We can grab lunch before we stop in to see Hal in his office."

LIDDY SET HER BAG down by the door and walked into the kitchen a little before five that afternoon. I had just placed two marinated chicken breasts in the oven and was stooped down in front of the open refrigerator door to collect salad fixings when Liddy sat down at the kitchen table, a coy look on her face. I juggled an armful of vegetables as I kneed the refrigerator door shut. Her coquettish look followed my every movement to the counter. Her hands rested on the table, fingers interlocked.

I grabbed a knife and the cutting board, and began chopping celery and carrots. Over my shoulder I said, "How'd your day go at school? How's Phoebe and John doing?"

Liddy bypassed my dithering line of questions. "Theo Phillips, I'll be happy to answer your patronizing questions after you answer mine."

"Pray tell, what's on your mind then?" I knew full well what she wanted to talk about.

Liddy left her seat at the table, soft hands extended as if she wanted an embrace. She then clamped her hands onto my cheeks as if she planned to apply Mister Spock's Vulcan mind meld on me. Her eyes measured mine. "You still can't tell me anything?"

"About Gus?" My head attempted to swivel against her firm grip. "No, not yet. I'm sorry."

She dropped her hands from my face and kissed me. Exasperated, she begged in a soulful whine, "You will tell me before whatever this is all about shows up in the paper or, even worse, someone else tells me?"

Still holding the knife over the cutting board, I smiled, leaned over, and kissed her forehead. "Promise. Now let me finish. Arnie asked me to lead the service tonight if he isn't back in time."

Liddy pursed her lips. "And you can't tell me why Arnie *might* miss tonight's service and why he asked you to step in for him?"

"Go sit down. Dinner won't be long."

Arnie called as I put dinner on the table. He assured me he'd try to be there before the service ended; the hardest part of his visit with the Archers appeared to be over. Arnie sounded relieved when he said Maddie proved to be a godsend after Gus' confession had infuriated Phillip, who'd stormed out of the room. He then explained that the clanking and clinking noise in the background was Maddie fixing the table for dinner so they could continue talking.

"Arnie, anything said about Pepper?"

"Right after Maddie calmed Phillip down and he returned to the room, Hank broached the question with Gus. It seemed Hank felt oddly relieved when Gus showed him his watch."

"And Hal? How has he been handling all this?"

Arnie paused for a brief moment. "He has said little. Hank and Phillip did most of the talking. If you ask me, he knew, or at the least surmised, the possibility that the rumors of Gus and his mother would come into the light someday. It wouldn't surprise me if Harold had said something to Hal before he'd died."

"Is it possible that's why Hal offered little resistance to Pepper's claims when she arrived in town?" I asked louder than I should have. Liddy's ears perked up.

"What's going on, Theo Phillips?" Liddy walked closer.

"I can hear Liddy. You haven't told her, have you?"

"No," I said as I felt Liddy breathing on my neck.

"You might as well. Liddy's relationship with Pepper might prove instrumental when Gus visits Pepper tomorrow. Think she'd go with us if I get Judy to sub for her at the school?"

Liddy whispered, "You can tell me the whole story after you hang up, but if he can get Judy to fill in for me, I'll go."

"Arnie, she'll go with you."

"Great. I'll tell Gus. There's a chance Phillip might be willing to go too. I'll call Marie tonight. Remember, just read the notes I left about Saturday night's Cooperative Fellowship Music Jamboree. I know you can handle the prayer time. Mary will do the rest. Thanks, Theo. I'll talk to you and your wife tomorrow."

Liddy stared at me as I hung up. "Can you explain now?"

"Sit down. I'll tell you all about it over dinner."

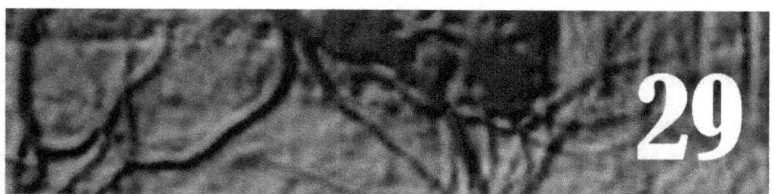

AT LEAST FOR TODAY, BALMY GULF BREEZES BROUGHT SOUTH Georgia a little reprieve from the sweltering heat wave. As a result, not long after Arnie picked up Liddy for their delicate meeting with Pepper at Marie's, I strolled into town. At the Elysium Emporium, Mandy motioned for me to come inside while I peeked at her display window.

"I haven't seen you since Jim's hospital stay," she said and walked from behind the counter. "Have you heard if they've identified Jim's attacker?"

"Not that I'm aware of. Mitch is still working on some leads."

"Well, I hope they catch whoever did it. Jay's been working himself silly at the lumber mill without Jim's help in the warehouse. Woogie's been a godsend, but he's not Jim."

"Woogie's a smart, hard worker, and strong as a mule, but I agree with you. He can't replace Jim's know-how."

Mandy all of a sudden beamed. "I want to show you something." She led me to the tabletop display in front of her store's bookshelves. "With the Independence Day Jubilee around the corner, I ordered extra copies of *Jessie's Story*. It's still hands-down the best selling book in the store. Would you mind signing these since you're here?"

"I'll be glad to, Mandy." After I had opened each book to the title page and added my illegible autograph, I said, "Listen to me. The reason these keep selling has nothing to do with me."

"I don't understand. Why would you say that?"

PURGATORY: A PROGENY'S QUEST

I pointed in the direction of Town Square. "Jessie's bronze memorial may lack its original luster but not his legacy." I placed my finger on Jessie Masterson's picture on the front cover of the last signed book. "It's been five-and-a-half years since this town lost Jessie. His exemplary story made the book possible. I merely had the honor of coming along for the ride."

"I never had the privilege of meeting him. But after I read your book, I felt as though I got to know him. Your book also gave me a deeper appreciation for this town's contagious, country-fried wholesomeness. I'm glad I moved here."

MARTHA YELLED OUT with a sarcastic smirk as soon as I walked into the *Sentinel* front office. "Dick Tracy's in his office waiting for you. Please help us get him to take a break from pursuing all these silly wild goose chases. We've got deadlines!"

"Where's Mary?"

Martha pointed to the breakroom.

"I'll see what I can do, but I've got to talk to Mary first." My crooked smile disintegrated Martha's curled-lip smirk. "Now that you look like the Martha I have come to love and adore, how's Mickey Waller working out for you?"

Martha's eyes lit up. "She isn't Tim, but she's a ball of laughs. She's going to work out just fine."

"Her mom seems like an awfully nice lady, too. I met her at the ER the other night when Jim got hurt. It's good to see new families moving to Shiloh."

Mary was seated at the breakroom picnic table staring at her notepad. I recognized her fretful, detached look. I had seen the same *oh my goodness, I think I'm going to be sick again* look more than once during both of Liddy's pregnancies many years ago.

T.M. BROWN

"How's the Editor-in-Chief today? Your mom thinks your father has left the reservation with Zeb's limo caper."

Mary forced a closed-lip, reluctant smile. "Good morning, Theo. At least I hope it's going to get better. My stomach is disagreeing with me this morning. I'm afraid to wander too far from the ladies room. On top of feeling like this, Dad dumped tomorrow's paper in my lap this morning."

I rested my hand on her shoulder. "This too shall pass, young lady. As far as your dad's Don Quixote quests, I'm afraid he'll always prefer to joust windmills. I'll see if I can get him to dismount his gallant steed long enough to roll up his sleeves and help you out. First, I have a personal favor to ask of you."

Mary looked up at me with a green-gilled plea. "Will it make me feel any better?"

"It might. Should you hear anything about Pepper and Phillip, I want you to sit on it for the time being."

"Anything particular about them?"

"Trust me on this. I promise I'll tell you later."

Mary did a double take but queasiness took over again. She took another sip of her Coke. "Okay, I'll let you know if I hear anything, but—"

"Well, there you are. Martha said you were here. What are you two cooking up? What's this about a promise?" Larry said when he walked into the breakroom.

I left my seat next to Mary and greeted Larry with a lighthearted chuckle. "Talking about promises, have you found out anything more about Zeb's limousine or Cyrus Riddell?"

Larry hesitated, examined Mary's doleful look, and then slapped my shoulder. "Come on into my office." He turned to Mary. "You don't look well, darlin'. If you need anything, call me. I need to talk to Theo about something."

Mary bit her lower lip and returned to her uneasy vigil studying her notepad.

Larry and I sat across from each other in front of his desk. "Tell me, have you heard more news from Mitch or Hal?"

"No, not yet. Why?"

"It took a little persistent digging, but I found out Cyrus Riddell has an interesting criminal past. He faced multiple racketeering charges in the Federal Court in New Orleans back in 2005. Katrina forced his trial to take place in Atlanta. The long and short of it is this: His high-dollar lawyer pulled a rabbit out of a hat and wrangled a reduced-sentence plea deal for money laundering. Cyrus got paroled after only five years in a medium-security Federal Correctional Facility in Altahama, Georgia."

I sank back in my chair. "So, this Cyrus character has a checkered past connected with organized crime?"

"Seems so."

"Can I have a copy of those articles and your notes? Mitch may already have similar information by now, but just in case."

"I thought you'd ask." He handed me a manila envelope from his desk. "Tell me, what's this about Pepper and Phillip? Something I need to know about?"

"Nope, not right now." I checked my watch. "I gotta run. Liddy's meeting me for lunch. I'll shoot straight over to talk with Mitch afterward." I waggled the envelope in front of me. "This should make for some mighty interesting conversation. I'll call you by tonight."

Larry held onto our handshake. "Did Arnie's absence last night have anything to do with anything?"

"I'll call you tonight."

THE UNDENIABLE VOICES of Cora and Barb cut through the babble of Bubba's busy lunch crowd when Liddy and Arnie sat across from me at the table with less-than-happy expressions. Cora swooped by with a pitcher of iced tea and two more glasses. She filled their glasses and topped mine off. "I'll be right back. Y'all take your time figurin' out what y'all wanna have today."

"I'm glad you two made it, but by your careworn faces I don't expect cheery news," I said to Arnie and Liddy.

Liddy eyed Arnie as he drank tea. He lowered his glass and then said, "I believe it'll be all good with Pepper, but she'll need a little time to process Gus' revelation. Even Marie felt unsettled by the news."

He looked at Liddy and smiled. "I gotta tell you though, I'm sure glad your wife volunteered to go with me. While she took a walk with Marie and Pepper, I got to speak alone with Phillip and Gus. Neither knew what to say when Pepper burst into a teary-eyed bout of confusion. One moment she seemed to accept the news and urged Gus to tell her more, but that only instigated another flood of tears."

Liddy tapped my forearm. "Pepper told Marie and me that she felt betrayed by her mother and, to some degree, Maude, too. She claimed as she got old enough to understand, her father's icy distance made her feel unwanted and illegitimate. She said Maude tried to explain his coldness had nothing to do with her, nor did Dixie's choice to virtually abandon her as she did. Pepper said she thought something was wrong with her."

"Understandably, more tears erupted when Gus confessed he didn't want to step in as her father. He said he had nothing to give her that she didn't already have," Arnie said.

Liddy chimed in, "At that point, Pepper sobbed the hardest and out of pent-up anger screamed at Gus: 'That's not true! You've filled in the blank my birth certificate failed to provide for seventeen years.' In utter disgust, she added she didn't want to be a burden on him or anyone else either, which brought tears to both Gus and Phillip. That's when Marie invited Pepper and me to go for a walk."

I began to speak when Mickey Waller walked up. "Excuse me, Mister Phillips. I hope I'm not interrupting y'all. Please forgive me. I wanted to say hello. That's my father seated over there. Is Pepper okay?"

I smiled at Mickey. "She's fine. Thanks for asking. Have you met Pastor Wright from Shiloh Baptist Church? And of course you know Miss Liddy."

Mickey shook Arnie's extended hand with a cute smile. "Glad to meet you, Pastor Wright." She then turned to Liddy. "Good to see you too, Missus Phillips."

"Have you and your parents started to attend a church in town?" I asked.

"When we do go, we're attending the Methodist church. I kinda like it there. Miss Thatcher and Coach Priestly go there as well," she explained.

Arnie said, "Doctor Matson is a fine preacher. Will your parents be going to the Music Jamboree Saturday night? Miss Thatcher will be singing."

"Yes, sir. I believe so."

"Has my little darlin' been talking your ear off?" Mister Waller stood behind his daughter wearing a starched blue oxford dress shirt with a solid navy tie. His athletic, youthful stature belied his years.

"Oh, no. Quite the contrary, Mickey and I are friends. I didn't think anyone could replace Tim Thompson, but Mickey sure is bound to be nearly as good," I said, chuckling and shaking hands.

"Mickey said you and your wife plan to be at the Jamboree out at Priestly Park Saturday night. We'd love it if you'd sit with us, Mister Waller," Liddy said with one of her inviting warm smiles.

"Please, I'm Roy. Vickie and I would enjoy that. We're still learning names and faces around town. Thank you. We'll be certain to look for you Saturday evening." He then guided Mickey toward the cash register.

Cora arrived at the head of the table. "I'm so sorry. I've been so busy today. What'd y'all like today?" After we ordered, Cora walked away shouting our order out to Cecil at the counter.

"How's Pepper doing? What about Gus and Phillip?" I asked.

"After Marie, Pepper, and I stepped back inside, Gus and Phillip asked Pepper to come back into town with them. The way Marie hugged Pepper, I have a hunch Pepper has found a new friend to confide in," Liddy said with a more promising smile.

"That's good news. So why the humdrum looks when you first walked in?" I asked.

"We talked on the drive here," Arnie said. "Liddy agrees there's still a lot in play with Pepper. We were concerned how she'll distill today's news and how it may play out with the changes about to happen within the Archer family. We figured it best to allow God to work on Pepper's heart as she adjusts and continues to settle into her new home and hometown."

After lunch, Liddy and I left Bubba's in our vehicle right after Arnie drove off to the church. I broke the news to Liddy about what Larry discovered regarding Cyrus Riddell's past, which displaced her lingering concerns for Pepper by the time we stopped at City Hall before going home.

HILLARY STEPPED OUT of Hal's office when we arrived. "Hal's not here. He left about an hour ago headed to the house."

PURGATORY: A PROGENY'S QUEST

"I suspected as much. Liddy said Phillip called this morning after they met with Pepper." I noticed the folder on Hillary's desk. "Did Mitch find out more about Cyrus Riddell?"

Hillary showed me the file Mitch had given Hal earlier that morning. "Hal said you may be interested in seeing this anyway."

I found much of the same information Larry had shared, but Mitch possessed the complete rap sheet: Riddell's criminal record also included a misdemeanor reckless endangerment conviction as a teenager, a dishonorable discharge from the Army, and he'd served nine months in the Orleans Parish jail for assault and battery. Mitch's notes included a circled, handwritten comment: Considered armed and dangerous.

Clipped to the front inside flap, Mitch included a copy of the Cassandra Davis certificate of parole from the East Central Georgia Residential Substance Abuse Treatment Center, dated February 3, 2011. A yellow sticky note read Savannah Department of Community Supervision.

Uttering the facts like Joe Friday from *Dragnet*, I said, "Cyrus Riddell appears to be a nasty fella. I'm afraid the Shiloh Police force is ill-equipped to deal with someone with a track record like his. Cassie appears to be on parole, and it looks as though Mitch has reached out to her parole officer in Savannah to find out more." In my heart, I prayed both of them had decided to vamoose to parts unknown.

Liddy shared her nervous look with Hillary. "This has been a long, trying day. Hilly, will you let me know how things went out at the Archer house?"

"Of course."

I handed the folder back to Hillary. "Let Hal know I saw this. I'm sure we'll talk more tomorrow."

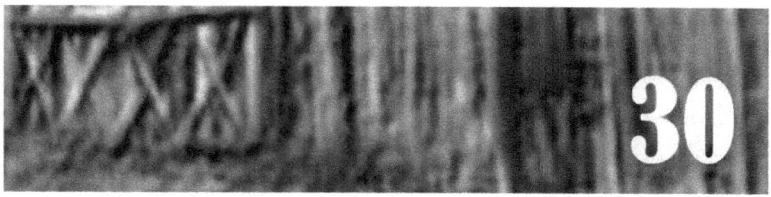

A LITTLE BEFORE DAYBREAK ON FRIDAY, THE TIFFANY READING lamp beside me illuminated my cozy confines as the first hints of dawn's arrival cast a ghostlike grayness beyond the bay windows. The passage atop this day's journal page came from Proverbs: *Good people detest the darkness of evil; the wicked abhor the light of goodness.* The relevance struck a chord within me so beneath the passage I wrote about my previous discussion with Pepper about Purgatory.

Everyone awakens each new day facing the relentless push and pull between right and wrong, good versus bad, light versus dark, and love versus hate. The conflicts within test our mettle. Without God's grace, no one can muster the strength, stamina, or stalwartness to resist evil's lure.

For this reason, I believe Purgatory is not some ethereal afterworld abode created to purify souls from a vast array of forgivable venial sins, as some religious traditions promote. The light of life is required to conquer the darkness of evil that invades each of us during our birth-to-death lifespan. I paused and contemplated my feelings toward Gus, Hank, Wilson, and even Dixie. I added: *Forgiveness demands no retreat, no regret, no reserve.*

Before I could respond to the phone ringing, Liddy yelled from our bedroom, "It's for you, hun. Larry. He sounds upset."

"Hate to bother you this early in the morning. Sheriff's Department reported a body found in Shiloh Creek downstream from the bridge that leads to Marie and John's place."

"A body? Who? What else did they say?"

"Don't know more. Can you finish your coffee on the way?"

Liddy stood next to me wearing only a nightshirt, rubbing sleep from her eyes. I stared at her bewildered expression. I cupped my hand over the phone and said, "Hun, think you can get Phoebe to pick you up this morning? I need to drive out to Old Mill Road. A body was discovered in the creek near John and Marie's place."

Liddy bobbed her head as she swept her hair off her face.

"Larry, I'll get right out there."

"Okay. Call me as soon as you find out what happened. No one's gonna intentionally drown in Shiloh Creek."

LESS THAN A hundred yards downstream from where Marie's gravel access road crossed Shiloh Creek over the decades old, rusted steel-and-timber decked one lane bridge, flashing emergency lights lit up both sides of Old Mill Road. Mitch stood amongst a cadre of law enforcement officers huddled near his white pickup. His vehicle's seldom-needed rooftop blue emergency lights and red taillights flashed smack dab in the middle of all the commotion.

Four Adams County EMS personnel muscled the corpse, now wrapped in a yellow tarp and strapped onto a red bodyboard, up the steep overgrown embankment. Yellow plastic tape cordoned off the area where the body was found.

Ringo sprawled at his feet, John Priestly leaned against Mitch's hood, arms folded. He had on a gray t-shirt, faded jeans, and sandals; peppered dark brown hair, uncombed and mussed.

John looked up and dropped his arms by his side. "Theo, what—or should I say who—brought you out here?"

"Larry, of course," I said, echoing the tone of John's tongue-in-cheek inquiry. "What can you tell me?"

"About five this morning, Ringo wanted to go out. Not five minutes after I let him out, I heard him howling down in the woods near the creek bed. I figured I better get him back inside before he woke Marie up in the main house. But he wouldn't respond to my whistle nor when I called his name. So I sensed something had to be wrong."

John pointed to the red flag stuck in the mud on the other side. "I found him on our side of the creek right over there. I waded into the creek as soon as I realized what Ringo got so riled up about. A man's body floated face down wedged in the shallows between those rocks. I liked to have jumped clean out of my skin when I rolled him over and saw the bullet hole in the side of his head. His eyes stared right at me. After I got my wits back, I dragged his body to the bank and hightailed it to call 9-1-1. By the time I returned, Mitch had already pulled up with a Sheriff's deputy's vehicle right behind him."

"Any idea who he was?"

"Never seen him before. Not that I wanted to stare at a dead man's face any more than I had already. Mitch told me he thought the body had not been in the water for more than three or four hours. That's about what I told three different officers who asked me pretty much the same questions as you."

Mitch tossed a clipboard through the open driver-side window onto his seat. He appeared relieved to be free from the GBI and the Sheriff's Department investigators. He joined John and me at the front of his vehicle. "Mister Phillips, I'm glad to see another friendly face out here. I presume you are here as a curious reporter for the *Sentinel*."

"John told me you got here first. I'm impressed."

Mitch said with a taut expression, "Tyler woke me at one-thirty to tell me a silver Chrysler 300 with Louisiana tags cruised through town. Said the front seat passenger could've been Cyrus

Riddell, and he noted a dark-haired woman in the back. He couldn't get a clear look at the driver. I asked if they had broken any traffic laws or gave any other reason to pull them over. He said no. I told him to call me if they continued to linger around town. But..."

Mitch paused. "The hair on the back of my neck bristled the more I thought about it. I sipped on a cup of coffee a little after four this morning sitting in my truck watching the Shiloh Lumber Mill. When the 9-1-1 dispatch came across the radio, I radioed Tyler that I'd respond and he should remain in town."

"Any idea who this guy might've been? Any connection to Tyler's call about the out-of-state vehicle that went through town?" The hairs on the back of my own neck stiffened.

"This is an ongoing investigation. I can't officially give you much more at this time."

John stared at Mitch with a tired smirk. "Then, off the record, can you tell the guy who found the body something? Did the wallet you guys pulled from his pants verify he had, by any chance, an out-of-state license?"

Mitch's hardened look relaxed enough to muster a sly grin. "I can't deny the possibility, but I can't confirm it either. I can tell you the GBI boys are running a background check on him right now. Look, as soon as I know something more, I promise I'll make sure you know."

Hank pulled his black pickup alongside Mitch's truck; Hal hopped out from the passenger side, deep furrows across his forehead. "Mitch, how's it going? How long before you guys know what happened and who this guy might have been?"

Mitch directed Hal toward the back of Hank's truck. While the two spoke for a few minutes, I knelt and petted Ringo. John knelt beside me and said, "Whoever this guy was and wherever he came from, he had interesting tattoos on his forearms and fingers.

By the expensive clothes he had on, I'd say he definitely wasn't from this neck of the woods."

As Hal walked toward us I heard him say to Mitch, "Call me as soon as you learn more about this Nawlins fella." Hal's crow's feet dug deeper into the sides of his face, and his jowls pulled at the corners of his mouth. "John, I hear we need to thank Ringo for getting us all out of bed so early."

"Heck, Hal, Ringo's still trying to figure out what all the commotion is about. In the meantime, the two of us are walking back to the cabin for some breakfast before I try to grab a nap." Ringo waggled his tail after John slapped the side of his leg. "You're welcome to join Ringo and me for some grits and eggs if you'd like. Unless you need me for anything else, I'm outta here."

"Wait a second. I'll drive you and Ringo. A cup of coffee sounds good to me," I said as I watched the EMS vehicle pull a slow U-turn on Old Mill Road. The driver turned off the emergency lights.

I glanced at Hal. "How about letting me know if you can share any news about this later? You know Larry's gonna haunt me until I give him something to put in the paper. A dead body doesn't show up in Shiloh Creek every day."

Hal forced an approving grin. "Sure." He grabbed my arm. "Thought you ought to know, I think we're going to be able to come to terms with the fact Gus genuinely did love our mother, and Phillip and Pepper should not feel any less of an Archer than Hank or me. We've got more to discuss, but I want to thank you for handling this delicate matter as you have. You're a good friend. We won't ever forget it."

"Thanks, Hal. I appreciate that. Your father would be smiling right now. We'll talk later. I need to run John and Ringo back to his house." Hank looked up from behind his steering wheel. We exchanged tired, half-hearted grins.

PURGATORY: A PROGENY'S QUEST

Hal yelled as I walked to my vehicle, "See you and Miss Liddy tomorrow night. We all are going to need some good music and laughter after this wraps up. Besides, there's rumor of a surprise guest we'll all enjoy."

Mitch climbed into his truck, turned off his overhead blue lights and emergency flashers, and stared at his clipboard.

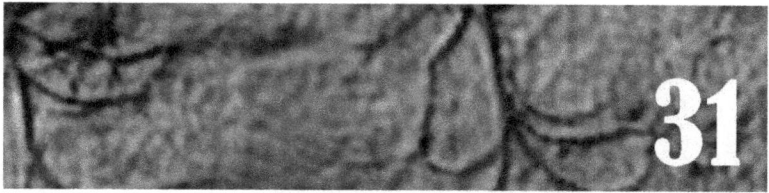

"I STILL CAN'T GET OVER THE FACT YOU ACTUALLY SAW THE DEAD BODY they hauled out of the creek," Liddy said, propped on her elbows in bed as I exited the bathroom before dawn Saturday.

"Like I told you yesterday. The EMS team had him wrapped in a yellow tarp and strapped down by the time I got there."

"But who was he? Did John tell you anything?"

"Liddy, I told you everything John shared with me, pretty much word for word."

"Poor John. The thought of him looking at that poor man's face. It kept me awake most of the night," Liddy said, then swung her legs out from under the sheets and climbed out of bed.

"I'll go make coffee. I've got a weird gut feeling that Mitch, Hal, and I all share similar concerns about who this guy might've been." I headed to the kitchen.

A few moments later, Liddy pulled her hair into a ponytail and was about to sit in her armchair. "Hun, Mickey's coming up the street. Will you fetch the paper? I'd like to see the Jamboree schedule for tonight. I'm curious who the special guest might be."

Mickey brought her bike to a screeching stop and popped her kickstand. "Good morning, Mister Phillips." She ran up the walkway with our morning paper. "Hope you don't mind. I overheard my mom and dad talking last night. What do you know about the dead guy the police dragged out of Shiloh Creek? Is it true he'd been shot?"

PURGATORY: A PROGENY'S QUEST

"Easy goes it, young lady. The authorities are still trying to sort out what happened. In the meantime, what you heard last night, unfortunately, is pretty much true."

"Holy smokes. Attempted car thefts, some dude toting a gun and chasing after Woogie, Mister Adams assaulted in his own backyard, and now a stranger shot dead. I thought when we moved from Birmingham things would be a lot safer in Shiloh."

"I wouldn't exactly call Shiloh crime-ridden either. We've got more than our fair share of honest-to-goodness law-abiding folks around here, and the town's police department is more than capable of keeping us all safe."

Mickey sighed. "Yes, sir. It's still pretty scary, though. Don't you think?"

I removed the paper's pull-out about tonight's musical event. "Now this is exciting, good news." I slapped the full-color advertisement. "Remind your parents to find us. We'll save y'all a seat."

"Thanks, Mister Phillips. See ya tonight." In one continuous motion, she swung her leg over the bike, snapped the kickstand up, and pedaled off.

Liddy cleared the breakfast dishes from the table while I lounged in our hammock on the porch. The *Sentinel* contained a cut-and-dried writeup—two paragraphs tucked below the fold on page three—about the body found in Shiloh Creek. Mary excluded specific details about the crime scene. She stated the still-unidentified victim was from out of state according to unnamed sources close to the investigation. Larry insisted yesterday, when I called in the facts as I knew them, that we should identify him as being from Louisiana, but Mary overruled her father. I argued in Mary's favor and promised that Mitch would tell us more about the victim's identity after they ran his driver's license information through GBI's database.

Pete's vermillion pickup roared into the driveway a little before ten. He hopped out of the driver's side and hustled to the front passenger door to reach up and help Mary climb out.

"Quit your fussing. I can still climb out of this rig on my own," Mary pouted, swatting Pete's hands, but then grabbed ahold of his hand anyway to step off the truck's chrome running board.

"Mister P, we didn't wake you from a catnap, did we?" Pete asked with his usual burly jovial charm.

"Nope. I was just reading the morning paper." I looked at Mary stepping onto the porch ahead of Pete. "It appears after our heated conversation with your father, you prevailed. I know Mitch wants to keep a lid on this until the investigators get a better handle on who this guy was and why he ended up face-down in Shiloh Creek."

Quite serious but looking well-pleased, Mary said, "There are moments like this when he regrets making me Editor-in-Chief."

"I, for one, am glad. There's no sense scaring the townspeople unnecessarily. It's bad enough the guy was found in Shiloh Creek, but to give too much detail without all the facts wouldn't have been helpful either."

Liddy opened our glass storm door. "Feeling any better? Theo told me you've been experiencing a little morning sickness."

Mary grimaced. "Yes, ma'am. It comes and goes. I now understand why it's called *morning* sickness."

Liddy pointed to the nearby rocker. "Sit down, young lady. Queasiness during your first few weeks is quite normal and actually a good sign."

"We stopped by to tell you that Mitch visited the office yesterday afternoon. An Adams County deputy had responded to a call from Megan's parents. A silver Chrysler 300 bearing Louisiana plates had been found smack in the middle of Mister Miller's pecan orchard. After they ran the plates, they found out

PURGATORY: A PROGENY'S QUEST

the car was registered to a Bayou Royale Trading Company in New Orleans. Mitch hadn't heard anything more about the victim's identity, but he insinuated the victim and Cyrus Riddell likely knew of each other. What do you think, Theo?"

I eyed Liddy's arched eyebrow. "Mary, it wouldn't surprise me in the least. I doubt your father would disagree also."

Pete shook his head. "Mister P, I don't get it. Mister Scribner's convinced a bunch of Russian mobsters are behind all that's been happening since the car showed up. Is that even possible? Organized crime right here in Shiloh? That doesn't compute to my way of thinking."

"I wouldn't quite put it that way," I said, though my gut began to knot up. "Look, the dead guy may well have shot himself. Lord knows why, but we can't rule it out. Let's not get ahead of the investigation. They've got a whole lot more tools at their disposal than even Mitch and Mary's father seem to have."

Mary eyed me with an inquisitive gaze. "Dad called *The Times-Picayune* this morning and found out a few things about the Bayou Royale Trading Company. It appears to have been a legit, family-owned enterprise with its main office at the Port of Orleans. After nearly fifty years as a thriving business, a private foreign trading conglomerate bought the company two years ago from the sons of the founder not long after he passed away."

"There you go. The company sounds legit to me. Let's remember we're not writing a Hollywood murder script," I said as a brief chuckle surfaced. "Pete, why don't you take Mary home so she'll be rested up for tonight?" I looked at Mary's feeble smile. "You're playing and singing tonight, right?"

Mary's wrinkled forehead relaxed. "You're right. Tonight will be a great way to get our minds freed up from all this cloak-and-dagger intrigue." She squeezed Pete's fingers. "Help me up. We've taken up enough of Theo and Liddy's Saturday morning."

Liddy wrapped her arm around my waist after we waved goodbye from the porch. "You're a bit worried, aren't you? You can't fool me, Theodore Phillips."

"Let's go see what time the Braves game starts," I said, and kissed Liddy on her forehead. "Why don't you call Marie and invite her and Pepper for dinner before we go out tonight?"

PHILLIP PULLED HIS Wrangler in behind Marie's pickup while I stood on our deck firing up the grill. Pepper got out and waved. Phillip honked as he backed out and began to pull away.

"What's for dinner, Mister Phillips?" Pepper leaned nearer to the open grill-top. Her braided hair and freckled cheeks were accented by the amber glow of the late afternoon sun hanging low on the horizon. Otherwise, she looked every inch like any other teenager in her blue sleeveless top tucked into a pair of jean shorts. The one exception: Maude's rosary threaded loosely through her belt loops with its crucifix dangling over her right front pocket.

"I'm about to throw on some of my special burgers. How's that sound? Liddy's also whipped up some of her potato salad."

"Sounds good to me. What makes your hamburgers special?"

"I added some Cajun seasoning when I made the patties. I thought you'd like that. Besides, I happen to know Miss Marie likes them that way, too."

"Yummy. Can I help?"

"Come on in. Let's see what the ladies are up to. This grill is about ready to cook some burgers."

Marie was topping off a bowl of banana pudding with banana slices and vanilla wafers when Pepper and I walked in the side kitchen door. Liddy grabbed a dish towel to wipe her hands. "We heard you outside, but as you can see, Marie and I had our hands pretty full getting dinner ready."

I grabbed the platter of seasoned burgers for the grill. "Pepper's eager to help, too."

"Yes, ma'am. What can I help y'all with?"

Liddy looked at Pepper's outfit. "How about you set the table? Dishes and silverware are already over there on the buffet." Liddy glanced at Marie. "Doesn't Pepper look nice? Are Tim and Woogie meeting up with you tonight?"

Pepper's dimples sank deeper into her reddening freckled cheeks. Marie said amidst giggles, "Lord have mercy, I wish I had looked that cute at her age. You best remind them boys who your brothers are."

THE CLOCK HAD struck six when the doorbell rang. Liddy had just grabbed our dirty dishes. "Will you get that, Theo?"

I opened the glass door and motioned for Tim, Woogie, and Mickey to come on in. "Marie, think there's enough of your banana pudding for these three?"

Pepper jumped up. "How'd you know I'd be here?"

Tim said, "I called your house and Hank told me. Hope you don't mind, Missus P."

Liddy yelled from the kitchen, "For heaven's sake, no. We've got plenty. Grab a chair. Theo can drive us all over to the festival after we enjoy some dessert."

Woogie said, "I heard there's going to be some music in the Community Center for us older kids."

"That's what I heard, but I'm afraid I don't know more," I said.

Tim said, "We saw Brent Cody's van and trailer pull into Priestly Park. They were off-loading equipment at the Community Center when dad drove me over to Woogie's house."

"I TOLD YOU we should've gotten here a little early," Liddy said with a told-you-so sigh. Before I turned off the ignition, our younger passengers, full of banana pudding, piled out. The unmistakable sound of the Gaither Vocal Band blasted from speakers around the park. Before the teenagers dashed off, Mickey told Liddy and me her folks had promised to look for us. Without another word, they weaved through the maze of parked vehicles toward the Betty Priestly Community Center.

I took Liddy and Marie's hands and we walked to the portable aluminum bleachers adjacent the pavilion's canopy. The vast majority of the folding chairs near the makeshift stage under the canopy had already appeared spoken for, with plenty of others vying for the few remaining vacant seats. The sight of all the folks milling about earned another told-you-so sigh and an elbow to my rib cage from Liddy. At the far end of the park, the Community Center's parking area gave every indication the news about Brent Cody singing for the youth had spread like wildfire.

Pete and his brother Andy joined us from behind the stage. I greeted Andy, who was cradling Jessie in his arms. "Megan performing tonight?"

"Yes, sir. Mary insisted, but she's pretty nervous. I know she's got a pretty voice, but she's not exactly comfortable singing in front of an audience. Phoebe, Mary, and Megan will be done pretty early. Can you save us those seats behind you?"

Liddy smiled. "If you let Marie and me watch Jessie for you."

Andy lowered Jessie into Marie's waiting arms. Liddy moved to the bleacher row above where we were seated to honor her obligation, but she nestled in right behind Marie and Jessie.

The Thompsons and Wallers waved as they broke from between the parked cars. I said, "Glad you're here. There's going to be standing room only by the time the show starts. We need to save those places beside Liddy for some of our friends, but there should be enough room for y'all."

Vickie Waller leaned over and shook my hand. "Thank you. You think Mickey'll be fine going off with her new friends?"

"Don't fret none. They'll take good care of her." I pointed to the Community Center. "Pepper and the boys agreed to find us as soon as their concert gets over."

In South Georgia, the sun didn't set much before nine in late June, so at eight o'clock the early music ensembles sweltered with everyone else. Some relief came when a slight breeze swept across from Shiloh Creek at the bottom of the hill below the pavilion.

Not long after the sun disappeared and the park lights took over, Hal took the stage to introduce the finale. "Friends, before I introduce our special guest tonight, how about a round of applause for all the local talent who have entertained us thus far this evening."

After the applause subsided, he said. "By the sound of it, the youngsters are enjoying Brent Cody and his band down in the Community Center as well. What do y'all think?" More applause erupted as Hank joined Hal on the stage. "I'm going to ask my brother Hank to introduce our final performer tonight."

Hank's wrinkled smile struggled all the more as he fumbled with the microphone. You would have thought Hal handed him a Jedi sword the way he looked at it when a loud squelch echoed from the sound system before he realized it was already on.

Hank said, "Folks, a good friend of mine who I met quite a few months ago happened to be traveling through on his way to Tallahassee for a scheduled performance at the University. When he heard what we had planned, he asked if he could take part. Ladies and gentlemen, I'd like to present, my friend and a damn good old-fashioned country troubadour, Mister Dave Jackson."

The audience stood as Dave walked onto the stage gripping his guitar. Hank pulled a stool out from behind a speaker for Dave to use onstage. For the good part of forty-five minutes, Dave Jackson's velvety baritone serenaded us. He ended with his trademark song, *By God, I'm Just a Good Ol' Country Boy*. When he finished, he bear-hugged Hank and shook Hal's hand. The applause seemed to never end.

Hal put his hands high above his head and said, "Thanks to all y'all for coming tonight. As you leave, there are several folks with white buckets. Please leave your donations for the Shiloh Cooperative Fellowship with them."

Andy started to grab Jessie from Marie's arms until Megan said, "Hold on a sec. Marie, would you like to come over tomorrow after church and spend the day with us? We could use someone to watch Jessie while we take care of some needed chores around the house."

Marie beamed, nodded, and then kissed Jessie before handing him to Andy.

I looked at Mary. "Did you know about Dave Jackson and Brent Cody?"

She glanced over at Hillary holding Hal's hand by the stage. With a smug grin, Mary said, "There are some secrets us gals can keep when it suits us."

Pete wrapped his arm around Mary. "We need to vamoose. You gotta be at church early in the morning."

"I wonder where the kids are?" I asked, looking toward the Community Center. "Their concert ended before Dave Jackson finished his set."

Vickie Waller grabbed her husband's hand. "Something's wrong." She pointed to Mickey and Tim running like scared rabbits straight for us, tears racing down Mickey's face. Tim tried to catch his breath as he bent over, hands on knees.

"They've been kidnapped," he gasped. "Someone stole Mister Adams' fancy car. Woogie and Pepper are in the backseat."

"Who drove off with Mister Adams' limousine?" I crouched down to capture Tim's attention.

"I don't know, sir," he said, still gasping. "I couldn't see who was in the front seat. All I could see was Pepper and Woogie looking out the back window."

Mitch pulled up and jumped out of his truck. "What happened?"

"Zeb's limo got stolen from the lumber mill garage. For some cockamamie reason, Pepper and Woogie were in it when it was driven off."

Mitch asked, "Which direction did the car head when it left the mill property? Think son! We need to act quick!"

Tim looked in the direction of the lumber mill and raised his arm to point. "It went toward the school, I think."

Mitch got on his radio and issued orders to Tyler.

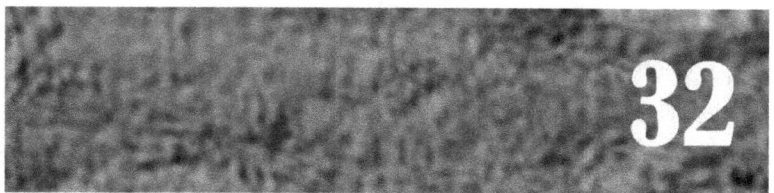

A CURIOUS CROWD GREW IN THE WAKE OF TIM AND MICKEY'S hysterical arrival. Many had begun heading to their vehicles by the time the commotion caught up to them. Even Dave Jackson stood beside Hank among the growing throng of onlookers until Mitch got riled and asked for help to disperse the swelling audience pressing closer with each breath. Joe Arians, John Priestly, and Pete Simmons attempted to encourage everyone to get far enough back so Mitch could do his job. Hal offered to open the Community Center as Tim and Mickey, along with their parents, reached the verge of coming unglued emotionally with so many eyes glaring at them.

Mitch barked, "Please! Get everyone back. I can't hear a word these kids are saying. Every minute we waste is costing valuable time. We need as much information as we can to locate that vehicle and, more importantly, Pepper and Woogie as fast as we can." He turned his attention to Tim's and Mickey's parents. "I know your kids are upset, but I need to talk to them. I need to know everything that happened."

Mitch eyed Liddy and me. I sensed he wanted our help to distract their parents while he interviewed Tim and Mickey. Liddy put her arms around Hannah Thompson and Vickie Wallers. I said, "Let's get out of Mitch's way. The quicker he can finish interviewing your kids, the sooner you can talk to them and find out what happened." We directed the anxious parents to take a seat on the front row of the nearby bleachers.

Heads turned the moment Tyler pulled up beside Mitch's truck, blue lights flashing. "Mitch, I did what you asked. Sheriff ordered patrol cars dispatched to all major intersections and issued an APB on the vehicle. I don't think there's any way they can get very far driving such a recognizable vehicle."

Camille stepped out from the passenger seat of Tyler's vehicle. "I just spoke with Mister Adams. Jay and Jim went to the lumber mill to secure the gate as you asked. He assured me they will not do anything more than secure the area and prevent anyone beyond the gate until we or one of the Sheriff's deputies arrive."

"Good job, Camille. Tyler, why don't you head straight over to the lumber mill and make certain no one, and I mean no one, enters that lot. That definitely also includes the Adams brothers. It's a crime scene until further notice. I'll be there as fast as I can."

"Yes, sir. I'm on it." Tyler jumped back into his patrol truck, executed a swift U-turn around Mitch's vehicle, and raced out of the parking lot, kicking up dust and gravel as he fishtailed.

Mitch motioned for Camille. "Please take Mickey over there." He pointed to the stage area at the pavilion. "Get her statement about what she saw and heard. Write down even the slightest details. I'm going to do the same with Tim."

Roy Waller eyed his wife's fretful look. "Mister Johnson, please, can we be with our daughter?"

"Of course, but please don't get in the way. Miss Gaines needs your daughter's undivided attention for the next few minutes."

John Priestly and Phoebe joined the Wallers on bleachers near the stage and engaged them in conversation while Camille sat Mickey on the edge of the stage with her back to the bleachers. Vickie Waller's husband kept his arm draped over her shoulder. Vickie's head swiveled between the stage and John and Phoebe while talking with them.

Liddy and I sat next to Ben and Hannah Thompson. Fortunately, they seemed far calmer as they listened without flinching to every word exchanged between Mitch and Tim. Mitch had positioned Tim on his tailgate and kept Tim's focus on him, not his parents. "Tim, this is important. Start with how you four wound up going to the lumber mill in the first place. I need you to walk through everything you saw, heard, and did. No detail is too small. Got it?"

"Yes, sir. I'll...do my best." Tim wiped sweat from his face.

Mitch stared at Tim and rested his hand on Tim's shoulder. "Tell me what you remember."

"Well, Pepper asked if we had ever been inside of Mister Adams' limo. We told her we had sat in it a couple of times when we worked together at the lumber mill. Pepper asked if we could take her to see it. We figured it would only take us a few minutes to run over to the lumber mill and show it to her and Mickey." Tim pointed in the direction of Shiloh Lumber Mill and then peeked at his dad's unsmiling glare. "I know we shouldn't have left the concert and gone over there."

Mitch glared at Tim until his focus turned back from his dad and mom. "Then what?"

"We knew the four of us could squeeze between the gate and the fence post. Jay had a habit of allowing a little slack in the chain when he locked up at night. The heavy chain and padlock is enough to keep most folks and vehicles out, but we knew better. When we got inside the warehouse, Woogie told me to stay with Mickey while he and Pepper climbed up into the rafters.

"When we were working at the lumber mill Woogie showed me how to climb into the locked garage that way. They snaked their way through the ceiling joists above and beyond where the wall separates the warehouse from the garage on the other side. Once on the garage side, he only needed to lift a drop ceiling panel and hop down onto the storage roof above the mechanical room. He promised to let Mickey and me in through the steel door that could only be unlocked from the inside of the garage."

"Why didn't he have Pepper wait with you?" Mitch asked.

"Pepper can be pretty insistent when she has her mind set on showing us she can do something."

Mitch cracked a momentary, wrinkled smile, as did Liddy, but she hastily clamped her hand over her mouth. Tim continued.

"Right after Woogie and Pepper made it into the garage, a flashlight shined outside. We heard hushed voices. Woogie unlocked the garage door as he promised but told us to go hide in the warehouse. I grabbed Mickey's hand, and we hid behind a stack of lumber. The sound of glass breaking caused Mickey to duck down, but I snuck to the door and whispered to Woogie. He remained crouched down at the partially open door and tried to get Pepper's attention, but she slipped into the car's backseat, leaving the rear passenger door open. Woogie shushed me before he pulled the garage door closed.

"I stayed by the door but almost ran when I heard the steel entry door inside the garage get pried open. I clearly heard two sets of footsteps enter the garage.

"Then I heard the guy grumble as the vehicle's doors were slammed shut while the other person tugged on the chain that hoisted the overhead door. I heard the woman tell the guy to hurry and start the car. The guy got into the driver's seat and cussed up a storm when the car's ignition would not turn over after trying twice. When the engine finally started, the driver shouted a few more cuss words before he revved the engine and drove out of the garage."

Tim paused too long, so Mitch got him started again. "Did you hear either of them say anything more?"

"Yeah. Outside of a lot of cuss words I'd rather not repeat, the driver said something like 'That old man could've at least put some gas in the tank. This piece of junk is darn near empty.'"

That's when I realized for sure the other person was a woman because I heard her ask, 'How are we gonna get beyond the gate?' The driver laughed. She climbed in. And they pulled out of the garage. I grabbed Mickey and we ran outside the warehouse and watched Mister Adams' limousine speed off. The padlock and chain snapped clean off as the gate flew off its hinges. I ran fast as I could to the street when the car's brake lights lit up down the road out front of the old cotton gin. The woman opened the front passenger door and then got into another car and followed the limousine. That's when I saw Pepper's head in the rear window."

"How do you know it was Pepper you saw?"

"When the woman got out, the inside lights came on. That was Pepper alright. I wasn't sure about Woogie until Mickey ran up. She told me she checked the garage, and both were missing."

"What did you do next?"

"I grabbed Mickey by the hand and we ran as fast as we could until we got back here."

"Is there anything else you can remember?"

"Yes, sir. Pretty sure they were the same ones we hid from out at the mansion a couple of weeks ago. Kinda hard to forget the man's voice. Why would they kidnap Pepper and Woogie?"

"I'm not exactly certain. I'd guess the guy and his companion didn't realize they had ducked into the backseat until they drove off." Mitch jotted down a couple of notes and then eyed Tim's parents. "Mister and Missus Thompson, why don't you take your son on home. Don't be too hard on him. Sounds to me like an innocent adventure that backfired."

Mitch mussed Tim's already scraggly hair and allowed him to hop off the tailgate. Camille walked up beside Mitch. "I've got Mickey Waller's story. Sounds like a rather wild tale. I guess they chose the wrong opportunity to sneak into the warehouse to take a peek at Zeb's limo. It also sounds as though Pepper and Woogie had the misfortune of choosing the wrong place to hide when our suspects broke into the garage."

"My take as well. We've got a long night ahead. You and I need to get back to the office after we visit Wilson Edwards. I need to tell him what happened with Woogie, and then I'll check on Tyler. In the meantime, let's hope this couple makes a mistake. It's possible they'll get picked up before they leave the county."

Mitch turned his attention to us. "I know this won't be easy for you, but the best thing you can do is go home and get a good night's sleep. Let's hope we'll catch a break by morning and have them two young'uns back home with their parents for breakfast."

I squeezed Liddy's waist. "Let's allow Mitch to do his job. We'll only be in the way." I then said to Mitch. "If you need anything or have any good news—"

"Go home. I appreciate all you've done and understand your particular interest with all this."

Hal drove up with Hank and Phoebe in his truck. "We'll meet you at City Hall. We'll stop over to see Wilson Edwards. You go on and head straight over to the lumber mill. There'll be no sleep for any of us until those kids are safe and sound."

The set of Hank's jaw made it clear he agreed. He grumbled from the backseat and slapped Hal's headrest. "Sitting here jabber-jawing ain't gonna find our sister or Woogie. Let's get."

Hal looked at us with a what-else-can-I-do expression. "Call you in the morning, if not sooner."

John pulled up beside our vehicle with Phoebe and Marie in his truck as the Wallers drove off. Marie looked out her open rear window with a half-hearted, tuckered-out smile. "Y'all mind some company? I don't know who's gonna get any sleep tonight."

Liddy didn't hesitate. "I'll have coffee ready in fifteen minutes. We could use the company."

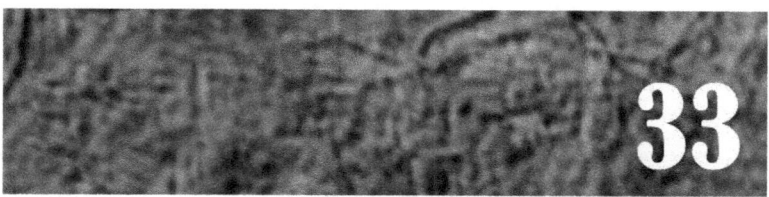

THE DOORBELL RANG THREE TIMES, FOLLOWED BY PERSISTENT rapping on the front door. What little sleep I had managed to get abruptly ended. I fumbled in the darkness and slipped on pants and flip-flops.

"What time is it?" Liddy mumbled.

"It's four-thirty. Stay in bed."

John plodded down the stairs from the guest bedroom and met me in the living room. "It's Hank Archer; truck's out front."

I flipped on the porch light, opened the front door, and unlatched the glass storm door.

"Sorry to wake y'all, but Hal's beyond frustrated. The Sheriff reported none of his patrols have turned up anything to help us find the kids or that blasted limo. They've pulled over every vehicle that even resembles the description of Cyrus Riddell's other vehicle as well. Hal and Mitch have concluded they must be holed up somewhere just outside of town."

John wiped his eyes. "Why do they think that?"

"When Mitch interviewed Zeb and his sons late last night, they confirmed Tim's account indicating the limo needed to find a filling station pretty darn quick. The red line on the ol' gas guzzler's fuel gauge tickled the E when Jay parked it at the lumber mill. He hadn't bothered to put any gas in it since then."

"Who's at the door?" Liddy asked, adjusting her robe in the hallway shadows.

"It's Hank."

PURGATORY: A PROGENY'S QUEST

"Well, let him inside. The three of you don't need to stand in the doorway." Liddy peeked over her shoulder. "Besides, Marie and Phoebe are coming downstairs anyway."

I turned on the foyer's overhead light. Hank squinted his dog-tired bloodshot eyes when he stepped inside. His long face made it clear he had managed even less sleep than we had squeaked in.

"Miss Liddy, I'm sorry to wake everyone. None of us are getting much rest until those kids are found and back safe."

Liddy pursed her lips. "Don't fret, Hank. We understand. So, what exactly do Hal and Mitch want us to do?"

"Mitch decided to organize search parties to scour every conceivable road within ten or so miles of town. He figures they could not have risked driving the limo any further. The Sheriff's deputies can't possibly cover all the back roads and possible places where they may have stashed the vehicle. He's convinced it's definitely Cyrus Riddell we're looking for, which also means Cassie Davis is likely the woman with him. She's familiar with all the out-of-the-way places they might be able to hide out. Hal's banking on the fact Cassie won't allow Cyrus to harm the kids, especially Woogie. But he also doesn't think Cyrus will let the kids go free until after they can make a safe getaway."

"That's a lot of speculating," John said.

"I agree," Hank said. "That's why Mitch asked me to fetch you and a bunch of others to begin searching right away. The longer this drags out, the more likely Cyrus Riddell may prove how desperate and dangerous he is. Mitch is also concerned it's not the limo they're after, but something in it."

Marie stepped beside Liddy and waggled her forefinger at Hank. "Hank Archer, you ain't telling us everything. What do you mean this fella may prove how desperate and dangerous he is?"

Hank stared at me before he turned a somber look in the direction of the women. "Mitch and Hal believe Cyrus may have shot the guy they pulled from Shiloh Creek. As it turns out, the murder victim—and yes we believe he was murdered—possibly was a Russian mob hireling from New Orleans."

All I'd read and heard about the car's history and Riddell raced through my mind. "Where does Mitch want us to go?"

"Right now, behind City Hall. He and Hal are waiting there to coordinate the search. I'm about to grab Pete, Andy, and their dad. Phillip already had rounded up Wilson Edwards, Hub, and Marcellus when I left to come here."

John looked at Phoebe. "Will you stay with Marie? Until they find the kids and this Cyrus character, she shouldn't go back out to the farm."

Liddy put her arms around Marie and Phoebe. "Let's go make some coffee."

Marie grabbed John's arm as he headed upstairs to get dressed. "Be careful. If you get a chance, check on Ringo if you get out that way."

Liddy stared at me while I tied my shoelaces. "Theo Phillips, no John Wayne heroics. You hear me? Here's your cell phone. I know it's nearly useless outside of town, but it'll make me feel better knowing you have it on you."

ZEB LISTENED TO Mitch's animated instructions from the passenger window of his Bronco as John and I pulled up. Camille's red pickup was parked next to Mitch's truck outside the rear entrance to City Hall.

When John and I stepped out of his pickup, we heard Zeb tell Mitch, "Curious why anyone thought the old limo was worth stealing. I don't care about getting it back. Heck, I'd let them have the blasted thing if only they'd let them two kids go free."

"Where do you want John and me to go?" I asked Mitch.

"Go inside. See Camille. She's got the instructions."

Inside the dispatch office, Camille had a map of the county spread out on Mitch's desk and looked up when we entered.

"Glad you're here." She eyed Jim and Jay standing on opposite ends of the desk. "Since Tim thought they drove toward the school, you two check River Highway toward Alexandria. Double check the school grounds and the stadium first. Here's a walkie-talkie. Report anything suspicious. Tyler's patrolling that side of town. Do not attempt to approach the suspects. Don't forget for one moment they are armed and extremely dangerous, and will likely use the two kids as hostages."

Jay handed the walkie-talkie to Jim. "I'll drive. You climb in the back."

Jim looked at Camille, gritted his teeth, and held up the radio. "I'll use this first, but if I get a chance to square off with this guy, he's gonna wish he had hit me a lot harder than he did."

Camille shot an exhausted, mindful stare at Jim and shook her head. "Y'all get going. Just mind what I told you."

As they left, Jay mumbled in disgust, "Come on, macho man. Let's focus on getting Woogie and Pepper back safe before you tangle with that maniac."

Camille motioned for John and me to step closer. "When Hank gets back, the three of you head out to Old Mill Road. We found the dead guy's vehicle abandoned out by Paul Miller's place. John, you know most of the backroads and properties out that way. Just be careful. Look for any signs. While it's still dark, you might notice a light or something else out of place." She handed me a walkie-talkie. "I hope you'll take charge, Mister Phillips. Please don't let either of them attempt something dumb—especially Hank."

I slipped the radio into my pants pocket. "We'll be fine."

By the time we left Camille in the office, Hank had pulled up next to John's truck. Pete, Andy, and their dad piled out of Andy's GMC pickup. Mitch instructed Pete to check with Camille.

Gus and Wilson stood beside Phillip. Hank tossed his keys to his youngest brother. "Try not to get it all scratched up."

Phillip opened the driver-side door. "Gus. Wilson. Climb in. Here come Hub and Marcellus. They can ride with us. We're going out River Highway and recheck the old mansion."

Arnie Wright arrived riding in Hillary's Camry. Mitch directed him to get with Andy in his truck. Pete jogged from the City Hall rear entrance as Arnie climbed into the backseat beside Sam. Pete yelled, "We're headed to River Road past the Archers' place. She wants us to also check the mill warehouses on the north end of town."

John lowered his window. "Hank, get in. Let's roll!"

Mitch got in his truck as Camille locked the rear door to City Hall. She stopped by her pickup, reached in behind the seat and pulled out a pump-action shotgun. She slid in the front passenger seat of Mitch's truck. Mitch stuck his hand out the open window and waved his radio. John gunned his engine and drove out of the deserted parking lot. Mitch pulled off in the opposite direction.

Larry Scribner honked his horn as we turned onto Washington Street. He pulled alongside and looked up at me from his Buick's driver-side window. "I heard all the chatter on the scanner. What can I do?"

I leaned my head out. "Mitch has us checking possible hideouts in the area. Get with Mary and make certain she stays calm. Pete's riding with Andy, Arnie, and Sam. You and Mary need to focus on getting tomorrow's paper ready. Let's hope the headlines will be good news. Stay close to your scanner. Try to reach me if you hear anything useful."

PURGATORY: A PROGENY'S QUEST

I sensed Larry wanted to ride along, but I felt it risky enough that Pete had volunteered. Mary didn't need her father also poking around in the dark for a couple of criminals affirmed to be armed and dangerous.

NO ONE HAD reported any encouraging news by the time Camille reached us on the radio shortly after twelve. John, Hank, and I had combed every conceivable paved, gravel, and rut-filled dirt road. John even maneuvered his four-wheel dually over a couple of farm trails that the two vehicles we were looking for could not have possibly navigated without getting stuck. Camille broadcasted lunch could be picked up at Bubba's before we were to stop back by City Hall. Her voice sounded as drained and frustrated as the three of us felt.

John pulled over to the side of the road and eyed me in the rearview mirror. "Wanna head to town and get some lunch?"

"I guess so. We've covered every possible road and trail you two know about out here. You've taken me to check out old houses, barns, and rickety sheds that only vermin, snakes, spiders, and stray cats would call home."

Hank had his foot propped on the dashboard and brooded. "They couldn't have just vanished."

John massaged the top of his steering wheel. "Let's stop by my place and grab a cold drink first. I gotta check on Ringo anyway. We can swing by and grab some lunch before we find out what Mitch has up his sleeve next. Maybe the Sheriff's helicopter has noticed something."

With a dejected look Hank tipped his ballcap. John pulled off of Old Mill Road onto the gravel road crossing over Shiloh Creek and through the woods to John and Marie's property. John knew the farm and the pastures well. He had been raised on the farmstead until his mother and father moved back into town to the same home Liddy and I had purchased.

John's recent-built cabin sat nestled amongst the pecan grove on the property not far from Marie's farmhouse. Right after John's vehicle cleared the woods, he had me get out and unlatch the pasture gate, allowing him to drive across the field to his cabin rather than take the circuitous gravel road past the farmhouse and barn. I likewise jumped out once more on the other side of the pasture and unlatched the gate near his cabin. After we climbed out of the truck, John let out a shrill whistle and called Ringo's name a couple of times.

"Where's Ringo?" John asked as he looked around. "Oh well, maybe he's down by Marie's place. Come on inside. I'm pretty sure I still got some cold beer in the fridge if you prefer, Hank."

I radioed Camille and reported we had stopped at John's place for something cold to drink and to check on his dog. Hank sprawled on John's leather sofa and sipped on a beer. John sank into the matching adjacent leather armchair, stretched his legs out onto the coffee table, and likewise sipped on a can of beer.

"John, your AC feels mighty good," Hank moaned.

I slid a frosty can of Coke across my forehead. "That feels good, but it could be a lot worse out there. John, do you mind if I use your phone to call Liddy?"

"Knock yourself out. Just leave a quarter on the counter."

Liddy passed the news to Marie and Phoebe that we were at the farm taking a break. She tried to sound encouraging, but her voice wobbled when she told me they were playing cards and watching an old Humphrey Bogart and Lauren Bacall black and white movie on the television. When I asked which one, she admitted she hadn't really been paying much attention to it. When I hung up, I heard Hank snore. His hand hung limp above his empty beer can now on the floor beside the sofa.

"John, I'm going to stretch my legs and look for Ringo. I'll see if he's up by Marie's place or sprawled out in the shade of the barn. I'll leave the radio on the kitchen counter in case Camille or Mitch try to reach us with any news."

"Okay. We'll head out as soon as you get back. Looks like Hank can use a few minutes of shut-eye anyway. I might even close my eyes for a few minutes until you get back."

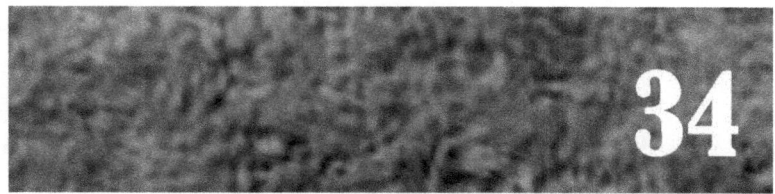

THE FOOTBALL-FIELD-LONG STROLL UP THE DUSTY GRAVEL ROAD
felt a lot farther than usual. The lack of sleep, growling stomach,
and the high-noon sun shortened every stride. I walked in the tall
grass along Marie's weathered pasture fence rather than feel the
crunch under my feet on the narrow drive between John's cabin
and Marie's farmhouse. The thought of Hank and John snoozing
in the cool confines back in the cabin stirred me to glance back
more than once. Yet, each passing minute unnerved me even
more. The sooner I could return with Ringo, the sooner the three
of us could climb back into John's truck and continue our search
for Woogie and Pepper. Checking my watch only added to my
anxious frustration.

Stonewall, Marie's cantankerous mule, lived up to his
reputation as he watched me from the corner of the fence
extending from the barn. His hoary brown and black snout
protruded over the top rail of the fence. His ears perked straight
up as his long black tail swatted his hind-quarters. His otherwise
devil-may-care indifference appeared out of sorts when I reached
up and petted his snout. "Hey, Stonewall. Good boy. Have you
seen Ringo?" Stonewall jerked his head side to side and snorted.

"Steady, Stonewall. Steady," I whispered, surveying the barn
and Marie's front porch for any signs of Ringo. Nothing seemed
out of place. Even Marie's homemade fork-and-spoon wind
chimes hung lifeless on her side porch.

PURGATORY: A PROGENY'S QUEST

I cupped my hands around my mouth and hollered, "Ringo, come here, boy." I expected him to come scooting from the deep recesses of the barn or from beneath the shade of Marie's shrubs which lined her house. I called two more times, and each time listened for Ringo. I walked to the chicken coop and to the edge of the woods and then returned to the house still expecting him to come running. But nothing stirred. I stood by the barn and yelled one more time, "Ringo, here, boy. Come on, Ringo."

Stonewall jerked his head as his whole body pivoted toward me when a loud clank reverberated from inside the barn. I yelled again, "Ringo, come here, Ringo!" Ringo's head and then his whole body squeezed through the gap of the weather-beaten wooden doors and the barn's red dirt floor. Once he found his footing, he howled and bolted through the pasture fence, startling Stonewall in the process. Ringo ignored my attempts to call him and made a beeline for John's place. I turned and started to walk back when a woman screamed, "No!"

I froze and stared at the barn door Ringo had come out of in such a big hurry a moment before. Ringo's persistent howling as he raced through the pasture distracted my attention for a second away from the barn. I could no longer see Ringo, nor any signs of John and Hank from my vantage point. I only made out the sun-faded green roof of John's truck out front of his place.

A part of me wanted desperately to chase after Ringo, but I knew what I heard. I knew it couldn't have been Marie's voice. The closer I got to the barn door, the harder and faster my heart pounded. The dust-filled, hot air felt harder to breathe. I knew this end of the barn provided entry to the maintenance and tool area where Pete often worked on Marie's outdated farm equipment. I remained still outside the door and listened for any more sounds inside. I gripped the door latch and squeezed. When the lever released, I eased the door ajar. The mixed, musty smell of hay and diesel I had expected carried with it a whiff of torched metal. I opened the door a bit further and froze as soon as I recognized the gold and red embossed emblem on the trunk of Cyrus Riddell's black Cadillac.

"Step on in, hands first," Cyrus snarled from the other side of the door. "Don't make any heroic moves or cry out, Mister Phillips." My heart stopped, but I took a deep breath before I stepped inside. Once again, I stood face to face with Cyrus Riddell, though this time his filthy, unshaven appearance, dark sunken eyes, and harsh words caused a fear I'd never felt before.

"Now turn around."

I stared at the limo on the other side of his Cadillac, and asked as calm as I could, "Mister Riddell, are the kids okay?"

"Shut up. Those miserable stowaways are just fine for the moment. Now put your hands behind your back."

When the coarse rope fibers dug into my skin as he secured my wrists, I jerked to free my hands. That's when I felt the cold business end of his pistol press against the back of my neck.

"Look, Mister Phillips, I'm tired, irritable, and far too short on time right now to fool around with you." He pushed the barrel into my neck so firmly I felt my pulse pound against the gun's bore. "Do you understand me? For the sake of those two brats, as long as you cooperate, the three of you will continue to be okay. If not...well, you're a smart man from what I've heard. Do I need to say anything more?"

"No. All I desire is to get the kids back to their families safe and sound."

"Now that we understand each other, stand still." Cyrus yanked on the knot binding my wrists before he grabbed my elbow and shoved me toward the back of the barn.

I noticed Zeb's black limousine had all four doors pushed open and its rear seat removed. Pete's oxygen-acetylene torch rig was near the vehicle's rear chrome bumper. Cassie Davis sat on a wooden bench with her head down beside the toolshed door. She looked up and rubbed her cheek; long, unkempt dark hair veiled reddened, deep-set eyes. The wrinkled and faded caramel-colored, long-sleeve blouse she had on matched her scarred, emaciated, once-youthful face. Her chocolate eyes held a preoccupied, glazed stare.

"Open the damn door and quit whimpering. Your brat got what he deserved," he barked at her. Cassie got up and dug into her pants pocket. She fiddled with the lock and thankfully pulled the door open just as Cyrus used his foot to propel me into the toolshed. I stumbled forward and struggled to regain solid footing on the earthen floor. With my hands tied behind me, I wedged my shoulders against the back wall and stabilized myself before I looked back at Cyrus.

He pointed at Pepper and Woogie, tied and gagged, sitting next to one another on the dirt floor at the other end of the toolshed. "Like I told these two, if you behave, you'll be okay."

His black whiskers glistened from beads of sweat streaming down his smudged cheeks and forehead. He stepped back to close the shed door. His final stare left a cold chill.

Slivers of sunlight flickered through gaps and knotholes of timeworn boards along the barn's back wall. Woogie and Pepper looked scared and helpless. They had their backs up against a tool bench. Pepper's wide eyes stared at me, petrified, as she struggled to speak through her gag. Woogie's head hung between his upright knees.

"Shush. It's gonna be all right," I whispered. "Listen, Ringo's fine. He bolted for Coach Priestly's cabin. It won't be long before Coach and Hank come looking for me."

Pepper's dread-filled stare eased as she allowed her bowed shoulders to sink back, but her eyes remained fixated on me.

"Woogie, I gather that's your mom. Why'd she scream out before? What happened just before Ringo ran out of here like his tail had been lit on fire?"

Woogie raised his head. He had a nasty gash over his right eye and a red and swollen cheek.

"You okay, son?"

He nodded, eyes seething a volatile combination of anger and fear. The door swung open. Cyrus' broad shoulders occupied the entire doorframe. He rested his right hand on the grip of the semi-automatic stuck in his belt. He narrowed his eyes and leaned toward Woogie. "Young man, be thankful I promised your momma nothing bad will happen to you, but I can't say the same for your two friends here."

"By the look on his face, I'd say your notion of nothing bad happening doesn't appear to mean much," I snarled.

"That was his own doing. He tried to trip me when that blasted dog got loose."

I stared into Cyrus' hardened glare. "Look, I don't know why you needed the old limousine so bad. In fact, I don't happen to give a hoot nor a holler, but it's obvious by the shape it's in now, you don't plan to drive it out of here."

"Shut up, old man," Cy snapped back. "That's my business. Besides, I got what I came here to get anyway." He patted whatever filled the right pocket in his stained dress slacks. "We're about to leave this godforsaken backwoods country-bumpkin hellhole. Unless the three of you give me a reason to change my mind, I have no intention of leaving here with more blood on my hands. Just don't make the same mistake a former associate of mine made recently."

He squeezed the wooden grips of his black semi-automatic, pulled it from his waist, and pointed the blue steel barrel between my eyes. "Am I making myself crystal clear?"

Pepper sniffled and moaned into her gag. Woogie thrashed his head back and forth.

"Yeah, I understand. Now, how about removing their gags and let them have some water?"

Cyrus lowered his gun and sneered, "You surprise me. I thought you'd be pissing yourself silly about now. Tell me something. Why did you come out here? Who's with you?"

I swallowed the dry spit in my throat and mustered what courage I had within. "The owner of this farm is at my house. She asked me to stop out here to check on her dog."

Cyrus eyed Woogie. "About that. I've got a score to settle with Mister Macho here and that mangy mutt." Cyrus looked at the scratches across his left forearm. "Until then, they can have their gags off. But hear me plain. I don't want to hear a peep coming out of this room." He slipped his gun back into his belt and leaned over, loosening their gags. As soon as he slammed the door shut, he barked at Cassie, "Get yourself cleaned up and bring them a bottle of water. We need to be ready to leave shortly."

Cassie whined, "I need some more. Cy, you promised me."

"Do what I told ya first. Until we get out of here, you're gonna have to suck it up, little lady. Now get a grip on yourself. If it weren't for the fact you were from here, I'd never have brought you. You're becoming more trouble than you're worth. I have half a mind to leave you here with your brat in there. Now, go clean yourself up and do what I told you."

In the meantime, Pepper scooted in front of Woogie and he removed her gag completely. They switched places and Pepper likewise untied Woogie's gag.

Pepper started to speak, but I shushed her and whispered, "These walls are thin. Okay?"

"Yes, sir. I'm sorry," Pepper whispered and then muttered to Woogie. "Are you okay? Your face looks really sore."

"I've been hit harder on the football field." Woogie masked whatever pain he felt with a cocky grin.

"You think you can untie my wrists?" I knelt in front of Woogie to allow him to work the knots Cyrus hastily cinched in the coarse manila rope bindings. After a couple of minutes of tugging and yanking by Woogie, though his own hands were still tied, I felt my bindings slacken.

The door unlatched just as I sat down near Pepper. "Here's a bottle of water." Cassie glanced at Woogie's swollen face. "I'm sorry, Kevin. This isn't what I bargained for. He promised all he wanted was to get his hands on what he got hired to deliver to New Orleans."

"Would you mind unscrewing the cap?" I shrugged, indicating my hands were still tied behind my back.

"Sure. Here you go, son." Cassie peered at Pepper with what seemed like genuine concern. "Don't fret none. If all goes well, y'all should be home by tonight."

"What the hell's going on in there? Get back out here, Cass!" Cyrus barked beyond the door.

Cassie turned and snapped back with a tinge of sarcasm, "I'm doing what you asked. I'm coming."

"Thank you, Miss Davis," I said. I witnessed Cassie's compassion toward the kids and hoped it was real. She hesitated, peered back over her shoulder, but said nothing further before she closed the toolshed door.

Cyrus snarled at Cassie in between the sound of car doors being opened and slammed shut. By the amount of noise they made, I sensed Cyrus must have believed my story. I twisted my wrists all the way free and inched toward the door in hopes of making out what Cyrus and Cassie were planning to do next.

"Psst! Psst! Theo, it's me, John."

I spun around to find where John's voice came from.

"Theo, over here."

Woogie called out, "Coach."

I scrambled over to Woogie and put my hand on his mouth. "Shh!" I got to my feet and saw one of John's eyes gawking at me through a large knothole in the back wall. "Where's Hank?"

"He ran back to my place to call for help. He'll be right back. How are you and the kids?"

"We're fine...considering." I looked down at two promising smiles. "Woogie helped get my ropes loose, but I didn't want to risk untying them yet. Cyrus has a gun tucked in his belt, and he seems to enjoy pointing it at people. I think Cassie's the only reason he hasn't done anything rash yet. He's all but confessed that he killed the guy you found."

"I'm going to see if I can get into Marie's place. Her double-barrel should be over the mantle. I'm not crazy about the prospect of a bunch of Sheriff's deputies rolling in here in a few minutes. Sounds to me as though Cyrus won't give himself up without a fight. That'll put you and the kids in harm's way. I'll be right back. Hang tough and play it smart. We'll figure something out."

I sat down as soon as John disappeared and grabbed the ropes that once bound my hands. I had to appear as if my hands were still tied behind my back.

"I'm scared, Mister Phillips," Pepper whispered as she began to sniffle, her head nestled against my arm.

I realized she held Maude's rosary crucifix between her fingertips. "Look at me. We're not going to let anything happen to you." I stared at Woogie. "Am I right, Woogie?"

"That's right, Pepper. You can count on Coach Priestly. He and your brother will get us out of here." The words got Pepper to manage a half-hearted, almost-believable grin. Thankfully, she didn't bother to notice Woogie's grimace when he uttered his encouraging words.

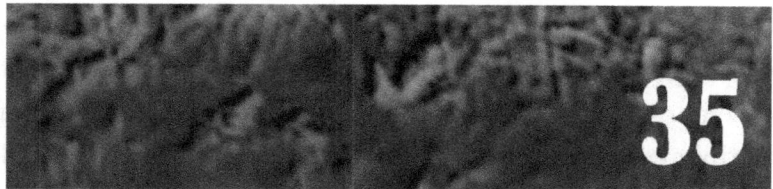

35

THE NEXT FEW MINUTES FELT LIKE TIME HAD STOPPED. CYRUS AND Cassie squabbled at each other on the far side of the limo while I freed the kids from their ropes. I heard the rumble of John's truck in the distance and peeked through a large knothole on the back wall. Hank was behind the wheel of John's green dually barreling headlong toward the barn through the knee-high pasture grass.

"Listen carefully. Whatever happens, stay close to me." I pulled Pepper and Woogie to their feet. "If I say run, don't look back, just go as fast as you can. Get out of the barn and don't stop running." I grabbed Woogie by his shoulders. "I'm counting on you. Whatever you do, don't let go of her hand!"

"Yes, sir." Woogie reached for Pepper's hand and they interlocked fingers.

A moment later, the whole backside of the barn shuddered as Hank rammed John's truck into the rear barn doors. Tools and hardware toppled off the shed's shelves, edging Pepper and Woogie closer to me. I grabbed the still-locked shed door handle right after Cassie began screaming and Cyrus fired his gun.

I took a step back, kicked the shed door open, and poked my head out far enough to see what had happened. Hay bales had toppled from the overhead loft and landed on top of John's truck, which had plowed two-thirds of its length into the central part of the barn. Dust and shreds of hay floated throughout the barn. I could not see Hank in the cab.

John yelled from the front of the barn, "Stay there!" He then popped up from behind the hood of Cyrus' Cadillac and fired

Marie's shotgun. The load of birdshot missed its intended mark and peppered the barn's timbers, diverting Cyrus' attention momentarily away from Hank. Cyrus ducked behind the open rear door of the armored limousine; Cassie cowered behind its rear bumper.

"Whoever you are, I've got seven rounds to your remaining one," Cyrus bellowed before he fired two rounds at John. One bullet ricocheted off the Cadillac's hood.

Woogie tugged on my arm. "Listen. I hear sirens."

When I heard them in the distance, I realized I needed to get the kids to safety.

John yelled at Cyrus, "It sounds like the cavalry is about to arrive. I like my odds at the moment."

"I don't give a damn. I'm not going back to prison," Cyrus barked back.

No matter what might happen in the next few minutes, I didn't want Pepper and Woogie to become hostages—or worse, human shields. I grabbed Woogie's arm. "It's time to go. Stay low and take Pepper out the front door when I tell you." I pointed to the door I'd entered the barn through.

Cassie's eyes filled with horror when she saw Woogie crouching beside Pepper next to me. I then heard Hank kick open the passenger side door of John's truck. He scrambled and stuck his head out around the front of the truck. As soon as Cyrus turned and fired at Hank, I screamed, "Run!" Woogie and Pepper scampered hunched over along the wall toward the door. Cassie stood and shrieked, "No!"

"Stop! Don't make me shoot," Cyrus hollered as he saw the kids nearing the door.

A metal sprocket had spilled from the shed shelves and lay in the dirt by my feet. I grabbed it like a baseball and flung it with all my might in Cyrus' direction, but my errant throw just bounced off the limo's hood. I ducked behind the shed door when Cyrus reacted and fired in my direction.

Cassie raced past me toward Woogie and Pepper and screamed, "Cyrus, no! You promised."

John stood and discharged his second barrel at the same moment Cyrus pointed and fired in the direction of the kids. This time the birdshot sprayed the limo's bulletproof rear door window, but some of the pellets tore into Cyrus' arm and shoulder. Hank bolted from the protection of the truck and charged Cyrus as he was recoiling from the sting of pellets. Cyrus swung his wounded arm around and pointed his semi-automatic at Hank. John grabbed the barrel end of the empty shotgun and charged at Cyrus with it raised over his head.

At the same instant, I reacted out of instinct and bolted toward Cyrus and yelled, "Hank, no!"

John heaved the double-barreled shotgun at Cyrus. It flew end-over-end and struck Cyrus' extended arm as he fired. Hank clutched his shoulder but kept his feet.

Cyrus turned his gun toward John. I screamed *Stop!*, raced from the toolshed, and dove across the trunk of the limo reaching for Cyrus' shoulder when I heard the gun go off. Cyrus and I tumbled to the ground. I landed face first and my forehead smacked the barrel of the empty shotgun. John held onto Cyrus' arm and ripped the semi-automatic from his hand. I scrambled to one knee, wiped dirt from my eyes, grabbing the barrel of the empty shotgun in a two-handed grip, prepared to help John. That's when I saw blood.

Hank writhed in pain curled up on the dirt floor a few feet away. John lay across Cyrus' chest. The wood-handled semi-automatic lay beyond reach. Mitch walked up, smoking pistol still in his hand. He squatted beside John and Cyrus and I went to check on Hank. Camille already hovered over his blood-stained left shoulder, but he managed a grin as she applied pressure on his wound with her hands.

"Theo, you saved my life. How's Pepper and Woogie?"

Mitch helped John to his feet and inspected the blood across his chest. "You're mighty fortunate, Coach. Sure you're all right?"

"Yeah, I'm fine," John said, staring at Cyrus' blood-soaked lifeless body.

From the other side of the vehicles, Tyler yelled out, "We need some help over here."

John and I followed Mitch to where Pepper knelt on both knees beside Woogie as he stroked his mother's dark hair. An EMT confirmed what we all feared—Cassie died in Woogie's arms. The EMT said, "I'm sorry, young man."

Woogie wiped his eyes, moaning. "Momma."

John knelt and ran his fingers through Woogie's dark hair. "No matter what anyone might say about your momma's past, she sacrificed herself to protect you."

Wilson Edwards watched Cassie's body being lifted onto an EMS stretcher then ran into the barn. "Where's Woogie?"

"He's over here, Wilson," I said.

Woogie embraced his father. "I don't understand, Dad."

"Kevin, this may be hard to understand right now, but your momma's finally at peace." Wilson tenderly walked Woogie out of the barn with his arm draped over his son's shoulder.

I walked out of the barn and was beginning to take stock of all my bruises and scrapes when Pepper walked up. "Are you okay, Mister Phillips?"

"I think so."

"You've got a nasty cut above your eye." I pulled out my handkerchief, but Pepper took it from me. She dabbed my left eyebrow and wiped the blood from my cheek. "It's not too bad, but you oughta have one of the medics take a look at it anyway."

I held my handkerchief over my eye. "Yeah, I will. Where's Hank? How's he doing?"

We snaked our way through all the vehicles that had raced to the scene and found Hank propped up on a stretcher next to an Emergency Medical Services vehicle out front of Marie's house.

His face lit up when he saw Pepper. "They told me you and Woogie were fine, but his mom didn't make it. That's a shame to hear. She not only tried to protect you and Woogie...her actions kept me from getting hurt far worse."

Pepper floated her hand above his bandaged shoulder. "Does it hurt?"

"I've been shot a lot worse than this."

Pepper looked confused when Hank and I chuckled.

"Hank, I hear you're gonna be just fine," John said with an odd look at Hank and me. "You do know if you hadn't raced off so fast, I could've told you where I kept my rifle in the cabin?"

Mitch walked up. "The Sheriff's deputies are going to need your statements."

"Can someone around here get us something cold to drink and maybe a sandwich in the meantime? We're starved."

Mitch patted John on the back. "Sure thing, John, but I've got a question. Who's gonna explain to Marie what happened to her barn? That is your truck holding up the back wall, smothered beneath all those busted bales of hay, right?"

Pepper giggled as she held onto Hank's hand.

Mitch began to walk away but looked back. "Anyone want to know why that maniac was so hell-bent on stealing the vehicle?"

I blurted, "Whatever it was, it fit in his pants pocket."

"How did you know he was after a bag of uncut diamonds?" Mitch asked.

"I didn't, but he had patted his stuffed pants pocket and bragged he recovered what he came to get."

Hank asked, "How much can a pocketful of uncut diamonds be worth?"

Mitch shrugged his shoulders. "I'm no jeweler, but when I handed them over to investigators a few minutes ago, their reaction confirmed they were worth a whole lot more than what I might earn in two lifetimes."

"Here comes trouble." John pointed to Hal and Phillip walking up between the EMS vehicle and Mitch's truck.

"I spoke with Camille and Tyler. They told me my big brother was the kamikaze driver who darn near destroyed Marie's barn and then took a round in his shoulder charging a loaded gun," Hal said with a wiseacre smirk.

"I only did what needed to be done to protect our little sister," Hank gloated as Pepper hugged Phillip and then Hal.

"John, what did you do with Ringo? Is he okay?" I asked.

"Holy smokes, I gotta run back to my place. I put him inside my bedroom before we left. All this commotion is sure to have gotten him all riled up."

I smiled at Pepper, "If it weren't for Ringo, who knows how this might've turned out."

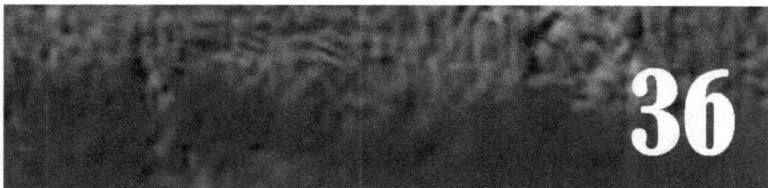

36

STIFF SHOULDERS, CHAFED WRISTS, AND A SWOLLEN KNOT ABOVE my eye requiring three stitches kept me from getting comfortable. I tried to sleep in, but the tantalizing aroma of eggs, bacon, and fresh biscuits became too tempting to ignore.

Liddy poured a cup of coffee and handed it to me with apologetic puppy dog eyes when I entered the kitchen. She gnawed on her lower lip, then said, "Will you forgive me for being so upset at you last night? I just couldn't handle the thought that you could have been killed."

"I knew you'd be upset. If it'll help, the same thought had crossed my mind during the night."

Though I survived the ordeal pretty much unscathed, those final hair-raising minutes played over and over throughout the night in frame-by-frame slow motion. Each time I tried to conjure what I could have done differently. My mind wrestled with the conundrum fate had placed me in, though I did not have the benefit of hindsight at the time.

On the one hand, I couldn't escape the haunting notion I caused Cassie's death when I dispatched Woogie and Pepper toward the door. However, Mitch tried to reassure me before we left Marie's place last night, the fatal bullet that struck Cassie landed precisely where Cyrus had intended and well before she had reached Woogie and Pepper. Still, I couldn't help but second-guess my decision.

On the other hand, Mitch emphasized that had I not dove over the back of Zeb's limo when I did and grabbed Cyrus, John more than likely would've been Cyrus' target and not Cassie. I awoke still trying to absorb the reality of those horrifying seconds. In the end, I knew decisions were made beyond my own control which, in the frantic heat of the moment, led to Cassie and Cyrus dying.

As soon as I sat at the kitchen table, Liddy joined me and pleaded, "Theo Phillips, you didn't exactly tell me everything that happened yesterday, did you?"

"Why?" I muttered, chewing on a morsel of biscuit.

Liddy showed me the front page of the *Sentinel*. "The headline reads, 'Shiloh Police Department recounts heroic rescue of two local teenage kidnap victims.'" Liddy lowered the paper and glared at me. "Shall I keep reading?"

I slurped more coffee to help wash down the dry biscuit that was suddenly stuck to the back of my throat.

Ruffling the paper, she asked. "Are you listening to me? According to Larry's article, Mitch attributed the quick-thinking and courageous actions of John Priestly, Hank Archer, and Theo Phillips to preventing a far more tragic outcome. It says..."

> During the intensive manhunt that began late Saturday night, Mitch Johnson, Shiloh's Chief of Police, received a brief radio call from Hank Archer at about 1:30 Sunday afternoon reporting the whereabouts of the two subjects and their two teenage hostages. Shiloh's Chief of Police arrived first on the scene and heard the exchange of gunfire inside the barn on Marie Masterson's property off Old Mill Road. When he entered the barn, he saw Hank Archer had been shot and lay exposed on the ground. When the male suspect attempted to shoot unarmed John Priestly and Theo

Phillips as they charged the suspect,
the Shiloh Chief of Police shot the
armed male suspect.

Liddy placed the folded paper at my side of the table. "The story you told me failed to mention you and John charged this guy while he had a gun aimed at you."

"It wasn't quite as cut and dried as Larry reported. Besides, it seemed more like one of those out-of-body moments. I saw the two kids turn back from running out the door when Woogie's mother got shot. And Hank was laying helpless on the ground after he'd been shot. And John had just thrown Marie's empty shotgun at the guy and ran at Cyrus to save Hank. I-I-I just reacted without thinking, hun."

I gave her a *youunnerstan'doncha* look and reached across the table for her hand. "I gotta say, God must have answered my prayer because I still don't know how I leaped across the back of the limo and grabbed ahold of Cyrus like I did. All I remember is hearing the final bullet fire. I feared John had gotten shot as I tumbled to the ground holding onto Cyrus. The next second, Mitch was standing over us holding his pistol."

Liddy got out of her chair and buried my head in her bosom. "What am I going to do with you? Worse yet, what would I do without you?" She squeezed me tight and rocked back and forth as she mumbled, "Thank you, Lord."

I lifted my head from her embrace and looked up with a grimace-laced leer. "I'm sorry, but my head's still pretty sore."

"I'm sorry. I reacted without thinking." She giggled as she gently stroked the boo-boo on my forehead.

"I'll live, but I'd rather not pop any of those stitches. Tell you what. Let's get dressed and head over to the hospital and check on Hank. He twice risked his life to save ours. First, when he crashed John's truck into the barn. Then when he raced toward Cyrus after John fired his last shot."

Liddy ran her fingers through my hair. "Such an irony. Hank and John risked their lives to protect one another. I wonder what Harold Archer and Jessie Masterson would've said if they were still around to witness this day?"

"Maybe, just maybe, they did more than witness what happened," I said.

VICKIE WALLER SHOOK her head as she greeted us at the nurse's station. She touched the edge of the bandage covering stitches on the lump above my eye. "By the look of things you apparently did get caught up in that Wild West rescue of Mickey's friends yesterday, Mister Phillips. I don't know what to say. When I read this morning's paper, we were shocked to see your name."

Liddy giggled. "Seems as though Theo failed to tell me everything last night, too. I learned just this morning more of what actually unfolded."

"Both of you quit your fussing. I'm just glad it's over. Mitch, John, and Hank were the real heroes. How's Mickey?"

"In light of everything that took place and fretting over Pepper and Woogie, she's fine. Tim's parents stopped by the house yesterday. My husband and I got to know them better while Tim and Mickey hung out in the yard. You ought to know we prayed together as soon as we heard of Pepper and Woogie's rescue. By the time I heard that Hank Archer got admitted, no one knew any more details than two died at the scene."

"There's a tragic proverb that says something to the effect that *the wicked devour themselves and are never satisfied until they taste their own blood.* I believe that played itself out yesterday. Knowing you prayed is much appreciated. Like I told Liddy this morning,

I felt God watched over us, which, oddly enough, reminds me. Any chance we can visit with Hank?"

Vickie grinned as she pointed. "Just follow the noise as you head down the hall. You can't miss his room."

The fact that Hank's left arm had been immobilized mattered little to him. Pepper sat at the foot of the bed beside Hillary and Maddie hovered at the head of it massaging his right hand. Hal and Phillip stood in the hall just outside the door.

"How's our hero behaving?" I asked.

Hal smirked. "Getting smothered with attention. Doc Lucas told him he'll need reconstructive shoulder surgery after the swelling subsides in a few days. That bullet ripped through shoulder ligaments and shattered his clavicle. After Doc installs a little hardware to repair his collarbone and anchors it back with a few sutures to the damaged ligaments, he'll be good as new after three or so months of rest and rehab."

"I thought he was planning on leaving Shiloh?" Liddy asked.

"Shucks, Miss Liddy. He's our prodigal big brother. After the three of us talked, Hank intends to ask John to help him build a cabin like his on the plot of land Dad deeded to him anyway."

Maddie waggled her finger at Hank. "You best mind them doctors, Harold Archer the Third, or I'll pin your ears back like I used to do when you scampered around my kitchen floor in your muddy bare feet wearing nothing more than cut-offs."

Hank shrugged and glared at Hal until a spate of belly laughter erupted from all of us.

"Liddy and I won't stay. I only wanted to see how you're doing and to tell you thanks again for what you did. I know your father would've been proud."

Hank stretched his hand out toward me. "Theo, you were the real hero." As I grabbed his hand, he squeezed tight. "Miss Liddy, you've got a real-to-life John Wayne for a husband. I never knew he had a bad-ass side to him."

Liddy tried to hold back her chuckles. "Me neither, Hank."

Hank smiled at Pepper. "What do you say, lil' sister?"

Pepper gripped my arm with both hands. "As far as I'm concerned, Woogie and I wouldn't be here today if it wasn't for Mister P. You should've seen him stand up to that brute and then leap over Mister Adams' car and wrestle the guy to the ground."

Hank blurted, "I've witnessed him firsthand stand his ground before. He's got more grit and grace than any man I've ever known, and I've been around a lot of tough Army Rangers in the heat of battle. None of them had anything on my friend Theo."

"Y'all mind if I stick my head in here a moment?" Gus asked. "I'm pleased to hear you'll be okay, Hank. Seeing as Theo's here too, I want to thank both of you." He exchanged smiles with Pepper. "Since the Mayor's here, I best scoot back to the office."

Pepper left Hank's side as Gus disappeared back down the hall. "I'll be right back."

Liddy patted Maddie's hand sympathetically. "Why the long face? Are you alright?"

"Yes, Miss Liddy, everything's gonna be fine. God works in mysterious ways to make all things as they should."

Hillary took Maddie's other hand. "This is supposed to be my father's cue to say something profound, but since he's not here, I'll be the one to say *Amen*, Miss Maddie. Everything happens to fulfill God's greater good and always in his perfect timing."

"Watch out. Here come Zeb and Jim." Hal and Phillip stepped back to allow Jim to negotiate into the room with Zeb, foot propped in the wheelchair.

Zeb said, "We parked my cursed old black albatross in Pete's garage. He swears he can put her back together as good as new. I hope Doc Lucas can do the same for you, Hank."

"Well, that's what he promised. I thought you intended to get rid of that good-for-nothing relic after all that has happened," Hank said with a curious stare.

Zeb laughed out loud. "Heavens, no! That vehicle is now more valuable than ever. Can you imagine all the tall tales the old heap will stir up? I'm ready to start looking for my next vehicle to add to my collection." Zeb looked over his shoulder as Pepper returned. "Besides, I expect to be toting this good-looking young gal in the parade next year."

Doc Lucas raised his voice from down the hall. "In case all y'all forgot, this is still a hospital. Time to break up the family reunion. Nurse Waller still has to check on our patient before he gets the needed rest I ordered for him."

AFTERWORD

OUR SONS CALLED FRIDAY MORNING TO RECONFIRM MARIE'S address. They had agreed to meet us there. John and Marie had asked us to lend a hand with last-minute preparations for Phoebe's birthday party. By the time we ventured across the noisy loose timbers spanning the stream cutting through Marie's property, we realized we were not the first to arrive.

We saw Pete, Andy, Jim, and Jay working feverishly on the backside of Marie's barn. They appeared about ready to rehang new barn doors. All the new boards surrounding the opening provided a fresh reminder of the extent of the damage inflicted when Hank crashed into the back of the barn.

Right after I parked, Liddy bee-lined for Megan and Marie, who played with Jessie near the kitchen stoop. I wanted to talk with Zeb, who was seated on Marie's front porch.

"Where's your wheelchair?" I asked.

"Doc said it'd do me some good to walk a little bit if I didn't overdo it and used this blasted cane." He waved a wooden cane that looked more like a war club. "Heck, it beats the wheelchair."

"Where did you get your cane?"

"You like it?" Zeb handed it to me. "Mandy ordered it for me. She called it an authentic *sha-lay-lee*—some sort of fancy Scotch-Irish walking stick."

Sam shut the lid on the smoker. "Your boys still bringing their families for the holiday weekend?"

"Yep. They assured us they could find their way with their smartphone GPS programs." My lighthearted chuckle voiced my skepticism. "I expect them to call for more traditional directions when they discover their GPS may not get them all the way here."

John yelled from the front of the barn. "Theo, come check out what the fearsome foursome got done."

When I caught up with John inside the barn, I surveyed where everything had taken place. Marie's Massey tractor occupied the end of the barn where the vehicles had been. Once again, the familiar musty smell of hay and diesel permeated the dust-filled air. I sighed in relief when I noticed the dirt floor no longer showed remnants of blood spilled the previous weekend.

"Mister P, come take a look," Pete said from atop a stepladder. He tightened the last bolt securing the barn door's hardware.

John patted my shoulder. "Looks a darn sight better than my truck. What do you think?"

As Pete hopped down from the ladder, he said to John, "After I get done repairing Zeb's vehicle, I'll make sure your truck's front end will look better than it has in years."

"Thanks, Pete. No hurry. Marie told me we'll have Pepper's Buick out here as of this weekend."

I gave John a curious look. "You're going to drive her car?"

"You didn't hear? Marie invited Pepper to move out to the farm with her. Her brothers all think that's a great idea as long as she agrees not to forget how to spend time with them. I heard Maddie nodded her approval since Hillary will move out there in another month."

"Does Liddy know?"

"I imagine she does now."

"What about Hank?"

"It'll be three or four months before Hank's cabin will be move-in ready. In the meantime, he'll be busy with his rehab. But I also don't want you or Liddy to fret about Pepper and Marie. I'm not leaving my cabin." John dug into his pants pocket, pulled out

PURGATORY: A PROGENY'S QUEST

a blue velvet pouch, and dumped an engagement ring and wedding band into the palm of his hand.

"About time. Are you going to give her the engagement ring this afternoon for her birthday?"

He tapped an envelope sticking out of his shirt pocket. "Got our wedding license right here. Arnie's going to marry us this afternoon. It's a surprise, but I've already popped the question."

"You two going on a honeymoon?"

"I arranged to take her for a whole week to Saint Simons Island. We leave this afternoon."

"Are you going to see Nick while you're there?"

"Not exactly. He'll be here shortly and will hand me the keys to his house. He decided to spend some time with his twin nieces while visiting Joe and Missy for a couple of weeks."

The rattle of toolboxes and ladders turned our heads. "Guys, great job. Thank you," John said.

Andy pointed to the brand-new wide-open sliding barn doors. "You and Mister P want the honors of testing them out?"

John grabbed one side and I grabbed the other. We slid the doors closed and latched them.

"Good as new. Now, I'm getting hungry. How about you, Theo?" John said, ushering us out of the barn and toward food.

THE DELICIOUS AROMA of pork and chicken cooking slow in the smoker filled the air and guests continued to arrive.

Pepper followed behind her brothers with Maddie in her car. Hillary arrived a minute later with Arnie and Judy Wright. Not long after, Larry and Martha brought Mary with them.

Joe Arians also arrived with Missy and their red-headed twins, Lizzie and Lucy. Wilson brought Woogie, Tim, and Mickey. Ray and Kay Abernathy arrived a little before one o'clock followed by Mitch riding in Camille's red pickup, which earned a wide smile from Pete.

Marie yelled from the kitchen door, "Theo, your boys just called and they're five minutes out. Their GPS couldn't find where to turn off Old Mill Road after they left town."

Sam hollered, "Supper time."

I helped him bring platters of cut-up pork and chicken to makeshift picnic tables we set up out front of the farmhouse. Marie, Liddy, Maddie, Jeannie, and Susanna brought out a mouthwatering array of serving bowls and plates of side dishes. Judy and Hillary filled everyone's glasses with iced tea.

Thankfully, our sons followed Nick riding in Phoebe Thatcher's vehicle. Our younger son, Tommy, and his wife, Kari, climbed out of their van right after Teddy, Sissy, and Buzz bolted straight to Liddy and me. Junior and his wife, Stacey, followed behind Bubba and Conrad as they caught up to their cousins already laying claim to seats at the table. Nick walked straight up to John and nonchalantly handed him his house keys. John then took Phoebe by the hand, and they sat next to Marie and Zeb at the head of the table.

Long after Arnie had offered grace and bowls and plates had been passed for seconds, John stood, stuck two fingers between his lips and whistled. Even Ringo poked his head up as the clamor of convivial chatter went silent.

"I want to thank all y'all for being here and sharing this very special day with Marie, Phoebe, and me. This is Phoebe's birthday party, but it is also about to become another extra special day." John turned to Phoebe and took her hand as she stood beside him. "Phoebe, I have two small gifts for you."

He dug into his pants pocket, pulled out the velvet pouch, loosened the drawstring, and first placed the diamond engagement ring on her finger. Pent-up tears of joy streamed down her cheeks. She wasted no time and embraced John, but he tilted his head back and chuckled. "I ain't done yet. Don't you want to know what your other gift is?"

Phoebe looked confused. "More? What in God's name could you possibly give me more than this?" She stared at her engagement ring sparkling on her hand.

John took the envelope from his shirt pocket and handed it to her. "Open it." While she took care to unfold it, John dropped the wedding band from the pouch into his hand.

Phoebe did a double take and then grabbed a napkin to wipe her eyes. "Don't I have to sign it or something to make it legal?"

"Got it covered. As soon as we leave here, we swing by the courthouse in Alexandria. The clerk's office is expecting us."

John smiled. "I'm not partial to a long engagement. Since you now possess our wedding license, and I happen to have this other ring with me, would you allow Arnie to marry us this afternoon? We're already surrounded by a church full of friends and family." He looked at Kay Abernathy. "Our boss already approved Mary to sub for you next week." Kay's smile said it all.

"Where are we going?" Phoebe asked.

John held up Nick's house keys. "Saint Simons Island."

Nick shouted from the far end of the tables. "I just got the hot tub serviced, and there's a golf cart in the garage you can use to get around while you're there."

Liddy nudged my ribs with her elbow. "That sounds so nice. We oughta think about taking a long vacation to the shore ourselves. I think we deserve a little peaceful getaway."

I whispered, "I like how you think."

Before dessert, Arnie led John and Phoebe in their vows. Then Marie, Hillary, and Judy brought out three chocolate sheet cakes with plenty of vanilla ice cream.

While Phoebe enjoyed showing off her rings, I joined John on Marie's porch. He sat in the porch swing with his eyes closed and a goofy smile on his face. He had a suitcase at his feet.

I walked up. "Are you okay?"

"I just needed a second to be by myself and thank God before we left. I'm glad you're here. I've got to thank you for being the friend you have become. If it had not been for your words of encouragement this day may never have come." He got to his feet and wrapped his arms around me. "Let's grab a bite to eat when Phoebe and I get back."

We then heard Zeb yelling, "John, your pretty wife is looking for you. I think she's ready to leave for her honeymoon."

John threw his suitcase into the back of Phoebe's Peugeot station wagon. Then, in a hail of rice, John opened the passenger door for Phoebe and raced around the car to slide in behind the wheel. As they drove out of sight, I looked at the abundance of friends we had been blessed with since we first arrived in Shiloh not even three years ago.

Pepper and her new friends played with our grandkids near Stonewall, Marie's cantankerous mule. I stood next to Liddy and said, "Pepper looks at home at last. It's a shame she had to lose the only family she ever knew to discover her real family."

Pete yelled, standing beside his truck. "Hey, Mister P, you old geezers want a rematch?"

He reached into the bed of the truck and tossed a football for me to catch. Liddy waggled her finger at me after I caught the ball and eyed Arnie, Sam, and Larry.

"Sure, let's see who else wants to play."

~

THE END

~

T.M. BROWN

ACKNOWLEDGEMENTS

WHAT BEGAN AS a challenge by my wife Connie to write a story my grandchildren might cherish has exceeded my wildest expectations. God willing, Theo Phillips and his wife Liddy may yet share more adventures before I truly retire. In the meantime, *Purgatory, A Progeny's Quest* is the third adventure in the Shiloh Mystery Series, which also includes *Sanctuary, A Legacy of Memories* and *Testament, An Unexpected Return*.

How did the quest to publish one become three and possibly five? A host of family, friends, and talented folks is my response. I cannot possibly name all of them here, but they know who they are—I remind them at every opportunity. But the inspiration for each of my stories rests with my grandchildren Noah, Brannon, Natalie, Eli, and Dillon.

A special note of thanks goes to my wife's cousin, Kay, and her late husband, William Frederick Wallace. Fred took Connie and me on a tour of his notable vehicle collection during a family reunion at their mountaintop home in Pennsylvania in 2018. He introduced us to the armored Cadillac limousine that I decided right away needed to be a part of my third book. Sadly, Fred lost his battle with cancer a few months after our visit, but the memories we share of Fred stretching back to before Connie and I married in 1973 always remain.

Finally, my biggest shout-out goes to the thousands of folks I have met and communicated with since *Sanctuary* came out in 2017. Next to the constant affirmation from my five grandchildren, reviews and comments from readers like you weigh more precious to me than awards or recognition my novels have received.

ABOUT THE AUTHOR

T.M. BROWN, Mike to friends and family, embraces his Georgia heritage thanks to the paternal branches of his family tree. Mike recalls his childhood when, on many warm Sunday afternoons, his father drove the family beyond Stone Mountain to his great uncle's farm.

Though the dust-filled, red-clay backroads beyond Snellville, Georgia, have long since become paved thoroughfares, Mike fondly recalls getting bitten by barbed wire pasture fences, sipping cool well water from a ladle, and getting scrubbed in a washtub near the front stoop of Uncle Kerry and Aunt Monk's old farmhouse.

Retired since 2014 from the 9-to-5 life, Mike and wife Connie reside below Atlanta near Newnan, Georgia. Creating his fictional rural town of Shiloh and its cast of memorable characters has conjured up many near-forgotten memories, and thanks to recollections of his Pop and Poppa, the truth they espoused to Mike as a young man resonates in his stories. *Purgatory: A Progeny's Quest* concludes the Shiloh Mystery Series. Nevertheless, Mike promises that Theo and Liddy will find their way into new stories about their further adventures soon.

ALSO BY T.M. BROWN

Sanctuary (Palmetto Publishing, 2020)
Testament (Palmetto Publishing, 2020)

You can find out more about T.M. Brown
by visiting these sites:

Website: TMBrownAuthor.com
Facebook: @TMBrownAuthor
Instagram: @T.M.Brown.Author

The author would love to hear from you.
Please email him at:
mike@TMBrownAuthor.com

T.M. BROWN

PURGATORY: A PROGENY'S QUEST

T.M. BROWN

PURGATORY: A PROGENY'S QUEST

T.M. BROWN
PURGATORY, A PROGENY'S QUEST
BLUE ROOM BOOKS | DECATUR, GA
978-1-950729-19-7

9 781950 729197

Please visit the publisher of this fine book at
BlueRoomBooks.com to see the lineup of our other authors and
the wide variety of excellent books of
memoir, fiction, children, and nonfiction.

www.ingramcontent.com/pod-product-compliance
Lightning Source LLC
Chambersburg PA
CBHW071230190726
48292CB00007B/2219